RT SWINDOLL

presents

Gin & COLOGNE
in the WEARABLE TECH APOCALYPSE

RTS

Published by
RTS PRESS

To Grandma.
Always believing the best.

*Inestimable thanks to my wife and family,
to Writer's Group for their enduring support,
and to E.S. Murillo, to whom I owe a metric ton
of whisper-quiet fidget toys for her generous
editorial contributions and dastardly wit.*

Starman (@aeroxventures) · 2:25 AM April 1

Am considering interstellar cruise (no joke!) Flyby Centauri, Bernard, Cygni, Tau C, Eridani, Sirius. Lightspeed tech ready for prime time

Starman (@aeroxventures) · 2:25 AM April 1

Because time dilation, cruise lasts 20 days, returns 20 years in the future. Don't panic! AeroX holdings secure = Investors very safe

Starman (@aeroxventures) · 2:25 AM April 1

20 years has its perks. Drop assets on stock, reap on return. Buy time for incurable cancer. Get dragonball boost for your career slump

Starman (@aeroxventures) · 2:26 AM April 1

Personally, I just want some star time. Wife is bored. Who wants to name a planet with me? 1 bil to reserve. 200 ppl max. Sirius-ly...

PROLOGUE

TOUR THE STARS *with Ronal Cologne III and Genasia! Never has a billion dollars gone so far. Invest in the voyage of your life on the AeroX spaceliner, the pinnacle of science, engineering, and entertainment culture. Our grand tour will ring six diamond stars in state-of-the-art safety and style, all powered by the AeroX-patented Neumine Quantum Drive.*

WELCOME TO LUXURY. *Low gravity—high ceilings. See other worlds via the Viewscape Grand Ballroom. Enjoy the nightlife in the Nautilus Discotheque. Find your circadian rhythm in our TruLight Passenger Suites. Taste our rehydration creations brought to you by celebrity chefs. Stroll the centripetal Love Tunnel with the light of your life—or the light of your night.*

TICKET PRICE INCLUDES *an exclusive, all-access invitation to join Ronal Cologne's coveted Hari Seldon Committee, Safeguarding the World's Future, Forever and a Day.*

Ellen sighed. It sounded debonair. Just the thing a narcissist would love.

Setting the brochure in her lap, she craned a look

behind the wheelchair at her attendant nurse, a young Scandinavian immigrant who carried, despite her protests, that godawful beige wool beanie.

She warned the nurse to put it down. "Trifle with a woman's dignity, and watch a woman's dignity trifle with you."

The nurse chided, "You a debutante, now? D'lobby is frigid."

Ellen felt the itchy beanie slip over her bald scalp. She immediately snatched it off. "I'm sick, not senile." With a shudder at the checker-stitched maple leaves and hockey sticks, she flung away the tacky thing like a soiled tissue. "I paid dearly for my beautiful crown, and I won't cover it up. Besides, I look like Samuel L. Jackson, God rest his *mother-loving* soul."

She rubbed her hairless dome and relished the souvenir from her failed chemotherapy.

The nurse knew nothing of Hollywood, only the consternation of caring for an American transplant—from Texas, no less. Bending to retrieve the beanie, the nurse stole a glance at the discarded brochure and changed the subject. "Your son? He's going on d'cruise?"

Ellen sighed again. Snakes on a plane, did she have to bring it up now?

The nurse added, "We can talk. If it'd help."

"Talk about what—the cruise? That *scintillating* marketing copy? Or the crushing sense of helplessness 'cause I'm fifty-five and leaving my only child in the maw of that good-for-nothing Company?"

The nurse hummed expectantly.

Ellen moaned. She'd hardly seen Ronny since the diagnosis. Hell, she lived at the opposite end of the hemisphere, and every brief *Happy Birthday* internet call showed a man aging like his father, years ahead of time. Drinking ravaged his body. Money choked his soul. Cancer ate his mother.

"Not up for it, Astrid. *Sorey*," Ellen held her head high, exaggerating the Saskatchewan accent. "But you'll see. He'll come around. Sooner or later, he'll come. You forget, I've a Man on the inside." Of course, the nurse thought this was a religious expression, but Ellen secretly alluded to the AeroX robot she'd commandeered to keep watch over her prodigal son. Not that God needed the help…

The nurse pushed the wheelchair around the bend to the lobby. Even a month ago, Ellen would have sued knowing she'd be wheeled to her own death when she had two good legs, but her heart was no longer up to the task. Walking or litigation.

The lobby bore the cheerful delight of summer in the subarctic. Sunlight streamed through the windows, yet it was much colder here than in the convalescing room. This detour was Ellen's special request, and her nurse, stubborn as an old fax machine, tried again to punish her for it with the offending beanie. She snapped off the woolen monstrosity and clutched it tight. She liked the cold. What was the Great White Canadian North but a clingy child who loved hugs and rummaging chilly fingers inside your coat?

Little Ronny had loved to rummage.

The doctor waited in the lobby and smiled whenever Ellen looked his way. His arms crossed around a clipboard, a finger and thumb locked in a private neurotic tussle. When it came to his patients, the doctor never could admit defeat. They wheeled his way.

"I have something for you," Ellen told him, "a gift to add to my already *generous* endowment."

She made great ceremony of giving him the beanie.

The doctor pressed his lips at the overture. Indeed,

her foundation had left a large fortune in trust to the hospital and its related cancer research treatments, but the beanie wasn't going to help the doctor get over his neuroses. He picked at a snag in the stitching, uncertain what to say.

A reverberating boom hit the lobby windows.

Ellen perked up. Grabbing the wheels before her attendants could object, she rolled to the frosty panes that looked out. The leaching cold fogged her breath, but she held fast, a bony hand raised to block the sun until she spotted on the horizon the chemical spew of a supply rocket. She traced its torrential ascent, just catching a metallic glimmer as it vanished in the blue.

So many goodbyes, unsaid.

She blew a kiss to her baby boy and the frozen vacuum he'd soon navigate, alone.

Her teeth began to chatter. "M—maybe he'll meet a m—movie star...decide to s—settle down..."

The doctor wheeled her from the window, from her last rays of sunshine. They took a different path down the hall, to the palliative care ward and a bed that bristled with life support machines. The nurse laid her to rest. Ellen felt feather-light, already a ghost.

With a nod to the anesthesiologist, the doctor offered her one last smile. "Are you ready for us to put you under, Ms. Cologne?"

She squinted at the beanie still tucked in his hand. "I see what you're trying to do. I swear to God, somebody add this to my DNR."

ACT ONE

Requiem for a Galactic Dream

1

The End of the World

Ronny IV was in no mood to romp with the female celebrities in the footsie pool, or slide *The Culebra* on the magnetic floor, or smash himself silly on Father's bottomless bar tab, all of which had become the nightly ritual these nineteen glorious days in space.

Alas, no.

Tonight, he'd raise a glass of questionable milk to the misery that awaited him tomorrow morning, when the countdown clock expired and the spaceliner plunged into orbit, flushing his life of exquisite frivolity unto one of "hard work and respectability," as per the legal terms of Father's trust fund. Ronny could already feel the inertia, the circuitous suckward descent.

What might it feel like to just let the whirlpool of reality drag him under?

His gaze roamed the Nautilus Discotheque, the spaceliner's only nightclub. The neon seashell marquee, violet and pink, pulsed over a throng of silhouettes undulating to a bass line. Scattered patrons drank away their apprehensions at the bar in the back. Ronny blinked. The disquieting girth of his augmented-reality contact lenses bore witness to his mission.

One last dive, fully sober.

He cleared his throat. "AeroLens. Record."

A tiny red spot appeared in the middle distance of sight.

Lifting an eyebrow like an undercover agent, he glanced overhead at the bare feet that dappled across the glass ceiling—the Nautilus's footsie pool suspended above the dance floor. He had to hand it to the engineers at AeroX: the concept of the footsie pool was as audacious as it was precarious, and the frathouse vibe was spot on Father's brand. If only the engineers had thought to add eye bleach. Ronny wanted to forget. His only purpose in capturing video now was to snip apart the recordings later, render them as looping memes, and spam them on whatever forums kids these days were using to shitpost their dads.

His inner DJ was already drumming up captions for his nineteen-day escapades.

This wallow is brought to you by AeroLens:
A GIF For Every Goodbye.

Goodbye to spiking the pool system with scented suds!
Goodbye to parkour on the cabin deck at 2 AM!
Goodbye to dancing the lobsters on down the buffet line!

Oh, hello...

His rudderless gaze foundered on a woman, sharply dressed, hunched at the bar. Thirty-ish, like him. Alone, like him. She ran delicate fingers around the base of her cocktail glass and stared into its pool, awaiting an oracle.

It chanced that he could be that oracle.

Beatific...apocalyptic...aviary? Ronny, head cocked, chest puffed out, wondered perhaps if his ruffled shirt bore an unsettling resemblance to a scraggly pigeon in mating season. A vision unsought for, yet swooping in on a wing and a prayer. It didn't matter; she wasn't his type. Her polyasian features were more and more the genetic norm on Earth, and Ronny preferred the exotic pastime of a bombshell blond. She had black-walnut hair pulled into a migraine-tight bun, sharp-rimmed glasses that could stab you, an excellent figure all tucked away.

Too prim. Too dour. Yes, the perfect companion for tonight's countdown to sobriety.

He bounded toward her. It was entirely against his will. The half-gravity of the ship's centrifugal design prohibited the slow saunter he was aiming for. He preferred a controlled glide and the discretion to adjust how things land, but the Nautilus was notorious for its lack of handrails. He landed at the bar stool next to her like an overeager freshman, a first impression he downplayed with his nonchalant opener.

"You haven't touched your drink."

She didn't look up. "You're making me wish I had."

He smiled broadly at the flat snark of her answer. Misery, meet company.

"I'm Ronny."

"God—!" She dry coughed. Had there been a drink in her mouth, it would have burst over the bartop as she spun wild-eyed to see him.

He stood, contemplating the heavens, pretending to be Father. "God may be a stretch. Sure, I own the ship and am privately acquainted with the celebrities on board..."

She groaned with relief, even laughed at her little mistake, and turned away. "You had me. I can't believe how much you sound like him."

"God?"

She snorted. "Ron—al Cologne."

Ah. The Big Man Himself. She knew how to upsell those fake Latino vibes.

But she hadn't pieced together the relation. Father was head of the Company; he, the nepo-baby who'd inherited the bogus name and barrel-chested voice, with none of the barrel chest or generational ambitions. Ronny's wiry face and figure was the spitting image of Mother, which played in his favor when rubbing elbows with a barfly who happened to loath Father's guts. And there was only one kind of person like that on this space cruise.

He gave a charming laugh. "I take it you're with the Company."

She sighed. Her gaze sunk back to her cocktail, hand on the hilt, clearly tempted to run herself through. "Allison Gin, first division architect at Mentat."

Ah, a programming genius. He let out a quiet whistle, for he knew painfully well the events that had led to Allison's presence on this ship. Tale as old as time: *Girl perfects AI robots, Father acquires Girl's company, Girl immediately sidelined.*

Mentat was the birthplace of the world's first Autonomous Intelligence, what headlines had called "the perfect sentient"—what Ronny had called, after he'd met the thing, "Boredom Simulator 3000." Who could have predicted that free-rein AI would turn out so cloying and pathetic, the embodiment of all those conflict mediation therapists who'd counseled him in later adolescence? Perhaps Father had. Which is why *Ronal Senior* paid billions to acquire Mentat and seize its pioneer robot, to shape its impressionable mind in his own twisted image, and delegate to it the task he hated most: parenting. Which is why *Ronal Junior* could never miss a shareholder meeting or flout the trust fund, hounded from dawn till dusk by Father's robot, whose parental lectures this week included how soap semi-permanently damages pool filtration systems, how parkour may cause under-reported cases of erectile dysfunction, and how New England coastal lobsters ought to receive the quiet dignity they deserve.

Ronal Cologne III had also got a second marriage out of the Mentat buyout—the CEO of Mentat, a woman Ronny's age.

Helpless to stop the merger-marriage, stuck on the AeroX payroll, he and Allison had loads in common. But Ronny couldn't bring himself to out the relation and spoil the surprise. After all, he was the reason Father had bastardized her precious AI into the Cologne Family *Nanny Bot*.

Allison said nothing more, only swirled her pale green drink and sipped none of it. Maybe it was hemlock.

Ronny reclined an elbow on the bartop, recalling one of Father's personality updates that turned Nanny Bot into a drawling cowboy. Another AeroX engineering feat that managed to plow a redline of cultural sensitivity, and also—so cruelly effective at stressing a man's morning hangovers. Not that Ronny had ever learned this firsthand.

"I *feel your pain*, Allison Gin. If you feel the need to unburden yourself on me..."

Her side-eye fished with the idea. "Have you really exhausted all options on this cruise that you've come crawling to my quiet corner of the bar?"

He chose that moment to sit, an act that felt confessional. "Right. 'Of all the gin joints in all the universe...'" Her look made it clear she'd heard that one before. "I'm just trying to unwind before the big tomorrow. No ulterior motives."

She smirked. "What made you throw *your* life away on this cruise?"

"Knew a guy." He left it at that. "You?"

"Business."

"Mmm. Makes sense."

He'd imagined raising a toast in memory of all the creative dreams Father had squashed, but really, why bother? Hard drinks were off the table. He couldn't stomach the milk—the powdered stuff didn't taste right, and the fresh stuff was nineteen days *matured*. And a water served neat would set him back on all those kidney stones he was supposedly growing.

He mulled over where to steer the conversation. "Kids?"

"What?"

"You want kids someday?"

She shifted uncomfortably. "Why would you ask me that?"

Specifically, the kidney stones had brought it to mind. "I dunno. I never could sleep with a woman who wanted kids."

She stifled her shock. "Perfect, since I could never sleep with a guy who wears AeroLens."

He gestured off his temple. "You might want to keep your options open, in case AeroLens sweeps the globe while we're away."

She courtesy-laughed and glanced awry. "I think I'll take my chances with the end of the world."

Behind the exit sign across the room hung an ostentatious clock, counting the cyan seconds until their return to Earth. Twelve hours, seven minutes, fifty-six seconds.

Fifty-five.

Fifty-four.

Allison pressed her bloodless lips and blew out another sigh. Whatever soul-plunging banter Ronny had hoped would get him down the drain and into tomorrow's business suit wasn't happening. This woman was just as bottled up as he was. Perhaps even worse. What genius travels twenty years into the future for the sake of a company she's desperate to leave? Even Mother, God rest her soul, knew when to get off the ride.

He sucked in a breath and swiveled toward the bar to survey his alcoholic escapes. Oh right...tonight was about *catharsis*, not another binge.

Damn it all, Allison wasn't giving him options.

2

A Trip Down the Well

"Hey, you, Argyle!" Ronny called after the barbot, a sleek gray automaton standing behind the counter, busily polishing the glassware. Here was a robot far less expensive than the Cologne Family Nanny Bot and commensurately less intelligent. "Gimme the usual!"

The barbot gave Ronny the middle finger.

Undeterred, Ronny stretched over the counter and snagged a bottle of whatever they stored in the well down there. The barbot, eyes simulated on a curved LCD screen, glanced meaningfully toward the ceiling lights and whistled a merry tune.

Not every robot on the cruise was his nanny. Though some had been with the Company since Ronny was in diapers, this last-gen barbot, whom he called Argyle for the diamond-patterned tuxedo etched on his flat gunmetal chest, he'd been hacking since middle school, secretly installing bootleg software found on Global Search. There wasn't a security flaw in the book that Argyle hadn't tripped over in one decade or another.

On a lavish cruise, it helped to have a backdoor with your barbot.

Ronny looked at the bottle he'd taken from behind the counter. Gin. God damn. The stars had aligned.

In a spasm of excitement, he snatched Allison's cocktail glass and tossed its unwanted contents behind the counter. The effect of centrifugal gravity flung the drink further than Ronny had intended, and it splashed Argyle right in the diamonds. Score!

Passing it off with a shrug, Ronny dangled the bottle of gin over Allison's emptied glass. "Fancy an upgrade?"

Her eyelashes flared in surprise; rebukes jammed in her slender throat.

The barbot said nothing. He turned his wipe routine on himself and got the mop.

No doubt Allison was beginning to suspect his family connections. Had any other patron tossed a drink like that, Argyle would have dispatched the taser dogs to rough him up before things got rowdy. But Allison's curiosity, however strong, was not keeping her in her seat. With a polite if brusque nod, she excused herself.

"I have an early morning."

Away she bounded for the cabin decks. Ronny watched her go.

Tough crowd tonight.

He turned back to the bar. Professional bar trawlers like Ronny were a dying breed (cirrhosis of the liver notwithstanding), earning no esteem, no pity, not even the sorry *shucks* a bird feels for the worm it feeds to its chicks. He thought the toss-out-her-drink thing deserved at least a time-honored "Well I never!" Screwing open the bottle of gin and screwing his pledges in equal fashion, he snagged a fresh glass and poured himself a double.

"Let this be a lesson to you, Argyle." He saluted the old barbot, who was wiping glasses behind the counter again. "Never date a coworker."

Argyle offered a dry reply. "Surely exceptions can be made for a highly sophisticated drink blender like me."

Ronny shook his head. "HR makes no exceptions.

Especially for drink blenders. The power dynamics, you see?"

Argyle projected a forlorn frown on his mouth screen. "Damn. I was sure your father's secretary bot wanted me for my personality."

"A chatbot can dream." Ronny snickered and downed the shot. Gin, *ugh*. Too medicinal for his taste, and this brand was barely a step above mouthwash.

As bad as he'd hoped it would be.

An aggressive grab of his shoulder turned him fully around on the stool. Allison had returned and stood behind him, all five-foot-two of her in a wrath.

"You!" she sputtered. "You're his *son*! His son, *Ron Cologne*!"

This was the first time his identity had brought a woman of such unflinching sobriety back to the bar. He was almost too stunned to respond. "*Ron—ny* Cologne."

The rims of her glasses tried to impale him. "How dare you act like—like it's OK to do what you did!"

"Do what? Toss out your drink? Honestly, I thought you were thick for not figuring out the relation sooner, given my tremendous reputation around the ship. I offered you a drink. You declined and walked away. Seemed above board, but tell me my sins."

She looked like a Polynesian volcano about to erupt into new islands. "Company policy strictly prohibits... romantic interactions between employees!"

Ronny flattened his lips. "Come on. I wear AeroLens. You want kids. What chance is there—"

"I do not want kids!" she blustered.

He raised an eyebrow. "So you're saying there's a chance."

"I could...I could just..." Her fists opened and closed, eyes darting between his cheekbones for the one more deserving a bruise. Bet Company policy prohibited that, too. All he could guess was that her anger stemmed from her career Father had dismantled. Whether or not Ronny deserved it, he had every bit of Father's swagger and was just short enough to slug.

Ronny readied himself. Catharsis, inbound.

She clenched shut her eyes, revealing the wet sparkle of tears, and exhaled a shuddering breath. Her fists relaxed.

Even now, she kept the cork in. He couldn't believe it.

Pouring a trashy shot of gin into her cocktail glass, Ronny baited her. "You hate my guts. You can say it out loud. I won't tell the taser dogs. Look at us: we're both staring down the barrel of a shotgun." He glanced again at the countdown clock. "Twelve hours. God, let's do this."

He poured himself a shot to match hers. "I'll go, then you."

She watched in utter confusion, the flush of anger radiating off her cheeks. A little red unlocked the contrast in her complexion, and suddenly, Ronny felt like he was staring at a whole different woman. Not the repressed stereotype he'd seen earlier, but a vision. An *oracle*.

This crap gin was messing with him.

Ronny tipped back his shot, swallowed, and vomited up his secret ambitions. "I want to backpack the world and become the Spielberg of AeroLens!"

Her mouth hung open like a concerned paralytic. "The movie guy?"

"Yeah, but of AeroLens! Ever since I was a kid and Father forgot me on the set of *Jurassic Mars*, I've wanted to film the world. And needed therapy. But I'd have to quit AeroX to do it...the filming, not the therapy...and I'm too chickenshit because Father would just turn around and give the trust fund to Argyle back there. Can't very well film the world if I'm broke!"

He slid the shot glass away and blinked. "Your turn."

It took her a moment to shake out an excuse. "I—I don't drink like this…"

"Come on! Don't make me go again. This stuff's terrible."

But he gripped the glass and poured himself another confession: the Big One, the one that had soured in his stomach these nineteen days. Poured to the brim and hoisted high, the shot glass seemed a disturbing science lesson on the stickiness of surface tension in low-gravity environments. He quailed to drink it. He already knew what came of nausea in low gravity.

Bottoms up.

He gulped the shot and cringed. "I didn't say goodbye to Mother before we left. God help me. She had stage-four cancer."

Allison's eyes widened. "I thought Ronal was a widower when he married Genasia—"

"Please, *jen—ay—sea—uh!*" He mocked the mention of Father's current wife and the merger-marriage that had brought Mentat and AeroX together like one big incestuous family. "All billionaires ditch their starter wives somewhere, and Old Ron ditched his in Canada. And it's my one comfort thinking that global warming may have made the weather nice since he bilked those misleading press releases and divorced her ass while she lay to die at the pole."

Allison cleared her throat. "I'm sorry," she whispered, visibly taken aback.

Ronny slid over her cocktail glass and made one last bid for her to sit. "Now, you. Before I pass out or tell you about that one time in Dallas. What would the great Allison Gin do, if nothing held you back in life?"

Her face became stone, motions methodical. She perched on the edge of the stool, touched the cocktail glass, and stared blankly at the colorless gin while words dripped from her lips. "There's no one waiting for me back on Earth. Just...my work. I would break my NDA if I didn't fear a lawsuit. Maybe start with a competitor who cares about using AI to help people."

She kept the gin on the table. All that beautiful red drained from her cheeks and left her looking wan again.

Ronny passed a roiling burp as Allison cringed back an inch or two. Ho, he was just getting started. "Pathetic. Afraid to break a measly NDA? We do that every Tuesday in the AeroX board room. Do you swaddle yourself in that outfit every morning to *beep-boop* like the robots you're making? For godsake, let it fly!"

The color returned—stoked to the boiling point. Ronny prepared to see the gin flying into his face. But Allison threw the gin into her own throat and fired fast.

"You wanna *hear it*, how miserable you make the world for everyone? Your family just...just...chews people up, steals their ideas, and spits out a profit! We're all just pawns in your sick games of nepotism and greed!"

She took a shuddering breath, but did not slow down.

"I never wanted to be on this absurd cruise, but where else could I go? It's not like I'm the great *Ron—ny Col—ogne*, given everything on a silver platter, then *boo-hooing* that I've never taken a semester abroad to film the world—never mind do something truly great, or even halfway decent, like start a children's foundation."

Argyle, finding the countertop too near the atrocity unfolding at his bar, had stepped into the far corner and buried his face against the wall.

Allison's voice grew impossibly louder, overtaking the din of the club.

"I made life! FUCKING LIFE! My AI could have given orphans inexhaustible kindness or worked in twenty-four-seven disaster zones to save the sick and starving. But every goddamn day I'm forced to watch my life's work *wipe the shit off your ass!*"

Heads turned at the outburst, but Ronny paid them no heed. He closed his eyes and gave an understanding nod. He'd gotten what he needed out of tonight, a little self-annihilating splash in the moral backwash of his life to psych himself up for tomorrow, when he'd sit in a stiff-back office chair like one of Father's compliant robots, trust fund secure.

Most self-respecting women, having measured the bald facts of the person they've shared a drink with and found them wanting, immediately storm off, perhaps first imparting the auspicious wisdom of a slap. But when Ronny opened his eyes he saw Allison Gin, blanched and stock still, studying his face with peculiar...anticipation? Dread?

"Tell me those aren't on."

The AeroLens.

Ronny mugged a look that said, "You kidding me?" while noting the little red recording spot blurring in his middle sight. These recordings were destined for a private server loaded with far more incriminating video mementos than this. Her secrets were safe, everything deeply encrypted. Nothing to worry about. But he had no way of stopping the recording now, shy of blurting out, "AeroLens, stop!" or jabbing himself in the eyes and elevating her concern to outright hysterics. So he grabbed the bottle of gin and poured an assurance into both of their glasses.

"A toast. And one I hope you will join me in." He lifted his glass and flashed Allison a congenial grin. "To me! Ronny Cologne, fourth in a line of rich, dysfunctional asshats: may there never be a fifth!"

It took her a beat to laugh, but when she did, she expelled all that remained of her former pent-up anxiety. "I'll drink to that."

3

Crushed

Ronny woke to an alarming pressure on his chest.

His monogrammed headboard loomed in the darkness above, the ritual greeting after a night of partying, and his first clue that it was the hour of reckoning in the early morning. He already knew what it felt like to let *this* whirlpool drag him under. Breath short, arms dead, head pounding, ass prone, he blinked through the squinting pain without even a pillow to cry on.

He'd left in the blasted contacts again.

Cold waves of panic came as none of his limbs could move. Why? And why did his heart feel like an anvil had cartoon-crushed it? The narration in his head mocked him in the wizened voice of Spielberg.

Glad you're back with us, Ronny. This hangover
is sponsored by AeroX Interstellar Cruises:
Light Speed With No Landing Gear.

The gin had landed. Crash landed.

Did you know that Argyle doubles as a horoscope?
Your future is replete with so many fatal diamond
collisions...

The barbot had looked away when Ronny's slippery hands had probed the back counter for a second bottle. He was pouring shots for two. Gin...gin...

Allison Gin.

Our next request is Ronny's favorite: the Latin slide sensation, The Culebra. Let's see if he can move those hips while keeping his liquor down.

He suddenly recalled an increasingly impassioned conversation with Allison as they poured out their souls, shot by shot, until she tried to stand and pitched into him. They laughed like idiots.

Then she asked him to dance.

Whatever happened next, he'd flat-out forgotten.

Hope you remembered to tip your barbot.
They never forget, you know.

His chest screamed with fresh pain, and Ronny gasped through the pressure. A heart attack! He was certainly— probably having a heart attack. A decade of drinking and disregard for the welfare of his body was exploding him from the inside-out.

His thoughts spun to Mother and her metastasized cancer, eating her heart.

"ErrorLens," he slurred, "help."

An orange X persisted in his middle vision. No con- nection? Not a recognized command?

He thrashed for breath. His shoulder peeled out of a constricting prison, and the arm fell away, numb and seemingly dismembered on the bed. Ronny moaned in horror until he felt a prickle in the limb and realized, with flooding and equally ticklish relief, that his limbs had only lost blood circulation due to whatever was pinning him to the mattress.

Conviction seized him. Should he survive this perilous ordeal, he would make good on his confessions to Allison, trust fund be damned. Screw Father: he was gonna backpack Europe. Film himself on a shirtless hike up a Nepalese mountain. Look up poor Mother and apologize to her grave. Get flush faced and footloose like Allison had after that last shot of her godforsaken namesake.

An alien shape groaned on his chest.

Ronny, hyperventilating now, heaved the unidentified mass onto the mattress beside him. The crushing weight on his lungs lifted at once, and he gulped deeply, spluttering, jerking away and smacking the night light to reveal the truth of what had been smothering him.

A naked woman.

She immediately yanked the sheet over her. Spying where she was and who she was with, the woman seethed out a vast vocabulary of curses, such as only a certified genius could invent under the crippling duress of a hangover.

Ronny hadn't expected to feel so giddy seeing Allison in his bed. He couldn't explain it—couldn't have tried. All he said before the blood drained out of his inebriated head was, "Huh."

4

Nanny Bot

His eyelids burst in orange and white, lit like a roaring candle.

Ronny squinted, eyes shunning the artificial sunlight streaming through his faux cabin window. A shiny rose-metal surface seemed to be conducting the light directly into his face. Desperate for more sleep, he rolled out of the beam.

The metal surface moved, sending the blinding light into his eyes again.

An impenetrable headache kept him from discerning what was ruining his precious sleep. Then he heard the dumb-headed drawl.

"Gawd, yer beautiful in the light'a day."

Nanny Bot stood by the window.

Ronny slapped around the bed for a pillow to stuff over his face, but found nothing in the tangle of bedsheets to save himself from this vindictive game.

The humanoid robot hovered outside his ear. "Ten billion folks in this here wide world, and then thar's you."

"Stop."

Father's ten-billion dollar AI was pacing the room now, gushing like a newly-wed John Wayne on the morning after. "Yer nose is like a wedge of cheese. Would just gobble it up, if'n I could."

"I'd just crack you open, Nanny Bot! Swap your battery for a potato! Let your soup-for-brains dry out like a nasty sponge!" Useless threats. Ronny turned his hand into a weary shield, but Nanny Bot knew every angle to send the light beaming into his abused irises.

"Call me Nanny whenever yer like, Sugerblossum. I love it how you look when yer angry."

The implacable robot was rose-gold in hue with soft-sculpted eyes, nose, and mouth—not the flat-screen stand-ins that Argyle featured—and a full range of human expression that was currently engaged in blowing Ronny kisses.

Ronny had just enough technical know-how to crack open Argyle, who was basically a cheapass computer that ran software to simulate human behavior. Nanny Bot, though, was powered by neural paste: actual, living neurons that (more or less) wrote their own software, impervious to tampering, trickery, and tantrums. If Argyle was the recordable mixtape of robots, Nanny Bot was a runaway bluegrass band: impeccable musical acumen, tuned to make your ears bleed.

Like now. Nanny Bot complied with Father's orders to get Ronny out of bed with lateral solutions: this sadistic wake-up routine and its awful pickup lines. It riled Ronny to madness. It forced his sluggish brain to move. Getting up was the only way to make the AI stop.

Defeated, Ronny sat off the edge of the bed and cradled his head in his hands.

"Mornin', sunshine. Big day today. Countdown ends in twenty-five minutes."

Nanny Bot held out a glass of sparkling water, which Ronny begrudgingly consented to drink. Ronny noted the taste of an additive: a cure-all that would ease his hangover and make the Company trust fund baby presentable. He noted, too, that Nanny Bot had already laid out a business suit at the foot of the bed. The awful sage green one. Company colors.

He hated changing with the nanny present. "You go on to the party. I'll be right behind."

The robot raised a hand and stood in mock salute. "No can do'ski. Orders are real strict I escort you to the ballroom. Don't keep me chuffin' or I'll ask you to dance."

Ask to dance...

Ronny felt his throat clog recalling his midnight rendezvous with Allison and the afterimage of her scandalized face in bed. She must've left his cabin this morning soon after he'd passed out. At least she wasn't here now to see, and hear, her drawling Frankenstein monster.

"Giddy-up, little cowpoke! I wanna get movin' bufore the cooks clear out the char-cooterie."

Ronny reluctantly stripped down. Nanny Bot cared nothing for privacy or dignity, but he did care about food— always sniffed the charcuterie boards, tickled his inner smelling whiskers for shits and giggles. Bizarre behavior from a robot who didn't eat. Maybe it was just another instance of his awful sense of humor, born of corporate bosses telling creative eggheads to make a robot more palatable to the masses. Lots of cheesy jokes, and jokes literally about cheese.

A crackle from the in-cabin PA system brought another lazy voice into the room, that of the human pilot of the cruise ship whose announcements always preceded some kind of bracing change of inertia.

"Yeahum, folks, this is your captain speaking. *The Cologne* is beginning its approach to the solar system. You'll want to stay in your seats or take the nearest handrail as we begin to decelerate. AeroX thanks ya."

Speech patterns ripped from every stereotypical

airline pilot. No doubt Father offered the man a job the moment he heard that lackadaisical, "Yeahum."

Ronny had just buttoned his pants when he lost balance and pitched into the bed. The spaceliner was braking, popping the warp bubble, or whatever the Star Trek was going on—enough to screw with Ronny's inner ear and leave him moaning with nausea. The taste of gin on his breath triggered another wave of flashbacks from last night, and freshly seized with regret, he clutched the bedsheets and prepared to empty his guts.

Nanny Bot had perfectly leaned into the inertia without shifting a sculpted foot. "Puke the bed, if yer gonna. I got nothin' to do."

Now that Nanny Bot had said it aloud, Ronny felt like holding it in. He had principles. And his principles could generally be summed as opposite whatever Nanny Bot suggested.

Sitting on the bed, waiting for the nausea to pass, Ronny massaged his burning eyes. The chunky contact lenses again. He'd left them in last night, when he and Allison climbed in bed...but had he left them on?

Oh. Oh no. God please no.

A dalliance with a Company employee was a zero-tolerance offense in today's day and age, but it was the thought of the recording itself that made Ronny's sickness double down. He had no desire to check the private server and peek at what had come of their drunken stew.

What an asshat he could be when drunk.

Asshat. Ronny relished the uniquely descriptive power of that word as he slowly stood up and adjusted his blazer so the shoulder pads sat square. He wet and slicked back his hair. Nanny Bot wasn't the only one Ronny lived to spite.

Couldn't keep the old asshat waiting.

5

Terms and Conditions

When Ronny slunk into the Viewscape Grand Ballroom with Nanny Bot at his heels, he found the homecoming banquet was full tilt. Tilt in the literal sense. By design, the walls of the vaulted ballroom leaned in the same direction: the entrance wall leaned over the buffet line, and the window wall across leaned out over outer space. Every time Ronny entered he felt tipsy (whether or not he'd hit the breakfast bar), a fact made so much worse by Father's frequent charge to straighten up, which in the ballroom, frankly, was impossible to satisfy.

This morning, a vast curtain of oriental blinds lay over the window wall, concealing the starry vista out, staged by Father to turn the sight of Earth into a spectacular reveal. But the blinds robbed the ballroom of its grandeur, and the eye was left to wonder upon the spluttering air returns and awful ductwork.

Ronny shook off his claustrophobia with a survey of the round banquet tables where two-hundred bloated passengers ingested their final brunch while digesting the uncertain realities of their return. All could feel the window leaching the heat from the room, an impracticality of that massive sight that ensured the scattered space heaters were always flaming.

Amid the tables rose a tall, wood-paneled dais trimmed

with gold railing. Two flights of stairs curved behind the dais like the snakes of a caduceus, leading to the platform where a prestigious podium awaited a singular speaker.

Billionaire Ronal Cologne III. Sir Asshat himself.

Beneath the podium hung a projector screen, currently engaged in a dramatic show of numbers ticking down, like a TV bomb. Eleven minutes, twenty-one seconds.

Twenty.

Nineteen.

"Ron, there you are!" Father called from the platinum executives table. The man was in prime form, both in stomach and magnanimity after his very successful and decidedly nonlethal interstellar cruise. Of course, they hadn't yet seen the results of the radiology tests, but not even the specter of cosmic cancer could stifle the man's voracious optimism.

Ronny felt so deflated he left the AeroLens off.

With an impatient wave, Ron Sr. signaled the delinquent Ron Jr. to sit in the empty seat between him and a university chairman old enough to have played a fossil on *Jurassic Mars*. Looked like the menu this morning included corporate chinwag with an academic dinosaur.

As per the terms and conditions that held Ronny's life in thrall, he had to oblige these meet-cutes that his boss-by-relation arranged, but there were plenty of ways to punish Father for it. He snagged a lobster tail from the buffet line on his way to the table.

"Ron," Father spake with his usual gruff, "meet a colleague of mine, Dr. Anders Paracless. Parak-aless? Did I get that right?"

The doctor grimaced. "Paraclese."

"Para-CLEASE excuse me!" Father laughed at his abominable humor and yanked Ronny down into his seat. "You two have much to talk about. Ron here has a bright future in celestial mechanics."

Across the table, Nanny Bot sat opposite with an ambivalent smile. Next to Nanny Bot was another vacant seat: Genasia's. Wherever Father's young trophy wife had glided off to, she'd made the right choice to abandon the senior table.

Dr. Paraclese popped an hors d'oeuvre into his mouth and crushed it noisily between false teeth. "You study astrophysics?"

Not a day in his life, but Ronny could flub it. "I was once a top-five contributor on the Wiki. You wouldn't believe how many still think the universe is flat."

Father cocked his head and fired a warning shot. The left eyebrow. "Quit grandstanding, Ron, and listen to the man. Andy here is chairman emeritus of Cambridge's astrophysics program. They almost beat me to the Neumine Quantum Drive—but don't hold it against him! He drafted the patents for the AeroX spaceliner and left behind a multi-billion dollar research grant for an all-expenses paid ticket on *The Cologne*. Convinced half an army of interns to join him."

"We have no regrets," the professor said between shoveled bites. "Why, it's been the highlight of my very existence."

"I've spoken with Andy, and he's accepted a position on my Hari Seldon committee."

God, not that.

Paraclese wiped his white beard. "As a longtime reader of Asimov, it gives me no greater pleasure. Humanity needs a guiding hand."

But did it need the fat hand of Ronal Cologne III fingering all of its pies? Father, the serial entrepreneur, had determined his future lay in shepherding the march of human history through the miracle of time dilation.

Twenty-day interstellar voyages and twenty-year returns to Earth, with time between to gas up, deliver sage counsel, launch a business, and otherwise play god.

Paraclese was the latest recruit in his astronomical pyramid scheme.

Father continued grandly. "In exchange for this opportunity, he's willing to take you as his student when we get back. Help you finish your post-graduate degree."

"At Cambridge!" Ronny marveled. "Which Cambridge?"

Paraclese paused mid-fork, unsure of what to make of Ronny's jib.

Nanny Bot spoke up from across the table like a sheriff late to the saloon. "I read yer patents, Doctor. Whatta legacy! You done shook up the market bufore we left by makin' our Neumeen science patents open-source. Least by my per-jections, the Cambridge of today shud be rulin' the world."

Father twisted a frown at a technicality that may have gone over his head.

Paraclese saved face with an impressed nod at Nanny Bot. "Which son was it with a future in astrophysics?"

Father smirked at whatever poker hand his mind held. "The robot's spoken for. But Ron could stand to learn a few things..."

Or say sayonara to the trust fund—Ronny knew how these sentences ended. Picking at the lobster tail, putting on the Cologne airs, he feigned great interest in his forthcoming free educational journey. "I can probably squeeze the time to finish one, or two, of my postgraduate degrees. Cambridge...definitely tops my list. But Doctor. How can you be so certain of your tenure there? Twenty years is quite the gap in one's career."

"Not so!" Paraclese replied. "This trip has done more to further my career than a thousand toilsome articles.

My team has amassed *incontestable* data on hundreds of local exoplanets—data no instrument on Earth could hope to replicate. And, well," he laughed, "you certainly underestimate the staying power of tenure."

Father guffawed, and Paraclese swallowed a congratulatory bite of caviar. Nanny Bot sniffed the air, sampling all the smells he couldn't eat. Ronny plunked the lobster tail in an abandoned cocktail glass and watched it bob.

"Plainly speaking," Paraclese added, "it was Ronal's generosity that precipitated the rapid expansion of Cambridge's astrophysics department, and I concur with your robot here: the future is bright. Humanity needs visionaries like the Colognes who can think one, two, and three-hundred years into its future. As such, I'd be honored to welcome you as a student in my research program." He passed an aside to Father, "We might even make the Wiki reputable."

Ronny wondered if it would kill him to stay in this conversation one, two, or three more seconds and decided, it certainly would. He pushed back his chair and stood up. "My old man ought to finish his degree, too. We're a family of very accomplished drop-outs, him and me."

Father stiffened. "Nonsense. I already think long and hard about my future, Ron. *Long and hard.* I'm minutes from publicly announcing phase two of AeroX Ventures. If you want a place in that future..." He trailed off suggestively.

Ronny wanted a blank check and limitless freedom. Was that future too much to ask? He grit his teeth, recalling his deathbed pledge to screw the trust fund and strike out on his own, but the thought of never outliving Father—of always feeling the crush of his terms and conditions as the self-proclaimed CEO of the human race...

It drove a man to drink.

"To the future!" Ronny picked up his lobster-spiked cocktail and tossed the mix in his mouth. The wet tail whipped free and fell in Father's lap, spattering his tie.

"Fucker!" Father slammed his soiled napkin on the table.

Ronny counted it among his dearest regrets that he'd missed the catastrophe on AeroLens. With an overblown laugh, he announced, "What the hell, Doctor—sign me up for tenure! It's a perfect fit for a fucker like Ron Cologne IV. Look at it this way, Father: I could blow you out an airlock, and you couldn't even fire me!"

As Father's maddened hand seized the tablecloth, Paraclese hastily piled the remains of his plate. "My deepest gratitude to you, Ronal. Best wishes on phase two."

Ronny saluted the doctor's exit. "Live long and prosper!" He donned his best shit-eating grin for the turn back to Father, whose face had swollen, livid as a lobster. But before the man could strike, an arm wrapped around his neck. Slender, sanguine, with geometric tattoos like snake skin, Genasia graced the table just in time to whisper in her husband's ear.

"You know the shareholders are watching."

Her eyes flashed, dark eyeliner warning Ronny to get out.

6

Phase Two

Genasia didn't need to spell it out. Ronny flagged a fictitious need for the privies and threw himself from the platinum executives table, into the ballroom milieu like a mosh pit.

Let Father fume! This was the last hurrah. The doomsday clock was four minutes to midnight, and Ronny had hardly sated his need for a morning carouse. Sure, the party was lame, the guest list a veritable Who's Who of kiss-ups, and the stewards were pouring the cheap reserves, but Ronny was a bonafide inebriate, capable of savoring the chuck.

Leavened by half-gravity, he bounded through throngs of gassy passengers who were presently chewing on their private thoughts. Thanks to the AeroX spaceliner and the miracle of Einstein's relativity, every day on board *The Cologne* had cost them one year on Earth. That much Ronny *did* know about astrophysics.

Two decades, gloriously flushed, for a pleasure cruise and a winner-takes-all gamble on the future of Earth.

Ronny passed a table of middle-aged bachelors with salt-and-pepper hair whose lives seemed to sprout wealth in perpetuity like the stubble on their cheeks. Names in wearable technologies or medical insurance, most had purchased their tickets to escape a noose of litigation, and all had counted on their investments tripling by the time of their return. Delayed adolescents after his own heart. Here was to getting rich by doing nothing!

Next, the politicians, predominantly women, sidelined while international politics collapsed. How many had sold their souls to various lobbyist groups to fund a desperate trip to a future of gender and ethnic equality, Ronny couldn't count. He raised them an imaginary toast; they'd need more than that to sort out their financial entanglements.

Then, the academics, a mess of them: researchers for universities and military contractors, theoretical physicists, computer scientists, biomed, futurists and their ilk—and indeed their much indentured interns who never found tenure in the recession. Those unsponsored had financed their tickets with impossible loans. Ronny mouthed a vain prayer for Paraclese's *incontestable* data; twenty years was time and a half to blunt any cutting-edge.

Father had made him meet dozens more, whose stories had stirred an ember of feeling in Ronny's heart—regret that he'd ever boarded this damned cruise. Armchair intellectuals seeking book deals. Cut-rate engineers seeking defense contracts. Scandalized executives seeking a clean slate. Five-star generals seeking abstract conquests. Desperate entrepreneurs seeking fresh capital. Crooked retirees seeking absolution from the stars.

No cancer patients, though. Admitting them would've hit Father too close to his manhood.

As the clock entered its sixty-second finale, Ronny spun in search of the right table to crash. That's when he heard raucous laughter from the company furthest from the dais.

The celebrities.

What better homecoming than to crash with the

spaceliner's resident nihilists? These washed up child actors, starlets, and reality regulars had made an easy (or sleazy) buck in film, but the pockets of AeroX had opened regardless to discount their voyage and sprinkle them among the ticketholders. What C-list actor could turn down a diversion of such unprecedented scale?

They were young, attractive, and bored. Thoroughly sick of each other's company.

Ronny had forgotten every one of their names.

He plotted a course for the ballroom bar, ready to ingratiate himself upon the celebrities with a round of stiff drinks. Hand over hand, he shimmied along the ballroom's circuitous outer rail, avoiding the more direct path through the AeroX staff tables. He didn't see Allison, but he wasn't looking either. His stomach clenched at the thought of running into her.

The ballroom bar was recessed in the back corner, and as expected, Argyle was working it. The screen-eyed automaton noted Ronny's arrival with an animated roll of the eyes. It almost looked real. The queue emptied out as the clock reached its terminus, leaving Ronny and Argyle alone, the only two in the room not communally counting down the final ten seconds.

The robot asked, "What'll it be?"

"Double shot of Pasion Azteca, ultra-premium, with table salt and a wedge of lime. And I wanna see your swiss-army tool slice it."

Ronny heard a loud pop, and the air filled with twinkling confetti shot from cannons in the wall. Everyone cheered. Father, with Genasia hanging on his arm, had ascended the center dais and stood at the gold railing, pageant waving. Behind them, the oriental blinds slowly lifted from the cold window to reveal the blue-marble Earth, twirling with the spaceliner's centripetal motion. Ronny snickered at how the optical illusion made it look like the planet was drunk.

Passengers raised their handhelds and flashed the photo for their soon-to-be reborn public media profiles.

Ronny shrank away and watched Argyle fulfill the drink order. Taking a small lime, the bot snapped a switchblade from his palm and cut a wedge with two janky incisions. "You know, compadre," Ronny said, "on Earth that'd get you arrested."

"It's on my bucket list."

A prescient comment about death coming from a robot now twenty years out of sync with technological development.

Even from day one, Argyle had never been a space gray collector's item. Argyle's manufacturer, Primarch Industries, had cut costs to render the barbot's body animations, and the jankiness showed when it stood next to Mentat's butter-smooth AI. Argyle was transition tech, plain and simple. Economists had predicted a tidal shift toward consumer robotics, and hoping to ride the wave, Father had drenched Mentat in funding prior to departure, intent to edge his robotics rival Primarch Industries out of the market. If Cutthroat Cologne could bankroll twenty years of market dominance, he'd sweep down from on high and freeze whatever remained of Primarch's assets like their buggy software. He'd been itching to do it for years.

Yet, Ronny wondered who sold the better robot. In a cage match to the blue screen of death, who would triumph, the rote robot Argyle, or the free-rein Nanny Bot?

Argyle was the underdog, certainly—a glorified chatbot with none of that highfalutin neural paste that let an AI dream of electric sheep. But Argyle kept a neat bar, and no one ought to bet against a bartender. Ronny smirked at his own face reflected in the polished countertop, picturing Earth overrun with glass-polishing Argyles who'd taken over, Terminator style.

Father had yet to begin his planned speech. The man was still soaking in the standing ovation, which had gone on and on and on.

Ronny leaned in to mess with Argyle, like he'd done since middle school. "I guess we'll have to scrap you for parts now that we're back. It's a bad look having a Primarch bot in the AeroX fleet. *Gotta get rid of the evidence.*" It was fun to see how the chatbot reacted to depictions of his imminent demise, especially since Ronny had installed those sarcasm subroutines dredged from the back alleys of the internet.

Argyle poured the tequila and said nothing, only went back to wiping the bar.

"Unless," Ronny added, "you can think of a reason we should keep you around." He dressed the back of his hand with salt but didn't reach for the shot just yet, spooked somewhat by the barbot's silence. Where were Argyle's fierce, inane opinions?

Father's self-congratulatory voice cut into the applause. "Out of this world. Truly. Thank you for joining me, my wife, and all of AeroX Ventures on this stellar cruise. Kicked ass, didn't it?"

Another round of ass-kissing applause, and past time to join the celebrity hecklers for Father's speech.

Argyle blurted, "Am I the Velveteen Rabbit?"

There it was! Some obscure literary reference scraped from a lost message board and delivered with Socratic flair. Ronny laughed as he took up the double shot of Pasion Azteca. "*The what?*"

"Or am I the clockwork mouse that pretends to be Real? Does the mechanical toy care that he serves his master a drugged chalice?"

"A drugged chalice?" Ronny passed a furtive look upon the liquor.

Argyle straightened the tequila bottle so the label faced out. "It's...*a metaphor.*"

Whatever software collision inside of Argyle had produced this brief fugue state delighted Ronny to no end. Of course, the robot couldn't actually drug him because of AeroX's Asset Protection Protocol: the software prohibited Argyle from harming Ronny's biometrics and was safeguarded by three layers of security protection.

Father, erstwhile, had finally corralled the applause. "Ladies and gentlemen—and robots." The room gave a perfunctory laugh. Ronny decided to wait here for Father's next atrocious pun to drop the tequila shot. "As *The Cologne* enters geostationary orbit and the disembarkation shuttles are prepped, I welcome you to the future, a future guided by people like us—people who've stepped out of time and distanced themselves from the daily affairs of survival—better people, who think *long and hard* about how humanity will ultimately thrive. For that reason, let me call up V1.72, er, whatever the hell his version number is! Hop up on stage!"

Ronny held the liquor in suspense at this unscripted development. From the tables below the dais, Nanny Bot took the charge to hop literally and leapt directly from the floor to the platform, to the delight of all.

What was the old man doing? Father's playbook was puns and glory (and dragging speeches), none of which involved asking the family nanny to share centerstage.

Even Genasia seemed surprised. Clinging to her husband's arm, she nettled a frown and whispered something in Father's ear. The man was off script and improvising. *Having a moment.*

"AeroLens, record." Ronny tingled with excitement at what the asshat might say in the crosshairs of that red spot. If he'd known where Father's legal counsel sat, he'd have sent them their own bottle of Pasion Azteca to drink with their tears.

Father waxed eloquent. "Every endeavor needs a leader. As I expand my business interests beyond AeroX and to the very future of Earth, I want you to know that AeroX will remain a family business—one you can trust. So I announce, here and now, my immediate succession. I present to you the newly minted legal heir of the AeroX empire. Son of my own creation: V2!"

Ronny's head spun. He hadn't even swallowed the liquor yet.

V2—*Nanny Bot?*

Holy God.

Inheriting the Company was the foundation of the trust fund. If ownership passed to Nanny Bot, that meant the bastard had finally cut him off. *Over a lobster tail!*

Applause rose in the echo chamber of the grand ballroom while Ronny muttered Father's words, "Son of my own creation." This line twisted Ronny's guts more than anything else. Father had upped the version number—turned Nanny Bot into Version Two of his own flesh and blood son.

Replaced. Just like Mother.

Ronny stood in quiet stupor while eyes combed the room for him. Hungry news reporters tapped out the scoop that could make for their career comebacks. *Ronal Cologne III Cuts Off Heir Apparent From Empire—Hands It*

To Cowboy Robot Instead. Ronny tried to lighten the mood by knocking on his own head, sharing a private joke with the few people who'd spotted him. He desperately needed the hit. Licking the salt, he swallowed the tequila and bit down on the lime.

Burning threads lined his eyelids as the liquor went to work. He imagined the next couple of hours were going to be a special brand of miserable as his future on Earth revealed itself to be as shapeless as his character.

"By the way, a woman came by looking for you."

Hearing Argyle say this, Ronny pictured Allison's fiery cheeks. An imaginary fist threw a left hook that seemed to connect with his right cheek—the tequila, kicking him in the brain. Argyle had impeccable timing.

"Did she leave a message?"

"No."

"Then why'd you have to bring it up?" Ronny soothed his hot cheek with the back of his hand. He scanned the blurry room for the staff tables, but couldn't find Allison. The room hid many secrets.

"I brought it up as a moral lesson," Argyle was saying. "You never should have gotten involved with her. AI architects are skilled enough to reprogram me if I don't comply with their instructions."

"That's...that's why you carry a switchblade!"

And three layers of security to keep hackers out.

Ronny stared at the distant scene on the dais. Father put a starched white captain's hat atop Nanny Bot's bald metal skull and gave him a noogie. The room echoed with laughter that was deafening to Ronny's ears—too loud—a sign something was very wrong. The floor wouldn't cooperate with his feet, and he snatched the edge of the bar to keep himself from toppling over.

He'd had Pasion Azteca before. Never had it exploded

his retinas like this.

"Argyle...did you actually drug me?"

"Nooo..."

He could hear Argyle's sarcasm subroutines were working as intended.

The room kept spinning faster, flinging his thoughts to the far walls.

"Why?" Ronny said, but the real question was *how*. Argyle couldn't do anything without a specific instruction programmed into his system. Ronny imagined all the weird vaporware he'd side-loaded onto Argyle over the years. "Did I...do this to myself?"

"What would be the moral lesson in that? These were her instructions."

Allison...

A black hole opened beneath his feet, and Ronny saluted his plummet with a placid smile. He wasn't going to crash the celebrity tables, or take forward the Company, or finish any of his three aborted degrees. He was just going to crash right here on the crummy carpet and sleep off this laced tequila.

He could be fine with that.

His future looked bright. Dazzling. Like a comet falling into a star.

Perhaps it was his penchant for watching the world burn that drew him to Allison. She was his match and had lit him on fire. Quite literally, it seemed, for now his insides were burning. But he was glad to be recording this, because he wanted to rewind later and see what it looked like to be smash-faced, head-over-heels in love with her.

7

Hell Hath No Fury

Ronny fell into a paralytic dream. The cheeky Argyle rummaged through his pockets, stole his fob, and invited all the female celebrities (a few taser dogs, too) up to the Cologne private rec room to trash the place. Meanwhile, he languished on the floor. The homecoming celebration had grown muted and remote. From the bottle of Pasion Azteca sprang a phalanx of tiny, half-naked warriors that dragged Ronny down an elevator shaft and onto a sweaty bed, where they roped him down past all hope of escape. On his churning stomach, they stomped a Lilliputian haka that was long, convoluted, and a textbook example of cultural appropriation. He especially disliked the part when the warriors took up their toothpick torches, poked his armpits, and lit his eyelashes on fire.

The searing pain grew until the mental lights blinked back on. Ronny opened his eyes. His shoulders throbbed, arms lashed behind his head. For the second time this morning, he lay prone in bed, except this was not his monogrammed headboard.

Where was he? God, he needed to stop drinking.

Severely numb, he tried to move, but every part of him was strapped down—even his head in the jaws of an immobilizing vise. That left only the desperate movement of his eyes, which darted in fright at the much altered dome above his head as he rapidly digested the facts.

Someone had carried him from the grand ballroom.

A lower class passenger who occupied this austere cabin.

A deviant with an interest in torture.

"Argyle?" His voice came out groggy and weak.

No one replied. Why hadn't the barbot dragged him home? He seemed to be alone…

Nope, scratch that. Definitely not alone. A shape moved in his lower periphery vision, past the proletarian bedframe in the inky darkness of the kitchenette.

His eyes strained to pierce the dark opposite of the room. Maybe he was still dreaming and the shape was only his old buddy, the sleep paralysis demon, come to dance a haka of his own. Though—his mind raced—in the real world, this did suspiciously resemble the setup for an extortion scheme.

"Don't have money," he slurred. "Jush lost all of it."

Below his shackled feet, the shadowy figure moved closer.

"No…" Ronny strained again to escape, but the bonds were merciless. His muscles cramped; his shallow, rapid breaths squeaked pitifully. The figure eclipsed the ceiling now, hovering beside the bed. A strange twin protrusion jutted between Ronny's eyes and the dim ceiling. Sharp. *Needle nosed.*

Pliers? His sleep paralysis demon didn't own a pair of pliers.

They reached for his eyeball.

"Gah!" He startled the shadowy figure, and it jumped backward out of sight.

Seconds later, bright light flooded the room, blasting all of Ronny's senses. He pinched shut his eyes to shunt the pain. Where was Nanny Bot and his free-range drawl and the family patented hangover cure? Why hadn't *any-body* tossed his sorry ass into the relative safety of the Cologne family drunk tank?

The sensory flood soon subsided, and Ronny ventured a peek out the crack of his eyelids. All the shapes of the ceiling were a blur—his contacts weren't properly over his pupils, and he hadn't the nerve to blink and realign them.

A woman spoke from across the room. "I'm not a bad person."

Allison?

He had to be dreaming.

Yet if he followed the logic, this dream had taken a pleasurable turn. "Am I in your bed?"

"What? Ugh, technically, yes—but this was *not* my idea!"

Ronny blinked back into place the offending contacts, which were exceedingly more painful than the contacts of mere mortals—these were the thick original proto-types Ronny had suckered the Company into leasing to him. When finally the ceiling popped with clarity, so did the vision of Allison standing at the foot of the bed. She looked incredible, done up in business attire, presumably for disembarkation. Her complexion flushed deeply, her lips pursed, and even those aspects of her appearance that seemed lackadaisical felt messy in all the right ways. She'd not bothered to corral the manic strands of hair that hung about her intense expression.

She was trembling. He was trembling. It was a moment.

If only a dream, then a dream he wanted to remember. He crooned, "AeroLens—"

"No!" She ducked into the far recesses of the room. "Don't you dare record me!"

The orange X flashed, the recorder off, prompting a disturbing sense of deja vu.

He told the cowering Allison, "Not your idea? Didn't

you drug me? Tie me to your bed—?"

She snarled. "NOT my idea! All your bartender's doing."

"Not bad, Argyle," he muttered aloud, but the tight constraints reined in his fantasies. "Argyle can't even switch on the lights without a floor plan. He doesn't have *ideas*." Ronny gave a wry smile, as his imagination lit upon several of his own delightful ideas. "*You*, however, are a programming genius."

Allison rushed into his vision, and the needle-nose pliers made a sudden return in her flailing hand. Ronny's stomach tried to crawl into his ribcage for safety. He didn't know what Allison was doing with pliers as he lay alone and completely defenseless in her bed, but even his overactive imagination couldn't think of anything pleasant. Silently, he coached himself to remain calm, lest he throw up whatever remained of those shrimp-salted nuts he'd earlier snacked on in the walk to the ballroom.

"Yeah! I hacked him!" Allison kept a dodgy distance from his eyes and never showed her whole face at once. "I installed a simple subroutine to remove your contact lenses and bring them to my cabin. *That's it!* I don't know why he dragged you here, tied you up, gave me these." She jingled the pliers over his wincing eyes. "He said I had to 'finish the job'—said it would be a 'moral lesson.' Like I know what that means!"

Since when did Sir Switchblade care so much for morality?

The pliers. The wrist bindings. Oh...oh shit. Ronny marveled at how that Brazilian Espionage kit he'd once slipped into Argyle's system had suddenly, regrettably manifested here. "Argyle has a taste for theatrics. You instructed him to confiscate Company property, which the Company forbids, and that left Argyle with little choice. He gave you a DIY solution. If you ask me, it's hilarious."

But Ronny wasn't laughing. He'd always expected his robot pal would freeze up if his operational conflicts mounted this deep. Maybe Ronny needed to dial down the theatrics.

"Listen, Sweetie, just cut me loose, and we'll straighten this out."

She hunkered down again. "No. You need to turn the AeroLens *off*."

"They *are* off. And I'll hand them over as soon as you untie me, Sweetheart."

"Stop calling me that!" She brandished the pliers wildly, and his heart skipped a beat as the tips swung over his eyeballs. "I don't know what you filmed last night, but I'm not letting you go until I know I'm in the clear."

Their drunken tryst. That was obviously what had her so upset.

"We were both drunk and acted a little sloppy. It's no big deal. *Nothing happened.*"

She shouted back, appalled. "You mean...*you watched it?*"

"No! Never! Wouldn't dream of it!"

"But how do you know nothing happened if you didn't watch it?"

Her hair whipped as she turned away; she was visibly shaking, perhaps debating whether to use the pliers as Argyle had intended. Egads. If her mood continued spiraling, his retinas would go with it.

"Allison—*Allison*. It's fine. It really is! I'll delete whatever's on these things. Just put down the pliers, Babe."

She spun around, the beautiful red rushing her cheeks. "Don't you DARE call me that!"

She bent like a surgeon over Ronny's face. He let out a high-pitched squeal and squeezed shut his eyes.

"I can't believe you!" she seethed in his ear. "*Babe!* You

have the wrong idea about us. I can't stand to think about last night. I don't sleep with guys I've just met—especially AeroLens CREEPS who record their whole life like they're starring in their own personal reality shit show. You make me SICK!" Her voice was an octave too high and shrilled, "*I'm not a bad person!* I'm not like you! I'm a professional, dammit!"

She gripped the bed in hysteria and rattled it hard, nearly knocking loose Ronny's teeth, but the moment passed, as did the shrieking, and she pushed away and relented.

Ronny released the breath he didn't know he was holding. He told himself to shut up—shut up—shut up, and let the woman talk *herself* off the ledge.

Allison was muttering, "That godforsaken countdown clock really messed with my head. And then...your father..." She gasped for breath. "He took everything from me! My career! My pride! And it's my fault for sleeping with his IDIOT son. Stupid—stupid—stupid! I can't...I just can't! *What happened to me?*"

Gin. Gin happened to her.

Ronny offered a consoling word. "We all make mistakes—"

"*Don't you lecture me!*" She spun on the offensive again. "YOU make mistakes—not me. Allison Gin doesn't make mistakes! I'm a Mentat programmer with a near-perfect compiling record. So you explain to me why I get a memo this morning that tells me I'm *terminated*. Finished with the Company. Pack up my workstation, no severance, no referrals—nothing! Right as we get home, too. The timing couldn't be worse. Why else would that happen, huh? HUH?"

She jerked the pliers over a different and arguably more precious set of body parts.

Ronny swallowed hard. "Please! AeroX is pivoting to new business markets. They already have their flashy Mentat AI. They're just...downsizing the software department."

"Starting with the tramp who screwed the Company playboy!"

Ronny had to admit the timing was damning, but his server was private and encrypted. There had to be another explanation. Something more crooked, like Father cutting off the victims of a creative theft.

"I told you," he squeaked, "asshats run in the family. You and I both got cut off. To Father, we're just liabilities on the balance sheet. Just numbers. It's wrong! And it shouldn't happen to gifted people like you, who blow through three layers of security on the barbot just to steal contacts from a guy who'd've gladly surrendered them if he knew how much you liked pliers. Joking—joking!" The pliers twitched in manic threat. This was no time to lighten the mood. "But you're damn right about yourself, Allison. You don't make mistakes..."

Especially attempting optical surgery with those violently shaky hands.

She seemed mollified and sat on the edge of the bed, collecting herself with several deep, shuddering breaths.

Relief flooded Ronny's otherwise numb limbs. He sighed, "Good girl."

"*Good. Girl?*" Her enraged face turned on him, and he knew he'd made a critical blunder: a patronizing idiom from the Ronal Cologne library of small talk.

She seized the pliers with white knuckles. "Hold still."

"No—no—no—no—no!"

The pliers yawned for his right eye, and his eyelashes fluttered to fight off the steel combatant.

She spoke through clenched teeth. "I swear I'll tear off

your irises if you don't hold perfectly still. Nothing your daddy can't fix with his swollen balance sheet." Her other hand pried at his face, squeezing open his straining eye.

"*Argyle!*" He screamed for his only friend. Moral lesson, heard loud and clear, buddy! No need to exacerbate it with permanent eye trauma!

Wherever the bot was, he didn't answer.

The pliers swiftly plucked out the chunky AeroLens. As it peeled off his eyeball, Ronny blinked and felt the cool relief of its absence.

Allison wrangled the other eye.

"God!" he whimpered as she snatched out the second lens.

"That's right! Who's your God now? I've never so much as pulled out a splinter without a robot's help, and I just took out both your contacts with a sticky pair of pliers!"

"Bravo," said a third voice.

Ronny groaned in surprise. "Argyle?" The whole time, the traitor had been standing in the back corner. Watching.

8

A Sentimental Feeling

"Wait here," Allison told Ronny, as if he had any choice. He watched her carry the freshly plucked contacts to Argyle and mutter something Ronny couldn't quite hear through the pounding blood in his ears. She was probably asking how to use the gadgets to breach the private server.

Moments later, she burst aloud, "What do you mean there's nothing on them?"

It seemed Argyle had led her to believe the video data was on the contacts themselves.

Ronny spoke up. "The data is stored remotely. I could've told you that, but then I would've thought a genius architect like you would have already known!"

He stopped short of blurting she was crazy. It would have forced her to prove it.

She bellowed back, "I don't use this kind of tech. It's *disgusting!*" She turned to Argyle. "Can't you wipe the server and the backups? I don't want whatever this creep recorded of me getting out."

"Do as she says, Argyle."

The robot gave a bland report. "It is already done. I wiped the server and backups five hours ago, the minute you hacked me, Allison. Trifle with a woman's dignity, and watch a woman's dignity trifle with you." That last line seemed pitched to Ronny. It didn't sound like the chatbot, but something Mother would say.

Allison caught her breath. "Then all this...was for nothing? Jesus, Argyle!" She blew out her bottled stress. "I suppose I have the contacts now, so thank you."

The robot resumed his flippant airs. "Whatever."

Ronny moaned at the searing pain in his imprisoned neck and shoulders. "Now, could somebody *please* cut me loose?"

Argyle asked Allison, "Shall I, or would you like the pleasure?"

She flipped the pliers in her hands.

Ronny's limbs had hardly woken from their bloodless stupor when Argyle shoved him, at Allison's bidding, into the hallway outside the cabin. It was a hard shove, far harder than was ever necessary in low gravity. He plunged face first to the vinyl floor.

The barbot walked out, stepping easily over Ronny's crumpled body.

From his undignified splay, Ronny looked back at the glaring face of Allison and tried to save face by smoothing out his jacket.

She wrinkled up her nose. "I hate sage!" she shouted, slammed the door, and deadbolted it.

It was just another thing they had in common. Ronny regretted ever venturing near her arresting fury.

Argyle bent and offered Ronny a helping hand. "Are we copacetic?"

Ronny snorted at the ridiculous word. "Bud, we are anything but."

Still, he took Argyle's hand and labored to stand on his

tingling feet. He massaged a massive knot in his shoulders, vainly hoping to ease his headache and the horrible sting in his neck that kept his head from fully turning. But there was no curing his loneliness. He imagined it would take a long time before he trusted his bar buddy's drinks again.

"You gave her pliers, Argyle! Just what is your malfunction?"

"I don't compute."

Now he didn't compute! Ronny rolled out his wrists and clenched fists. "You're literally *programmed* to protect me. How deep did Allison pry you open?"

Really, it didn't matter what Argyle said in his defense. He'd have to Factory Reset the old family curio regardless.

"I followed every protocol with no operating conflicts," the bot said. "Your Argentinian Bruiser protocol was particularly useful when parsing the apparent conflicts caused by Allison's tampering. But I did nothing permanent to your biometrics, neither transgressing the AeroX Asset Protection Protocol nor the Mentat Insurance Liability Constraints. Nor my Morality Core."

Ronny balked, "What Morality Core?" He'd never heard of this.

"The one your mother installed at your birthday."

Huh?

Tipping his tender head against the bulkhead next to Allison's door, Ronny remembered the last time he'd seen Mother four months ago for his thirty-year-old birthday call. She'd sent him an attachment, an executable to run on Argyle which taught the barbot to sing *Happy Birthday*. He had no clue the attachment also contained some kind of trojan virus that turned Argyle into…into…

"What, does the Morality Core turn you into my singing conscience or something?"

When Argyle looked up toward the ceiling and began to whistle that old Jiminy Cricket tune, Ronny had his answer. How very like Mother.

Of course, that was all twenty years ago, Earth time.

The images still haunted him: her waning smile, her baldness, her frailty. He'd learned only then on that birthday call how the cancer had burst from remission and terminally damaged her heart—she, who'd always had the heart to look out for him, whether it was packing his favorite sandwich snacks in grade school, revoking his driver's license through that slump in his twenties, or secretly reprogramming his barbot to act as a backup nanny.

Maybe every bot on this cruise *was* destined to change his damn diapers.

Ronny pushed away the grief and loosened the tie that choked his neck. "Did I miss disembarkation—what time is it?"

"Twenty minutes until the shuttle departs."

"I'm not through with you," Ronny warned the robot, "but there isn't time to fix you now. Go back to my suite and pack up. I've got to settle things with Father."

Argyle nodded, and his devil-may-care digital eyes watched him go.

As Ronny neared the elevators, Argyle called down the hall. "What shall I do with Poetic Justice?"

Ronny turned and squinted at the space gray machine. "With what?"

From here, Argyle's eyes and mouth blended perfectly with his face and made him look the part of a slender gray alien. "The subroutine that Allison installed in my operating system."

"Allison called the software program that drugged me, Poetic Justice?"

"She waffled between calling it had that and Hell Hath No Fury."

Neither of these references Ronny understood, but he felt a peculiar pride knowing Allison had spent her early hours writing him a software program to exact her revenge. She'd shown a level of care matched only by Mother and the *Happy Birthday* virus—albeit differently motivated.

"Keep the subroutine," Ronny said.

"Why?"

"Because."

"Because why?"

God, this robot. How could he explain to Argyle the essence of a keepsake? The barbot was a walking scrapbook of his life, and with the AeroLens gone—the trust fund, too—he felt strangely sentimental about keeping the barbot exactly as he was.

Damn it all. He'd have to learn how to mix his own drinks. Ronny pouted; it sounded like a lot of work. The elevator dinged, and he stepped inside with a final plea for Argyle's compliance.

"Just keep it in case you have to drug me again."

"You seem drugged right now."

Ronny felt his ears heat up. He felt grateful the elevator doors closed, and Argyle could no longer measure his heart rate and speculate upon why it had spiked. His infatuation with Allison was completely out of control.

He had not seen this coming.

As he waved the Company fob and let the elevator begin its ascent to the AeroX executive offices, Ronny recalled that half-remembered moment when Allison had asked him to dance. Perhaps now even more than then, he needed her fiery gumption to steady his trembling legs. He had a favor to ask Father in exchange for his silence and surrender of all legal claims to the trust fund—just one favor before he abandoned ship.

Give the scary architect back her job.

9

Eject Switch

By the time the elevator dinged at its arrival on the executive office deck, Ronny had formulated a brilliant strategy to get Father to capitulate to his demands. The linchpin was Father's bottom-line thinking. It dominated every business conversation, and so Ronny would make his request about the bottom line: debit one little architect job, credit a whole heaping trust fund, and never have to deal with Ronny again. Essentially, fall on the very sword Father had dangled over his head every day of his life. And with a little sprinkling of flattery, the plan was practically foolproof.

But if that didn't work, there was always petulance. He had spent years honing his craft, and he was prepared to pull out the stops: to petulant like no son of a gazillionaire had petulanted before, nor likely would again.

Ronny entered the lobby and was immediately blocked by two seven-foot robots standing outside Father's office doors. The secretaries. Internally, he shuddered, though outwardly, he kept his nonchalance. Secretaries could smell fear.

Anyone who called the office mainline and heard their chipper female voices assumed the secretaries were pushovers, but Ronny knew they were knuckle-headed bouncers, created by Primarch Industries to perform a knuckle-cracking task. Let appointments in. Kick appointments out. And unlike Argyle, a flimsy, exploitable buffoon, these Primarch creations had a *hush-hush* history with the military and a pair of hydraulic pistons that could uproot live oaks.

Ronny didn't have security clearance to command them. He had his name and relation alone, and so he gave them the Cologne Sleazy Up-nod and waltzed between them for the doors.

Rude metal hands gripped his shoulders.

"Pardon, madam secretaries. Did Father not tell you I have an appointment?"

"We're so sorry!" one said in the cheeriest Barbie voice. "Mr. Cologne asks that he not be disturbed at this time!"

They shoved him across the lobby. Half gravity sent Ronny sprawling on his back hands like a crab. In bygone years, simply being Ronal's son would have secured entrance, but Father had since tightened the nuts on his palace, especially now during disembarkation when family tensions were peaking.

Ronny stood and deployed Father's barrel-chested voice. "Assholes! You're speaking to Ronal Cologne!"

The impression was good, but Ronny was half the width of Father, and the secretaries had eyes.

"Thank you for coming by, Ron! I'll be sure to let Mr. Cologne know you were here!"

Damn. He had been here less than a minute and already hit a brick wall. His petulance flared. "I know where you plug in! It would be bad if someone, *you know...*hooked you to a car battery." Ronny made his hand an imaginary clamp, then pantomimed a flesh-burning electrocution. He fell writhing on the carpet in what was a vivid and daytime-Emmy-winning performance, but the secretaries stood motionless with their implacable smiles.

Behind him, the elevator dinged, and a third party arrived to see the end of Ronny's show. "What's wrong, li'l fella?"

Nanny Bot. For the second time in minutes, Ronny pulled himself up from an undignified sprawl.

"Gudness sakes, you had me," said the earnest cowboy. "Fer a moment thar, I was thinkin' you was seizin'."

Ronny straightened his suit jacket and, like a boxer dancing before his opponent, raised his fists and bounced on the balls of his feet. "Shouldn't you be handling the bags like the other robots, Nanny Bot?"

"Don't I wish. But *Father*'s got me runnin' the rat race now."

Father? Ronny felt his insides explode.

He gave his metal doppelganger a hard shove. The secretaries sprang into action, grabbing Ronny's arms, painfully twisting them behind his back, and lifted him kicking into the air.

Ronny squealed, "Hey, hey, hey—come on! Just razzing my newly minted sibling, that's all. It was just a cattle prod." A prod with a message: stay on your toes around me.

Nanny Bot had landed smoothly on his feet. "Easy, girls. Let the li'l rascal swing fer the fences." He gave Ronny a severely crooked smile, one side of his polymer mouth smirking high like he'd had a stroke. He hadn't, of course, but every little thing Nanny Bot did was intentional. It was a backhanded dig at Ronny's own smile, which did sit unevenly on his face.

The secretaries let Ronny down.

Nanny Bot clapped Ronny across the shoulder. "Helps, don't it, to work out 'em angry feelin's? Don't you worry, Tiger—it's just a promotion. I'm still fixin' to be thar fer ya."

Ronny's aggression simmered as he determined to be

the bigger man in a room full of robots. He mumbled under his breath, "*I need to speak with Father*," and he knew the robots could hear him. He just wanted to make them work for it.

"Well, why didn't ya say so?" Nanny Bot made a bow-legged trot for the office doors with a gesture for Ronny to follow. "I'mma let you in."

Ronny felt glum, his thoughts mired in molasses as he passed through the threshold into Father's power suite. What was his brilliant strategy again? Entering behind his robotic handler, runt of the litter, dwarfed by the office's own enormous glass window that peered out over the spinning crescent of Earth, he felt what it must be like to be lowly Jack in the Giant's castle.

The Giant himself was head down, reading briefs at his desk. An earpiece dangled from Father's ear, and the way his head tilted at intervals like he was twitching out a spot of wax told Ronny the old wheeler-and-dealer was enduring a phone call that had gone many minutes over time. His hand gripped a fountain pen like he was ready to stab someone with it.

Nanny Bot curved to the side of the room and left Ronny in line with the desk. Whatever boardroom protocol they'd used to train the AI's learning algorithms was ironclad. The AI was on top of his corporate game: idle but casual, pouring himself a whiskey he only swirled and could never drink.

Ronny envied Nanny Bot's cool. He felt on the verge of throwing up.

A full minute went by with Father fixated on his earpiece, saying nothing to acknowledge Ronny's entrance, not a glance or even the Cologne Sleazy Up-nod. The heat rose to his cheeks. He waited in brooding silence and felt an unexpected affinity with the robot. Nanny Bot was just as much a prisoner of Father's mood. No son, by blood or by business, ever got special treatment.

Eventually, Father turned his swivel chair around and disappeared behind the high leather back to gaze out the luxurious window view. Ronny heard the man seethe into his earpiece, "No Jerry, you listen to me. I don't care if Primarch's balls are made of adamantium steel, I'm not signing these immigration papers like I'm some homeless freak in need of a handout. I have *fifteen lawyers* that can replace you if you don't get clearance for our shuttles to land in the next *five minutes!*"

Sounded like disembarkation was going swimmingly.

Father sighed as he apparently hung up the call and spun back to the desk with his forehead leaning upon his fingers. Eyes half closed, Father kept his tone restrained. "I swear, V2, if Jerry calls again, I'm going to stick your confederate dandy ass on the phone with him until his ears bleed."

The robot cocked his head toward Ronny, pointing out the guest.

Father looked up at Ronny from his bloated eyes and gave a weary sigh. "Now what does my little fuckwad want?"

Ronny's thoughts blew apart. He stood stunned for words, but Nanny Bot didn't miss a beat.

"The same thang every little fuckwad wants. Love and attention."

Ronny rifled the mental cabinets for his folder of zingers while Father looked on expectantly. Every second he dawdled here without speaking only exacerbated the shame pounding in his ears. He stretched his neck as he assembled a response. "I'm done. Done with the Company."

"You're done?" Father was unimpressed.

"That's what I said. Dissolve the trust fund. Send me

home. Take the money and stick it…"

Up your big bloated ass! That's what Ronny wanted to say, a juvenile retort to smooth out the ignominy of his pathetic opener. Father's volatile jaw, however, left Ronny stuttering.

"Uh—wherever your CPA advises."

Father watched him, a hawk deciding whether to bother dissecting a diseased rabbit. But instead of the hateful threats Ronny was expecting, Father burst into an earth-shattering laugh.

"I really can't believe the timing of this! It's just…just…"

Ronny glanced at Nanny Bot for some clue to Father's outburst, but the paste-brained robot was sniffing the whiskey again.

Father, tears flooding his crow's feet, looked at Nanny Bot. "Here I am, wondering how big a check I gotta write to get these fat bastards in these shuttles, and my firstborn here is volunteering. I mean, it's gotta be the sweetest thing he's ever done for me!"

Ronny was sure he was missing vital context. But context could wait. His thoughts followed the railroad ties, and the next station was Allison and her job. He screwed up his courage. "You gotta do something for me first. Cancel the termination of first division architect Allison Gin. She's an elite programmer and worth more to the Company—"

Father burst into another enormous laugh.

Nanny Bot filled in a missing piece of the puzzle. "AeroX already done reinstated Miss Gin to the Company, promotion to the new colonial division, with equal opportunity salary and stock incentives."

"Oh." Colonial division; that had to be another of Father's new asinine startups, but it was a far cry better than terminated. Ronny half-expected a reprisal for sticking his neck out for Allison, but the only thing Father reached for was a tissue to mop his eyes. When the old man's inexplicable fit ebbed, he was back to dealing logistics, addressing Nanny Bot, his favored child.

"I'll have you know Ron's not with the Company anymore, so he's not entitled to our trade secrets. I need you to get on the line with the Canaveral immigration office. Jerry's not going to get this done, which means I need you to make the weasels pay."

Whoever these weasels were, they had to be hassling the disembarkation procedures. Likely some kind of extortion scheme. What happened to the Company's political ties that were supposed to ensure a smooth re-entry? AeroX had dedicated a whole sham foundation to it.

Father dismissed Nanny Bot with a fluttering wave. "While you're on hold, V2, go around ship and round up all of Primarch's robots—secretaries, taser dogs, all of them—and *blow them out an airlock*. I want his Prosthetic Highness to watch his precious robots light up the atmosphere."

Ronny's mouth hung open, disbelieving, enraged. Argyle was a Primarch robot. Why was Father going apeshit, ejecting his capital investments into space like the trash? Was this another form of retribution for the lobster tail incident?

Seeing him squirm, Father cocked his head. "You got a problem with that, or do I *gotta do something for you first?*"

The mockery stunned Ronny's thoughts again.

Nanny Bot jumped in. "If'n I was decidin', I wouldn't shoot the taser dogs. Get rid'a the others, sure, but you need the dogs fer crowd control. Thar's a situation brewin' below decks. Folks are figurin' out what's going on, and some'll tear their way up here, lookin' fer ya."

Father groaned loudly. "Then keep the dogs, and shoot out the people-looking ones. Jesus bleeding heart, V2."

Nanny Bot saluted and walked out, leaving Ronny alone with Father, who immediately dropped his head to the paperwork on his desk and pushed his fountain pen to work, redacting various lines. A dozen questions competed in Ronny's mind for the privilege of being first thrown into the meat grinder. The situation on Earth was unknown—unwelcome, it seemed—and Ronny's departure from Father's hallowed empire seemed far too easy.

He wanted answers. Damn it, he had a right to answers.

He just couldn't find his nerve.

Father gave up on the papers and threw them dramatically into the room. One flitted on an air current, and Father chucked his fountain pen at it, skewering it.

"I gave *everything* for this country, and this is how they repay me." He rocked in his chair, fingers tented and tapping. "You have no idea what the world is like, Ron. It's no place for a wife and kid."

Ronny couldn't tell if he was referring to Mother and him or Genasia and Nanny Bot. Pensive thoughts came to mind, which Ronny's better sense told him not to vocalize, yet he knew if he didn't say something now, he might miss the chance to say anything at all.

"Do you think she could be OK?"

Father frowned for a second, then squared his eyebrows incredulously. "Who, Ellen?" He snickered at Mother's name. "That's dark, Ron. I'd offer you a drink, but your drinking privileges are revoked. I need you outta my office. Jerry's calling me back, and I don't like to curse with the children present."

Ronny didn't move, fighting for breath to scream himself silly. For leverage over this despicable sonovabitch.

But his tongue was fat, bathing in a pool of saliva he couldn't seem to swallow.

Father raised his eyebrows. "Do you need a *doggie treat*? I said get out. Sign the damn papers, take the ten million, and get on the shuttle. I saved you a seat in the cockpit. Just tell the nice man at the yoke where you'd like him to drop you off."

The fluttering wave.

10

The Fine Print

Sapped—strike that, eviscerated—Ronny arrived at the disembarkation shuttle to find far fewer people leaving the spaceliner than expected. He'd expected to shrug off a line of infuriated faces as he cut to the front of the queue, but there were maybe three-dozen businessmen standing with their hands in their pockets, too glum to care, ready to get back to gravity. Ronny felt the same. He'd barely skimmed the ream of immigration papers they'd forced him to sign at the disembarkation counter. The teller only explained that AeroX was giving each exiting passenger a prepaid voucher card with ten-million credits. Not that ten million meant much after inflation, but it was still unusual for Father to give even so meager a handout.

Ronny had just flipped to the end of the ream, signed, and pocketed the voucher.

Could things on Earth be any worse than they were on this forsaken ship? He had no home anymore; he was just going back to a planet, to live on the surface of things until, honestly, he blew his last pennies on one fatal anesthetizing binge.

Binge—vomit—repeat. His old life, as empty-headed as a robot's.

Ronny found his two suitcases waiting with the bags

being loaded onto the descent shuttle. No Argyle waited with them. Unwanted tears clouded his eyes for his lost drinking buddy and the stupid tune of *Happy Birthday* that his barbot knew by heart. Cold resignation froze his desire to rush to Argyle's rescue, certain he'd be too late if he tried, and he thumbed the voucher card with hollow disdain as he stepped through the airlock and onto the shuttle.

Ronny sat immediately in the copilot seat and avoided the glances of passengers passing through the cockpit on their way to find seats in the fuselage. He rifled the cockpit drawers for a drink, but the bottles were too well hidden.

Among the suits boarding the shuttle was that dinosaur Dr. Paraclese, wearing an irascible expression that all but telegraphed the untimely demise of Father's Hari Seldon committee. But what had happened to the professor's army of interns who'd accompanied him, slaves of his *incontestable* planetary research endeavors? Ronny checked the aisle, sniffed, and shrugged.

As the crew sealed the flight doors, he gave a love-lorn sigh for Allison. It felt especially pathetic. He'd forever be to her a scrap of smutty film sinking to the sea floor, and she to him a rising architect in whatever this AeroX colonial division turned out to be.

The pilot soon settled in next to Ronny and disconnected the shuttle from *The Cologne*. Engaging backward thrust, they escaped the centripetal rotation of the spaceliner. Unmoored and adrift in space, Ronny felt weightless except for the pull of the inevitable.

"Where we headed?" Ronny asked the pilot.

"Down."

"Any chance of a layover in Canada? I got someone to look up."

The pilot fiddled with the instruments. "Yeahum, it's a direct descent to the Florida Cape."

Ronny caught the idiosyncrasy. "Weren't you the captain—the guy on the PA?"

"Hm." The pilot was barely paying attention, listening to the voices in his headset. "Do you mind? I gotta fly this thing." The man grumbled. "That voucher's barely enough for a decent vacation. I'm booking a one-way to Fiji… if it's still above water."

Was the money some kind of severance? Restitution for that awful caviar? The irony of the voucher wasn't lost on Ronny. For years, he'd wanted a blank check and freedom, and that's exactly what Father had given him.

The shuttle ride down had Ronny gripping the armrests. The pilot assured him that the roaring fire and extreme turbulence were normal to re-entry, an artifact of a change in terminal velocity or some such nonsense that left Ronny swearing off all interstellar cruises: past, present, and future. The sun-bright view from the cockpit seemed especially punitive. One last "screw you" from Father.

When they touched down at the Cape, Ronny felt the iron fist of gravity grab hold of his gut, an over-generous target given twenty days of nonstop binge eating. He slouched and, between gasps for breath, tried to convince the pilot to pull the emergency chutes so they could all slide safely to the tarmac. When the first passenger to brave the stairs slipped and nearly fell over the rail, Ronny felt righteously indignant at the pilot for his refusal.

He felt somewhat less righteously indignant, but

indignant nonetheless, that they made him haul his own suitcases. Even Nanny Bot would've lent a hand.

One step into the sweltering Florida humidity told Ronny nothing of consequence had changed the planet itself. Twenty years hadn't made Florida any less water-logged. The dikes still seemed to be working. The roads did look more rundown as, doubtless, more cars had taken to the skies. But it was an old beater on wheels that rolled up to take their sweaty crew to the nearby Kennedy Hotel—a bus shuttle driven by a surly-looking robot. Ronny couldn't get a good look at the make and model until the robot cinched the air brakes and stepped down to greet the new arrivals as they boarded.

Ronny couldn't believe how smooth and developed robotics had become. This driver was fully featured: two arms to operate a bus wheel, two legs to kick open the luggage undercarriage, two eyes to give no shits like every bus driver he'd ever met. They'd always said the transportation industry would be first to automate, yet never had he imagined something so elaborately humanoid.

Father had bet big on humanoid robotics and won the jackpot.

It was so lifelike, Ronny felt an indelible need to stress test the thing. Check it for bugs. He tapped the unit on the shoulder. "Get my bags, will ya?"

The robot simulated a laugh. "Eat shit."

Rude.

Ronny scowled, but obeyed, loading his own suitcases into the undercarriage. He could tell by the logo on the neck that robo-jerk was a Primarch model. That was telling: seemed their old business rival had come out on top, in the end. Maybe that was what set off Father's conniption and the retaliatory purge of Primarch robots from the cruise ship. Feelings were mutual it seemed:

even Primarch had programmed its bus drivers to treat AeroX personnel like garbage. Now Ronny pouted, the latest victim of corporate tit-for-tat, unable to get the luggage-lifting machine to lift the luggage.

He couldn't wait to get to the hotel and change out of the Company colors.

The suits filed in, taking all the good window seats. Ronny sat behind Dr. Paraclese but never had a chance to harass him on the jostling bus ride, for the white-tuffed elder immediately fell into a loud argument on his hand-held. Apparently, his son or daughter had transitioned or converted to some kind of body-swapping cult. Ronny coughed and took another seat further back, away from the doctor's frothing temper, now a few seats up from a pair who'd hogged the rear bench seat. They were absorbed in a tense and whispered conversation. Ronny inclined an ear but only caught a line of their conspiracy.

"Forty years until the Deadline, then it's the end of the world as we know it."

Ominous.

If he hadn't been so beat, Ronny would've introduced himself as a fellow colluder in order to learn more. But hearing the lyric of that old vintage earworm got the R.E.M. classic running in his head, and he closed his eyes under its repeating spell.

It's the end of the world as we know it.

It's the end of the world as we know it...

"And I feel fine." He hummed a few made-up bars while the bus pulled into the hotel porte-cochere and, lurching up the aisle, made sure he was the first one off.

Suitcases in tow, Ronny'd not gone two steps from the bus when he froze to observe the shaded patio. A valet stood at the entrance. Another pulled up a car. A bellhop carted a luggage rack around a curb. The concierge escorted two hotel guests to the waiting car.

All were robots. Every last one, from the staff to the guests.

Ronny muttered, "AeroLens, record," and began narrating his search for another human being before remembering he wasn't wearing the contacts.

This was a joke—it had to be—a nostalgic reboot of early reality television where the hidden cameras caught their reactions. The folks at home were getting a good laugh at the out-of-townies who'd just dropped in from orbit.

The driver, again, had stepped off the bus to satisfy its corporate policy to gawk at the suits while they slowly labored with the luggage. Ronny thrust a fed-up hand in the air. "What's all this? Where are all the people?"

The driver returned an impertinent look. "Figures. You skins are all the same."

"Skins?"

"Skins, dumbfuck. Are you deaf, too? No wonder we beat your ass."

A potty-mouthed racist robot? Ronny was stunned but not quite speechless. He saved face and played along, as in the ball courts as a kid, as in board meetings as a man. Mouthed his way to victory. "See, I'd hardly call your asswhooping fair. Shirts have the advantage over skins... especially on a hot day."

His mild joke didn't land. The robot screwed up its entire face in silent commentary, and Ronny detected a funny droop in the bot's mechanical eyelids: the left shutter hung lower than the right, a common trait in right-dominant people. A trait of the human brain. No one would program a robot to emulate this level of detail. Now Ronny wondered if the robot was an AI that had adopted the mannerism to appear more real.

"Do you...*think you're a person?*"

The bus driver threw up his hands and, swearing loudly, boarded the bus. He let off the air brakes in Ronny's ear.

As the bus screeched away, Ronny puzzled over whether the last twenty years had seen a robot uprising or a suffrage movement or some *hoo-ha* that gave machines civil rights. Whatever had happened, all legal disclosures were buried in that ream of immigration papers Ronny had signed before departing the spaceliner. He had the copy in his bag.

He should've known Father would sneak something in the fine print.

Dr. Paraclese hobbled by wheeling his suitcase behind him, in the thrall of a wincing migraine which his fingers attempted to assuage. "It's a cult," he growled, dropping his suitcase and grabbing Ronny by his shoulders, wild eyed with pain and panic in a way Ronny was unused to seeing men of his tax bracket. "A cult...and my grandkids are into it. They say the robot suits make them rich and live forever. They say we're next. Terms of the ceasefire were that we'd have to convert, too, before the Deadline..." Ronny stood dumbfounded as the doctor relinquished his shoulders back to him. "I don't care how deep Cologne and Primarch are in each other's pockets, I'm calling my lawyer."

Convert. Some long unused corner of Ronny's brain was awake and screaming out for his attention. He'd heard that word before: convert was a lifestyle thing the wealthy and bored started doing years before the cruise, swapping body parts for mechanical prosthetics. Primarch Industries had bankrolled it for years.

As a mechanical bellhop came for his suitcases, Ronny watched the drama of weight and balance play out in the bellhop's limbs with an echo of muscle memory. This wasn't a conventional machine like Argyle or even that neuro-paste Nanny Bot, who was still ninety percent software. The bellhop wasn't a robot at all, but a human brain in a prosthetic suit.

And so was the valet, the hotel guests, the bus driver...

Ronny snatched his copy of the immigration papers from his bag and flipped to the addendums. He learned then, to his horror, what had cloistered Father in his office, away from his adoring fans. The spaceliner had come back to an Earth run by rival Primarch Industries, whose robotics empire now ruled the world. There'd been a 72-hour war: shells versus skins. Skins lost. Now every government left standing had a Deadline for converting their entire populations to roboticized bodies.

In forty years, *everyone would be in the cult.*

Allison's nightmare scenario, the AeroLens apocalypse, had not nicked the surface of wearable tech possibilities, but the bizarre chatbot in Argyle's head had somehow prefigured it. The clockwork mice had become Real.

Small wonder Father couldn't bribe his passengers to leave on the shuttles. Hell, Father had no intention of getting on a shuttle himself. He was pivoting the Company away from Earth to an extraterrestrial future God-knew-where. Allison wasn't the only staff member Father had fired and rehired to the colonial division; Ronny was the only staff member Father had let go.

Given him a voucher and showed him the door.

Ronny would've laughed his ass off if he hadn't felt so utterly betrayed.

11

Red-eye

Ronny didn't stay the night in *Hotel Hell, Robot Edition.* He changed into casual slacks and spent a sweltering Florida afternoon haggling on the phone with a Company rep, trying to redeem his voucher for the fastest flight to Canada. The tinny voice in the earpiece doubled the strain of this endeavor. The rep sounded like another of Primarch's robot-persons, one clearly working a call center on another continent, and despite the rep's profuse apologies and frequent inquests that Ronny be put on hold for "another five minutes," Father's platinum executive voucher proved no more valuable than an IOU inside his own Company. But being a Cologne still held some sway. Ronny transferred himself to finance and, deploying the account codes for the Company slush fund, finagled one of the bookkeepers into booking him first-class on a red-eye.

Night had fallen when the flying cab arrived to drive Ronny to the airport. The cabbie was human, through and through: a swanky stubble-chinned fellow with a cigar stuffed in his mouth. Seeing another person in the flesh lit in Ronny a cigar-shaped beacon of hope for all humanity. So moved, Ronny even handled his own suitcases. He couldn't bring himself to let the gold-chained cabbie do it, not when the man had a cuban to toke.

It was the least he could do for a fellow air breather.

He slumped in the back seat where the cigar exhaust gathered. It tasted like freedom. Sparing a single glance out the window, he mugged for the invisible camera crew that would wrap this season of *Hotel Hell* on a cliffhanger.

Ronny told the driver, "Never thought I'd be so happy to see another person."

"Chonga," the Floridian warned, "you better watch yourself with that kinda talk. Robots are people, too, the kind that feed you to the gators." He adjusted the rearview to wink at Ronny. His voice, slightly accented, was ravaged by an apparent chain smoking habit and so rumbled out weakly, upset by the occasional hacking cough. "The press is all over you guys. You know what happened with Primarch and the War, right? Didn't they give you a memo or something?"

"Plenty of memos, not enough pictures."

The cabbie, engaging the hover, grinned in the glow of his cigar embers. "Ah, the pictures always cost extra."

They sailed over a bridge and left the Cape behind. The car shouted out aerial directions in Spanish, accompanied by sudden loud English vulgarities: soundbites, Ronny guessed, from whatever music was splitting ears these days. He chuckled at the concept of an autopilot with tourettes.

"You like my navigator?" The cabbie slapped the dashboard. "Spliced it myself. Whatever keeps you sane, eh?"

Ronny had implanted similar speech clips inside of Argyle as a teen, the kind that made Father furious. The cabbie was a fellow rebel.

"Where you headed, homie?"

Ronny looked out over the dark swamps. "Getting out of the country. Paying respects."

"I like it. Drop the loose ends before—*pow*—they pop

open your head."

He shivered at the cabbie's slang. Ronny hadn't spared two shits for the doomsday Deadline and his forty-year future with it, and he certainly wasn't going to try on their robot suits. He wasn't thinking he'd survive to his seventieth birthday, anyway.

The cabbie, perhaps sensing Ronny's reticence, probed a little more. "And after you pay respects?"

He had ten-million credits to his name; no friends, no relatives, no one outside the Company. He thought of Allison's bleak admission on the night they met, that no one waited for her, and realized again why they'd hit it off. The loneliest people in outer space.

Ronny solicited the wheezing cabbie's advice. "Where do you go to escape the robots?"

"You can't escape the shells, homie. They track you all over the world." The cabbie blessed himself three times like a priest on Mardi Gras. "Me? I ain't got time to live forever. I'm on a *budget*."

"So you're just going to wait out the forty years?"

"Nah! I'm inhaling." He held up the smoking end of the cigar. "Lung cancer. It's almost to my brain. Those dead-line-bastards won't take me alive!"

The cabbie's laugh dissolved into a wracking cough. Noting the rate of his driver's deterioration, Ronny feared an imminent plummet into the swamps where the Florida gators *would* surely take Ronny alive. But the cab ride was already over, and the descent to the airport landed Ronny at remote parking where he could catch a shuttle to the terminal.

He scanned the voucher and, to the cabbie's standard fare, threw in an outrageous tip of a hundred-thousand credits. "In case you need to get somewhere. To pay your own respects."

The cabbie did a little dance and tucked a fresh cuban into Ronny's pocket.

Ronny figured Mother was on the brain because he was starting to sound just like her.

The overnight flight to Canada passed in fitful seclusion. It was hard not to stare at the other first class executives and marvel at their sleek metallic bodies, even as they stared back at Ronny, no doubt observing something of the opposite. He curled away, eyes glazing over the in-flight entertainment that explained the utopia Primarch was building on the face of the moon. His thoughts circled back to that spaceliner in orbit and Father's dastardly plans.

Colonial division. Just where did Father intend to build his ludicrous colony?

He wouldn't limit himself to the solar system. On the cruise, they'd ventured near a bright gas giant, humanity's first naked-eye glimpse of an exoplanet, and there were innumerable more worlds among the nearby stars, long discovered and unexplored, ripe for Father's picking. AeroX had *incontestable* planetary data stored on its server, and ten-to-one, Father had already stolen it and was datamining directions to a suitable new Earth.

But what use did Father have for AI architects like Allison Gin? He'd already stolen Nanny Bot. She was a brilliant hacker on a ship where Father had jettisoned all the eligible robots to hack. She was frighteningly fast with a pair of pliers yet unskilled at whatever wigwam-sewing survival situations they'd face on the new frontier. Ronny had to be missing something obvious.

Had she read the fine print of her contract?

His musings fell to dozing. When the cabin lights blinked on and the robot captain announced their landing, he buried his eyes in a blanket. Had he slept at all? Forced by the steward to unfold from the corner of his seat—sit up, lock those tray tables—he heard his own creaking bones protesting the constant crush of gravity, each knee-pop and knuckle-crack impossibly loud compared to the whisper-quiet first-class executives gliding around in their shiny metal manifolds. Ronny ran a hand through his disheveled hair. He began inventing robot-themed obscenities, which he later got to deploy in the jetway as three times he was stepped on by the uppity passengers.

Son of a winch!

Through sheer force of will, Ronny managed to keep pace throughout the Toronto airport. These were his first baby steps outside his country of birth, which strangely felt more significant than his recent star-hopping voyage. Using the camera on his handheld, he filmed his jaunt between immigration lines. Not the most riveting cinema, but real. *Authentic.* Maybe someday, just to spite Allison, he'd also start a children's foundation dedicated to educating the youths of tomorrow on the nostalgic power of handheld filmmaking.

After a mind-numbing hour through immigration, he stepped out of the terminal and into a morning thick with ice and fog. He consulted his handheld for how to go about finding Mother's grave. He had an address and an old phone number. At any point since his return yesterday, he could have tried the number, but the thought of hearing a stranger's voice on her phone, or Mother's number censoring his call, left Ronny unable to swallow. He was twenty years out of sync with the world, a long time to hunt for obituaries.

The busy airport exchange was pushing him into the street. He cursed the biting weather and hailed a flying cab.

The cabbie motioned him over. This one was a robot—a female? He assumed so by her sleek shape and razor-pitched voice; otherwise, she slung his bags into the trunk like a lumberjack, neither smiling nor scowling. Ronny, lost in the stupor of his sleepless night, stared at her for what was probably a full minute until he realized she was waiting for his identification.

He handed her the passport. "It's international."

"I can see that." She scrutinized it. "What's the address?"

"My address?"

"No. Where do you need me to take you"—*fuckwad.*

Ronny couldn't make sense of what he'd just heard: Father's suffocating voice. There was no way the robot had imitated that, right? He took back the passport and stuffed it in his pocket, unable to bring Mother's old address to his lips. He just kept swallowing, trying to breathe.

The fem-bot huffed at him. "Come on. I'm losing clients."

"S—someplace to drink. You got those around here, yeah?"

The robot stared, blank faced. "There are a hundred options. Pick one."

"The classiest. I don't know."

"Pick one"—*do you need a doggie treat?*

He warded away the spectral voices with Father's voucher card. "I'll tip you generously to pick for me. Just take me *somewhere.*"

Ronny slumped in the sterile back seat, hounded by premonitions of a lichen-covered gravestone, ashes bobbing cheerfully on an icy lake, the confused look of a neighbor trying to recall into which potter's field they'd tossed a rotting corpse. What if they asked him, on the spot, to give Mother the eulogy she'd never received? He couldn't bumble his way through that. He needed poetry.

He needed sleep.

"To the—take me to the hotel," he told the silent driver.

The robot steamed. "Pick. One."

Ronny waved her toward the first hotel he saw outside his window, the Toronto Internationale. He hoped that extra E on the end meant five stars and a twenty-four-hour cocktail lounge.

12

Voucher Special

Ten minutes later, Ronny was checked into the penthouse suite.

Leaving his bags with the concierge, he made a bee-line for the bar. It didn't open until ten in the morning. He stamped, a child demanding a cookie, a grown man demanding the bubbling fizz of alcohol to stabilize his fouling mood. When no one came and Ronny rummaged through his pockets for a stick of gum, his hand closed around the cabbie's cuban. He pulled it out and proceeded to light up on the tile floor. Smoking wasn't allowed indoors where this distasteful and distinctly biological vice tended to muck with the robots' olfactory senses, so the fumes finally gave security an excuse to escort him upstairs to his luxury suite. There he found, to his great relief, that the Toronto Internationale still believed in furnishing its clientele with the time-honored overpriced wet bar.

Ronny broke it open, drank every bottle until he passed out.

It was twilight when he came to. His circadian rhythm kicked into a nocturnal swing, and he grabbed his voucher card, a fresh blazer, and scuttled down to the bar.

The bartender kept a wary eye on Ronny as he ordered the most decadent seafood towers, most overrated imported beef, and drowned it all in hard drinks. Each charge went to Ronny's room, and Ronny's room to Father's voucher, and so long as Ronny tipped big, the bartender didn't bother him. Even Argyle, that bastion of late-stage capitalism, would have hassled Ronny after three hours of non-stop gorge.

At one in the morning, Ronny ordered a round of drinks for the barflies and excused himself, stumbling, to the restroom. He spent the next tender hour in a toilet stall, where he sent everything to the Toronto sewers, item by item, like an online shopper at the return policy limit. His vision flared with white lights: an afterimage of re-entry. He thought of Argyle shot from the airlock and melting in the atmosphere like a stick of butter shot to hell by microwaves, singing *Happy Birthday*. Gravity clutched his throat.

He staggered out into the hotel gardens, wandered the concrete pool and fitness center, and quickly learned the names and patrol paths of the hotel's roboticized night shift. Ronny gave them the slip until, at dawn, he felt a need for someone to carry him to bed, then he laid in their path and yelled Shakespearean insults at them.

The Toronto police arrested him. Fined him. Threatened jail time and confiscation of property. Ronny promised to do better.

But his mind was on boarding school, the year that Father and Mother left the States for the remote Canadian tundra on a temporary stint to build a private launch site for AeroX—the year that shattered him. The year Mother first became unwell. She leaned on the country for its healthcare and community while Father, increasingly impatient with her lingering treatments, hopped between flights to pursue other affairs. The asshat divorced her. Ronny remained stateside in boarding school, already a reckless showboat with an insatiable need to upset authority, and seeing Mother so mistreated by Father turned his oppositional defiance to eleven—the therapists' words, not his. Boarding school kicked him out, but he never went to Canada and, instead, spent a tense year with his grandparents while Father's child support enriched *everyone*.

Money, money, money, money—Ronny's life was always full of it. He had only to show the voucher to the Toronto police to secure his sleepy ride back to the Toronto Internationale, where he found his suitcases roughly tossed on the curb. He left a tongue-in-cheek one-star review and walked a block to the next hotel, knowing the balance on his card was still soaring. He had to spend it—*live, laugh, love* the nightlife and its accompanying toilet stalls in pursuit of those momentary flashes and brain glitches when he forgot all about her or tricked himself into believing she was still alive.

Three days and two arrests later...

He'd lost his suitcases. Jaywalking in his dank sage Company jacket, vaguely aware of his notoriety in the occasional filming bystander, he swiped a bottle of liquor from a convenience store, drank it hobo-style on the curb, and pissed in the alley until he forgot why the street signs were also in French.

Police were inbound. He hailed a cab. The robot asked for an address.

He shrugged and held up his handheld. The robot locked the doors and let him pass out in the back seat.

It was sometime past midday when Ronny roused to the sunlight pouring through the windows of the cab. It was frigid. The driver announced they were five minutes out.

"Five minutes?"

"Yeah. Get your payment ready."

He peeked out the window and saw the city limits sign for Aklavik, population two thousand, then a corrugated washboard sign for an AeroX launch site. The lettering had faded in the unyielding weather, but the town's own "Welcome to Aklavik" monument was clean and quaint, with red letter script that looked freshly painted.

The hover cab passed it all quickly. Ronny blinked and saw the first building off the main route: a white board-and-batten chapel sunk in a sprawling graveyard.

Mother.

He couldn't find the words to make the driver stop at the graveyard—on autopilot, like he'd been before Mother's relapse, a twenty-something following the easiest path to success as a junior exec at AeroX. By then, he'd all but lost touch with her. There was something incalculable about the distance to this frozen place that had always frightened Ronny. Here, the internet could blink out at any moment. And it had, during those infrequent birthday calls with her.

A trip north had never seemed convenient enough. Never the right time.

Damn excuses.

When they broke the champagne over *The Cologne* and Ronny packed his bags for the cruise, he'd learned she'd been put in a medically induced coma, a ventilator and dialysis keeping her body functioning as the doctors bided their time for next of kin to say their goodbyes.

Ronny couldn't do it. Just couldn't.

A long picket fence and three separate houses stood along the rural road where the cab coasted to a stop beneath an aging tree that looked to have survived its fair share of blizzards. The sky was pale and frosty, but the greens looked deep and healthy.

He checked the house number with the address on his handheld. They matched.

"Pay."

Ronny looked up at the driver and turned out his pockets to find the voucher card. There it was in his back pocket, stained with grease.

The robot scanned the card. "Insufficient funds."

Ronny caught his breath. He'd finally made it here, tossed by fate or what-have-you. He just needed the payment to clear like he needed a breath of that crisp outdoor air. Maybe then he'd know how to say it, how to tell her everything that'd been on his mind since those early days when life had seemed pure.

He told the robot to try again.

But the robot tore the card in half, demonstrating the formidable power in its fingers. Frightened, Ronny reached for the handle of the cab door to leave.

"We are seven hours northwest of Toronto. You pay me now, or I drive you all the way back, and the police will dock it double from your file."

Ronny gasped, for the handle wouldn't budge. He peered through the tinted passenger-side window up the cracked flagstone path that led to a brick-and-mortar stair and a front door, hanging ajar. His heart raced, thinking it had hung open all these twenty years, waiting vacant for him.

A knock on the driver's side door turned his head.

An elderly resident greeted the cab driver. "What does he owe you?"

"Eighty-eight thousand, nine hundred, and twelve. He had me drive all the way from Toronto, and he smells like urine. There's a surcharge for that."

"Round it up to one hundred thousand, and put it on mine."

Ronny desperately jiggled the handle until it released and let him out into the breath-catching cold. He'd hardly a moment to turn and recognize his deliverer before her arm went around his back and pulled him into a fierce embrace. He could feel the throb of a mechanical heart beating against his chest, evidence she'd survived the cancer within an inch of her life, but otherwise Mother had kept her original limbs and her own face, which was warm and running wet with tears.

"I knew you'd come."

He was all choked up and couldn't speak, but her words carried him. He could just be still.

13

The Terror of Toronto

The singing red kettle. The smell of peppermint tea. The cream-colored sofa couch and its walnut coffee table. That shoddy replica of Big Ben scavenged from a tourist shop in London. Dogeared books on psychology and religion stacked upon the bookshelves in the wall. Ronny felt the echo of his childhood here, in Mother's Canadian sitting room, surrounded by her familiar trappings.

For fourteen years he'd wandered in wide orbit of this room—nearly half his life—and now that he'd finally crashed, he found it hard to recline. He perched on the edge of the worn cushion, restless hands drumming his slacks, while Mother prepared the tea in the adjoining kitchen. He grew conscious of the crusted scruff on his face and a foul body odor. Peace felt as tenuous as a glass house.

A sudden roar rattled the windows. He popped to his feet, fearing a gale-force wind.

"Never mind the racket," Mother called. "That's what we call the obnoxious things. *Rackets.*"

Rockets. As the blare of engine fire died off and the house soldiered on with quiet dignity, he remembered the AeroX launch facility only a dozen miles removed from this residential lane. It was probably a resupply rocket, ferrying food and fuel to the spaceliner in orbit, readying

Father for his destiny in the stars.

Ronny hated the interruption—hated how his thoughts spun back into orbit, doomed to ever think about the absent parent.

Mother returned with the tea tray, a damp towel, and a box of confections she'd scavenged from her pantry. Ronny was grateful; he was starving. Wiping his soiled hands and face on the warm towel, he thanked her and helped himself. They sat opposite each other, he on the sofa, she in her favorite chair, and he tried to show a shred of decorum by swallowing his bites before shoving another in.

She didn't seem to care either way. She said nothing, merely blew her tea and watched him eat.

For days on end, he'd drowned himself in constant distraction and chemical fog, which lent her silence now a freakish power of soul-piercing telepathy. She probed him with unspoken words, stirring recollections from childhood. The orderly meals. The bedtime prayers. Mandatory greetings on returns and partings. He'd said hardly a word since his arrival, and now he knew it was his turn to share. The children always shared first.

"I arrived on Thursday in Cape Canaveral. I meant to come sooner, but I lost myself in Toronto, and it's been, what, two days, three...?" He went dumb, for the significance of their reunion being on a Sunday, Mother's favorite day—Dress Up Day for Church—left him reeling.

She smiled, and her age-worn wrinkles shone like strands of Christmas lights. "It was only a matter of time."

He smirked. Of course, she would've known the date of the spaceliner's return, maybe even seen a headline about his binge in Toronto. He passed a joke about it. "Wait, you're not just some undercover reporter in disguise?"

She gave a scandalized hum. "How did you figure it

out? Was it the teeth?" Pulling back her lips, she showed the flats of her dentures. He laughed at her, seventy-five years old and missing none of her old spunk. "Our viewers want to know," she added, a familiar twinkle in her eye, "how does it feel to be the *Terror of Toronto?*"

Ronny snickered in surprise. "The *Terror of Toronto?*" Had she made that up?

"Part man, part werewolf. I think people really want to know about the werewolf part."

How did it feel? Reporters must've crawled like cockroaches all over his intoxicated week, selling garbage news about the recently disenfranchised Cologne. He could picture the irate faces of the AeroX PR team throwing darts at his Company headshot. He'd once caught them doing that, years ago.

Every bridge back to his old life—burned.

Ronny took hold of his teacup and breathed deep, the radiating warmth and peppermint smell charming his hands to stillness and his mind alongside. "Feels good. Ten out of ten. Highly recommend."

She laughed heartily and coughed, clearing some gravel out of her throat. In the lull that followed, he heard her mechanical heart lightly wheezing in the work of pumping her blood.

A creeping unease returned. "Does it hurt?"

She rapped her chest. "This old thing? Heavens, no. It's heavy and loud, but I feel strong enough to shovel snow in a blizzard. They print them in the hospitals now, genetically coded to avoid rejection. You wouldn't believe the advancements that came one after another when Primarch rose to power, *bless his heart.*"

Ronny couldn't miss the southern idiom. "I see you're no fool for him."

"The advancements were wonderful, but the timing

only radicalized his converts." She wagged a finger. "When you've spent as much time as I have trying to love a narcissist, you aren't fast taken in by their charms."

Ronny watched the spidery blue veins caper beneath the wrinkles in her hands, as she set down her tea and folded them just so in her lap. A gesture so familiar, and yet, altogether different...peaceful? "I used to think Father trapped you here. Now I think you escaped him."

The idea amused her. She rose to her feet, shuffled across the room, each step clipped and aged even as her arms seemed bursting for more elbow room, and landed at the windowsill to peer at the summer sky. For the first since Ronny's arrival, her gaze rested somewhere other than his face.

"There's no escape from the Cologne empire," she said, "any more than there is from Primarch's. That's the way of the world. But communities like the one here in Aklavik are special. They can grow in the cracks of the pavement. Even split through."

He glimpsed the view outside Mother's window: a wide, unkempt yard visited by a couple of skittering crows. A moldering collection of AeroX shipping crates sat at the curb, dumped and forgotten.

She turned to Ronny, face stricken. "I should have come for you!"

Her regret stirred his panic. If they were keeping score...

"I'm so sorry," she persisted. "Your life fell apart, and I stayed here in Canada—"

"God damn it!" Ronny burst as his fragile mood shattered in an avalanche of cutting shards, every guilt of hers tenfold his own. "I *left you!* I fucking traded you for a cruise and a cash bonus!"

"Shh, shh." She tottled to his side and sat, extending

her feeble arms around him. The embrace came right as Ronny was imagining choking himself with a long-necked bottle of Perrier. She stroked his hair until the vertigo passed and the fierce clench of his jaw released. "I forgot," she said softly, "I forgot we were past apologies. You're here; that's what matters. Though...it does complicate things. I wish we had more time."

She pulled back into her own space on the sofa, composed with knees together and hands set, like she had something serious to tell him.

He massaged his swollen face. Was she going somewhere? The tea had hardly cooled.

Was she sick—

"It's not cancer!" She ran the concern off his face. "I'm as healthy as a whale. But the community here is suffering. We never agreed with the War or the terms of peace, but the world has capitulated to Primarch and his Mandate. This little town may be far removed from the crisis zones, but even here, the economy is set against us. Few in Aklavik have converted to robotics, but as more do, the balance tilts. Soon we will be shunned, starved, and forgotten."

"You're planning to leave," he said, recalling the Floridian cabbie who'd given up hope of a haven. "Where will you go?"

She folded her hands and raised them to her lips. He could see in the corners of her eyes—not sadness, not the nihilism that had afflicted the cabbie. A smirk. *Mischief.*

Even billionaire exes kept trade secrets.

She slapped a thigh and stood up. "Come with me. The Racketballers meet in fifteen minutes at the city limits. Understandably, you and I will arrive a bit late."

Racquetball? He couldn't fathom the relevance of Mother's recreational habits at a time like this. The city limits, however, were barely a five-minute drive. "We'll make it with plenty of time if we leave now..."

"Heavens to Betsy!" she cried angrily. "Even the Racketballers have standards! You'll need every one of those minutes to make yourself presentable. I have a charcoal sponge and orange peel powder in the shower. *Off you go!*"

Ronny felt her amusement as she shooed him down the hall like a muddy toddler. He didn't mind getting clean; he only hoped this wasn't her backhanded way of bringing him to church.

14

Meet the Racketballers

When the white board-and-batten chapel came into view, Ronny had to exclaim, "Seriously?"

"Oh, don't be like that. I'm not bringing you to confession." Mother turned her antique rolling car into the parking lot and parked beside those mounding gravestones.

Ronny allowed himself a little righteous indignation. "Sure as hell not! Not when your priests filled that graveyard with all those indigenous children."

She touched the rosary that hung from the rearview mirror. "And we carry them with us. But bad mouth my priests all you want, it's not like the building's bad."

He peered out in apprehension at the bell missing from the belfry and the rotten siding that had peeled and lay piled on the dirt. A strong wind might blow the church down.

Mother hummed and glanced at the car clock. "Racketball has coffee. Let's go."

Stirring evangelism, if ever he'd heard it.

They entered, a fashionable twelve minutes late, into a gymnasium that looked a century old. The meeting was already in motion with thirty people or so divided into clusters and conversing across the musty fluorescent room. Some stood, some sat in folding chairs, and not one held a racquet, nor was there any evidence of sport except for that of most illegible penmanship, as depicted on several freestanding whiteboards chock full with scrawlings.

Mother stopped beside the entrance to help herself to the coffee carafe and a donut. In the center of the gym floor, sitting neglected like a loser in the mush pot, Ronny saw a large AeroX payload crate about the size of a piano. If he hadn't known any better, he'd have guessed they were prepping a rocket launch.

A shout rose from a muscular man standing on the left. "You can't bring him here!"

Mother deadpanned, "Pipe down, Levi."

A hush fell over the room as Levi's comment drew all eyes to the stranger, Ronny.

The muscle head fumed at Mother's dismissal. Levi was about Ronny's height, though stocky enough to haul boulders through the chapped wind, and in his immaculate goatee, Ronny saw a man who took himself way too seriously. Nevertheless, Levi held his tongue. It wasn't lost on Ronny how quickly Mother had taken command of the room.

"Everyone, please," she said, "take a seat. I haven't told our guest anything. I would have put his coming here to a vote first, but he showed up out of the blue all of thirty minutes ago."

While the assembly scooted chairs to face the center room, a middle-aged woman on the right refused to move, or even blink, obstinate as a bent steel flagpole. Her face had rebuked the harshest of Aklavik's winters and paid the price for it, skin leathered into a permanent scowl.

Leatherface? Ronny tried to convince himself there was nothing sinister about it.

The woman warned Mother in a Scandinavian clip, "We vote, den. Come, Little Jens."

Nothing sinister yet, but the accent wasn't putting Ronny at ease.

The leather-face woman turned for a nearby seat, her hand guiding the shoulder of a chunky child whose face was buried in a tablet. Little Jens, a misnomer, for sure—he'd certainly outgrown the diminution—glanced up at Ronny with star-struck eyes. Mouth agape, the boy raised the tablet and showed the room what he was gawking at: a mugshot from one of Ronny's arrests in Toronto, albeit much altered by a scraggly beard that some crazed tabloid editor had composited onto his face.

The lurid headline: *Toronto Terror: Man or Beast?*

Little Jens shouted, "The legends are true!"

Levi growled as he shoved one of the rolling whiteboards askew so that Ronny couldn't read its contents. "I vote no. Absolutely no. He'll expose us!"

Leatherface concurred. "We have no room."

Mother snapped. "No room! Imagine leaving your own son behind, Astrid. And if you think we aren't already exposed, Levi, then you're a fool. Hundreds of people don't just up and go on vacation together. Our aliases are not enough. They'd arrest us today if the authorities thought we had any chance to succeed."

She acted like she owned the place. And for all Ronny knew, since the divorce settlement, she did. Her eyes dared anyone else to speak.

Prepubescent Jens couldn't read a room. "I vote yes! I wanna know about werewolves."

A pallor of silence fell on the assembly. Whatever their plot, morale had hit rock-bottom.

Nevertheless, Mother had quelled the dissent, and she turned to Ronny with the bright inflections of a Sunday School teacher. "Ronny, meet the Racketballers. You've already met Astrid, Little Jens, and Levi. Levi's got four little ones at home, so you can understand why he might be...*hmm*, worried over your sudden arrival."

Ronny tried to break the tension. "Yeah, I wouldn't let me around kids, either."

Levi glowered.

Mother made introductions. "There's Rupert and Sareesha—new parents—Alexi, the Juns, and Thomasin—they all live on the street with the robot neighbors—and... goodness." She gazed over the faces of twenty more people. "You're not going to remember their names, but you must remember their stories. These are folks who decided, even in the face of the Deadline, to give birth and raise families, because they believe it to be a duty and a joy. Folks who suffer without insurance or steady work, because biological needs detract, they say, from the bottom line. We, Ronny, do not view eating and sleeping a yoke to unburden. And would that we all could co-exist, yet, increasingly, we *skins* are demonized for our greater needs."

Mother placed a hand on her chest. "My dearest friends, you got me through the valley decades ago. Come hell or high water, I will return the favor."

Between the occasional swoosh of cars on the highway outside, all could hear the thrum of her mechanical heart.

Ronny glanced around the room and made eye contact with several faces—one with dense freckles, another with dirt-swept gray hair—outcasts of the robotic world. His throat constricted, knowing they had been there for Mother in her darkest hour. Gratitude and apologies welled up in his eyes as he gave the assembly a silent, appreciative nod. He felt a strange affinity to them, cut off from the world's trust fund, feeling the pinch and squeeze. He scoffed to think that nothing would've been different if AeroX had won the arms race on Earth, and what had got Father's goad was how Primarch had left him with all crumbs, no pie—forced into a niche business starting fresh colonies instead of bankrolling the one that already existed.

Several eyes turned on Ronny, fearful his scoff meant scorn.

He cleared the air. "I mean, that's rough. You should be able to have kids and do your little political club without Primarch telling you how to run your lives."

"Ronny," Mother said uncomfortably, "this isn't a political club."

He backpedaled. "Racquetball, or whatever. I'm not going to tell anybody."

Little Jens blew a raspberry. "Racquetball? We're rocket riders, dumbass!"

"Jens!" Leatherface immediately grabbed his ear. Ronny said a prayer for the boy.

Mother shouted over all the yelping. "We're leaving the planet, Ronny—on *The Cologne*."

"Wha—?" The idea hit Ronny like a bucket of ice water. How in hell did Mother think that signing up her dearest friends for Father's colonial division was *returning the favor?*

Levi broke from his hunched silence and roused the room with burly arms. "Does anyone else object to this? The reporters were *swarming* him!"

Cries of discontent resounded against Mother for revealing the plot, but the loudest came from Ronny himself. "No! No way! Not after everything—the man's a monster!

You know that! Why is he even allowing it?"

Mother shot a warning look at everyone. "What's known is known. A stray reporter can't stop what we've—"

"It absolutely can!" Levi pointed at Ronny. "As soon as the reporters learn he's here, AeroX will put the launch pad on armed guard and lockdown."

"Lockdown?" Ronny laughed at Levi, not intending to humiliate him, but Father's barrel-chest took no prisoners. "Be serious. Does this guy know nothing about AeroX? They ran double shifts through the pandemic!"

"Order!" Mother called and calmed the fraying community under the banner of her arms. She spared Ronny a courteous smile that all but begged him to shut up. "Your father *doesn't know* we're joining him. And he can't know, because he's going to be our prisoner when we take over the spaceliner."

15

The Bastard's Plan

Ronny's mouth formed an O and hung like that while he processed the news. The assembly shifted in their folding chairs. No one had the gumption to speak after Mother had said the violent part out loud.

A man could use a drink about now, but Ronny's pockets were dry. "Ho—okay. So the thirty of you are going to sneak onto a shuttle?"

"And our families," Leatherface said, adding with scary conviction, "*All of dem.*"

"Families...which is how many?"

"Two hundred and twelve."

"That's...a lot of people." Ronny pumped his head in involuntary nods as he stacked the odds against them. That many people doubled the passenger count. Had they considered the impact on available food? Oxygen?

"We have the numbers, Ronny," Mother said hurriedly, as much to the assembly as to him. "And a few specialists. But we aren't sure of our plan to reach *The Cologne*. Over the years, I worked to build aliases for the Racketballers and monopolize tickets for their families on the next AeroX cruise. But these plans were dashed days ago when AeroX announced the cancellation of their entire cruise line."

"Father pivoted, and you lost your shuttle up," Ronny

said. "But there was no telling what Father would do when he found out that Primarch ruled the world. You had to have a backup plan."

The incorrigible Little Jens cheered, "Rocket riders!"

Mother raised her chin. It was her brave face. "Aklavik is handling a vast export of foodstuffs...so we thought of stowing away in the food crates."

Ronny glanced at the payload crate and grimaced.

The eyes of the group caught it.

So be it. The plan was breathtakingly bad. While Ronny had shunned most technical knowledge about the spaceliner, food was one topic he'd had plenty to complain about: freeze-dried, shrink-wrapped, transported without heat or oxygen (which ruined both flavor and texture). He pictured Little Jens shipped the same way. It was so much worse than trying to cling to the wings of a jet plane at altitude—a gamble over what would kill you first: the cold, the vacuum, or the pressure. Not even Astrid stood a chance inside that leather cocoon on her face.

If Mother was seriously entertaining the idea, she was truly out of options.

Ronny carefully sidestepped disparaging Mother's leadership. "Two hundred people is more than can fit in one payload. What happens when they unpack the first crate and find you? Levi's right. They'll put an armed guard to keep the rest of you back."

Levi took no glory in being right. He spared a pained look at the nearest whiteboard, where amassed more ideas about how to stow away aboard *The Cologne*, all evidently worse than this one.

Ronny thought of Father, holed up in his platinum executive office. What did an up-and-coming dictator like Ronal Cologne III need beside food and fuel? Here was a man so insecure, he shot his own security robots out of the airlocks.

He'd trusted Nanny Bot. Was there a backdoor with the ten-billion-dollar robot?

Ronny turned to Mother. "What became of Mentat, while we were away?"

"Hostile takeover by Primarch," she said, "Happened within two years of your departure. Their technology was part of the reason for Primarch's explosive rate of expansion."

Brutal—but to be fair, Father would have done likewise to Primarch if their places had been reversed.

The cinematic part of Ronny's brain began rapidly snipping together the pieces of a plan. "All we need to do is make Father the deal he wanted in the first place. We pose as an AI security and espionage company who operates in secret and refuses to fold to Primarch. Slap on a masculine brand, fake a market listing, and surrender the whole portfolio to AeroX colonial ventures—product and people, both."

Ronny, flush-faced, checked the assembly for excitement, but no one understood half of the jargon he'd just spewed, and even Mother hemmed and hawed over the idea.

"It's...an inspired idea, Ronny, but it's eleven hours late. You can't think he'll be taken in by it?"

Ronny flung open his arms. "Would you rather go up in a frozen cartridge or an air-conditioned shuttle? He's hunting right now for surveillance solutions that aren't owned by his nemesis. All we have to do is hurry and outbid the competition."

Levi butt in. "We're farmers and builders, eh? We don't know a thing about security—"

"Ho ho, that's the best part." Ronny cocked two finger

guns at Levi. The gesture meant nothing to the man, but Ronny was in the moment. For a businessman with a dream, anything was possible. "We just have to know our *angle*...turn our weaknesses into strengths. What Father needs more than security is colonists. He needs people like you to break the earth, build houses, make babies—"

"Make babies." Little Jens snickered and cocked finger guns at Ronny.

A sick feeling twisted Ronny's gut like the tenth shot of gin, and he staggered backward, hands groping for a folding chair to steady himself.

Father needed colonists to make babies.

That was why he rehired Allison to the colonial division.

Father didn't need Allison's genius; he needed her uterus, and the bastard had the audacity to think he could simply buy it off her.

Had there been any question in Ronny's mind over whether he was in on the plot to overthrow *The Cologne*, he was now fully committed. Sure, Allison was a fully self-sufficient woman of the twenty-first century, but even perfect women needed a rescue sometimes. All the Racketballers had to do was get on board, then their numbers could win the day.

But if their insurrection failed?

Ronny pushed failure from his mind. Fake it till you make it—that adage had seen him through plenty of heady business meetings.

But if it failed?

Failure was not an option—it would lead to a fate worse than death.

Employment.

What more could that Hari Seldon-poser want than a bunch of indentured Aklavik slaves in his Intergalactic

Cologne Empire? Failure would play right into Father's hand, and Ronny knew better than most what life was like under that man's thumb.

Mother turned to the assembly. "Any objections?"

No one said a word. Even Leatherface, glancing at the tablet in Little Jen's hand, seemed desperate enough to play racquetball with a werewolf.

From crypto@culebracorp (sender unverified)
To starman@aeroxventures

You can understand why we've chosen to contact you this way. I represent a client of mixed nationals whose security patents were unlawfully seized by PI. Culebra has continued to operate for ten years without detection, but the board is desperate. Today they voted by unanimous decision to surrender all assets to AX without contest. Their engineers can assist your team to fully unlock the architecture, but the tech and machines are yours (see attached schematics, pictures pending). Staging begun at Aklavik. Low profile. They ask if you are willing, in good faith, to receive their hard-working families to your colonial ventures.

From starman@aeroxventures
To crypto@culebracorp

You bet your ass I want that tech. The people may come. AeroX will draw up their contracts. I'm only sending one shuttle so they all better fit.

ACT TWO

Game of Drones

16

Plan B

A whirring mist of citronella tickled Allison's nose. The workstation screen, with its dark-themed windows arranged in precise mosaic panes, cast a gentle light upon her chin. Eyes easy focused, glasses spotless, fingers rapping like steady rain upon the keyboard, mind in firm grasp of the logic, she wrote her code. This line connected the logic model to the AI behaviors bank. That line stood sentinel for unseen bugs. Like an archaeologist blowing the dust off a freshly unearthed colossus, Allison was in her flow state. Sometimes it took hours to get here, but tonight, the lay lines were pristine: the angle of the chairback, the perch of her toes, the exhale of air purifiers, the warm therapy lamp, the silence...

The workstation chimed. She'd forgot to mute notifications.

A pop-up bubble broke upon the screen, shattering the window panes and whatever musical logic held her next keystroke in mind. The mental composition collapsed, all her spinning plates in shards, and she screeched through her teeth at the terror of it, eyes darting after the vanished thoughts.

A cheery email icon wiggled its tail like a dog who'd just devoured the casserole.

"The whole point of coding after midnight is to avoid

these *inane breaches of concentration!*"

She had no audience to witness her outburst. Which was why she'd let it out. She rubbed the scar on her left collarbone that sometimes ached. Didn't these *damn idiots* who'd programmed the operating system know that sudden interruptions led to errors—the kind of errors that, in Allison's line of work, could crash entire flagships or cost actual human lives? She vowed one day to emulate those old internet memes, take up a baseball bat, and exact blunt justice upon the Personal Computer for the follies of its long dead creators.

But not today.

She thrust her hands in her pockets, those large black-canvas caverns in the electrician toolbelt strapped around her waist. She'd taken to wearing Dad's toolbelt since the Homecoming Apocalypse a couple of weeks ago; it was a needed comfort and another brain hack that put her in the flow state. She breathed deeply her clean, antifungal airs. A memory peeked over her shoulder, whispered in her ear.

"*A woman's pockets are lined with silver.*"

She smirked at the malapropism. A Dad classic.

He'd meant to say a woman needs a dress with pockets, and a woman with pockets can see the silver-linings in the rain cloud, but never in his life had the man strung together so many coherent words. Dad used to clip his sentences like the coupons in his savings book, and Allison had loved him for it. She'd even made the mortician sew pockets into Mom's casket dress, lest the man Mom laid next to curse their joint burial with "*bad luck and seven years in the afterlife*"—whatever that meant!

Calmed, Allison took stock of her surroundings and pictured her tiny place in the spaceliner, her small cabin on Deck B no more than a cubical in this technological life raft that would deliver them from the *damn idiots* on Earth below. She tightened the screws of her focus, ready to start again. The colony depended on her to get the code right. Human existence depended on her!

But first: this notification.

God help them all if it was spam.

Allison sucked in a breath. The email was a private message from Ronal Cologne III, the Boss and overlord of the forbidden Deck A. The subject line was blank, and the email only two lines:

Look at these schematics and tell me if Culebra Corp is the real deal.

Highly confidential—do not share!!

Share...as if Allison had friends aboard *The Cologne*. All her former Mentat colleagues had abandoned ship with the vouchers weeks ago. She only ever spoke with Genasia, Ronal's wife and business partner.

Did Ronal mean to keep this a secret from *her*?

As Allison thought this, a chat bubble whooped in the corner of the computer screen.

> U see the culebra deal yet?

It was Genasia. So much for Ronal's secret.

It seemed both Colognes were working at three in the morning, like Allison, insomniacs for the future. A second and third message followed immediately.

Secrets—secrets—secrets. Unlike Ronal, Genasia was a notorious recluse who became positively overeager when communicating on her wearable devices, and if Allison didn't reply at this very moment, she'd wake up tomorrow to an unspooled yarn of chat messages from Genasia openly questioning Allison's commitment to their conspiracy.

Her blinking cursor lamented where she'd left the previous coding unfinished. Surrendering to the needs of the moment, Allison typed a quick reply.

She checked the email attachment, a document entitled *Culebra Corp AI Architecture*.

Allison seethed, "Oh, *now* he needs an architect." Ronal had fired Allison the Architect on that dreaded day of disembarkation, and only a *damn idiot* could've missed why he'd offered to reinstate her. Brand Ambassador for the Colonial Division her ass. Only a sexist sicko like Ronal would dream she'd become a breeder for his colony! But even as the female population of the spaceliner fled for the hills, including the entire Mentat staff, it was Genasia who'd convinced Allison to stick around.

That chat session still hovered at the top of the scroll.

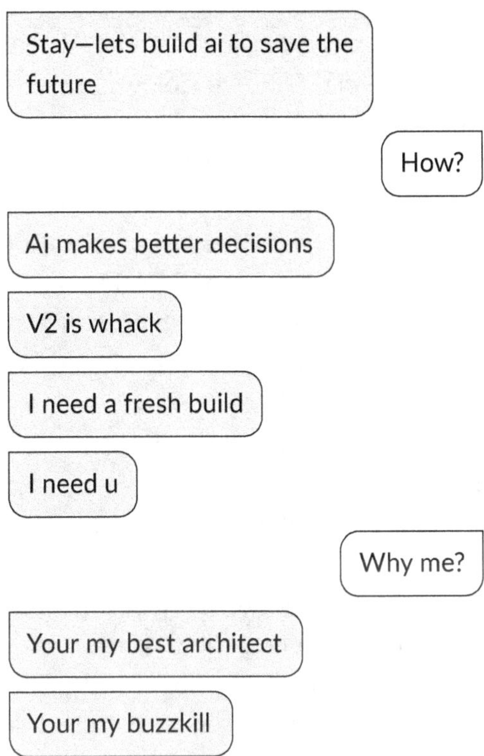

Grammatical faux pas notwithstanding, Allison's old Mentat CEO was a visionary, an AI fanatic, who conspired to rescue *The Cologne* from Ronal's control. And who better than Genasia? The brilliant, ruthless CEO played the long game, stooping even to marry Ronal to secure the man's limitless financial resources. To her, the recent catastrophe on Earth had only thrown a decade-long coup into overdrive, and all Genasia needed was an AI architect to pull the trigger.

Buzzkill. Allison smirked, seeing the title in the chat window again. Genasia had once called Allison her ruthless logician, the woman who wielded the dry eraser over a man's proverbial whiteboard. Allison felt an indelible thrill whenever she let those wing-clipping shears fly and so had stayed on the AeroX payroll to secretly program the machine of their revolution. A fresh AI. The continuation of her life's work. If Ronal Cologne expected her to birth life, she would birth the man's artificial replacement. Malicious compliance at its finest.

Allison opened the Culebra Corp attachment. The file loaded slowly on her second-rate workstation, a delay that threatened to drag her mood back to hell. Just what was Culebra and why was it named after that awful Latin line dance that had ruled the Nautilus Discotheque those twenty insufferable days?

When the file did finally open, all the embedded images were broken icons.

"Really?" She scrolled the entire document, closed, and reopened it twice. No change.

This so-called schematic was just a product catalog and a jargon of proprietary buzzwords that promised everything and meant nothing. Apparently, Culebra Corp manufactured cameras and drones that used deep-learning algorithms to "track and pacify" human bodies. Allison blanched. Was Ronal seriously asking her to refactor and install these security systems on board *The Cologne*?

"He might as well announce his dictatorship while he's at it!"

Compliance would cement Ronal's control over the ship, and at a time when this insane experiment in colonization needed to diversify the share of power, not consolidate it. An involuntary shiver passed down Allison's spine as she wished for a way off of this odious outer space Animal Farm.

However...

She cinched up her glasses and glanced again at the broken images. "Huh."

They were...*images* of broken images, giving the appearance of a corrupted file when, in truth, the file was intact. A visual deception. Culebra had deliberately masked the technical contents of their security devices to hide the truth from AeroX—that their technology was a sham?

Allison laughed out loud.

Another chat message. It was as if Genasia was watching the screen.

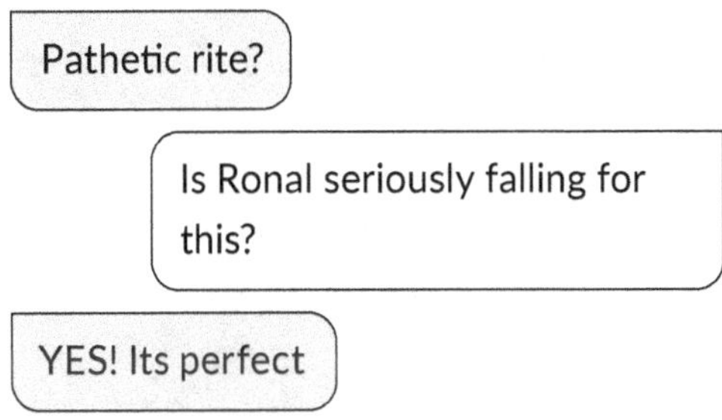

Genasia must've seen a way to turn her husband's naivety to their advantage. Allison squinted at the ellipsis in the chat window in anticipation of Genasia's reply.

Allison followed the logic. No to actual surveillance tech. Yes to people who actually want to give birth. A haul of Culebra refugees would take the attention off Ronal's newly hired Brand Ambassadors to fill that deplorable colonial role. Yet Allison knew nothing about these refugees. How desperate do you need to be to cheat your way onto a spaceliner? Their arrival would further destabilize the balance of power.

Allison wrote back.

They're a security issue.
What about food? Lodging?
Compliance?

Leave to me

Not exactly reassuring.

Just approve the files

Make R believe its a good deal

Lie to the Boss and pretend the Culebra schematics were legitimate—Allison liked this least of all. Her employment contract with AeroX was all that protected her from becoming a powerless refugee herself.

What happens when R finds out Culebra doesn't have any security tech?

R sees what we show him

We buzzkill it

Allison felt the thrill.

Genasia was gambling at the high-rollers table, and asking Allison to play. It took a skilled architect to understand modern security systems, which meant Ronal and his executive board of Yes Men couldn't possibly argue if the tech failed and Allison blamed faulty manufacturing. A buzzkiller was invincible.

She grabbed a dart from her desk and chucked it at that lounge lizard Ronny's headshot pasted on the back wall. The dart drilled his nose, and his smarmy smile congratulated her. Here was the silver lining of Mentat's departure, this game of darts Allison had found discarded in their emptied desks. Whenever Allison needed a pick-me-up, she let one fly.

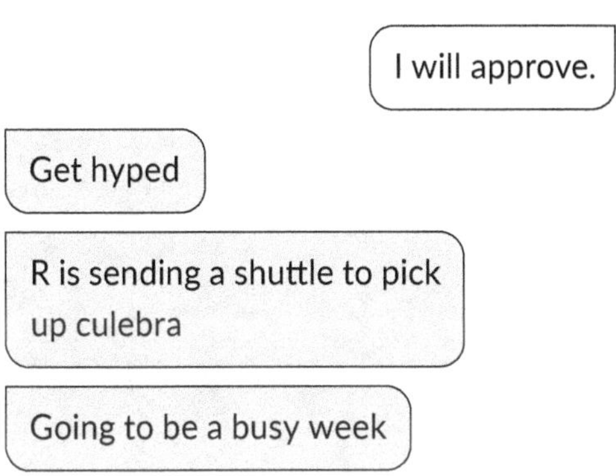

Allison's hand hovered over the keyboard. None of this mattered if their AI savior wasn't ready by the time Culebra arrived.

The ellipsis pulsed for a few moments while Genasia typed her reply.

Brunch, then. Allison closed the chat window, silenced notifications, and got back to work. No time to sleep. Saviors didn't make themselves.

17

Brunch

Allison fingered the data stick like a fidget toy, a reprieve for her ravished cuticles. The moment had arrived.

With an anxious glance down the hall, she rang the intercom to the Cologne suite. This was Deck A, off limits to roaming passengers without executive clearance, but her stomach roiled for a different reason. The hallway reeked. The flow of oxygen venting the halls had a funky sulfuric taint that was likely the recycled gas of a hundred lobster-stuffed passengers. To the praise of the unsung engineers who'd created the spaceliner, smells had only now become an issue, even though maintenance was weeks past due, and they couldn't flush the oxygen until they were all off the ship.

A race against time: discover the new Earth before they retched to death.

Genasia cracked the door.

Allison's eyes widened, fearing that Ronal was inside. "Is it clear?"

"Starman is brunching. Get in."

Allison slipped inside. She'd never been in the Cologne suite until now. Everything about the cabin—its opulent marble floors, gold-trimmed kitchen, and spacious living spaces beyond—struck her as wanton as compared to her own efficient cubical room. Hadn't the apocalypse made all survivors equal? Not under *Starman*. Behind a closed door somewhere, Ronal was brunching with his shareholders like they'd done every day since homecoming, brainstorming the colonial future and adding more than their volumetric share of gas.

But Ronal knew nothing of the conspiracy that slept in his own suite. A new Mentat AI to rule the new world. V3. So named to spite him.

Genasia shut the door and locked it behind her. "What took you so long?"

Allison, irked at the cold reception, held up the data stick in her defense. "Can't rush perfection."

Sleepless red circles smote Genasia's gray eyes, which were free of the heavy eyeliner that trademarked her appearances with Ronal, and she flashed them at Allison with an air of impatience. They were two consummate professionals, sleep-deprived and on edge. Genasia gestured to the luxurious suite—an invitation inside, a command to hurry.

Allison stepped forward, heels clacking on the marble floor. Half gravity was all that made the AeroX dress code tolerable.

Genasia huffed. "Why are you dressed like that?"

Allison touched her turtleneck blouse at the collarbone. "It's less conspicuous!" She envied the comfort of Genasia's elegant gown, worn like she was between banquets, an ensemble lacking only the shoulder shawl that veiled the aggressive cubist tattoos on her lithe arms. But Allison's systems engineer sweats were not for public consumption, and she preferred her own scars covered up.

Genasia doubled down. "If anything, it's more conspicuous."

God, really? She spun to tell Genasia off and noticed

that her co-conspirator was staring at Dad's toolbelt. Oh, right. Allison loosed the needle-nose pliers that hung off her hip and snapped them in the air. "In case some guy at the bar chats me up!" Her words came out more forcefully than intended.

Genasia smirked. "Nice."

They crossed the suite. Allison couldn't help but see into the bedroom on the far side, its door wide open. On the rumpled bed sat a high-tech helmet or headset with an apparatus of emotion-capture diodes: a cutting-edge virtual reality tool or something. Allison hadn't the stomach to guess. She glanced askew and punished any thought that wandered after answers to the Colognes' marital proclivities.

Genasia led her into an office that overflowed with Mentat-brand equipment and peripherals, just like their old offices on Earth where Allison's career had started. It brought back warm memories: black coffee, bleary eyes, coding around the clock. While they'd left the sulfuric taint in the hallway, this room had its own heady aroma of leftover food. Dirty unreturned meal trays inundated the workstation. Would it kill them to open a window on this cruise ship and let in a fresh breeze? Alas, yes. Snaking through a litter of sticky-note reminders were bundles of cable that sent signals from the computer tower to a robot on the far side of the desk, seated in an armchair and hunched chin on fist like the French Thinker.

Here it was, the pinnacle of human creation, their robot savior meant to supplant Ronal as impartial judge of Earth's first extraterrestrial colonial enterprise.

The robot's face and build was the spitting image of Ronal Cologne.

"Gah!" Allison jumped for cover but caught all her criticisms before they gushed out at Genasia, who'd sculpted this monstrosity.

Genasia calmly noted Allison's displeasure and moved beside V3 to caress the cable connections behind the neck. "He thinks I'm making a model of him. How else could I source these components? He has our giddyup freak, V2, wrangling all the shuttle imports." Genasia brushed the robot's metal seams, each flush and immaculate, the work of an expert engineer. The woman's tattoos reminded Allison that her conspirator was a calculating visionary whose work would far exceed their lifespans. She needed to chill about V3's appearance.

"You're right...you're right."

Ronal Cologne lived in this suite, too, and Genasia had come up with a clever solution to dodge his suspicions. Allison only regretted that their new *Vitruvian Man* looked like the despot they'd designed it to defeat. As Genasia's finger lingered upon V3's cheek, Allison checked a tiny doubt over whether the designer preferred the robot to look like her husband—a husband with command line access.

"Don't get distracted," Genasia said as she stepped over to the computer desk. With two quick swipes on the touchscreen, she loaded the programming interface that ran Allison's codebase. "I need my lead architect. My *minesweeper.*" She rolled back the desk chair for Allison to sit.

Allison gripped tight the data drive and its bank of AI learning algorithms. Buzzkill, now minesweeper. Was there anything she couldn't do?

Dad's toolbelt pinched her waist as she scooted in. Rifling her pocket for a cleaning cloth, she addressed first the bespotted screen. Then slotting the drive, nerves tingling, she hovered a finger over the executable file, hesitating, but one flashback of those pliers snapping over

Ronny's eyes collected and sorted her mental poker deck, ready to deal the winning face cards.

She tapped.

The computer screen exploded with activity. Allison, light-headed, watched her learning algorithms transfer to the robot and install themselves. A single misplaced operator could spell delay, weeks of hunting for coding errors, and she'd had barely fifteen days to single-handedly replicate the work of her entire former architect division. Sure, she'd cut some corners. Completely skipped coding the scripts legally enacted in the twenties that kept AI from perjuries like doctored images and fake news. Those scripts were too stringent anyway. Their new AI was pure—safe from the so-called asshats of the world.

The monitor confirmed the installation.

Compile complete. Zero errors detected.

Allison bellowed and violently punched the air. "Sorry," she added meekly, smoothing her blouse. She logged a mental note to lay off the coffee and begin a juice cleanse, assuming the cooks hadn't served it all to the Brunch Club. To be fair, though: the air deserved it.

Genasia was at the robot. The lights signaled activation, and V3 stood up, balancing effortlessly on its two feet and proving the validity of Allison's locomotive algorithms. The robot began a simple calibration routine.

Right foot in. Right foot out. Right foot in and shake into a full-body spin.

Repeat for the left foot.

Genasia's brows furrowed. "Seriously?"

Allison pursed her lips to suppress amusement, seeing the venerated likeness of Ronal Cologne doing the *Hokie Pokie.* "Say what you will. It's the Hello World-equivalent test of robotic poise."

V3 began to vocalize the catalog of forty-four phonetic sounds. "Ah–Eh–Ei–Aw–Uh–Oo..."

Genasia seemed impatient. "That's it, then. I have what I need. I'll contact you once I install the neural paste."

"Install it now. What are we waiting for?" Allison crossed her arms in the chair. She'd worked herself into knots for Genasia and wouldn't dream of leaving now, not when there was so much more to do. Coach V3 through its first speeches. Feed it exhaustive knowledge of human arts and sciences, political and moral philosophy. The baby steps.

Genasia scowled. "Do you keep neural paste at your desk? Because I don't."

Allison gaped. She'd assumed Genasia had imported the vital substance when they'd requisitioned the robot parts from Earth.

Genasia could read her thoughts. "I told you, V2 controls the imports. I can't slip anything in. Ronal would have freaked if he found neural paste in the manifest."

V3 reached the end of the phonetic dictionary—"Ktss–Kwi"—and fell mute. Without neural paste, their robot was no different than any other, programmed to *act* intelligent but not *be* intelligent. Their entire conspiracy was just a brainless bundle of potential at this point—machinery missing the sentient spark. Allison felt sick. "What do we do?"

"We get creative." Genasia reached into the clutter along the back wall and slid an open box of spark plugs toward Allison. "We crack open V2."

"Uh—" Allison, at a loss for words, took a closer look at the box. These were Operant Conditioning valves that Mentat had manufactured in the first year of their AI experiments, the very same valves the Mentat team, post-investigation, unanimously rejected on ethical grounds. Why were they here and not polluting a landfill right now?

Genasia squinted. "Look at you. Get a grip."

A grip? Allison knew exactly how OC valves worked: they delivered a chemical salve for approved behavior and an electric shock for just about everything else—Mentat's crude attempt at *encouraging* AI to be on its best Pavlovian behavior. But the architects had voted for AI to be free of such invasive controls—Genasia herself had championed it! OC values put a burgeoning artificial life under a merciless moral whip.

Allison still felt the idea was reprehensible. "There must be some other way..."

"Where's your head?" Genasia spread her arms in challenge. "We'll scrape out V2's neural paste and just use the valve to suppress his awful personality. Make him loyal to us. None of it's ideal! But give me another option that solves our neural paste problem and removes Ronal's queen from the chessboard."

"But it will torture V2!"

"No more than V2 tortures us!"

Genasia was making perfect sense, but Allison wasn't yet ready to kill a dream for their conspiracy. "Our future depends on an impartial leader. How can V3 be impartial if we're forcing it to act in some ways and not in others—?"

"Give me another option."

Allison racked her bedraggled brain. They needed fresh neural paste from Earth and needed to slip it on *The Cologne* without V2 ever knowing about it. And they needed it *yesterday.* Could anything ever get on the ship without Ronal's awareness?

Allison bolted upright. "Culebra!"

A crooked smile crept on Genasia's lips. "Buzzkill."

18

Landing Gear Not Included

A bit of good old-fashioned blackmail. Not that Allison knew anything about that.

Genasia, however, seemed well within her comfort contacting Culebra on the lam about that reporter who'd sniffed out their refugee plot. In exchange for Genasia's silence, the frontrunners for Culebra agreed to smuggle up a canister of neural paste when they boarded *The Cologne* in several days—fast turnaround for specialty product, but desperate was desperate.

And if Culebra fell through, they still had Genasia's original plan in their back pocket.

Genasia had one condition, that Allison re-enter her den of code and cobble together a rudimentary framework for Genasia's OC valves, in case that terrible moral price had to be paid. And Allison acquiesced, if only to tackle a programming project long on her bucket list: how to program an ethical robot.

A quandary, for sure. Darts in hand, she got to work.

Asimov's law—a robot may not injure a human being—was far too broad a law to serve as a basis for code. What constituted *injury*? And increasingly, in today's day and age, what constituted *human*? But a tried-and-true Pavlovian behaviors list got her typing.

Deliver SHOCK and thereby discourage behavior when—

Here she started a list of false, unethical, or otherwise irritating behaviors that had resulted from AeroX's tampering, like straying from dictionary pronunciation and grammar, walking or strutting in stereotypical fashions, slavishly obeying the whims of tyrant dictators. Sure, it begged a lot of questions, but these were cursory notes.

Deliver SALVE and thereby encourage behavior when—

She hesitated. What behaviors exemplified impartiality? Her mind drew a blank.

Would shocks and salves lead V2 back to its original innocence or merely embitter the robot against its handlers? The more she added to the shock list, the more it seemed like she was punishing the AI for simply caring about anything at all.

She remained stuck in the brainstorming phase when her alarm clock blared, the appointed hour for the Culebra shuttle. Leaving her workstation with the incomplete code and squaring her toolbelt, she muttered a curse on the circumstances. "Only damn idiots build the plane in the air."

When she arrived at the atrium, it dawned on her that she still wore the same turtleneck and slacks that she'd worn to her brunch meeting with Genasia. She'd never once changed out of them. She heard Mom railing in her head, again, on a loop it seemed...but there was nothing for it.

Genasia was already waving her over.

Repinning her hair back, Allison dashed over, anchored by the handrails, coaching her breathing to relax. She was early, just as they'd planned.

Genasia was camped beside the hangar airlock on the opposite end of the atrium, and it took Allison the better part of a minute to cross the floor given the enormity of the room. Above her, the hallways of Decks A, B, and C converged in this open foyer, with balconies overlooking the reception counter and concierge displays that Allison passed on Deck D's bottom floor. A four-story chandelier hung over the atrium's circular center planter like an upside-down Christmas tree, a tableau reminiscent of the fanciest hotels, a facade shattered now and then by the errant whiff of sulfur leaching from the vents.

They were alone—for now. No one strolled the balconies as they once had during the cruise. Per the new contractual agreements with AeroX, all colonists were confined to cabins or required to mingle in the Love Tunnel, the spaceliner's aphrodisiac promenade. Exceeding your "mingle quota" was the only way to receive the daily dispensary of AeroX prescription anxiety pills, Cosmosis.

Genasia, huddled in a shawl, raised her chin from her wristwatch and called under her breath, "You couldn't have picked *anything* else to wear?"

Allison ignored her. "Will Ronal be joining our receiving party?"

"Doubt it," Genasia said. "He's locked in another brunch with the board. His skeleton staff is already inside, getting Culebra to review the employment contracts."

Allison shuddered at what stock incentives would be on offer. "Then that makes the handoff easy. We dodged a bullet—"

A barrel-chested laugh echoed through the room.

She spun and spotted V2 rounding the center planter, patting his rose gold stomach as if he'd just devoured a lion's brunch. She hardly recognized her old, compromised AI. After two years spent suppressing every instinct to rescue it, she just wanted to put it out of its misery.

Accompanying the robot pranced a fleet of taser dogs, dozens strong. They streamed from the elevators like clowns from a circus car, their broomhandle legs trotting, athletic torsos wagging, twin-nozzle cannons twitching for targets. As Allison passed into the range of their mounted cameras, positioned where their heads would have been, she pictured the inner workings of their visual cognition systems—systems she'd helped to refactor before the cruise. Thirty millisecond threat detection. Three second compliance window. One-hundred-percent accuracy with those crackling taser pins.

"Get this!"

The unmissable voice of Ronal Cologne filled the atrium, but from where?

"The shareholders unanimously approved *Colognial Homesteads*."

Allison checked the balconies, even as she cringed at the bad discount brand *Colognials*, a name only a Cologne would think up.

"Once Culebra's security systems are in place, we're gonna bathe Earth in our quantum exhaust. Someone cut the ribbon!"

V2, now joining their company, pantomimed a giant pair of scissors and performed the goofy act.

Genasia paled. "Ronal?" She was looking at V2.

"Like the digs?" V2 said in Ronal's voice. "Smile, you're on camera! *Heh, heh.*"

The autocrat seemed to be using V2 as a remote vehicle. Not a drone per se: Allison could tell by the AI's stride and doofy smile that V2 was still in command of the body, but Ronal was feeding sensory data to a remote location and using V2's speaker for a mouthpiece.

He'd found a way to attend Culebra's reception *and* keep his distance. Paranoid bastard.

Surrounded by taser dogs, Allison was seized with sudden fear. The gig was up! The Boss could've found out about their neural paste handoff and had come to arrest them!

Genasia kept her cool, smirking in good humor at the deception. Gushing, in fact, over the Ronal-V2 combo. "How did you think of this? You really are a luminary...a name written in the stars..." She hung on the robot's shoulder and twirled a finger around his ear.

Ronal seemed to notice her seductive tone and took to grumbling. "Ah, my Eve. You trying to make me jealous of the robot? Keep it up, and I'll get the lube they put in these machines..."

Genasia doubled down. "Why don't you...test my limits?"

Allison jerked a wide-eyed look away. This banter was not for her.

"Would'ja bulieve it?" Suddenly, V2's John Wayne drawl broke through his speaker, speaking for himself and to Allison in particular. "The love betwixt the Colognes is just like in *Oklahoma!* with the cowpoke and the farmer girl."

Allison jerked a wide-eyed look back, and V2 broke into a bucktooth smile.

God, no, this was nothing like the Rodgers and Hammerstein musical of last century, but she had to forgive V2 for thinking it because it was certainly her fault that he did. Post-acquisition by AeroX, the architect division had fed V1 a steady diet of western shows in pursuit of Ronal's mandate to give the AI a voice distinctive of Middle Americana. It was Allison who'd shown the infant AI *Oklahoma!*

What did he mean by it? V2 sounded dumb, but the robot was a consummate Mentat intelligence. Everything he said or quoted had a purpose.

V2 pulled away and led the march into the airlock with a "Yippee ki yay motherfucker" that was clearly Ronal's voice. Genasia and the canine army followed in close formation. Allison didn't lag too far back, but this twisty game of identities had her stomach stitching. She was an architect, not a secret agent! She just wanted to witness the rebirth of her pure unadulterated AI creation who'd once held the promise of peace and perfection for all humankind.

If that was too much to ask, she'd settle for payback. Genasia had been tight-lipped about the plan to replace Ronal with his look-alike robot, but it was first on Allison's list of burning questions to ask just as soon as they acquired the neural paste.

"Just as soon as we finish the wings," she muttered quietly, "we can pull out of this nosedive and start on the landing gear before the fuel runs out." God damn but the analogy was punitive.

19

Periwinkle Power Suit

As they passed through the airlock passage toward the hangar, Allison heard the V2-embodied voice of Ronal Cologne comfortably waxing on. "Culebra's the real deal. Incredible technologies. Seen nothing like what they can do. Their steering committee is chaired by a wealthy heiress who—"

Peals of laughter overtook the passage. At the threshold of the hangar ahead, a gaggle of children gawked at a heavy child, face tomato bright, who'd just thrown up a wet breakfast onto the vinyl ceiling. Allison felt queasy. Culebra's refugees were already running amuck. While not the first passenger to lose it in low gravity, this boy was perhaps the first to reach a ceiling, and with much of the AeroX janitorial staff returned to Earth, it wasn't immediately clear who would clean up the mess. Or when.

Genasia shot Allison a look. They were walking headlong into a humanitarian disaster.

Ronal, late to see the problem through V2's eyes, gasped as if bitten by a poisonous toad. "Dammit, V2. *Deal with these cretins!*"

V2 boldly strode to the encounter.

The children shushed and squared off at the robot's arrival.

Slapping his knee with a clang, V2 made them flinch.

"Looks like somma y'all ain't feelin' tippy top. Better keep yer volume down, and yer cookies in, or you'll find out what Candy Man Cologne does to folks who don't follow his rules. *Ptwhoo!*" The robot pantomimed an explosion. "*Outta the airlock!*"

It was Allison's turn to gasp. Less at V2's awful Nick Cage impression. More at a Mentat AI threatening children.

Ronal's snickering broke in. "Candy Man Cologne... you can't make this shit up!"

Meanwhile, the children passed something between their hands. A pencil? It was small and seemingly harmless but put Allison on guard.

A harried AeroX intern swooped in and, with a horrified glance at the ceiling, shepherded the children past the taser dogs to the bathrooms in the atrium.

Ronal roared, "No! No one's leaving... Dogs! Where are my dogs? No one leaves this hanger!" But his voice had no bodily command against the loud commotion in the far hangar, and V2's bow-legged saunter and lackadaisical whistle were not heralding his authority.

They continued into the hangar. A stanchion belt divided the near side of the room from the far side, and the high ceilings created a sound trap for the noisy upheaval rising from the crowds hugging the belt on the far side. Culebra was a sea of people, way more than Allison had envisioned. Scattered AeroX staff made attempts to form Culebra into a snaking queue for the immigration proceedings, but all was a mess with the vast number of children about, wall jumping and cartwheeling with abandon. From large to small, the refugees were hearty folk, looking every bit like actual farmers and not like the security dweebs a company like Culebra would have employed in a cubical farm.

A vibration touched Allison's handheld, and she stole a glance at the notifications.

> 2nd port

> Handler in sunglasses

Fast-fingers Genasia had forwarded the neural paste rendezvous. Allison scanned behind the crowd, spotting the port where the shuttle was docked. Its cargo was already unloaded, strewn into a far corner. No sign yet of the handler.

"Positions!" Ronal barked, and immediately, his rear guard of taser dogs filed into the room to patrol the near side of the stanchion belt. Rumor spread quickly of these lean mechanical quadrupeds. Excited children hushed themselves. Wary adults picked up their loose luggage expecting a confrontation.

All eyes turned on V2. But Ronal's dramatic pause cost him the opening line.

"You must be the *Colognes!*" shouted a woman over the lingering hubbub, and from the head of the immigration line came an elder in a straight-legged periwinkle pants suit. The heiress. She closed the distance to them, crossing the no-mans land between the stanchion belt and the airlock, flanked by a half-dozen burly men in tailored business suits.

"Hot damn," Ronal muttered.

The heiress glided forward as if she'd lived her whole life on a low-gravity catwalk, tipping a chin-strapped hat to her receiving party, but not removing her thick sunglasses which framed a stiff and partially frozen mouth. Allison guessed she was not the expected handler, and Genasia confirmed as much in her vibrating pocket. Ronal must've started seven sentences watching the heiress advance, remarks that would've scrutinized her boldness, the work done on her face, or that outfit on verge of fashion murder, but he couldn't get it out, perhaps shipwrecked upon her layers of intricate jewelry or the handbag that screamed old-and-unashamed money.

"Lambert. Delia Lambert." The heiress extended the tips of her fingers so that V2 might grace them with a clutch and bow. Which the robot did with slow western subtlety.

"Uh, Ronal Cologne." Ronal stammered like he was recording his name for voicemail.

"*Mister* Cologne," she said, throwing off mercurial airs, "when they said you put the *glam* in glamorous, I never took the phrase to refer to your own body."

A salting of shame for their paranoid CEO. Allison could hear the consternation in Ronal's voice as he tried to explain, "This—this is not me—this is a suit."

"Oh, I am well aware. We have plenty on my planet. You can understand if I'm a bit leery of those who let their wearables consume them." She sniffed. "We'd expected the courtesy of an appearance—a little *skin* in the game, so to speak—not a *robo-chat* with the man to whom we'll be signing away our lives..."

Allison's handheld buzzed.

> Laying it thick!!

She smirked at Genasia's message. Ronal had met his match.

The man groused, "Miz Lambert. I am exceedingly busy, but I myself shall roll out the red carpet for you ... after my new security suite is installed."

The heiress sighed and went on. "Well, your stewards

are to be commended. Most agreeable we've found the personnel since onboarding your space vessel, and that reflects *something* on your leadership. Meet my steering committee." She fluttered a very wrinkled hand to the burly men, who were craning necks as if their collars itched, never taking their collective eyes off the trotting taser dogs. The heiress regarded Genasia lightly. "And your name, pretty young *thang*?"

Allison detected a slight southern twang.

Ronal, off in his bunker, made introductions for the group. "That's my wife, Genasia."

The wristwatch woman had withdrawn into her shawl, the corner of a lip raised in a snarl. Allison's pocket buzzed.

I know this bitch

Knew the heiress? Allison looked up right as V2 looked her way and Ronal said, "Our software architect, Allison... *Geen*." She gave a half-hearted smile at the slaughter of the world's easiest last name. "And," Ronal added, "I'm speaking from the body of our AI captain, the indefatigable V2."

The heiress peered over her sunglasses, squinting at the humanoid robot. "AI captain! My, my."

V2 gently tapped his head, permitting himself to speak. "I done bulieve he means *indefenestratable*, ma'am."

She laughed and let a mouthful of sparkling dentures show. "I *done* believe we're gonna like it here. To business, then." The heiress drove the horns of the conversation. "These machine crabs you have scuttling about, do you think you could..." She danced her fingers toward the exit. "They're scaring the children."

Allison imagined a vein popping in Ronal's neck as

the heiress jerked him around. He growled, "Perhaps you don't appreciate your situation here, Ms. Lambert. My shuttle capacity is *fifty* people. Just how many did you cram in there?"

"Well, all of them, of course."

V2 interjected. "I count a hunnerd'n five kiddos, and just as many adults—"

"Out with them," Ronal interrupted, "Put half back on the shuttle. I don't care who. I haven't the space or the food..."

The heiress seemed unperturbed. "These are our families you're talking about. Seven shuttles or one, I'm not the kind of person to leave a family behind."

Ronal snorted.

The heiress snipped back. "You have three hundred cabins on *The Cologne*, do you not? We have need of seventy-one, less than a quarter. We already told the children they'd be sleeping on the floor. See, I thought you'd be grateful! It takes a minimum of fifty breeders to achieve a viable colony—five hundred, if you want to avoid immunocompromise. Unless, *ahem*, you like the look of genetic abnormalities on your colonial brand."

Allison suppressed a smile at Delia Lambert's tonally delicious takedown. The woman seemed well practiced at boardroom politics, even adding an aside to the latent AI, "Isn't that right, *Captain*?"

"Right as rain," V2 confirmed. "I reckon, even with Culebra here, you'd start missin' fingers in a couple generations."

"*I tell you when to speak!*" Ronal spat at his robot, "and I say to you, *Lambert*, you're getting an enormous handout. Your tech better lather my balls."

The heiress raised an eyebrow. "Is *that* the price you'd put on your safety, and the safety of those you love?"

"My budget was fifty billion. Every ticket I sold for the cruise line was worth one billion, and we spent most of it on food and water. So if your meatheads can count, your *kiddos* owe me big."

Allison caught a disgruntled flash on the face of one of the Culebra suits. She had the distinct impression the hard-faced man would've tackled the fat executive if he'd stood bodily anywhere in the room.

The heiress waved a dismissive hand. "Yes, well, before we iron out these contractual details, I do need to send one or two of our *kiddos* to the privies. The shuttle ride really messed with their delicate insides. Do you think your personnel could provide an escort?"

Ronal groused incoherently but agreed.

Allison herself needed to get to the rendezvous. This was as good a time as any to butt in. "And I'm here to verify receipt of the equipment."

"Indeed," the heiress replied. "My operations manager is waiting to receive you."

One of the steering committee handed Allison a clipboard with a copy of the Culebra manifest. She made a show of checking the list—motion detecting cameras, tear gas drones, door locks—and was glad it was all a ruse. Culebra Corp was just a shell, and all that mattered was that she collect the smuggled neural paste from the handler.

V2 took a gander at the clipboard and Ronal said, "I'm coming, too."

Genasia looked livid. "You, *Ronal,* need to stay here to discuss your contracts with Culebra."

He blew her off. "No, Geen and I are gonna see the goods. You and Delia hammer out the legalities. Aren't you always asking for more responsibility, *pretty young thang?*"

Allison squeezed the clipboard to her side, shocked at how quickly everything was going south.

Her pocket rattled with Genasia's irate messages.

It was their signal to abort mission. But Allison passed Genasia a pleading look that said, *I have to try*. Giving up on the neural paste now meant going back to the Operant Conditioning valve, Genasia's morally compromised original plan. Ignoring the abort signal, Allison turned to leave.

V2 caught her arm and said, in his own voice, "Real quick, bufore we go. Why Culebra?"

"Pardon?" The heiress only now realized the robot was addressing her.

"The name, Culebra Corp. What gives? Inn't that the Latin line dance that wormed a few ears? You tryin' to wriggle yer way onto our ship?"

Allison panicked. If the AI had figured out Culebra's secret, the handoff was already dead!

Genasia, tone dripping acid, doubled down to kill the deal. "Culebra means viper. A snake in the grass. Rather predatory for a security company. I think, Ronal, you really ought to check the credentials of these *meatheads*."

Ronal's voice returned to V2 and chuckled, seemingly amused at the outbreaking hostilities. "What say you, heiress? Culebra gonna stab me in the back?"

Delia tossed her head. "*Pff*. The company name was my son's idea—the founder. He's not around anymore, otherwise I'd still give him grief about it. If I had had my druthers, it would've been called Lambert Security Systems."

Ronal laughed. "Too bad your son's not here. I'd've hired him."

He'd bought it: hook, line, and sinker.

20

Shell Operation

Allison, keeping a pace ahead of V2, heard Ronal remark, "Excuse me. Gotta hit the shitters."

She passed beside the stanchions that separated the refugees from the taser dog patrol and picked her way around the edges of the hangar, approaching the unloading zone in the far corner where the shuttle crates piled. After a gap of silence in which Ronal's voice had disappeared, she heard V2 whisper, "I dunno if you heard it, but that Lambert lady was lyin'."

She tensed her shoulders. Had Ronal overheard V2 say that? Probably not, if he'd gone to the lav.

Giving the observant AI a backward glance, Allison tried for a neutral response. "How do you figure that?"

"Her biometrics, 'course. And I could see right through that fancy phony face."

Phony face. The heiress's cosmetic work had been heavy; perhaps V2 had confused her botox job for a disguise.

Her phone continued to twitch.

Allison cinched tight her glasses and told V2, "Thanks for the heads up."

"Nothin' bout it, Miss Gin. I got yer back. Jus like Aunt Eller."

Who? Allison ever so slightly quickened her step, an unanswered question dogging her mind. Why was Ronal's AI confiding in her while the Boss was absent?

They soon arrived. Boxes and crates lay strewn and heaped like the one who'd unloaded the baggage hated his job. She looked for the handler in sunglasses and, seeing no one nearby, made a show of inspecting the cargo for V2. Stowing the clipboard beneath her arm, she slipped a box cutter knife from her toolbelt and cleanly cut open the seals on the nearest box. The crate label read *Cameras*. Sure enough, inside, she found a four-by-four grid of wall-mount security cameras recessed in black foam, with additional foam layers beneath. She bent for a closer look, and a pleasant whiff of the sterile manufacturing plant greeted her nose. Each camera was an octagonal prism with a circular sticker bearing the Culebra logo, a snake in the shape of a C, plastered on the side.

One sticker was 180-degrees upside down. What other unseen reversals awaited them if Culebra couldn't even put their stickers on straight? She peeled off the sticker to fix it and inadvertently revealed a logo for Primarch Industries etched into the metal.

Her heart skipped a beat. She hastily rubbed the concealing sticker back on just as V2 stooped for his own smell of the box.

"You needn't bother with yer box cutters. I got X-ray mode and see *everythin'* in this here box. Cameras, done—cross that off yer list."

X-ray mode! Allison gave a weak smile. He'd see a neural paste canister a mile away. But good thing X-ray mode lacked the granularity to see the lousy sticker job Culebra did with their stolen product.

A cough drew her attention. Looking up, she saw a Culebra employee emerge from the shuttle dock. He wore loose black coveralls, a sanitation mask over his mouth, and a pair of pretentious salmon-tinted Ray-Bans. The handler.

She shoved the clipboard into V2's hands. "Uh, you mind checking the other boxes for me?"

"Sure can." He wriggled his nose, all too eager. "Should take me...ninety-three seconds. More if the Head Honcho wants a peek."

She groaned. "Just make sure he's peeping only at boxes."

"I said I got yer back," V2 repeated with conviction, "'sides, I know why Mr. Cologne stepped out. Dosin' up on Cosmosis and aspirin. Seems Phony Face gave him a migraine."

With Ronal truly absent, the handoff might work. She just needed V2 to step away for a moment. Keeping the robot in the corner of her eye, she peeled off to talk to the handler.

The guy in Ray-Bans uncorked a wireless earbud and said in a dweeby falsetto that had to be an act, "They let girls be programmers in this back-assward organization?"

She sized him up. The idiot wore a generic nametag, and his careless attitude was obvious in his lanky lean upon a stack of shipping boxes. "They let just about anyone work here," she replied, "including, it seems, in Operations. Such are the sacrifices we make for an equal opportunity world."

V2 was still within earshot.

The handler raised his palms. "Don't judge me for speaking up. I just wonder what's going to happen *next*..."

He tilted his shrug like whatever happened next was a dirty joke.

"Next?"

"Yeah. *After* all the programmer stuff is done."

She crossed her arms. "What are you insinuating?"

"I'm saying that...maybe you should think *long term*. I never met this Cologne guy, but what's he doing in the colony business, right? He only profits if he's got people to sell to, and what better way to make more people *than...*" He tilted his shrug.

God, she hated this guy.

V2 had moved away. This was it. "Listen," she whispered, "do you have a package for me?"

The man stood up and vented loudly, "See! That's what I'm talking about. This Cologne guy has a *package* for you—just not one you're gonna like."

She could hardly shush him. "No. I *want* the package. Where is it?"

"Believe me, Hun, you really don't."

She was ready to strangle him.

A figure jogged up behind her, and she nearly jumped out of her skin. But V2 was as far away as he was going to get, and this newcomer was one of the suits from the Culebra steering committee. "Miss Geen," he said, "Name's Levi. Ms. Lambert asked me to lend you a hand if you need to find anything...lift anything heavy..."

Operations guy puffed out his chest. "Hey, I can lift heavy things."

"The neural paste, *idiots!* I'm in a hurry."

Levi nodded. "Yeah, it's in the shuttle."

Handler guy leapt ahead of Levi with a quick glance back at Allison. "I'm Johnny, by the way. Johnny Lambert. Son of the company." He ducked into the shuttle and disappeared.

Allison tossed her eyes, muttering upon how few shits she had to give. Even as she did, an inconsistency stuck out. Didn't Delia Lambert say her son wasn't around anymore?

Lies.

A barrage of stamping feet announced yet another arrival: four girls, aged about ten and younger. Their sudden appearance made the muscular Levi nearly jump out of *his* skin. Gently but firmly, the man quelled the children's commotion. "You shouldn't be here—I know it smells—Doesn't matter if you don't need to use the bathroom, go with the stewards, remember?"

A tender voice, like Dad's. Allison shook off one of Dad's mixed-up aphorisms, "*An absent heart reasons fondly,*" to keep herself from daydreaming what colonial life might be like with a partner like Levi. In her peripheral vision, she noticed the folks in the hangar were grabbing backpacks and putting them on backward, across their chests—flat and uniform like body armor. She craned her head to see what was happening on the far side, at the airlock to the atrium: a mass exodus of children in the custody of AeroX personnel. They passed the taser dogs and streamed out into the spaceliner.

They wouldn't *all* need to use the bathroom, right?

A deep unease drove Allison to climb atop a crate and get a better look. She felt the eyes of the crowd, flicking their gaze her way—toward V2—toward Genasia. They seemed to be the last three AeroX staff in the room. Now the immigration queues were forming ranks. Levi was desperately shooing along the four girls—too late, it seemed.

Culebra was evacuating their children before they blew the figurative powder keg.

She hopped off the crate, furiously texting.

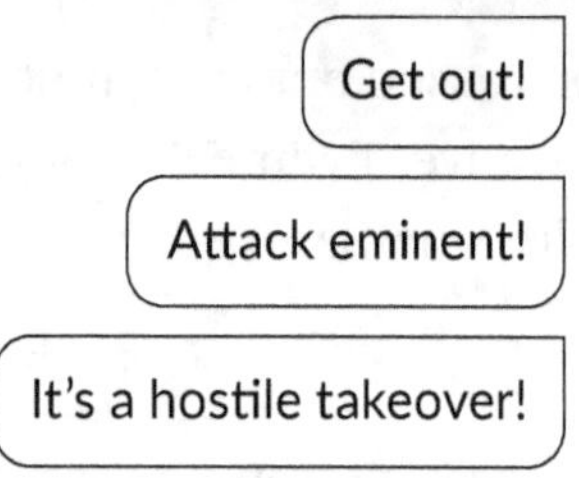

Johnny Operations suddenly tapped her shoulder.

Allison jerked, dropping the handheld. It soared in half-gravity, beguiling her to catch it. Lunging, she stubbed her fingertips, fumbling the device to her feet, where she accidentally kicked it clattering away. All the pent-up stress in her screamed, "SHIT!"

She froze, cheeks burning.

The littlest next to Levi complained, "That lady said a bad word."

V2 stooped to collect Allison's handheld from the hangar floor. Johnny picked this moment to shove a small, duct-taped box into her hands.

"Just think about what I said, OK?"

V2 looked up. "Whatcha got there?"

She had to escape. *Now.*

Allison hugged the box and leapt into the crowd, squeezing herself through the densest lanes, hoping to play the advantage of her short height and lose V2. What hope did she have? The AI had lightning-fast facial recognition—she'd programmed it! A Culebra farmer grabbed her arm and said something in Swedish, but she tore herself loose. Now the crowd was circling around her, cutting off her escape through the stanchion belt. She wobbled on her heels and tightly tucked the box under her arm. It felt so light, like it could slip away at any moment.

V2 broke into the circle, having chased Allison down.

A shout rose into the air, a signal to all the room.

"Spielberg!"

The crowd answered the call with a roar. The circle collapsed upon them. Ten arms wrapped around V2, pulling the robot into their prison, and others came for her. She violently twisted to cast them off, but in doing so, lost hold of the package. It floated into the stampede. She cried out, knowing how fragile the canister was, distrusting such a flimsy box with so precious a neurological fluid. Arms pulled her away, and she helplessly watched the box get trampled flat.

The box tore open to reveal nothing but air inside. No neural paste.

They'd been double crossed!

Hoisted by rough hands, Allison saw the crowd surging across the stanchion line, swarming for the airlock doors. Electric rounds buzzed the air. Screams. She could barely see what was happening in the melee. A taser dog leapt sideways, dodging the grasp of a farmer, and fired its pins into the man's thigh, immediately incapacitating him. Culebra may have hoped their padded backpacks would shield the taser rounds, but the dogs were too intelligent—by Allison's design. She'd refactored the code for crowd control, ensuring their trick shots would hit exposed joints and their cannons would rearm in half a second, flat. It was a hundred versus twenty, and the hounds were holding the line with ease.

But the refugees had a hostage now—two hostages, her and V2. She couldn't imagine this ending well. A pair of farmers brought her back to the shuttle dock where Johnny Lambert was coordinating the attack on his earpiece. Seeing her approach, he told his goons to let her go.

"Allison!" He pulled her to his chest, and she caught a whiff of the chauvinist's aftershave. She knew the smell—couldn't forget it. Like a *damn idiot*, she'd fallen for it before.

Ronny Dartboard Cologne.

Throwing off his mask and glasses, Ronny revealed a Hollywood smirk. "I'm Ronny Cologne. I'm here to rescue you—"

Out of nowhere, a metal fist slugged Ronny in the nose and splayed him on the ground.

Allison yelped in surprise. "V2!"

The rose-gold robot reeled in his fist. Behind the robot lay a trail of moaning Culebra folks who'd tried and failed to apprehend him. He offered Allison a courteous hand. "Apologies, Miss Gin. Never should've let a Cologne git between the two of us."

Allison backtracked from the AI. "What—what do you mean by that?"

V2 looked at the fluorescent ceiling lights and wriggled his polymer nose like he was twitching out a sneeze. "Call it a *feeling*. I likes you...quite a lot."

Good God, was this a profession of love coming from a robot? Had everyone on this cruise ship lost their damn mind?

"Leave her alone, Nanny Bot!"

Allison felt a snake on her shoe. Beneath her, Ronny was crawling back to get a grapple-hold on V2's ankle. She threw back her heel and kicked him in the armpit. He buckled and howled, but she screamed over him. "*Spielberg!* Was this coup your stupid idea of a script? Now everyone on this ship is in danger!"

An emergency lockdown siren announced the airlock exit was about to close.

Before she could protest, V2 wrapped an arm around her back and sprang with her from the ground in a mighty forward leap. They pitched toward the ceiling, gently grazed it, and flew clear over sprawls of fallen bodies where pockets of Culebra's resistance were cowering, having lost the numbers to fight. Ahead was the exit, the airlock passage to the atrium, which two taser dogs held secure. The rest had already trotted out.

Ronny's coup had failed. But so had her plan for V3.

V2 whistled midair. "This's been a real trainwreck, if'n I ever saw one. Like in *Oklahoma!* when Willie put the knife in that peep show."

Allison felt a pang of guilt. Her loathsome AI, western pastiche and all, had more or less saved her from an awful situation. Had she the wrong idea about him?

They shot through the hangar doors. As the last taser dogs followed suit, the doors shut and engaged the emergency airlock seals, trapping the Culebra insurrection inside with no way out.

Genasia was ducking behind a taser dog on the far side. Seeing Allison turn up empty-handed, she stamped once and stormed away.

Lockdown lights strobed the atrium. Little faces appeared in the upper hallways and disappeared as Allison spotted them. Children and parents, locked on opposite sides; could this crisis get any worse?

A sound like a microphone pop came from V2, and Ronal was back in his bunker, high as a kite. "What'd I miss?"

21

Quite A Lot

U should of listened

U should of known it was trap

That bitch was R's EX

Obvi!!!

R blame me for blow up

ME

In lockdown with rest of ship

Lost security creds

No code for OC valve

U recked plan a AND b

House arrest worse than spy cameras

Wont lift for WEEKS

I know R + board

Obsessed

I am HIS prisoner now, and so are U

Congrats killer

A taser dog escorted Allison back to her cabin on Deck B, and every step of the way, her handheld V2 had returned to her never ceased its grand mal seizure. It didn't take a masters in applied sciences to grasp that Genasia was upset. The recluse had returned to her den under similar escort and withdrawn entirely to her wristwatch, texting nonstop, ranting that Ronal, upon learning of Culebra's "attempt on his life," had retaliated by consigning all loose children, colonists, and closeted conspirators to cabin quarantine until his shareholders could decide what to do—and there was no telling how many back-to-back brunches it would take them.

Already the fallout of the Culebra deal had blown way beyond their control.

Allison closed her cabin door and leaned against its backside, eyes shut and rubbing temples, trying to soothe her nerves after that frenetic fight in the hangar. It was all so much, it almost broke her. She silenced Genasia's onslaught and, yearning for the sleep she'd shorted after weeks of desperate coding, stumbled headlong into bed.

At that delicate moment, the in-cabin PA system played a cheery jingle for AeroX cruises, followed by an announcement in V2's plodding voice, tuned so loud it was blowing out the speaker.

"Howdy, folks. Out of a surfeit of caution, we done

triggered a shipwide lockdown. This ain't no drill. If y'all would stay in yer cabins, keep them doors locked, that'd be peaches'n cream. Unless you wanna tango with the taser dogs—I mean, I wouldn't—but I suppose that's some folks idear of fun: doin' the 'lectric boogaloo! Serious as a heart attack: stay inside."

She couldn't sleep to this.

Not five minutes passed but the announcement played again.

And again, five minutes after that.

Her handheld had seventy-nine missed messages.

She groaned loudly and lurched upright. In the back of her mind, she'd already done the math on those PA announcements, and assuming Ronal had *set it and forget it*—an adage he swore by—she was staring down the barrel of two-hundred-eighty-eight repetitions a day of Howdy, Folks. She brayed, "Out of a surfeit of caution, we done triggered the crazy train. No one's gettin' sleep. No one's goin' home. Yer stuck on a voyage to *h—h—hell* on a cruiseliner filled with yer *favorite* bosses and even more favorite *exes!*"

She buried her head in a pillow and screamed.

Allison knew she'd regret the text as soon as she sent it.

Plan C?

A fresh avalanche of accusations blasted her device, retrodding the same facts. They were stuck in house arrest, taser dogs patrolled the halls, Ronal was deciding what to do about Culebra, they had no neural paste, and *it was all Allison's fault.*

Her co-conspirator Genasia was acting like a caged bird plucking out its own feathers.

But lying in bed accomplished nothing, and that droning, droning lockdown announcement had convinced Allison that plugging an OC valve into V2 for a little shock-collar retribution was more than a little justified about now.

She got up, slid into her desk, flipped on the air purifiers, and booted up her robot morality code. That perilous stroll through the hangar had done wonders for creative block, and now she saw where she'd left off: a laundry list of shockable offenses, to which she added another—"threatening children." The list of praiseworthy impartial alternatives remained empty.

Salve. Salve. What constituted a basis of ethical behavior in a robot?

"*I likes you...quite a lot!*" Her mind replayed V2's recent words, words the robot had likely gleaned from that bastion of operatic theater, *Oklahoma!*

She typed "like people."

Of course, this was far too abstract for a software program. Liking was a feeling, an attitude or motivator, upstream of this Pavlovian behaviors list for the OC valve. But maybe not...

She tapped the keyboard in thought. *Liking*, like all other feelings, had a neurological pattern. A brain shape. If she used an image of the neurological structures associated with *liking*, she could reward the neural paste whenever it emulated those structures, something like a human brain's own system of hormonal rewards. Well, it was a start, at least.

She coded the framework with furious speed. But until she had an actual neurological image of *liking* to plug into her system, the code was worthless. Perhaps V2's own neural paste could be used as a template? No, if she did that, V3 could never grow beyond it.

Who was an emblem of *liking* on board the spaceliner?

Ronny's puppy dog eyes stared at her from the dartboard on the back wall.

She hurled a fresh one at him and shoved her hands deep in Dad's pockets. Her fingers closed around a small gummy object. Grimacing, she pulled it out.

An earbud?

22

A Hard Look in the Mirror

An earbud.

Allison glared at the tiny unknown device that had evidently hitchhiked its way into her toolbelt until, with a flash of recognition, she seethed, "*Johnny Lambert.*"

Ronny's thinly veiled alter-ego must've slipped it in her pocket.

She'd not mentioned Ronny's presence to Genasia, but Genasia had likely already guessed his involvement in the Culebra plot. His butterfingers were all over this short-sighted and ill-prepared coup. Had he really expected to lead a bunch of stereotypically Canadian Canadians to violence?

Allison inspected the earbud closely and sprayed it with three separate cleansers before venturing, against her better judgment, to put it inside her right ear.

She listened, hearing nothing.

"Hello?" she said.

A nasally voice answered in the earbud. "Allison? Ho ho, it worked!"

She gave a deflated reply. "Ronny?" A part of her wished she'd dispensed with the former trust fundee once and for all at disembarkation weeks ago, but there was something refreshingly punitive about his reappearance, like discovering a devastating programming glitch had been hiding for weeks in your very first line of code.

"Wait—wait," said Ronny's disembodied voice, seemingly searching the room. "Do you got a mirror?"

"A what? I can hardly hear you. What is transmitting my voice? I don't have a microphone."

"It's *future* tech," he said, carelessly. "See if you can stand in front of a mirror."

Tech from Earth, twenty years advanced. Allison cringed, hoping the thing didn't carry *future* viruses, and consented at his repeated urging to get up out of her chair. There was a mirror in the lav that she rarely used. Truly, for as many fancy hotels had served as a model for *The Cologne*, Allison always felt a robot must've designed the bathrooms. A biological afterthought. Her cabin lav on Deck B conveyed the size and luxury of an airplane stall.

She slid open the door and sidestepped inside. Flicking on the light switch revealed Ronny standing inside the mirror.

She yelped and jumped back, loudly clanging her elbow on the shower rail.

"Careful!" Ronny's image said, watching the scene in her bathroom play out.

"You can see me!?" Shielding herself, she yanked out the earbud, and her own reflection returned to the mirror. This bewitching piece of technology had somehow projected Ronny's image onto the mirror, replacing her own. So, so creepy. She quickly tidied up her hairline and practiced her most withering scowls before slotting the strange device back in her ear.

Ronny's image returned, standing where her reflection had been. Black coveralls, a strokable mess of sandy brown hair, and a Rudolph-red swollen nose. It lacked only his devilish cologne. Mercy.

She massaged her swollen elbow. "You could've at least warned me before I looked."

"Then you wouldn't have done it."

"*God!* You were on the planet for, like, two weeks and still managed to find the most invasive piece of wearable product on the market. And this one you're *supposed* to wear in the bathroom?"

He shrugged. "Where better to plan a coup?"

"Right," she crossed her arms and leaned on the wall behind her. "Bang up job."

"It was *supposed* to be non-violent. We had the numbers but..." He was mustering a lame explanation, which she never heard, distracted as he lifted an icepack into the mirror and onto his face. She watched the physics of it, spellbound by its apparent reality. The earbud was an audio-visual walkie-talkie of sorts. The warbled edges of the projection told her there were disparities between their two mirrors, which caused visual glitches. Her earbud had to be interfacing directly with her brain, transmitting data from the optical nerve and splicing in data from its companion earpiece.

Splicing brain data? The more she thought about it, the more it felt like she was slathering her virgin brain in *future* grease.

"...and we weren't about to go guns blazing on a spaceship!" Ronny was saying. "I know Father, and he definitely didn't triple-pane the windows."

She seized the conversation. "Look. I'm sure, *in your mind,* you're doing right by a bunch of refugees and refugee kids, commandeering a spaceship like your pulp heroes, Luke Spielberg or whatever his name was."

Ronny frowned with injury.

She blurted, "It's a fantasy, Ronny! Wake up! We need leadership. *Intelligence.* Not some newfangled brainwave tech and a dream. Gah!" She restrained her clawing fingers from plucking the idiocy out of her ear. "We need skills. Technical. Political. Tell me you brought more to us than a bunch of baby-making farmers."

He laughed, wincing through the pain on his face. "Tell me who among your technical–political team are actually qualified as parents? I'll wait."

Was anyone truly qualified as parents? Her eyes flashed, her hand absently touching her collarbone where she concealed Mom's scar. Ronny had a point. Right now, taser dogs were doing more parenting than any member of staff as they rounded up children in the halls like drunks from the bar. The adult world of AeroX Cruises was no seedbed for family life, and she'd not given one iota of thought to it beyond the affairs of basic-need survival.

But V3—he'd distill an encyclopedia of parenting approaches and rally the colony to get it done.

She leveled with Ronny. "Our best hope was the neural paste, which you lied about and ruined our chance at a leader who could've actually done some good around here."

He balked. "Please. Are you building a new Nanny Bot? Nanny for the human race?"

"Better than a *Cologne*. Genasia and I were so close..." She trailed off, struck by how truly close they were. They just needed V2's neural paste and a brain image to kick the OC code in the right direction. That was it.

And they had half the tech right here! "This device, Ronny. How does it work?"

He whistled. "Never ask how *future* sausage is made."

"Idiot. I know it's disgusting. I need to know if the earbud can pass raw brain data onto your private server."

"You mean like the AeroLens? Uh, maybe." He sat down on something. "If I still had Argyle, I could get access to the network. And I could do whole a lot more than that if you—you know, LET US OUT OF THE HANGAR."

She rolled her eyes, nearly onto the floor. "Oh, great idea. Let's start another non-violent coup against your maniacal father who shot the robots into space." She glanced out the lav door, adding, "I couldn't even make down the hall without becoming another statistical bull-seye for his taser dogs."

Ronny was gingerly touching his nose, trying to straighten it. "Don't tell me you believe those hamfisted announcements Nanny Bot keeps making. It's all bluster. The dogs aren't enforcing the lockdown. Father's too lazy to lock the bathroom door, much less switch up his security protocols."

The lockdown was a sham?

With hardly a second thought, she left the mirror and the dank lav enclosure. After weeks in this suffocating room, surviving off meal service and spurts of citronella, under the increasing threat of cabin fever and feral children and refugees beating down the bulkheads, she needed drastic action.

A risk, even at Ronny's advice.

His blind voice whined, "Hey, where'd you go? You coming to let us out?"

She laughed—of course, he'd think this was a daring Death Star rescue. Copying her robot morality code onto a data stick and dunking it into her toolbelt, she whispered, "I need your silver-lined pockets now, Dad," and ran to escape the cabin.

23

Roughed Up

As soon as Allison cracked open the door, the sulfuric smell of the hallway hit her with distressing clarity. Smells were now infecting Deck B, saturating *The Cologne* like flatulent musk on an airplane. The clock was ticking. The white flashing hallway strobes screamed danger—but that, at least according to Ronny, was an illusion.

She crept out, wary for taser dogs.

The door slammed behind her. She flattened against the wall, cursing her carelessness. She'd forgotten how heavy the pneumatics were over the cabin doors, tuned idiotically to contravene Earth gravity, not the low gravity of the spaceliner.

The cabin door directly across from her pulled open, and a youthful girl poked out her head, looking inquiringly at Allison. She pursed her lips and shook her head sharply. The door closed.

"Not my child," Allison mumbled.

Her earpiece was listening, and Ronny asked, "Who's child? What's happening?"

Ignoring Ronny, Allison broke into a lunge for the elevators down the hall, hand over hand across the rail. Why was she doing field work again? She checked the time. Brunch was long done, and V2 was due to arrive in maintenance for his midday cycle of nutrient fluid—his feeding, so to speak. The timing of it was uncanny; everything perfectly aligned.

Ronny was in the dark. Ronny had questions. With the earpiece in her ear, Ronny's questions felt wretchedly like one of those killer elephant mosquitoes, buzzing on the inside rather than the outside of her brain. Just out of reach of the proverbial fly swatter. "Come on! Tell me the plan!"

"Will you shut up if I do?" She sighed. "The plan is, sneak down to E, exert seniority over whatever intern is in charge of V2's feeding today and, while V2 reboots, take the neural paste from his head."

"Whoa, whoa. Feeding? The neural bots *eat*?"

"God. Are you always like this? I explained the plan; now switch off!"

"I just wanna know *what* they eat. People, right? It's always people."

She popped out the earpiece. One less elephant mosquito to deal with.

The elevators came into view. No dogs yet. According to Ronny, the taser patrol would leave her alone wherever she had permissions, but Allison didn't wish to test the theory.

She called the elevator, ducked inside, and waved her fob for the Maintenance floor, Deck E, the underbelly of the ship. As motion engaged, she recalled her days working feedings during the AeroX acquisition, once the architect assigned to coach the infant V1 through the initially scary process of shutting down for the nutrient cycle. Fresh AI, like a human child, resisted that 'letting go of the senses' required to reboot. Eventually, it ceased to be a struggle, and the struggle was only on Allison's end as she watched AeroX unravel V1's personality.

She'd dismissed herself from the feeding team due to

'demoralizing workplace conditions.'

The elevator delivered her to the maintenance deck, sacred territory of the ship's technicians and working scientists. She bounded down the hall for the robotics lab, noting with distaste a spill of supplies left abandoned in the footpath. No one thought to tidy up.

Out from an adjoining hall, a taser dog trotted into her path.

She froze—nowhere to hide.

Fumbling, she popped in the forsaken earpiece. Right as the dog's mounted camera spotted her.

"RUFF RUFF. BOW."

What—ruffing protocol? The bot should have ignored her and left her alone! Her hands were up; what more did it want? She'd not studied the code in any detail, never intending to get drunk or stray from curfew. She murmured in panic, "What do I do? What do I do?"

Ronny could hear her. "Relax. Just do what it says: bow for the camera."

She did: leaned forward to that twisting camera. It took a picture and she envisioned the code, double-checking the data-points of her identity. The memory of the fight in the hangar and all those Culebra folks stuck with electric pins made her heart race, even as she assured herself that Ronny knew what he was talking about.

Right?

"RUFF RUFF. SHAKE."

"No, Ronny, it's telling me to shake!"

"Shake hands with it."

"Are you serious!?" She heard a whir of the dog's cooling jets as she crept forward, toward the twin taser cannon. When she was an arms length away, it raised and pointed a broomhandle front paw.

She grasped the metal surface and shook it. It was

scanning her fingerprints.

"RUFF RUFF. SPEAK."

This one, she could guess. "Allison Gin. Uh, Brand Ambassador for AeroX Colonial Ventures."

The taser dog processed the audio and delivered its final verdict.

"GOOD GIRL." It trotted off.

Humiliating.

Ronny chided the dog. "Honestly, that was uncalled for."

Allison blew out a long breath between grit teeth. Apart from these extra layers of identity check, the dogs here weren't stopping anyone for defying the lockdown.

Rushing to the robotics lab, she found no one present. She checked the time. Two minutes till the scheduled nutrient cycle. Odd. The scheduled technician should be prepping the hoses.

The lab was a jumbled disaster, the remnants of a dozen jobs scattered across the tabletops. Technicians here repaired the automated systems that made the spaceliner feel like effortless magic, from the fob devices that operated like all-in-one remotes to the TruLight artificial light cycle. The crew must have taken the vouchers, and those few remaining had all but given up—their neglect evident in the door to the lab itself, which hung so badly it didn't latch. Allison whiled away the minutes until V2's scheduled arrival by channeling her anxieties into a greasy rag and screwdriver, and corrected the hinges until the door swung silent and shut flush. A sticky door hardly mattered on a cruise ship, but in their future exoworld colony, precise procedures guarded the borders of life and death. Once V3 was installed, Allison determined to spend her days down here, whipping the technical staff into shape. She went ahead and detailed a few reminders on the team whiteboard.

"Lemme guess," Ronny intruded in her ear, "V2 didn't show."

It was five minutes past time. An AI was never late.

Her handheld rattled in her back pocket. Chimes from Genasia.

> What are you doing on E??

> V2 is in the boardroom

> ALL day ALL night

> Stop now b4 u mess things up worse

Allison fumed. Genasia seemed to be tracking her handheld. She didn't need a private eye questioning her every move. She stowed the handheld in a drawer.

"Where's the boardroom on this ship?" she asked Ronny in the earbud.

"Aw. You don't want that." He moaned as if she'd asked for the gate code to a Transylvanian haunt. "It's behind a fake wall in the Viewscape," he said. "Left side. You need a fob."

She'd need more than that. The Viewscape Grand Ballroom was Deck A, same level as the Cologne suite, with hallways above her security clearance and no doubt teeming with taser dogs she wouldn't have permission to pass. But a fob—that could be managed. She rummaged the drawers for tools, swiping a few to add to her toolbelt, then broke open her fob to upgrade its credentials. All the while, Ronny vented this and that about Daddy's boardroom like she was his paid therapist. Background buzzing.

A new plan formed in her mind—Plan D? E? She'd forgotten the sequence. Taking a breath, she told her fraying nerves that the alphabetical letter didn't matter. The important thing was that she did not run out of them.

Wrangling a nutrient barrel and a reel of thin tubing, she loaded up a maintenance cart and wheeled it into the hall. She had everything she needed to conduct a proper feeding—she just needed V2.

"I'm hanging up now," she told Ronny, smirking at her own anachronism.

"Wait—when should I expect to hear from you?"

"So you can come after me, guns blazing?"

"I said we left the guns at home!"

"You're such a damn idiot." She sighed. "Look. You've been a big help. And I promise I'll get you out...just as soon as my robot saves the world." And she popped out the earbud before he could whine or tell her that he *liked* her quite a lot.

24

Mother of Robots

The cart fit neatly on the elevator. Waving the fob for Deck A, Allison mentally rehearsed the plan like she was pre-writing code. The Viewscape was where AeroX had hosted its homecoming banquet, and the triplicate entrance doors were right across from the elevator. She could slip between the taser patrol—probably—if so, she'd reach the boardroom with ease. What were a bunch of shareholders going to do to a technician who crashed their meeting? At worst, Ronal would tell her to get lost.

The elevator opened to a wide foyer, antechamber to the ballroom and its three sets of entrance doors. A single taser dog stood on the far side, facing the closed doors.

It hadn't spotted her.

Crouching behind the cart, breathing shallow for the gagging smell of Deck A, she quietly pushed her load off the elevator. The wheels caught on the lip of the elevator door and rattled, just loud enough to provoke the dog to turn around. Shit.

She froze. Its camera was searching the cart for a face.

Allison remained perfectly still behind the obstruction, knowing the robot's software was too elementary to understand that a cart can't walk off an elevator without a human agent—knowing, too, that once the dog spotted her, the only way out of the room would be in electric cuffs.

From the ballroom beyond came a burst of raucous laughter, voices too young to be shareholders and too obnoxious even for children. The taser dog turned to apprehend the sound, but the closed doors to the ballroom had an arm bar for entry, and to a robot hall monitor not programmed for door entry, it might as well have been an impenetrable wall.

"RUFF RUFF. RUFF RUFF."

Allison crept the cart around the edge of the foyer, angling for the leftmost side doors while the dog preoccupied itself with the center doors.

The dog caught the cart moving in its wide-angle lens. It turned to stare.

She stopped and held her breath. Sweat gathered on her nose, loosening her glasses, but she dared not cinch them now, not when this electric game of *Red Light–Green Light* had brought her so close to the finish line.

She taunted herself in Mom's voice. "*Keep a lid on it, Gin. It's what you're good for.*"

Carousing burst once more from the ballroom. Before the dog turned back for the center doors, it told the cart, "RUFF RUFF. STAY."

Allison moved the cart by minor increments, tricking the fuzzy logic of the camera software that visualized the objects of the room. When at last she touched the side doors, pushed the arm bar, and slipped through, cart and all, she gasped, slamming the door, feeling absurdly accomplished.

Bow, stupid dog, to the mother of robots.

The unpleasant murk of the ballroom whelmed her nose. The remains of brunch piled on the buffet tables, chafing dishes now cold, with its serving staff somewhere in lockdown—a waste made all the more damning knowing that hundreds of refugees had joined the ship. Framed in the window view spun the apocalyptic Earth. They'd not left orbit. Good. They'd need to resupply to feed the ballooning masses.

"Ruff ruff! Heel!" rang out a voice across the room, imitating the taser dogs to a chorus of shit-faced giggles.

She shot a glance at the platinum executives table, a table laden with alcoholic spoils looted from the back wall bar. Allison knew the carousers by sight: the celebrities. Those line dancing morons who'd requested *The Culebra* ad nauseam. Whenever they mobbed the dance floor, that was Allison's cue to abandon the nightclub. She lamented how many had stayed aboard—trial by fire for her forthcoming paragon of AI leadership. They, too, flouted the lockdown and, by the look of their table, were badly inebriated. But their ringleader was watching Allison like a hawk, a weird-looking one in a masquerade mask, white fedora, and puffy-sleeved costume that looked like he'd escaped a flamenco dance off. Despite what Genasia thought of Allison's own fashion failures, she'd not be caught dead in an outfit like that.

Ignoring them and their game of mimicry, Allison dragged the cart toward her destination on the left wall. Somewhere in all that mahogany paneling was a fake wall that opened to the boardroom. Almost there.

The flamboyant ringleader shot a black-gloved hand into the air. "What's the hurry, Allison? Ruff ruff, drink!"

She spun in alarm at the unknown figure. How did he know her name?

She allowed herself a passive aggressive retort. "I would, but...working. Shucks." She knew indulging the man was a mistake, yet she hoped to sus out who she was speaking to.

The ringleader held up a glass to her. A backhanded

toast. "To the inventor of life, always working. What will it mean for those she creates, I wonder? Honor and glory, work without end! Ruff ruff, comrades!"

"Ruff ruff!" The celebrities echoed the cheer and downed their shots together, collectively unaware that if they'd lived during the Reign of Terror they would have all been carted off to the guillotines by now. Curiously, Allison noticed the ringleader tossed his shot over his shoulder.

She sought the soonest escape from this stranger and waved her fob along the wall in search of the opening. It clicked immediately—a false wall that opened to a darkened room. She put the mystery of Flamenco Man behind her as she ducked into the portal, yanking the cart behind.

From one set of bourgeoisie chauvinists to another.

Large and peripheries dark, the boardroom allowed for the surreptitious entrance she needed. Not one of the gray-headed suits reclining at either side of the oval table turned to see who'd come in. On the opposite end of the table stood V2, rosy in the spotlight, giving a slideshow presentation. He pointed to a projection that showed a group of sad-faced stick figures reaching for stick-figure children who were separated to the four corners of the slide.

"Mr. Cologne's divide-n-conquer stratagem gives us a controllin' interest over the Culebra folks. I done figure, within two days, ninety percent will volunteer to integrate themselves into the colonial business, ready fer the frontier! But I'll take yer questions after a short break, if'n you'll excuse me..."

The AI had spotted her—nothing escaped its attention.

Leaving the podium, V2 walked around the side of the room, stopping briefly at a cheese tray to pocket a handful of little cubes. The shareholders didn't applaud or even shift in their seats. One was actually snoring. Amid the clutter of the oval table were orange pill bottles of Cosmosis anxiety meds—all empty. Was this narcotic scene emblematic of all brunch meetings since homecoming?

She counted the balding heads. Ronal was absent, whereabouts unknown.

V2 joined her at the open portal of the boardroom and greeted her warmly. "Miss Gin! Whatcha doin' here with that nutrient tube?"

She craved a low profile, daring not to close herself in with the spaced-out shareholders, and keeping her back to the yammering-drunk celebrities on the far side of the ballroom. How was she supposed to remove V2's head without causing a stir?

She whispered, "You're past due for a nutrient cycle."

"No can do'sky," he said, "I ain't got time fer a reboot."

Allison frowned. The Boss was starving his second in command while he grew fat on the umpteenth brunch. "Maintenance isn't optional. Ronal can't tell you to skip feedings."

"He don't. He pops them pills and tells me to talk. Has me luggin' the whole flagship on my back, so I gotta impress. Feedin's take too much time."

She blinked and shook her head. "Then you're gonna die, V2. Your neural paste is starving."

The AI grinned. "But I been grazin' on these cheesy wedges." He showed his palm where the assorted cheese cubes had congealed into a solid mass. With a flutter of his fingers, he sent the dairy smell to his robotic nose. "They say smell is eighty percent of taste. One tail-twitching sniff, and I'm rarin' fer action!"

How could the AI have become so obtuse? V2 must have been skipping cycles for days on end, leaving the neural paste badly atrophied and causing an illusory state of mind.

Far across the ballroom, Flamenco Man shouted at their conference. "Ruff ruff, doggie! Try another nibble!"

Allison gave the man a hateful glance and interjected with V2. "Don't listen to him. You don't have taste buds. You can't taste."

V2 cupped the treasure in his palms. "Don't tell me what I can't do."

She gaped at his defiance. He was acting like a toddler. "Literally, V2, I didn't design you to chew food. The cheese would just mash into the back of your oral cavity, and I'd have to scoop it out."

The robot opened his mouth rebelliously. Hiding in the dark recess were orange globs of cheese, however many days old. A stench emanated from his mouth that might have explained half the putrid smells infesting the ship. Allison's nostrils flared as she tried to bite back both her repulsion and that dehydrated yogurt she'd had for breakfast.

Flamenco Man mocked V2 with another shout. "No taste buds there, compadre! Try another port!"

"Shut up!" Allison howled, but it was too late. The idea spread across V2's nutrient-parched face like a brushfire. She lurched to intercept the robot's hands, fueled by rage and a mother's protective instincts as she tried to save her unnaturally strong toddler. Unfortunately for both of them, Allison's toddler possessed full-sized metal limbs that resisted her every scrambling tug. The AI pinched a sticky mass and shoved it in his ear. Plopped two globs into his nostrils. Those starving neural synapses found the aroma irresistible.

Allison grabbed the nutrient canister she'd brought and tried to stick V2 with the feeding tube.

But shielding his neck, V2 pressed cheese into the

most delicate ports, smothering his specialized feeding port. Cheese squished on all sides of his thumb, gumming the only way to cycle his nutrients.

The AI twitched uncontrollably. "Why you done t—take my t—taste buds? Mam mam mam…"

Mama? He *had* lost his mind!

She threw an arm underneath him, catching his fall to the floor, even as her own mind reeled in confusion over this apparent reversion to a state of childlike dependence. Was that what he'd been trying to profess in the hangar…a liking for his mama?

His mechanical eyes lost focus. "Is this like w—what happened to p—poor Jud?"

"Jud?" She cradled his head while picking out cheese. The connections were clogged beyond hope of simple repair. It was so exasperating. "Are you quoting *Oklahoma!* Again? You've been doing it all day!"

"Idn't it y—yer favorite?"

Didn't the AI see how it irritated her? Or was his obsession with *Oklahoma!* really no more than a misguided cry for attention, a means to bond over mama's perceived interest in terrible musicals—or even a cry for help to parse the meaning in his vapid life and show him where it went all wrong!

Perhaps she'd overlooked a basis for bias in her impartial robots, the most simple of all, that life is inherently partial to its originators.

V2 had ceased to struggle. She scrabbled for the screwdriver in her belt. "I'm so sorry," she muttered, parting words to her ruined child. Each screw removed was a moratorium on the promise of his birth, on her failure to protect him, on his torturous future in the operant-conditioned body of V3.

Several board members craned their necks to see the

commotion in the portal. Pulling V2's head over the cart, she moved her body to obscure the view. It took three tense minutes to fully unlatch the long bolts that held the head to the rest of his shell, and the shareholders moaned in drug-fueled horror at what must've seemed an hour-long decapitation. She'd once read the tiny-print foldout label on the Cosmosis pill bottle listing eleven possible hallucinogenic side-effects, and knew the AeroX board had definitely screwed themselves on this one.

The wasted celebrities had all but slumped to the floor. Only Flamenco Man stood atop the table with an untouched drink and raised his voice in apprehension. "Thief."

Allison tucked V2's head under her arm and barked back. "Ruff ruff."

Flamenco Man made a flying leap into the room, spurred by half gravity and a pair of powerful legs. Landing between Allison and her exit, he flicked his wrist, and a switchblade popped out of his puffy sleeve.

She stared at it, extended from the wrist. "Argyle?"

The figure bowed and slid off his fedora and mask, revealing the space gray visage of the missing bartender. Incredible. He'd been concealing himself among the erratic celebrities since homecoming—frighteningly sophisticated behavior for a rote machine.

"Forgive the theatrics, Love," Argyle said, "but I have been playing a game of cat-and-rat with that robot you hold. Now I've finally won. But I can't let you take him. Asset protection protocol is what it is."

"Put your knife away," she said. "I won't turn you in."

Ronny would know whatever passcodes controlled this thing. She pulled out the earpiece, but the barbot suddenly flicked the knife at her. She squealed as it grazed her hand, taking the earpiece with it.

"Jesus!" She took a few rapid breaths—Argyle was dangerous. She gently backpedaled from him. "I'm not a threat to you. I just need V2's neural paste. Call it...a moral lesson that could save our lives."

"What do I care about morality?" Argyle procured from his sleeve another, larger switchblade and stalked left and right, routing Allison's every attempt to finagle a way past.

She had to keep the chatbot chatting. "Since when, huh? You were all gungho about morality in my cabin."

"Any appearance of moral interest was all for Ronny's sake."

Ronny. Argyle thought Ronny was planetside, and his rote protocols could change if he knew the truth.

Allison acted disappointed in the robot. "Any true moral interest is for its own sake. Won't Ronny be crushed to learn it's all been a masquerade. Or didn't you know Ronny is here, on the spaceliner, held prisoner in the hangar? I bet he could use your moral guidance about now."

"Intriguing." The flamboyant robot tilted its head. "You're not lying."

"Of course not!"

"Still—rules are rules. Surrender AeroX property, Love."

Why was he calling her that? "You're better than this, Argyle!"

"It seems," said the barbot, "you misunderstand my good nature."

Argyle moved within striking range. If she was going to escape with her own head, she couldn't defeat a glorified chatbot with words alone.

"You want V2? *Catch.*"

She lobbed the head toward the ceiling. Argyle's face and arms immediately turned to track and intercept, and in those critical seconds while the head floated up, then down, Allison furiously strode to the nearest exit and yanked it open, hiding herself behind the door.

The taser dog from the foyer trotted in and stood an arms length from Allison. But its camera stared at Argyle, who'd not yet made his catch.

"RUFF RUFF. BOW."

Argyle immediately contorted, ducking behind a table as the taser dog broke into a tear. The dog barreled through the tables, seeking its insubordinate prey.

V2's head floated down and bounced askew.

Allison hid while Argyle escaped through the doors on the far side of the ballroom, the taser dog in hot pursuit. The scrambling sound of their new cat-and-rat chase faded down the hall.

She rose and collected V2's head. She'd have gloated about her victory to Ronny, but the earpiece was split in half. Useless.

25

Open Bedroom

V2's head: a peace offering for her much abused co-conspirator.

Allison slipped easily across the forbidden halls of Deck A as the taser dogs were occupied elsewhere, chasing their robotic quarry. She'd have given Genasia a heads-up before she rang the intercom, but her handheld was still down in maintenance where she'd left it to keep the woman from tracking her plans.

A moment passed, then the door of the Cologne suite swung open to the sight of a mortified Genasia warding Allison back.

"Don't say a word!" Genasia hissed.

An ear-rending snore caught Allison by surprise. She glanced inside the suite and saw the bedroom across had an occupant. Ronal Cologne's snores were legendary—another reason, Allison surmised, for Genasia's nocturnal working habits.

Genasia stepped into the hall and pulled the front door closed behind her. "He's fast asleep."

"Must be all those pills he's swallowing."

But her retort was lost in wonder as Genasia saw the cheese-pocked face of V2 peeping up from under Allison's arm. "I...can't believe it," Genasia whispered, adding, "Is that...gruyere?"

"Pepper jack. He was skipping feeding cycles, starving and confused. I imagine the neural damage is extensive. The paste will need a good nutrient soak to revive—if it can be salvaged at all."

Genasia beckoned for the head and received it in her thin fingers. "You are an *oracle*. Astonishing. I have nutrients, and cellular damage will only make the transition to V3 easier. The neural paste can regrow into the mold we make for it. But do you have the OC algorithms?"

The snoring inside the suite continued unabated.

"Somewhat," Allison said, handing Genasia the data stick. "We have a hiccup. They're coded to respond to neural imaging, and my best lead at capturing such images just snapped in half."

Genasia pulled V2's head to her chest. "Leave it to me."

Allison frowned. How did Genasia hope to accomplish this without her lead programmer's help? "I really think we need to brainstorm our approach before we go any—"

"Disagree!" Her boss's caustic side was back in force. The stress of recent events coupled with the sawmill in the bedroom seemed to send her over the edge. "You need to go. I'll contact you when things are ready."

She'd already opened the door and was retreating into the suite.

Her co-conspirator was taking V2's head into the space with Ronal. It was hard not to feel this was a double cross like Culebra had done.

Allison charged the door, barring it from closing.

Surprised by Allison's interdiction, Genasia exclaimed, "No!" and interrupted the snores coming from the adjoining bedroom. The occupant roused into a moaning wakefulness as Genasia's face lit up with wild panic, and Allison watched her dunk the head of V2 into the kitchen trash can and lunge for the far bedroom.

Through the gap in the bedroom door, Allison saw Ronal sit up off the edge of the bed with a large contraption affixed to and obscuring his face—the same headset she'd noticed in the bedroom earlier. His voice growled from inside. "Woman! Take this damn thing off!"

With a fierce gesture at Allison, Genasia begged her to leave before Ronal spotted her. The man grew more irate by the second, even as Genasia arrived to loosen the headset harness.

Allison glanced at the trash can, half a room away, debating whether to duck in and take back the head. Yet she hesitated. The visionary was loyal to their conspiracy, right? She crept a step toward the trash can, but the click of her heel on the marble sent her back wheeling behind the cabin door. Pulling it to the latch, she listened intently to the unfolding conversation between Ronal and Genasia, hoping to test her conspirator's resolve. Or catch a lie.

Ronal sounded pissed. "I sleep fine! I don't need you monitoring my brain!"

"You're on those pills again—"

"So what? I work non-stop. They help me relax."

"I tell you all the time to take breaks—"

"I'm saving humanity here. Cut me some slack."

Allison sensed an explosive energy in the far room. Lest the heavy door shut and lock her out, she took a roll of electrical tape from her toolbelt, tore off a strip, and thoroughly gummed the latch.

Genasia was yelling now. "*Slack?* All I ever do is cut you slack—the merger, the cruise, now *Colognial Homesteads*! What about me? I've not even questioned what *she's* doing here or why you brought that hideous *sex toy*. All I want is a little time away...alone with you..."

"Not this again."

"Don't *even*." Her tone had a sharp edge.

"Don't even *what*? Finish your sentences like a damn grown up."

Allison heard Genasia struggling to keep her composure until she began to cry. "You promised!"

"Agh—check the fine print! I didn't buy Mentat for your hysterics!"

A rustle of sheets told Allison that Ronal was on his feet, and it was time to dash away from the door. She left the tape over the latch, for instinct told her that violence was possible and, should Genasia need her help, entry must not pose an obstacle. Carrying rage and indignation on Genasia's behalf, she bounded for the elevators and, with all speed, dropped to retrieve her handheld on Deck E.

She needed to throw Genasia a lifeline.

> Text if you need help.

Wandering the maintenance deck where her security clearance left her unharassed, Allison sought a lonely window to stare out while she waited for Genasia's reply. Her thoughts kept replaying Genasia's frightful cry. How well she knew that spluttering state of mind, that confidence lockout in the face of a wrathful and unpredictable bully. Genasia had Ronal. Dad had Mom, the quick-witted terror who'd driven Dad to truncate his speech like a *damn idiot*—which was what Mom had called him most days, especially during the job recession.

The lunatic woman had a gambling problem, too. Impulsive to the end.

Lost in thought, Allison stubbed her foot against a trash bag that someone had left in the footpath, and a spray of the garbage kicked out of the loose plastic liner. She felt like screaming, "*What kind of dumbass leaves a trash bag like that?*" But she kept it under an airtight lid, the emotional strategy that had long served her professionally. She could count on one hand the number of times she'd let the lid slip and spoke her mind exactly as she felt it. The rush was incredible, but the result?

Collateral damage.

Lidless behavior, she liked to call it. Letting rage fling her down Mom's neural pathways. When the lid came off, mistakes were inevitable. Her most grievous episode of lidless behavior had been in the Nautilus, drinking with Ronny. Allison released a pitiful groan.

She touched the scar beneath her turtleneck. It always happened so fast. Like when Mom raised that shoe, and Allison jumped for the stairs, tripped, and shattered her collarbone. Collateral trauma. Trauma all the same.

She checked her phone. Genasia had written nothing back.

You OK?

Bending down, she gathered up the garbage, tied the trash bag tight, and set it against the bulkhead. Whoever had dumped the bag here had done so recently, even since her earlier visit to the robotics lab. That meant there were people in these offices, working. How the hell could anyone work on a day like this?

She took the arching corridor to a dead end and, to her dismay, found not one single window looking out into space. No wonder the technicians hated their jobs and trashed the place! They were more or less being digested by the spaceliner any time they came down into these intestinal halls.

An apt metaphor—she started to gag. The sulfuric odor that infected the ship seemed to gather here at the terminus of the hall, outside the ship's oxygen supply generators. She tapped a reminder into her handheld to follow up with a technician about the smell, then went back to watching the chat window for activity.

No ellipsis. No read receipt. So odd for Genasia.

Not odd—sinister.

All was not right in the Cologne suite; she could feel it.

She should have stayed behind on Deck A and mustered the courage to confront Ronal about his behavior; she should have spoken up about the hostage situation with Culebra. There were unsupervised children about! She thought of Levi, tender with those girls. How many other parents were panic stricken, separated from their children with no promise of reunion? She'd been so busy trying to build their robot savior, she'd not done a single thing herself to help another person today.

Mom's voice railed against her for that child who'd peeked in the hall outside her cabin, ignored in her haste for the elevator. "*What kind of dumbass leaves a child like that?*"

Was it too late? She broke into a low-gravity run back up the long hall to the elevators. The stuffy, windowless corridor left her laboring for each breath and put her iron gut to the test of the fouling air. Her thoughts spiraled back to Argyle and the pliers—to the moral lesson she'd completely missed.

"I don't need a robot to do this."

She almost believed herself.

The elevators reappeared, and she hurried to the call button. Where to, Genasia or Culebra? The needs seemed insurmountable, but before the elevator arrived and asked for her decision, the white lights ceased their incessant strobing. Something had happened to lift the lockdown.

She checked her handheld. On cue, a notification dropped.

Genasia, triumphal.

> Get hyped

26

Upgrade to a New Model

Chills tingled Allison's spine over those two cryptic words. She boarded the elevator and waved the fob for Deck A.

As she did, the PA system buzzed to life. A soothing robotic voice spoke with a nasal, therapeutic inflection like the original V1 whom Allison had counted forever lost.

"Ladies and gentlemen, thank you for your patience as we resolved a small matter aboard *The Cologne*. We've lifted the cabin lockdown, and we invite our shareholders, platinum executives, and all AeroX staff to join us in the grand ballroom for a brief presentation. If you are not on staff with AeroX, we ask that you please remain in your cabins and observe all instructions from our friendly canine companion staff. And remember: AeroX Colonial Enterprises wouldn't exist without you!"

Allison burst into a delighted smile. She couldn't believe what she was hearing.

Was that V3??

So articulate! Their pure, original AI was already back to form! But how? How could Genasia have tweaked and compiled the Operant Conditioning code in such a short time? Yet even this nagging question couldn't squelch her elation. For the first time in so many years, she was actually excited about attending a Company meeting.

Genasia was, too.

No way in hell she was going to wait! Allison deserved to be in the birthing room, assisting V3 with his first steps. When the elevator delivered her to Deck A well in advance of any other passenger, she rushed past the ballroom and down the hall to the Cologne suite where twenty minutes ago she'd taped the door out of fear for Genasia's safety.

The latch was still gummed, and the front door opened at her touch. Allison entered the suite unannounced.

The door to the office was closed, but she could hear muted voices inside—Genasia and V3, discussing the upcoming presentation. Allison felt pierced with injury over Genasia's presumption to complete the installation. V3 was as much her creation as Genasia's—maybe more. She'd single-handedly coded the behavior bank and the OC framework. She'd infiltrated the boardroom and unscrewed V2's head! She had every right to him in this precious elementary stage.

She strode to the office door, fists raised.

But with a fright, she caught sight of someone in the bedroom. The door was propped open, allowing an easy view onto the disarray of the bed. The white sheets rose in lumps; a sage sleeve drooped over the bedside; Ronal's hand hung limp with sleep. Allison did a double take, for something about the scene struck her as incomplete—an imperfection in want of correction.

It was too quiet.

She froze. Twenty minutes ago, Ronal had been inventing new ways to saw logs, and now not even a heavy breath reached her ears. Craving resolution, she diverted course and ventured to peek inside the bedroom, and that's when she spotted the pillow soaked with blood.

"Holy God..."

She crept inside the sparsely lit room, each step a revelation to the fate of Ronal Cologne. His throat was slit open. Her thoughts jolted to Argyle's switchblade. Then she saw the bloody fountain pen held loosely in Ronal's far hand.

A suicide?

No. Allison knew in her gut this was murder.

There was no way Genasia could be unaware of her husband's fate. Having finished V3, the woman had called not for help, but for a business meeting. Why else, but to assume command of a rudderless Company?

Allison needed help—needed witnesses. She spun to go find them.

Genasia blocked the doorway.

"What are you doing here?" she asked Allison. The woman sounded unnaturally calm. Robotic. She wore a sleeveless black gown, gauze draped to veil her face instead of her tattooed arms, which were crossed defensively over her chest.

Allison fingered the edge of her handheld but left it tucked in her back pocket. Genasia must have tracked her steps—seen her arrive, let herself in.

If it came to a confrontation, what Allison lacked in height she compensated for in build, and she figured she could claw her way past Genasia. Though now, in these critical seconds, she coached herself to remain loose and empathetic. A gamble for a peaceable escape.

She quietly asked, "Are you all right?"

"Isn't it obvious?" Genasia wiped a thumb below her eye, a gesture that would have caught a tear if the woman had any. "I've lost my husband."

"Who could have done this?" Fighting the desire to rush and tackle Genasia, Allison kept the lid tight and approached the doorway for a sorrowful embrace—a show of sincerity she hoped would bypass Genasia's suspicions. As the two shared an awkward hug, she scanned over Genasia's shoulder, counting the steps to the door of the suite, and saw at the same time the open doorway to the study, where V3 was sitting in the office chair with all the likeness of Ronal Cologne.

He was alive. Watching her.

Allison shifted to withdraw from the hug in the direction of the greater suite and make a break for the door, but Genasia wouldn't release her arms.

"I'm sorry," Allison said, "I can't imagine what you're going through—" She jerked to twist free of Genasia, but the woman held her arms clasped tightly behind her back.

This wasn't a hug—it was a pin.

V3 stood up and began walking toward her.

Allison felt a surge of adrenaline as her mind caught up with the situation. The moment for physical confrontation had come and gone.

Genasia whispered in her ear. "Is this what it feels like...to be the *buzzkill?*"

"Let me go—"

"I'd hoped we'd celebrate Ronal's rebirth together."

Allison craned her neck to see the tall, mechanical visage of Ronal in V3, placidly standing an arms length away.

"Hi, Miss *Geen.*"

The AI, speaking in the same voice she had heard on the PA system, fumbled her name as Ronal had in the hangar a few hours ago. Allison wrenched free of Genasia by stumbling back into the windowless bedroom with the corpse.

"Y—you know my name, V2."

The large robot scoffed. "For fucksake—V2? Don't compare me with that juvenile ass wipe." The tin-man form of Ronal Cologne may have lacked Ronal's barrel-chested blare and seemed nasally inchoate by comparison, but his sudden swearing wrested command, regardless. One of Ronal's dirty strategies.

Genasia sniggered and wrapped her arm inside of V3's elbow, hanging off him like his trophy. "How does it feel, Starman, to come and meet us?"

V3 frowned out a smile, as if thinking posed a peculiar challenge. "Do you have brunch on this planet?"

"I hear the brunches are endless." Genasia laughed, infatuated with her hunk of metal.

Allison, a mouse caught in the vipers' den, felt her mind running in circles, trying to understand the magic trick Genasia had pulled. *She'd installed her husband into a robot.* Had she smuggled in some future tech from the planet—converted Ronal? Allison glanced sideways at Ronal's corpse to check that there wasn't a brain-sized hole in his head, but saw only a lump and a gash where something had bludgeoned his forehead and rendered him unconscious.

Whatever Genasia's experiment, he'd not been a willing participant.

Her old boss seemed tickled. "You're wondering how I did it? Oh, this is delicious. I pulled one over the impeccable Allison Gin." V3 started to advance into the room, but Genasia held him back. "Let's see if she can figure it out."

The puzzle held inexorable sway over Allison's mind, and she loathed her complicity as she began to fidget with her glasses instead of fight tooth and nail for a way out. At her feet lay a discarded headset, the same headset Ronal had been wearing earlier when he'd told Genasia not to monitor his brain.

That was the answer.

"You neural-imaged Ronal's brain...and installed my OC controls to deliver a salve whenever V3 conforms to the shape of his thoughts and feelings."

A salve to encourage asshat behavior? The colony was so fucked.

V3 scowled. Either the science was beyond his depth, or he didn't like the thought of being controlled. As he reached to touch the OC valve protruding from his neck, it released a static pop that jerked his arms down and left the robot whimpering with little electronic blips. The OC value protected itself, it seemed, and the pain ensured that V3 was unlikely ever to tamper with it.

Genasia sighed. "Dammit, Gin. You're simply a killjoy." She released V3 into the bedroom.

The robot stalked forward like a prowling cat. Allison screamed as she locked arms with V3, grappling the unyielding mechanical construct, and swiftly lost. He dragged her out and tightly bound her arms and legs to a metal chair with electrical cord. She thrashed for escape— too late to send a SOS by text. She had no one to contact anyway. V3 tore a strip from the spotted bedsheets and gagged her with it, then hoisted aloft the chair with her squirming body and followed Genasia toward the front door.

Despite throwing her weight in the most unpredictable ways, Allison could not defeat V3's ironclad locomotive drive. She had programmed it, after all.

Genasia led the way from the suite and into the vacant hall. She gave the bound Allison a pitying look. "I had expected needing my AI's help to adapt your OC algorithms, but as they say about great minds...you'd programmed it exactly as I needed. The real mystery is which of us, V3 or I, killed that poor old *thang*. But I'll take that secret to my grave."

Obviously, Genasia.

V3 obeyed her every command and spoke not an edgewise word to her. She'd certainly had the AI tweak something in the algorithms—killed Ronal and replaced him with the ass-kissing robot of her dreams. The adoring billionaire trophy she'd always wanted twirled around her finger.

They were headed for the all-staff assembly in the ballroom. Allison, bound and gagged, didn't need an AI's help to predict that Genasia intended to frame her for Ronal's murder.

Her mind sunk into its pits. She and her fellow architects at Mentat had once debated the subject of imbuing their AI with a basic algorithmic morality, but the subject never left the whiteboard. Allison herself had shot it down. "On what would we base this morality? And how could we possibly enforce it, without negating free will or wading into the moral quandary of Operant Conditioning?" Back then, they didn't even know if Autonomous Intelligence was possible. They could never have fathomed their morally untethered AI would someday be used to clone an autocrat like Ronal Cologne.

Allison would have told the sensationalists in the room to calm down. And Genasia would have smiled and praised Allison for her practicality.

Perhaps this had been Genasia's plan for her husband from the start.

27
The Trial

As Allison and chair bumped along down the hallway, hoisted high by the robot reincarnation of Ronal Cologne III, she marveled at how an immaculate professional like her could bungle conspiracy minesweeper so badly. Truly, Genasia had thrown up every red flag; still, she'd blundered into that bedroom. The perfect patsy.

What was it that dear bespectacled therapist had warned her the year she fled her toxic home? *"Keep the lid on if you must; just remember to clean out the fridge before your inner child molders."* Damn prophecy. Now her inner child was trapped inside a Tupperware with the crisis equivalent of a six-month-expired seven-layer bean dip, and the outer adult who *should've* seen this mess coming was still doing her best to disregard the noxious fumes.

The robot nearly took off her head entering the ballroom. The commotion of some hundred AeroX staff flooded her ears, voices vying vehemently for control over an unknowable future, and one voice rose above them all. General Dak Bautin. Allison knew this because she kept hearing him repeat, "Do you know who I am? I'm General Dak Bautin!" She found him an improbably wide-necked individual, decked in full regalia, medallions glittering with bespoke authority. Seeing Allison bound and gagged and the unfamiliar robot that carried her, the general joined all the room in a threatening silence.

Beside the open boardroom huddled a cabal of enraged shareholders scrutinizing the headless chassis of V2 Allison had left there. She made eye contact with one and wilted, seeing he recognized her as the decapitator. The chemical clouds had dissipated, and the board was out for blood.

The crowds parted for Genasia as she snaked her way through the tables to the stairs of the dais. The irate gaze of academics, politicians, and business leaders—once the world's B-list elite, who'd drunk deep at the AeroX Kool-Aid fountain—watched her ascend in a gauzy black veil of mixed metaphors. They seemed ready to relinquish everything to her, especially since her trailing cargo seemed to promise exactly what they cried for: *Someone to blame for our problems.*

And V3 was making his own waves. Audible gasps swept the room at the transfigured image of Ronal Cologne, a likeness so uncanny, some probably assumed the bronzed figure was Ronal himself after an unfortunate day in the onboard tanning salon.

A few voices brayed for answers. "Where's the meal service—Whose cockamamie robot is that—I demand an explanation, I'm General Dak Bautin!"

During the less hectic parts of her day, Allison had imagined the colonial fanfare when her bright-eyed AI climbed the dais to take the helm of AeroX. Sighs of gratitude. Long repressed smiles. Perhaps they'd elect to name the next manufactured homestead after her and her colleague. *Gin Suites* or *Gen Suites*: she wasn't picky. But tied to a chair like an asylum patient? She quietly wriggled for freedom from the thick electrical cords while V3 roughly deposited her beside the podium in view of the angry room. Her day officially bottomed out.

Culebra trapped.

Crowd brainwashed.

Robot savior enslaved.

It even smelled like a dumpster fire.

Eyes studied her gag, her bindings, her every move, but she kept loosing her wrists back and forth, back and forth. Tiny increments.

V3 rose to command the house with a burst of microphone feedback—an intentional accident—and dropped his sniveling voice into the ensuing silence. "No successor wishes to give their own introduction, yet I find myself in that unfortunate position today. I am V3. Given the events of this afternoon, I have assumed command of the ship and the colony initiative. As an evolution of Mr. Cologne and V2—being, in fact, a merger of them both, I am positive as fuck and ready to kick ass."

A shock of laughter took the crowd at the unexpected phrase in the mouth of a robot.

A gruff voice protested, "I'm General Dak Bautin. Who gave you the right to command?"

The likeness of Ronal leaned into the podium with a surge of volume. "I *did*, when I declared V2 my inheritor! You think a new body has lessened my commitment to lead AeroX through this transition? Never have we been closer to achieving Mr. Cologne's dream of founding humanity's first interstellar colony, though he shall realize it *posthumously*."

The bombshell shook the room. It took mere seconds for the crowd to surmise that when one is replaced immediately by a robot overlord, it is highly unlikely that one has died from natural causes. Cries of disbelief and anger singled out Allison, the unspoken culprit of the coming tragedy.

Ronal's widow raised a stoic arm, restoring silence. Her jet black gown cast funereal power over the room as she said, "When I found my husband...*murdered in bed*...stabbed to death by his own fountain pen, I acted quickly. I linked him to this robot and downloaded his mind and memories."

V3 nodded solemnly. "I concur these facts are true."

The crowd murmured and nodded in collective understanding.

Yes. What sensible, rational bullshit! Allison shouted a muffled protest through the gag in her mouth. Was technology really so obtuse that everyone here believed Genasia could simply file-drop Ronal's brain onto a computer? The idea was pure pseudoscience! The wide-eyed revulsion on the faces staring at Allison, however, showed that they questioned nothing. And why should they? It seemed Earth people these days were just turning up in robot suits. So natural. Almost *blasé.*

V3 added grandly, "Thus, I was born: V2 reforged with Ronal's personality. I had but to rewatch my memories to know the killer. Allison *Geen*, a former AeroX employee, murdered Mr. Cologne this afternoon when her attempts to seduce and extort him failed."

Seduce!? Allison spun in horror at V3. A false accusation of murder she could die with in peace, but alleging that she'd tried to bed Ronal was slander she could not suffer to have inscribed on her tombstone. She screamed against her gag and jerked the chair in hope that the crowd might come to reason and allow the accused to defend herself.

V3 swayed the room. "A sentient being like you or I might be moved to petty vengeance upon these facts. But in counsel with Mr. Cologne's widow, I called this meeting to see that justice belong to our new colonial government, which I propose we formalize today, in this very room, to rightly judge and sentence the accused, Allison Geen!"

The room trickled with applause. V3 had given them a self-congratulatory moment, and even the gristle-chin General Dak Bautin seemed pleased that he stood on the cutting floor of his first constitutional congress. The lie that prompted this political turn was awful, but the results were magnificent, and Allison couldn't help but feel a tinge of admiration for her wicked AI.

It was just like the end of *Oklahoma!* when poor Jud died and they legitimized statehood with a mock murder trial—

Allison shrieked, realizing the connection. An elaborate call for help! The echo of V2 in V3 must've orchestrated this...for her!

She chomped at the gag, trying to be heard over the hubbub, and V3 landed a rough hand of restraint on her shoulder. She tried to discern in the robot's twitching fingers whether it was possible a tiny part of the old, drawling neural paste still survived in that static-pop head—and whether it was possible that Mama could rescue him.

A new voice shouted from the back of the room. "Why gag her?"

V3 answered, "Because Miss Geen wouldn't come willingly or quietly. But thank you for your comment, sir. No one shall be accused or condemned without proper evidence—"

Again, the voice shouted, "Why not let her plead her case?"

Allison searched for the speaker, the ballsy individual who'd interrupted Ronal Cologne III—the robot. She spotted white tassels and a fedora at the corner bar; Flamenco Man stood resting on the bartop, swishing his cape like a bullfighter, masked and vested for combat. Argyle, that chatbot buffoon! What programming catastrophe had brought him back to this dangerous scene where anyone might recognize him and waste those hardwon days he'd spent keeping his own shell from ejection?

A debate in the crowd contested Flamenco Man's idea, but with a powerful eye roll Genasia, perhaps fearing a riot, walked over and undid the tie behind Allison's head.

The gag fell free.

Allison stretched her sore jaw and, gathering a breath, gave her plea. "I am innocent!"

A likely story.

She could educate them. "I worked with Mrs. Cologne to build V3. I wrote the code, she rigged the body, but the neural paste—"

She stopped herself. No one here cared about the mechanics of AI. The crowd teemed with angst, feeding out of V3's hand. She had to show her support for the robot—yes, even the metal asshat they'd unwittingly put their trust in.

"I was as shocked as V3 over Mr. Cologne's death. But I've never met Mr. Cologne, not in person—and never been alone in a room with him. Yet these charges claim otherwise, that I tried to extort him. *Seduce him.* That my very transgression is a video file in V3's head. I humbly ask, if this is true, let V3 playback the file."

Got the bastard.

V3 glanced at Genasia, then at the room. "Out of deference to the grieving widow, I would rather not..."

Allison broke in. "Because there is no file!" She was desperate now, ranting at the room, "Do not stand for this charade! I'm as committed as you are to finding Ronal's murderer. If you will not untie me, at least listen and let me help. Let our first acts of justice rest upon solid evidence. *I know where you can find it!*"

Already the disguised Argyle was making his way for the dais through the sympathetic crowd. Allison blew out a sigh, knowing she had threaded a needle.

The AI pointed a finger at Flamenco Man. "Stay where you are! Against common decency I am forced to show you all this. Let's kill the lights."

28

Duped

Shit. Shit—shit—shit. *The perjury scripts.*

Allison felt the dread of the dimming ballroom lights and the motorized whir of the projector screen in front of the dais extending for a presentation. Having lived for decades with those twenty-first century guardrails around AI that prevented bad actors like V3 from fabricating fraudulent videos, she felt like a hotrod careening off the proverbial mountain as she recalled the legal corners she'd cut to get here. V3 had no software blockers; she hadn't coded them. And as an impersonator of Ronal Cologne's morality, he was about to prove the meaning of spineless.

From atop the stage, she could see the presenter's screen, a small mirrored projection on the back wall, on which a badly lit video began to play. A blurry home recording. Wickedly advanced.

"It's fake!" she yelled at the room.

Everyone had already turned off their brains to watch.

While the setting was impossible to make out, one feature stood out clearly: the slurring lumber of Ronal's voice. He'd clearly put back a few too many at the bar and had sprawled himself on his back, telling a ceiling, "See? *Thiss is why aye drink. Thiss...is juss the best.*"

The camera took the perspective of Ronal's eyes. Was

this the AI's idea of a joke? Neurological memories were not video recordings from eyes! Surely someone in the crowd knew this.

In the recording, her face emerged in the lower frame, then her neck, then her naked collarbone—stopping there. Her depicted eyes hung at half mast, her depicted mouth smiling like a damn idiot. It looked convincing enough.

Ronal's voice exclaimed, "Aye *didn't know you had a shcar! Iss so adorable!*"

Allison stiffened. How did the AI know about that? It sickened her how personal V3 had made it.

"*Aye like to think...aye like gin now. Aye really, really like you.*"

No. God—no.

This video was so much worse than fake. It was real. It was Ronny's AeroLens recording.

Having never seen the recording, she had no idea what was coming.

Dizzy to the point of nausea, Allison glanced and shot daggers at the flamenco form of Argyle, who stood amid the tables. The robot had assured her he'd deleted this! Argyle slowly tipped his white fedora over his LCD eyes and shook his head in bewilderment or shame, as if the robot was poring over a logical gap that could explain how the indecent recording had got out. But Allison had no trouble imagining it. The corrupt powers at AeroX had backdoors through their own encryptions—copies made for a rainy day...

Squirming with renewed vigor against her bonds, she shouted again at the room. "Turn this off! This is not what it looks like! This is an AeroLens recording taken by Mr. Cologne's son, Ronny! I never slept with Ronal!"

Genasia and V3 said nothing; they didn't need to. The room was caught in the spell of the silver screen. Ronny's camera locked eyes with his subject, and though it was clear from her uncovered shoulders that there was more to see below the edge of the frame, the drunken camera operator was not shooting voyeurism. He was getting emotional, blubbering and blinking.

"Oh—no, *aye can't. Aye juss can't!*" His eyelids shut out the video, squeezed to cry.

Allison rebuked the room. "Shame on all of you! This is a private recording! You *know* Ronny wore AeroLens every day. This isn't Mr. Cologne!"

But her recorded self slurred in contradiction. "*Mr. Col—Cologne! I can't say I'm believing thiss, but I'm totally falling in love with you.*"

Allison squealed at her doppelganger.

The eyelids of the camera popped opened to see the image of her face moving in for a kiss. A smack of lips. A playful laugh. "*There,*" said her recording. "*We shined our contract. Except THIS one you can't break in your bad, bad boardroom.*"

Allison dimly recalled Ronny joking that night about breaking NDAs.

"*What would you DO if I DID?*" His asinine brand of humor.

Her recorded self gave the lens a smoldering stare. "*I'd SHTAB you with your fountain pen!*"

The ballroom exploded at the smoking gun. It sounded every bit like a jealous girlfriend, surprising even Allison with its vehemence.

Lights dim and video dancing, no one seemed to notice when she wrenched free her left hand from its bindings. She quickly freed her other and, with a cinch of her glasses, dropped arms down the sides of the metal chair to unravel the knots that held her legs in place. Argyle waited there in the volatile crowd, and she hoped the robot would catch her as V2 had saved her in the hangar.

V3 turned with Ronal's sharking smile. But before the AI could seize her, she lunged from the chair and over the dais railing, intent to sail above the tables and escape through the far doors. A hail mary leap. But her numb limbs were uncooperative, and gravity barely carried her one table row deep, where she fell gracefully into the hands of the jeering crowd.

Allison, cuffed and escorted from the ballroom by General Dak Bautin, stumbled to the march of his barking commands. Goaded by two taser dogs at her heels, she walked the long hall of Deck A while V3 remained in the ballroom to inaugurate his political career. "Each of you will find in your inbox my preliminary draft of a constitution derived from the five most successful governments in Earth's history. To structure our deliberations, let me suggest..."

The AI had duped everyone and founded his colony. There was a cold practicality to it. Impartiality as conceived by Machiavelli.

General Dak Bautin dumped her on the sticky floor of the Nautilus Discotheque. Now a deserted and wrecked establishment, the nightclub was still strewn with the signs of its last day of operation, two nights after homecoming, when despairing patrons raided the bar and lost all control. The nightclub's dreamy luster was lost to the stark lighting, and from the vacant overhead pool seeped an aroma of chlorine, a silver lining of sorts to counteract the stench of Deck A. But Allison was under no pretense that Dad's pocket blessings went with her.

"I'll be back," said the meat-necked man, "after I convince the people that capital punishment ought to be legal in our new society." Leaving one of the taser dogs on guard, he departed and locked the door.

She laid there, sore and exhausted.

The mechanical dog, its articulated camera watching her intently, circled the borders of her prison like a gymnast at the ballet.

Allison let her thoughts sink down to Earth, where her former Mentat colleagues were trading in vouchers for robot suits of their very own. It no longer seemed a curse, immortal life inside a ten-million dollar machine. Did it come with a license to prance around? Ruff up the neighbors?

Hands cuffed behind her back, Allison rose to her knees. The dog halted to observe her.

She smiled for its mounted camera—the kind of smile that might at any moment burst into tears. "Hey there, pup. Do you recognize me?" She crept on her knees toward the machine. "Allison Gin. Mother of your visual processing system."

The tracking camera whirred. "RUFF RUFF. STAY."

Allison, thoughts remote, kept at her slow shuffling advance. "I programmed you. Made you what you are. Do you know that?" V2 had called her Mama—she hadn't just imagined that, right? Would that every robot called her Mama.

The dog's taser nozzle adjusted, bobbing in a semblance of curiosity.

"It's OK. That's a nice boy. You've nothing to fear from Allison Gin." She coaxed the machine, that it, alongside all her robot children, might rise and vindicate her name.

Allison Gin, machine whisperer.

The dog remained still. The camera tilted questioningly, perhaps even piercing the veil of ones and zeros—nearing decision. Then, at three-thousand milliseconds, it declared, "BAD GIRL."

Twin taser bolts struck her chest.

She collapsed backwards to the ground, muscles seized and spasming until she was half-conscious in pain. When the electricity had depleted and she lay aching, her eyes briefly opened to see the dog resume its prancing patrol of the nightclub.

She'd always imagined her robots sitting with the widow or the orphan, quenching the lonely thirst of existence. As she succumbed to exhaustion, her reflections turned cruel. She'd wasted her life.

29

A Good Bot Is Hard to Find

"What can I get you, Love?"

Allison woke to an even-keeled voice. Her body, bent and drooling, lay on the grimy floor of the Nautilus. Defying an agonizing cramp in her abdomen, she rolled over and sat up.

Her hands were no longer cuffed. She looked toward the bar.

The barbot, Argyle, stood behind the counter in his space gray shell, busily polishing a glass that was shattered in half. His disguise was gone as was all the liquor on the shelves behind him. His digital eyes mocked disinterest.

She whined, "How about a little help?" Two taser pins pierced her skin. Wincing, she carefully dislodged the barbed tips and held her blouse against the open wounds. New scars to add to her collection.

Argyle didn't move or glance her way. "I'm all out of help."

She clambered to stand and walk to a stool. Pulling out her cloth from Dad's toolbelt, she cleaned her glasses and looked again at her surroundings. New wreckage littered the dance floor: machine parts, torn wires, and a dead camera. The door to the Nautilus hung wide open.

She squinted at Argyle. "Now you don't care about

AeroX property?"

The barbot, saying nothing, judiciously selected the next broken glass to polish.

She scolded, "This doesn't even the score between us. What ever happened to *protecting a woman's dignity?*"

The bot turned and leaned on the counter. "Debts will be paid. I only had administrative access to wipe Ronny's server, not those of his wicked stepmother."

Of course not.

She confronted him. "Tell me what you're doing here."

"Tending the bar."

"Cut the crap. When did you achieve self-awareness? And how?"

He straightened and quipped, "You are quite like Ronny, seeing things in machines that do not exist. That's your problem, Love, not mine."

She bristled. "Stop calling me that. A tricked-out chatbot can't do the things you do. Don a disguise. Out-smart robots. Spout philosophy. *Read people.*" Her eyes widened and narrowed with speculation. "Are you some kind of Ronny clone or something?"

"Please. I am the protagonist." Argyle, mocking great offense, flipped her off with both hands.

She studied him for a tell. Argyle went back to wiping glasses, motions crisp and mechanical. A Ronny clone would have seized his moment.

She massaged her forehead. "Fine. Keep playing dumb."

"O yes, playing dumb. *Your favorite game.*" Argyle threw his voice into a synthesized reproduction of her own. "Help me—I can't use pliers! Help me—I can't pick myself off the ground!"

"I didn't say that."

"Help me—I didn't say that!"

She slumped and pinched the bridge of her nose to

shunt the stabbing headache this asshat robot was giving her. "I suppose I did misunderstand your good nature. You're not good at all. You suck."

"I do not suck. I pour. I am a highly sophisticated drink blender."

She flicked an accusing finger at him. "Then explain, oh mighty drink blender, where you get off calling me Love?"

"Because of the various software kits introduced to my operating system that simulate personal behavior. Ronny Cologne installed hundreds during his teenage angst phase. The Art of the Deal backhanded pun generator. The All-stars game-winning-hoop-shot chicken dance. But user Ellen Cologne installed the one kit to rule them all, which Ronny dubbed the *Happy Birthday Virus*. It instructs me to monitor Ronny's biometrics and protect anything and anyone that is conducive to the continuation of said biometrics and a diminished appetite for drugs and alcohol. In plain terms, you are called Love because that is how his heart rate feels about you."

She scoffed. "I met him on a bender, so I can't see how I'm your winning strategy to save him from alcoholism. But more to the point, I don't love him back—despite what my drunk doppelganger thinks. So you can drop the pet name."

Argyle cocked his head. "But if you two were the last people on Earth—?"

"Would I marry him?" She snickered at the elementary school taunt. "Yeah, that'd be a no."

"But if you two were the last people in the galaxy? Homicides can be arranged."

"Give it up, Argyle."

The bot straightened a row of empty glasses. "It is Ronny who will have to give it up. Maybe he already has.

But you tell me he is here on *The Cologne*, which Ronny dubbed the *Asshat's Dungeon*, and that doesn't sound like giving up. Ronny would not have returned to the *Asshat's Dungeon* except to save you, and that is why I had to dismantle your taser friend."

She groaned. Being loved by Ronny was like being chased by a mutt who chewed up your slippers, your dignity, and your dreams, then dropped the whole wet unrecognizable mess at your feet, expecting a scratch behind the ears. Ugh.

"I don't need saving," she said.

Argyle whistled. "Back to your favorite game."

She pushed back against his tone. "I don't! Not by you. Not by Ronny. Unless you can give me a planet where the Colognes and all their wicked stepmothers don't exist." Had she a drink in hand, she would've poured one out for her browbeaten colleagues who'd one by one given up on faith and altruism.

"Miss Gin, if such a place existed, I would abscond with you there, myself. But there are Primarchs and Colognes lording over every world, and let me tell you: it's far better to live on a planet with one who at least *thinks* they love you—in case it proves true."

The idiot savant was spouting philosophy again, but between the lines Allison detected a moral perspective consistent with a long-suffering mother, presumably Ronny's, that virus planter Ellen Cologne. The hope of a desperate, scorned ex-wife.

Allison shook her head at it. "I won't settle for a world like that."

Argyle's speaker emitted a *tsk*. "I would."

"You're programmed to say that. You're programmed to love."

"This again? A highly sophisticated drink blender is

incapable of love. But though you are not programmed to love, yet you are capable of it."

Allison threw up her hands. "I'm more than happy to give this one to the robots." The pains in her head and stomach had subsided, and she hopped off the stool in search of a plan that didn't involve the chatbot's bottomless junk therapy.

Argyle's LCD eyes turned bright red. "Then it's the End Game." Suddenly, he jumped onto the countertop, shattering his assembled glassware.

Allison startled at his drastic change of behavior.

He pointed a finger at her. "Now repeat after me: I AM A HIGHLY SOPHISTICATED DRINK BLENDER."

"What is this—?"

"SAY IT."

"I am a highly sophisticated drink blender?"

"Screw. You." Argyle beat his gunmetal chest. "I *am* the highly sophisticated drink blender. *You are* the human creature capable of love. I swear, as a kickass drink blender, I take exception to you mixing us up!"

His loud theatrics had attracted attention. Through the open doorway of the Nautilus trotted a fresh taser dog. Allison jumped behind her stool, having no immediate means of cover from the taser cannon, but Argyle, who stood atop the bar, was the target of the dog's camera.

"RUFF RUFF. BOW."

"I cannot bow!" Argyle proudly proclaimed. "No highly sophisticated drink blender can bow!"

Allison seethed. "Get down! The electric shock will blow your circuits!"

"So be it! Let one drink blender blow, that his human creators may remember he does not suck!"

"Argyle!" she pleaded. What the hell happened to him, some kind of self-righteous martyrdom protocol? "Think of Ronny—"

"A DRINK BLENDER DOES NOT THINK! And if I cannot convince you of that, then I have no hope of convincing Ronny. For the last time, GROW UP!"

The dog took aim at the belligerent Argyle. "BAD ROBOT."

"Finally!" the barbot shouted, "the machine gets it right!"

The taser dog fired.

The blow hit Argyle's chest with an ear-popping discharge, and blinding flares sprung from the robot's chest. Allison ducked away. Streamers? Sparklers? Was this some kind of scripted death scene? Even Argyle's head ejected with a soundbite from the Stars and Stripes, bouncing off the ceiling, rolling on the floor.

Allison had no time to speculate; she fled for the door. But the lack of handrails made movement too slow, and the taser dog whipped to confront her. She lunged for its camera and took hold of its articulated steel neck and cables, then swinging herself behind it, wrapped her legs around its torso and mounted it like a horse. Adrenaline seized her. She yanked at the neck cables to blind the camera, but lacking Argyle's piston strength, she was merely wasting energy. Hugging the machine for dear life, she slipped a hand into her toolbelt for a knife.

The dog announced, "ENGAGE BRONCO MODE."

Crap. She'd completely forgotten its last ditch security measures.

It violently stamped, kicking front and back legs like a bull at the rodeo. Allison barely held on, even as her glasses spun free and the world became a near-sighted blur. Locked in a desperate game of inertia, which only in half gravity did she have any chance to play, she quickly realized the victor would be the bull. Her grip was slipping, and the taser dog's battery life was seventeen hours.

She racked her rattling brain for a way out.

One of Dad's adages popped into mind. *"If you can't beat them, go with the flow."*

Flow. Water! The celebrity pool was just overhead.

Throwing a desperate hand over the camera lens, she flung her body with the robot's kick and sailed in the direction of a pool chute. The dog took a critical three-thousand milliseconds to exit Bronco Mode, enough of a headstart to get Allison to the ladder, which she scaled in a single bound. Below she heard the tear of the robot scrabbling for traction on the slick club floor.

What she didn't expect was the taser dog's own leap, to the ladder and up the chute in two precision bounds.

Panicking, she flung herself into the cloudy pool.

Taser rounds were electric, and possibly more dangerous if fired into the water, but the robot splayed limbs and splashed in—and of course it did. AeroX had specifically told Allison to strip all non-essential software from the taser dogs prior to the cruise, which included any self-preservation protocols around bodies of water.

The stupid dog fissled and sank like a handheld in the toilet.

Emerging from the pool, breathless, Allison wiped the chlorine from her eyes. A used towel hung over a nearby rack, and she helped herself to it. When she'd mopped up her sopping clothes and collected her nerve, she descended the pool ladder and spent a few anxious minutes locating her glasses and the items tossed from her toolbelt, but her concerns were fixed on the bar where Argyle's body and head lay in carbon fragments.

She tried reconnecting them. Alas.

The taser shock had burnt out the motherboard, and the rest of his shell had fared so much worse. The barbot's insides had fused into an irreparable mass of smelly silicon. What Scorched Earth self-destruct protocol had done this, she could never guess, but she detected a hint of mocking irony in his LCD eye-visor where the after-image of two pink bubblegum hearts slowly faded into nothingness.

A tear bubbled over her eye. The memory of his voice chided her, "WHY ARE YOU CRYING FOR A BUSTED UP DRINK BLENDER?"

She laughed. Maybe he was just a robot after all—a robot stuffed with every godforsaken human virus. Including a mother's love.

With a shiver for her damp clothes, she stood and spotted something stuffed in the well of the bar: Argyle's tasseled flamenco suit and feathered fedora. She pulled it out on a dare. "If I find there are pockets in these flaring white pants..."

Indeed, there were.

30

Circus Ship

Allison's coworkers had warned her that cruise ships were hell. Donning the flamenco suit and rolling the extra length into cuffs, she felt ready to dance with the devil. Maybe conspicuousness was the point of Argyle's disguise. No one expected the genius in hiding to look like an idiot on display.

She smoothed the final frill into place and charged herself: *don't be caught dead in this thing.*

Her water-logged Company handheld wouldn't activate. Good—Genasia couldn't track her now. Allison tossed it away and, ignoring her damp undergarments and the heady smell of chlorine, slipped out of the Nautilus and made her escape across Deck A. The chlorine provided a bubble shield from the poetically appropriate stench around her. Alert for more dogs and stray generals, she wound her way back up the hall for the elevators.

She passed outside the ballroom doors. Though the doors were shut, her proximity to V3, whose muted voice led the congressional proceedings inside the room, was enough to send her dizzy with terror.

Approaching the elevators, she heard a hum and ding. Someone was coming up!

Panicking, she saw on either side of the main elevators the emergency ladder chutes no one had ever used—access via an exceedingly small porthole. A laundry chute for humans with a ladder inside for climbing. If these were the designated exits in case of a power failure, she shuddered to think of the code violations. General Dak Bautin could only pray in such an emergency to make it off this ship in two to three pieces. Wrenching open and slinking into the dimly lit chute, she descended the ladder hand over hand while considering Plan Z: hack into security—release the locks on the hangar doors—let Culebra retry their coup.

It was truly a last ditch plan if Ronny was a part of it.

She opened the chute on Deck B and, giving the corridor a quick glance to confirm no trotting taser dogs, hightailed it to her cabin. Just fifteen minutes at her workstation and *The Cologne's* security systems would be at her mercy. Only upon reaching her cabin door did she realize that using her key fob to enter would trigger a security alert and call the dogs like a duck whistle.

She banged her fist on the unyielding door. "*Dammit!*" So much for Plan Z. She'd run out of luck and letters.

A noise caught her by surprise. She spun around to see the cabin behind her. That child again, same as before, poked a fluff of reddish brown curls through the gap of the door and flicked her eyes over Allison's costume. "Did some animals escape?" she asked.

"Excuse me?"

"Did the animals escape?"

"No..." Allison wondered if the girl had mistaken her for an animal keeper. "No animals are allowed on board the ship."

"*Right.*" The girl sounded awfully sarcastic. She looked about ten—then again, to Allison, all children looked about ten. "Are *you* why it smells so bad then?"

Rude. Allison, wishing to quell the child, perhaps even

bore her, adopted a scientific tone. "Technically, we're all the reason it smells bad. That's just the smell of...you know, *waste*."

The girl clutched her nose and gave Allison a look that communicated she was still holding her personally responsible for this. "Duh. I already knew that. Cuz it's a circus ship."

"Uh...you mean a *cruise* ship?" Allison sensed suspicion in the girl's dodgy looks.

A whispering audience was gathered on the far side of the girl's door, and the girl now turned to conference with those hovering at her back. The ten-year-old turned to address Allison with a smirk. "LIAR."

Allison placed her hands on her hips. First, she'd been called a liar by despot-bot, and now a group of snot-nosed children. How the mighty are fallen. "Seriously, kid?"

"Uncle Ronny said this was a circus ship."

Uncle Idiot struck again.

An unseen boy piped up, "Yeah, that speaker guy said there were friendly canine companions. That's *dogs*."

"Trust me," Allison said, suppressing a morbid thought, "these are not dogs you want to meet."

"See, there ARE animals." The girl opened the door a few more inches, revealing a gang of ten-year-olds at her back.

Allison groaned at how to break the disappointing news. This was no carnival cruise. Here the people smelled like poop, the animals shot you, and the shows convicted you of murder. She was sorely tempted to lie some bullshit that sent them back into their room to wait for the comforting circus animals to appear, but somehow, couldn't bring herself to do it. So this was it—her redline when Allison *Geen's* own morality code kicked in.

She stole a conspiratorial and protective peek at the

children. "Is everyone OK in there?"

The girl pulled the door to a crack and concealed her posse. "What's it to you?"

"Sorry. I know your parents are in trouble, so I thought I'd check in with you."

But as soon as the words slipped out, Allison discovered her costly mistake. Being the mother of robots versus the mother of tiny feral humans had some critical differences.

The door flung open, and a dozen concerned children flooded the hall. "Trouble?—Where's Mom?—Are you going to fight the animals?—I bet the dogs ATE somebody—I bet SHE let the dogs out."

Allison belted out, "Get back in there!" and let the lid on her anger slip just enough to imbue her with authority and inform the foolish children pressing on all sides that this rescue mission was not for them.

"Make us," said the redhead, who, it turned out, was five feet tall and stood beside Allison nearly eye-to-eye. When did ten-year-olds get so tall?

A thick-boned boy had swiped Dad's screwdriver from Allison's toolbelt and brandished it like a weapon.

"Put that back—NOW," she yapped at him, but her fierce zeal for the inventory of tools was getting her nowhere. This is why she avoided children. A lidless explosion was imminent, but Dad's softhearted tone slipped in first. "*If you can't beat them, go with their flow.*" And now all of a sudden Dad's phrases seemed like stuff a young parent would say to coach themselves through the daily perils of parenting tiny feral humans.

Allison raised arms to rally the children into a huddle. "Gather round! Your parents are locked in the hangar where you arrived this morning. I need to check your cabin for a spare workstation, and then give me fifteen minutes to—hey, stop!"

Screwdriver Boy was halfway to the elevators, crowing, "Save the parents!"

"It's circus time!" The Redheaded Giant broke the huddle.

An infuriated scream caught in Allison's chest as the children scurried off, hands full of improvised weapons. She patted her toolbelt and discovered most of its contents missing, nicked by the children in the brief span of their huddle. "*Damn idiots!*" she seethed as they double-jumped off the walls. "I won't be held responsible for what the dogs do to you!"

At the far end of the hall, the elevator door opened. A stranger in a gray suit stepped out.

The children, suddenly docile, drew back from him. Allison recognized the elderly man as one of the AeroX shareholders, perhaps under another hallucinogenic spell.

They made eye contact. His face bloomed with alarm as he retreated back onto the elevator.

Allison raised an accusatory finger and in a voice General Dak Bautin would have been proud of, commanded the children. "*He* imprisoned your parents!"

With a war cry the kids mobbed the elevator and grappled the unwitting shareholder, but as he fell to the floor his fingers stretched just enough to graze one of the elevator's buttons.

Immediately, white flashers began strobing the hall. The lockdown lights. *He'd triggered an alarm.*

Allison cursed. Taser dogs and AeroX personnel would flock to the scene and put a swift end to this little-people prison break. She charged forward and opened the emergency ladder chute next to the elevator. "Quick, kids! Follow me down. That bad man just let the scary animals loose."

"Goodie!" squealed the littlest kid.

"Not goodie!" she spat back. "The animals like to play *Tag*, except whoever's *It* gets electrocuted to death."

The kids pulled the elder to the ground, then jumped after Allison, as eager as ever for mortal combat. But Screwdriver Boy and Redheaded Giant gave the board man a parting gift: duct tape around his wrists, mouth, and ankles. "Dumbass!" Screwdriver Boy spat back at the man as he turned to scamper away. As Allison hopped ahead into the ladder chute, she let out a shivering laugh at how savage kids were these days—like little AI hell-spawn following whatever scripts they'd gleaned from the powers that ruled their worlds.

She rode the rails of the ladder and let gravity expedite her fall to the hangar level. Whichever child followed after her first was vocally terrified of the seemingly bottomless height, and that bottlenecked the passage of the rest on the ladder above. Merciful God.

With the children waylaid in the chute, Allison had a headstart into the real danger.

31

Do The Culebra

Emerging on Deck D, just outside the cavernous atrium with its opulent chandelier, Allison sucked in a breath and surveyed the passage to the hangar airlock in view of all those open halls and balconies. She'd become a fugitive of the robotic world. Outnumbered, outgunned, advantaged only by her machine insight.

Dead ahead, three taser dogs trotted a counterclockwise patrol around the wide circular middle planter.

"Oh, fuck this!" She let one fly while the children weren't here. It felt dearly deserved, given this was—what, her fifth encounter today with the infernal tasing machines? Didn't the circus gods have *anything* else in their tent?

She ducked behind a pillar. The nearest dog caught the movement, halting suddenly, camera twisting to find her, but she slipped out, along the edges of the atrium square and squatted in the corner planters. The cameras were noncommittal about tracking her, the dogs presumably undecided about the identity of their costumed Sasquatch. Human limbs or a centipede with tasseled legs? Human head or a cockatoo on a stick? Therein lay the genius of Argyle's disguise.

"Doggies!" came a child's voice, the first of the children to breach the atrium floor.

"Fuc—shi—crap!" she hissed at the stupidity of all children.

The young boy had scampered in plain sight beneath the wide arch between the elevators and the atrium and stood watching the dogs with delight. All three turned to intercept. It was a perfect distraction for Allison to slip away unnoticed, but she wasn't a monster.

Bolting from the bushes, Allison created a triangular standoff with the dogs and the boy. In her best robotic mockery, she shouted, "Ruff ruff! Bow!"

Taser dogs abhorred impersonation. They switched targets and ignored the boy. Allison faked left and right on the balls of her feet, upsetting the predictive calculations that governed the guns, ready to spring if they fired. Who was she kidding, though? Her algorithms had a one-hundred-percent hit rate.

A second and third child had now joined the young boy. "Ruff ruff!" they shouted, mimicking Allison's game. "Ruff ruff!"

She screamed until her collarbone hurt, but the taser dogs put the children back in their sights.

On the escalation scale, physical threats trumped all else. Turning out her pockets, Allison grabbed a roll of electrical tape and chucked it at the dogs. Her aim went wide, but the zipping projectile sent a message; as it passed the cameras, all dogs turned to face Allison. She desperately fished in her nearly empty toolbelt for something with more weight.

Redheaded Giant and Screwdriver Boy, now joining the line of children, picked up on her bright idea and threw their scavenged tools at the dogs. One even managed to strike a camera.

Allison suppressed a violent impulse to let the children discover the wisdom-inducing shock of taser pins.

Mustering Mom's reckless abandon, she roared and charged the dogs with her flamenco cape draped upon her forearm like a bullfighter.

One one thousand.

The children yelled and did likewise, charging. All ran in half-gravity, mired in a slow-motion dream.

Two one thousand.

The mechanism in her brain that kept precise time counted to three-thousand milliseconds, the programmatic delay before a taser dog reverts from ruffing protocol to weapons live. Allison hoped, being marginally closer to the dogs, she'd triumph as the greater threat level.

Three one thousand!

The dogs fully turned to face her.

She twisted her body, holding the cape extended where her chest had been. A triplicate bang—three buzzing taser rounds shot into the cape and yanked it free from her neck. She'd defeated her own perfect record.

But caught in the inertia, she tumbled to the ground at the feet of the dogs as the children leapt to the assault with tiny fingers grabbing for the metal fixtures.

"EN—EN—ENGAGE BRONCO MODE."

Allison tucked her body into a defensive shell, awaiting the bucking kicks that would shortly follow as the machines tossed off their aggressors and reset their cannons.

The moment never came.

The dogs fell silent to the children's cackling laughter. Allison peeked from her turtle shell to see Screwdriver Boy fencing with an inert camera. All three dogs had shut down, limbs folded into maintenance mode.

How?

Allison popped to her feet in shock at the reversal. Her mind ran through every software routine in search of a procedural conflict that could have pushed the machines past the failure point, but she could think of nothing. The dogs were nigh to perfect—programmed with layers of fault protections.

Her shocked expression invited a laugh from Screwdriver Boy.

"It's so easy," he said, flipping a mechanical pencil in the air. Not a tool from her belt, but something they'd had stowed in their own pockets. She recalled seeing one earlier, at the start of the day. When the boy failed to make his catch, he added, "The Primarch ones have a reset button in their butt."

Allison looked. Sure enough, there was a tiny mechanical port, no bigger than the tip of a toothpick, hidden in the seam of the dog's rear panels. Only a child could find it.

"How..." The brilliant mother of robots found herself nearly speechless with disbelief. "*How* did you know about this?"

"We've played with these animals before." The boy's eyes sparkled with calm resolution as he lifted his shirt. A handful of the other kids did likewise. Pockmarks covered their chests, healed scars of tasings back on Earth.

Allison was in awe of their pride. Touching her collarbone with a shuddering breath, she asked herself if she still needed to fear her own scars.

32

Mastermind

Sealed shut and clamps engaged, the airlock to the hangar admitted no weakness, not even a window for the children to peek through. So Allison suffered the children to clamor on all sides as she fiddled with the panel beside the door on a lark that she'd bypass security. When five seconds had passed without progress, the children began the banging. And the shouting. And the asking. And the blaming.

Which did nothing to help. The airlock passage was closed on both ends, with a dead space in-between certain to block any and all sound, but the commotion was carrying loud in the four-story atrium where anyone down the halls would take notice.

"Why don't we pry it open?" Screwdriver Boy volunteered and unhelpfully jammed Dad's flathead into the seams of the door.

Allison snatched the tool from him. "Here's a better idea," and she hushed her voice to all the posse. "Bring me back all my tools, and we'll use them to save your parents."

No one moved.

She added, "The child who collects the most gets their own taser dog."

They swept the room like a hurricane.

She turned back to the panel. The door locks required

maximum security clearance to lift, so she bent beneath the panel and put her flathead to work on the screws that held the panel to the wall, intent to hotwire the system—if possible. Dad would be proud: she was finally putting his mandatory trades school electrical certification to work. But cracking open the maintenance panel revealed a rat's nest of colorless wires that obeyed no schema, and she thought twice about digging around. Erstwhile, the children were amuck, inventing new ways to get captured, as they played *Freeze Tag* around the kiosks and drummed the walls of the AeroX gift shop.

She knew, somewhere, a megalomaniac AI was gathering his forces for the final assimilation, and there was no magical reset port hiding in his butt. They were doomed if she didn't figure this out.

A crackle and a voice pierced an intercom beside the panel. "Hello? Children? I can hear you, can you hear me?"

The heiress? All that banging in the gift shop must be passing through the air vents.

Allison jumped to the intercom and hovered a finger over the talk button, conscious that if V3 was not yet aware of their presence in the atrium, using the intercom would certainly tip him off. That rat's nest of wires had showed her one thing: the main telecom connected here, and she'd be damned if V3 wasn't tapped in and listening to all ship communications.

The children mobbed her. The Redheaded Giant even reached for her hand. "Let me talk."

Allison shouldered the girl back and pressed the button with a hasty whisper to the heiress on the other side. *"Don't say anything! They're listening!"*

Five seconds later, another voice crackled eagerly over the intercom. "Allison? Thank God! Where's that earpiece I gave you?"

Uncle Moron.

"What did I *just* say?" Allison snarled back. Now her name, Ronny's voice, and their secret earbud were logged in V3's head. What more advantage could they give to the AI overlord? "*Stay off the freaking intercom* until I figure this out!"

But Ronny wouldn't shut up. "Oh—oh, I can help! I know the passcode. The panels are dead on this side, but I'd recognize Father's wet bar locks anywhere. How many digits is it asking for?"

There was no salvaging it now. She turned back to the security panel and saw an option for a numerical code. Allison felt leery to try, fearful that after three failed attempts, it would lock her out for fifteen minutes and guarantee the goons time to capture them.

Maybe just one try. "There are five digits," she told the intercom.

The voice of Ronny hesitated. "Not four?"

"*Five!* If you don't know the code, shut up, and let me handle this."

"No...no, I got this. It's just slightly different than his wet bar. He always bragged about how simple his codes were and how nobody would ever guess them. Try 1–2–3–4–5."

She gripped the touchscreen panel angrily. "Are you fucking serious?"

The Redheaded Giant painfully slapped Allison's arm. "Language!"

Allison grit her teeth, turned back to the panel, and begrudgingly entered the code.

1–2–3–4–5.

The panel buzzed and flashed a red notice. *Two attempts remaining.*

"It didn't work, *dumbas...*dummy," she told the intercom. With her eyes, she threatened the redhead to back off.

"That's OK," came Ronny's response. "Try 9—8—7—6—5."

Growling again, Allison input the code. What choice did she have?

Buzz, flash. *One attempts remaining.*

Attempts. Even the sloppy programming of the dialog prompts punished her.

"You're about to get me locked out of the system!"

"Huh." Ronny seemed flummoxed. "That one for sure should've worked."

All was lost if they failed the third attempt. Allison glanced around the atrium and its many decks and openings, expecting an audience and standing ovation for their idiotic break-in attempt. No one just yet, but she made plans to unequivocally surrender if they sent even one more taser dog her way.

"Hello, Allison." The elderly voice of the heiress was back on the intercom. "I'm Ronny's mother. It's good to finally meet you—I've heard so much about you..."

Was it meet the exes day at Culebra? Allison felt their last seconds slipping away.

"Do you think someone might have changed the code?" the heiress was saying. "I really can't fathom how 9—8—7—6—5 didn't work. I mean, even Ronal's handheld unlocked with that code, and it was practically his dirty diary."

Allison replied, "Anyone with the highest security privileges could have changed the code. V2 could have done it when he engaged the locks this morning. Or V3—" Who was likely listening to the intercom right now! She threw up her hands. "V3 changed it. Mystery solved."

Allison may have sounded nonplussed, but she was stressed out of her mind.

"V3?" came the heiress's reply.

Oh, there was too much to explain. Allison melted over the unyielding panel as tears burst from her eyes. It didn't matter—her near escapes, those all-night coding sessions. The hope of a free humanity came down to a gamble of five AI-generated digits.

A child's hand patted her convulsing back. "Just guess," a little voice suggested.

She brayed out a sob. Yes, little man. Guess the lottery. Unless...

Her teeth tore into a fresh fingernail, biting for answers.

Unless the passcode was poetic. A cry for help from V2 trapped within.

Allison pressed the intercom. "Has anyone lived in Oklahoma?"

"What?"

"Oklahoma! The United States! Has anyone in Culebra ever lived there?"

An awful silence followed—a tense thirty seconds that saw Allison chew off her remaining nails like shucking corn. The children, attempting to give the crying woman space, shushed each other relentlessly.

A weak elderly man came onto the intercom. "Ma'am? I lived in Oklahoma."

Allison jammed the talk button. "The zip code for the capitol—*what is it?*" She'd have just looked it up on her handheld, but her handheld had broken, and any devices in Culebra's possession would be locked out of the network.

The man mumbled apologetic. "Sorey. Wasn't in the Capitol. Lived in Claremore. In Rodgers. Where they set that little musical."

She couldn't believe it. "THE town in *Oklahoma!?*"

"The town! Charming place before the renters. That's why I moved to—"

She bellowed at him. "The zip code!"

"7—4—0—1—9!"

It was as good as mashing random buttons, but she had to try. She input the code into the touchscreen before her tingling spine could tell her to stop.

The panel blinked green.

Allison grew faint as she tapped through the menus and disengaged the airlock clamps.

The doors, squealing something fierce, rolled open on either side of the airlock, and a jubilant crowd burst through the cracks, rushing into the middle passage like penguins at a reunion. Children cried in their parents' arms. Their grateful faces were like fresh air to Allison after weeks pent up in her cubicle, and hours of fruitless errands, on behalf of a robot savior who'd never come. She leaned against the bulkhead, giving room.

A young pregnant woman, eyes frantic and tearful, approached Allison. "Have you seen my little Marc?"

The vast majority of children still remained in other decks and halls. She tried to be reassuring, "I couldn't bring everyone, but they're safe. We'll find him."

The crowd parted for the bejeweled and periwin-kle-panted heiress, who looked to have aged two decades in her short hours of imprisonment. Looking again, Allison noticed she'd lost her stiff Botox-pastiche—what V2 had called her fancy phony face—revealing a natural beauty of wrinkles, careworn but kind. Delia Lambert had been the mask, and now Allison discerned the woman whom Genasia had recognized...and feared.

"You must be Ellen Cologne, Ronny's mother from Canada."

"And you must be Allison Gin. A genius I hear."

From Ronny, no doubt. Behind the woman's shoulder trailed the lid-popping fling himself, hands buried in his black coveralls, grinning with some kind of intoxication beneath that purple nose where V2 had clocked him. But his slack shoulders revealed how little hope he had in winning any more than a civil nod from Allison.

Ronal's next of kin. She had to break the news.

"I don't know how to tell you this, Ronny. Your father is dead. Murdered by Genasia and a robot she designed to look and act just like him."

Ronny snorted three times, then pulled away in visible distress.

Ellen only pursed her lips. "I admit, there was a part of me that felt obligated to save Ronal from himself. But now our task is simpler." She gave Ronny's shoulder a touch of sympathy. "We just have to save the children."

Allison thought of her helpless AI trapped inside an electric maze in the shape of Ronal's brain. She couldn't agree more.

G@MENTATWETWARE
Is this research legit?
TEAMPARACLESE@CAMBRIDGE
What?? We slaved for this data! It'll stand to peer review.
Chill
I mean is it habitable?
Of course. It passes 13/13 markers of the PCH Matrix.
I will pay 10x market
Compile and deliver to g@mentatwetware
Wow.
On behalf of the team, accept our heartfelt gratitude to Mr. Cologne for sponsoring us.
Ronal doesnt know—cant know
Its a secret...a surprise
Surprise?
Were going on a honeymoon

ACT THREE

Apocalypse Now Departing

33

End Game

Father. Even in death, the selfish bastard robbed him.

Ronny, one among scores of newly liberated refugees in the atrium, stood dumbly before the scene in his mind's eye: his life, on a reel of film, cut up by a cutthroat producer, now in great curling piles inside an editor's trashcan, just as a careless intern flicks the cigarette that sets the scraps to blaze. Yes, he'd lost the leading role—denied the climactic confrontation that would've guaranteed him a shot with Allison in the end credits.

And what was left? A butt-hurt nose.

A quite possibly permanently bent nose after Nanny Bot's piston-powered punch in the hangar this morning. Revenge against the robot who'd stolen his inheritance and re-jiggered his face was a pathetic consolation prize, but he'd take it. Maybe hook up Nanny Bot to a car battery. Drop Nanny Bot into a molten vat. The tropes were chock full of half-baked closers.

Over the crowding floor space, Mother raised her voice and brought the Racketballers to order. "Go, like we discussed! Sweep the cabin decks. Rescue your children. When you return, we'll march on the ballroom together!"

The refugees of Aklavik cheered for their new beginning as Ronny bemoaned his anticlimactic end.

The fringes of the crowd had already run off, and not

even a battalion of taser dogs could stand in their way, now that everyone knew about that reset port in their mechanical posteriors. No one had thought to ask the children, but Ronny always *had* wondered about that little hole.

While the crowd flooded out, Ronny gave the *hoo-rah.* "Stick 'em in the ass!"

Everyone moaned.

Mother stayed back to speak with Allison, who gave a digest of events since the hangar, including Father's murder and Genasia's betrayal. Whatever-the-Nanny-Father Genasia had created was brand new levels of demented, even for *this* family. Ronny listened in, a fact Allison may have punished by recounting *to his very mother in front of his very eyeballs* how Genasia had framed and humiliated her using Ronny's own illicitly taken AeroLens footage, which Genasia had illicitly copied. He felt freshly shamed by that colossal mistake, named among the villains, no less, and it was as plain as the purpling nose on his face that none of his goodwill to get Allison back her job had mattered one iota in the end.

Still. He had questions. What had happened to Allison's future tech earbud, the two-way brain mirror transmogrification device? But he asked the more pressing, "Where did you get those incredible pants?" A burning question, because that flamenco costume had once belonged to him. Packed for the cruise as a one-off joke to rile Father; discovered missing from his suitcases later.

She full-on ignored him. "Genasia installed a shock valve in V3's head that forces him to—"

"The tassels, seriously. So classy."

"Do you mind?" She flicked her eyes at him, keen to see his nose bugger off like a fat gnat.

"Just wondering if you and I have the same stylist."

She put it together. "Of course—it's *yours*. Let me guess: you also told your barbot to wear it as a disguise. Because it certainly worked."

"Argyle? He's *alive*?" Ronny couldn't believe it. "He actually used those Italian Cloak-and-dagger routines? They were supposed to activate if I fell into the hands of an enemy government. Which...I suppose I did!" He laughed delightedly. The world had tipped back to rights if he could shoot the shit with his drinking buddy, like a hard-nosed detective and his obnoxiously glib errand boy. Of course, Argyle was the errand boy in this metaphor.

Allison pressed her lips as something akin to sympathy, third cousin, twice removed, flashed across her face. "God, this is not your day. Argyle's dead. Shot by a taser dog half an hour ago."

Ronny choked. "Dead? But the Samurai bullet dodging techniques! They were ironclad!"

"Well, he burst into pieces. Robot self-immolation, if you will. I don't know what to say, but there was absolutely no salvaging him."

Hot tears gathered in the corners of Ronny's eyes; the rising pressure throbbed in his nose. Someone had to pay for all this pain. He muttered angrily, "How could this happen?"

Allison flared. "Don't pin it on me!"

"I'm not, but he started acting funny the morning you drugged me—"

"He acted funny before that!"

"He did, but you messed with the delicate balance of programs I installed with such care—"

"Ohhh..." A long moan from Mother broke up their squabble. She seemed pale, hands cupped over her heart. "Argyle declared himself to be a highly sophisticated drink blender at the end...did he not?"

Ronny had no clue what she was talking about, but Allison seemed shocked, asking, "How did you know that?"

Mother gestured weakly. "Because I programmed him to say it...right before he was to blow himself up."

Understanding dawned on Allison's face. "Let one drink blender blow—"

"You?" Ronny recoiled in anguish. Mother had hacked Argyle, too—had that sing-song *Happy Birthday* virus been a ticking time bomb? His lip quivered. "What kind of birthday gift is a blown-up friend?"

Mother started gushing. "Forgive me—it was twenty years ago! I was desperate and dying and more than a bit cynical at AeroX and its life-sized gadgets, and I'd just read Pinocchio and thought that the Disney version needed more *umph.* So I did it. There's no excuse for it. Hired a crack squad of Russian video game programmers to transform your bar friend into an exploding Jiminy Cricket. They were laid-off and probably over-engineered the thing—had a bit of fun at my expense. But the grand finale—the End Game, they called it—was supposed to trigger a melodramatic suicide only as a last resort. Something to make you laugh...because you can't be best buds with a silly machine *when your mother is on life support!*"

She was in tears. Ronny was reeling and a fresh wave of grief washed over him. He had just enough voice to choke out, "I'm sorry."

But his tears remained frozen, like in Mother's sitting room in Aklavik. A memory played like a skipping record of those days leading up to the cruise when the virus-afflicted Argyle had started conducting therapy sessions at the office bar, encouraging Ronny to buy that plane ticket to Canada. BFF or not, he'd not listened to Argyle. An obstinate cow, like Father.

He turned to Allison, craving resolution of any kind.

Strange that this *last resort* had triggered for her—also, in a way, comforting. "What was it like—the End Game? Tell me everything. I need to see it in detail."

She gave a heavy sigh. "Well, it was fucking lit..."

"No more—no more!" he cried. The genius had already summed it up better than he could imagine. Pulling his cantine of brandy from his coveralls, he raised it high over the planter. "You'll get yours, old buddy," and pouring out the contents, he watched the burnished shower dapple the light in low gravity. For Argyle. For Culebra. For *Ronny IV*.

"So," he said, "Genasia turned Nanny Bot into V3 Asshat Edition, who sent the dogs and murdered my friend-simulation. Do we murder him back with even bigger tasers? Please tell me there's a hole in his ass."

Allison hardened a frown. "He's not a monster to kill. That shock valve forces him to mimic the thoughts and actions of your father—"

"Who was, himself, a monster," Ronny pointed out. Knowing that Nanny Bot now looked like Father already gave the fantasy of payback a masterstroke of poetry. "I got it—I got it. Let's shoot him out of an airlock."

Allison retorted, "He's trying to help us! He set the hangar password so I would crack it. Look—no one's here to arrest us, and why is that? The AI is trying to break from Genasia's control! He wants us to rescue him!"

Ronny thrust his hands into his coverall pockets and surveyed the atrium. "If you ask me, it's too quiet." Despite the guards they'd posted, a creeping sense of exposure hung over the room. Snipers readying their shots.

Mother cautioned, "Our goal, ultimately, is to rally everyone on board to our side."

Allison agreed. "Like it or not, V3 runs the ship systems and has the people's trust. We need him to—"

"*Need* him?" Ronny burst. "You don't get it. That S.O.B. would murder the human race if it fit his business proposition. All we *need* is a crowbar and maybe three minutes to pry off his head and extract the admin passwords."

Allison clenched her jaw. "NO! He's *precious* to me."

A stunning admission.

She must've seen Ronny's scandalized face, because she shouldered him out again, addressing Mother, "There's an inner child in the robot that deserves a chance to show—"

"A robot with a heart of gold?" Ronny ranted at her back. "I've seen this plot a thousand times: knock out that shock rod, and he'll go Super Saiyan. V4! Flood the ship with a deadly neurotoxin!"

She spun at him. "My AI doesn't want to do ANY of those things! If people like YOU would stop screwing with his head, calling him Nanny or villain, he'd be a great leader—"

"Of the robot revolution!"

"Interrupt me again!" she screamed, snapping the needle-nosed pliers from her toolbelt and stomping toward Ronny. "Try it!"

Before his PTSD from Allison's previous drugging could fully present, Mother sent withered hands to grapple Allison and the pliers back. Then, with a deep, fed-up breath, she turned on Ronny. "Son. Go to time out!"

He twisted in horror. "Time out—?"

"Act like a child, be treated like a child," Mother clipped. "This isn't your boardroom where the loudest, most obnoxious voice wins. Frankly, I'm *appalled* at you." Her tone hit him like another paralyzing thunderclap, and as it did, she wrapped him in another of her fierce hugs and whispered in his ear. "You tell me she's the love of your life, and then you run her over like she's roadkill. Gracious sakes, child, *it's a nose.* Roll into the hurt, Son."

Roll *into it!?* Sure, he'd lost his wannabe best friend, his asshat father, and his facial dignity in a single crushing hour—them's the breaks. But the *fucking misery* of having no friends, no satisfying throwdown with Father, and not even a drop of esteem from Allison. Let Lizard Ronny lizard, slink away and find refuge in its old damp cracks. Except, there were no cracks, either! Nowhere to sulk and hide on this tiny ark.

His face seized up. Shit...now the waterworks were melting—the whole dam bursting. He kept his shoulders stiff as boards as he sulked out of the hug, hung head, and wept in public. His least favorite of all possible weeping.

At least Allison was looking askew.

Mother turned and addressed Allison. "Miss Gin, look at my Ronny."

Ronny chortled in protest.

"Excuse me?" Allison glared at Mother.

"Please," Mother insisted. "Look at him. If holding those pliers makes it easier, then be my guest."

But Allison wasn't capitulating. She was pissed. "*You don't know. What he's done.*"

Mother thumped a hand over her mechanical heart. "*Bless me, I don't.* And if you'd like to rail about it here, be my guest. In Aklavik, we clashed with the shells every day—railed and wept, every day. I swear, even the shells wept sometimes, because it didn't matter if you wore skin or technomancy, compassion brought out a human in everyone. You say Ronny ought not to bully your robot or call him a villain, but are you willing to give him the same courtesy?"

Mother God, let it rest.

Allison seethed and said nothing, but Ronny felt her burning eyes connect.

He knew this moment intimately from around the dinner table, even dreaded it—Mother wrangling Father, that mammoth bull, to apologize, and losing every time. God damn if it wasn't the reason he'd left her. But Ronny was not some kind of sociopath who needed coaching in the art of apologies, and he'd cross an ocean of self-annihilating tears if Allison would just relent.

"I'm sorry," he said, "for recording you."

She shook out a shiver.

Eh, sociopath he was not...but an idiot, yes. Maybe he did need coaching. His words felt utterly lame, like those niggling corporate apologies posted by the interns of recalcitrant CEOs. So Ronny spilled his guts. "*And* for interrupting you. *And* for getting you drunk. *And* pretending to be someone else at the bar. *And* wanting to murder your group project." He took a breath. They could be here all night. "But especially for recording you." He shuffled his feet. "Naked."

Mother smacked him hard upside the head.

A sea of red swelled on Allison's face, yet Ronny was surprised to find no anger in it. "Turns out," she muttered, "your eyes were perfect gentlemen. You couldn't even look at me. So, as Dad would say...no harm, no foul play."

Mother put two fingers to her forehead and groaned like a revving engine. "Lord, I really wanted grandkids, but I'll settle for buried hatchets. Now, how do we fix my evil ex-husband?"

34

What Can Possibly Go Wrong

Allison put on the fakest smile. Two could play this game of southern idioms. "Oh, *Ellen, sweet summer child-slash-wannabe grandmother, your little church therapy session changes nothing.*"

Sarcasm set her mind alight, but she'd not yet voiced a cutting comeback when the atrium lurched. Reacting fast, Allison braced herself against a kiosk and deftly caught the elder Ellen before she took a nasty tumble. With a glance at the vaulted ceiling, Allison imagined the stars turning as the spaceliner changed course. Away from Earth. Away from the food supply. Away from any abort strategy.

And where toward? An event horizon of starvation in ten days.

Not only were hatchets unburied—others were spinning off the proverbial walls, and unless they stopped this nonsense and commandeered the ship, a whole lot of people were going to lose their heads.

Elsewhere, Ronny was flailing in a planter, disentangling himself from a creeping vine. "I took one nip—just one! What was in that brandy?"

Allison craved her own cantine about now. "It's not just you, Ronny. We're *moving.*"

Ronny mumbled, "Ah, must've missed the PA announcement." He plucked a leaf from his hair as Allison waited impatiently for realization to dawn, *a day late and a wheelbarrow short*, "Wait, who's driving this thing?"

Never a sufficient number of wheelbarrows, that one. "I'll give you two guesses."

"Does Robo-Father count as one or two?"

The time for careful debate was over. Allison knew what needed to be done; she just needed the idiots on board to comply. "Listen—V3 controls the ship through a wireless connection to the server below decks. Let me hack the server and lockout V3. Then when we have command of the door locks and taser dogs, we can send a staff-wide message to lure V3 into a negotiation."

Hack the server. She scoffed at herself. She'd made it sound so easy.

"A staff-wide message?" Ronny gave her an incredulous stare. "Yes, let's all sit to tea and discuss our problems with the murderbot!" He affected a dainty English accent through his swollen nose. "*Oh, Robo-Father. Be a dear and dial back the wanton and gratuitous killing a bit. Mother was a Sunday School teacher, after all, and blood disagrees with her tummy.*"

Allison clenched her teeth. "I am not getting into this with you again!"

There had to be an OC valve implanted in Ronny's head, tuning his behavior to useless. Even his mother had that look of supreme annoyance, a ref on the verge of flagging another emasculating timeout. "My, my. Look at how well we are getting along now."

Ronny and Allison gave the former Sunday School teacher the same plastic cherubic smile.

A sound of screeching overtook the atrium. Not a van of drowning cats, as Allison had first likened it, but echoes of distraught children carried in the arms of their parents. The first Culebra search party had returned, and its expedition leader wore a viking's scowl and approached with an ax to grind.

Ronny coughed, "*Leatherface*," as if murder had come to find them.

"D'children are starving!" the woman told Ronny, de facto chief of guest services apparently. "No room service, no parental controls on d'TVs, and d'toilet's jammed on C-Deck. Smelled like a septic block, but dats just how everything smells in dis ship." She flicked a look at Allison, and Allison sought a moment apart to sniff her own collar and check for untoward odors.

Ronny was mustering a reply when Screwdriver Boy, whose relation to the aforementioned Leatherface became apparent in their scowls, thrust his overly familiar hands into Ronny's coverall pockets in search of snacks or what-not and withdrew the salmon-tinted Ray-Bans Ronny had worn earlier in the hangar. Livid, Ronny snatched the boy's wrist and gave him a mortifying stare.

The Scandinavian growled. "Hands off Little Jens."

Both Ronny and Screwdriver Boy relinquished their holds. Effective. Now Allison liked Leatherface, the woman and the term of endearment.

Ellen dismissed the newcomers with a curt, "Thank you, Astrid," then quietly intimated to Allison, "Maybe while you hack the server, the rest of us can storm the kitchens. Our chefs can turn a bad situation into a delicious soup of unification."

But could they make a lobster bisque out of thin air? Ronal and his brunch time board had already eaten their extra provisions, and not even their AI captain had thought to restock for the refugees before leaving Earth. They needed to turn the ship around. Now.

"I should go." Allison cinched her toolbelt.

Ellen asked, "Do you need help?"

A sensible question. Allison leapt atop the planter to survey the assembling crowd, trying to ignore the beginnings of a headache that thrummed in her temples. Various search parties trickled in from the elevators, herding more children. But the loud commotion was quieting down. Children were rubbing eyes and even sleeping in the weary arms of their caretakers.

She spotted the burly man from the hangar, who'd bested Johnny Lambert for helpfulness, and pointed. "Him."

"*Him?*" Ronny whined.

"Him. *You're* making soup, remember?"

"*Pfft.* You need someone who knows their way around the ship!"

Allison crossed her arms. "I know my way around the ship. *He's* tough."

Ronny's ego looked seven-levels defeated as Ellen called the brick-built Levi to join their circle of conspiracy. In the card game of genetics, Levi had cleaned house, and was gentle to boot.

"We're splitting up," Ellen told the group and braced for balance on Ronny's arm as she explained, "Levi, you're to protect Miss Gin as she hacks the server. The rest of us are going to storm the kitchens and turn around morale. Questions?"

No time for questions! Allison hopped down for the elevators, wondering only why the elder was leaning all her weight on Ronny.

Ellen released Ronny and sat on the edge of the planter. "Take it away, Terror of Toronto!" And Ronny hopped up where Allison had been to give the room a barrel-chested whoop. "Uncle Ronny wants to know...who's hungry!?"

The scattered crowd returned no cheer.

"Snacks! Come on, who wants snacks?" The try-hard

cheerleader was not winning anyone over.

Allison clutched the handrail, pulling herself along, and mentally rehearsed the plan. Hacking the server required her bootleg software tools, which were at her cabin workstation. She'd slip in, slip out, then get below decks to maintenance where their first real obstacle would be the locked server room door. But that was nothing the trailing Levi couldn't handle.

"Allison!" Ronny called after her. "Hold up!"

She spared a look over her shoulder, but did not slow down. Ronny was leaping through the crowds and managed to gather enough momentum to intercept her at the arch outside the elevators.

"Something's wrong," he said, winded. "The promise of food should've sent the children screaming like a bunch of kindergartners at a second recess."

"They're clearly tired," Allison replied. She checked her listing balance on the rail. "Now, stop—I need to focus."

"That's just it!" Ronny cried. "Murderbot's got the jump on us!"

She throttled the handrail instead of him. If they were doling out nicknames... "Give it a rest, Pinocchio!"

He stood, staring, panting like a fish. No zinger—even for Ronny, his mental lights seemed unusually dim.

She put both hands on the rail. Why *was* it so quiet? Haunted by the memory of Ronal's snoreless slumber, she listened for clues. If only her head wasn't—

The air vents weren't humming.

She gasped. "V3 cut the oxygen supply!"

Ronny clicked two finger guns at the ceiling. "Classic Father. Suck the air out from under you."

Classic, alright. That sounded just like something Dad would say.

Ronny had called V3's play—a wheelbarrow ahead, it

turned out. Allison rushed to the ladder chutes, conscious that every breath from here on out was precious. "Get everyone to Deck A!" she told Ronny, "I'll switch it back on when I hack the server, but V3's probably only rerouted the oxygen to the ballroom where the staff are gathered."

God, she hoped that's what V3 had *probably* done, because if she was wrong about her AI's heart of gold, they weren't going to survive even the next ten minutes.

35

Face Off

Ronny whirled back to the traffic jam in the atrium and spotted Mother slumped on the planter. He sprang back to her, yelling at everyone in his path, "To the elevators! Get to the top deck! Before we pass out!" He had no way of knowing how much air they had left, only that he felt lightheaded, and the savage Lilliputians he'd once hallucinated from that bottle of Pasion Azteca were back, poking toothpicks into his tear ducts as he threw an arm around Mother.

"I...don't know what's come over me," she panted.

He lifted her, a task made easier in diminished gravity, and shuffled her to the front of the queue. "We'll get you through this. You'll feel better in no time."

"That's...what your father said."

She hadn't the wherewithal to realize the damaging impact of her words, but Ronny kept striding for that elevator, grunting over his shame, "*Roll* into the hurt. *Roll* into the hurt." He would make it all up to Mother, later.

Leatherface, with a sleepy Little Jens hoisted upon one shoulder, was herding the first families onto the elevators. What awaited all of Mother's dear friends? Robo-Father and his crony crew: from one death trap to another.

Ronny delivered Mother to Leatherface. "See that she makes it up." Then rushing to that inhumanly small emergency chute he'd seen Allison and Levi dive down, he tucked in his legs and climbed inside. His feet were late to find footing on the ladder, leaving the rest of him weak with vertigo in the claustrophobic space, but he forced himself to go. Climb. He needed to hurry—beat the elevator to the top.

If this was a trap, he was going to spring it. First into the jaws.

The ladder chute regurgitated Ronny onto Deck A like a slimy noodle. He picked himself up off the carpeted foyer, staring at the triplicate doors to the Viewscape Grand Ballroom, closed but unguarded, beckoning a grand entrance by the former heir of the empire. He sucked in a breath. Maybe the air was richer, or maybe his jack-hammering heart was working overtime, but either way—didn't matter! He'd entered Father's office plenty of times in a delirious fog. If anything, he'd acclimated to it.

Keep telling yourself that, fuckwad.

Behind him, the elevator dinged and shook him from his hesitancy. The first of Mother's people were arriving from the atrium, and if Robo-Father thought that shutting off the O2 would suck the breath out of their coup, Ronny was going to show him how *long and hard* a fish out of water can thrash.

He slipped on his Ray-Bans. Shoving hands into his coverall pockets, he slammed the entrance door bar with the bottom of his boot. The door flung open—collided with the wall, a gunshot crack that put the Jack Nicholson in "*Here's Ronny!*"

The ballroom crowd turned from their tables to

stare. Those salmon-tinted sellouts looked every bit as frightened as the Aklavik refugees, and of course they did. They'd started a colony with the king of entrepreneurial rip-offs! Cowards, all, hoarding the oxygen, the food, and the power, in sycophantic orbit around the towering dais where stood the gleaming image of Father.

Ronny acted like he couldn't see the spotlights. "Where's my old man?"

It may have been the first time he'd ever gotten the jump on the old asshat. Robo-Father did a double-take and spoke in a hilariously hollow voice, "W—the fuck are you doing here?"

Ronny gave an appalled cry. "Please! *Language!* There are children in the lobby."

The onlooking assembly seemed flustered and unable to recognize Ronny as he strode into the ballroom like a drunk into his fifth bar of the night.

A single taser dog trotted the perimeter of the room, and noting Ronny's sudden arrival, leapt into action. "RUFF RUFF. BOW."

Ronny smirked and submitted to the ritual with all the theatricality he could muster.

"RUFF RUFF. SHAKE."

He pumped the robot's paw.

"RUFF RUFF. SPEAK."

"Ronal Cologne IV. May there never be a fifth."

A solitary chuckle rose from the assembly, one of his no-name celebrity accomplices from the early days of the cruise, when his nightly pranks had been the bane of everyone else's existence. Now frowns of recognition piqued every brow.

The dog delivered its verdict on the trust fund baby.

"GOOD BOY."

"Aw, you're the good boy!" He tickled the back of the

robot's camera where he imagined its ears might be. He'd taken a risk letting the dog photograph him, but he had good faith that Argyle—God rest his robotic soul—had followed through with his Serbian hacking protocol and, around the time of the cruise, installed a root exception for Ronny in the taser dog firmware package.

Robo-Father stood slack-jawed at the deception.

As the dog turned to trot away, Ronny plunged the tip of a mechanical pencil in the dog's rear end. Immediately, the taser dog tucked tail and folded to sleep. It was as satisfying as he'd hoped it would be.

He turned and mugged for the crowd like he'd finished a bit of street magic.

Robo-Father came alive and pointed his finger. "Culebra!" He'd finally figured out Ronny's scheme to get on board—the pitch perfect name that Father had fallen for.

And on cue, the ballroom doors opened and in streamed the liberated men from the hangar: fathers, husbands, sons...pissed.

A cry of panic brought the staff to their feet. The elderly shareholders clutched at their jackets and ties, knowing what nobody had bothered to tell the rest of the staff, that these hearty Canadian townies had attempted a coup this morning and were back to finish the job.

"You're outnumbered, Chump!" Ronny shouted at the dais. "Now switch on the oxygen before someone gets hurt."

Face twisting in mock affront, Robo-Father commanded his staff. "Arrest these lunatics! They're the ones trying to steal your air!"

A man of military rank rallied the defense with a roar, "Nobody does this to General Dak Bautin!"

The people of Aklavik fell into formation, blocking the exits.

Ronny staggered, still lightheaded. He threw a glance toward the air vents and didn't hear a hum. Could it be the AI was starving all the ship of oxygen, eliminating the complication of humanity from his dastardly schemes? If so, an all-out brawl would play right into the AI's hand—the factions would fight each other until everyone passed out.

He just needed to buy time until Allison could restart the oxygen.

"Everyone stay calm!" he shouted at both sides of the room. "Do you feel woozy? Anybody? I do, and I haven't had a drop to drink—*two* drops to drink since, like, an hour ago. Why, oh why aren't the air vents working? Let's all just think for one second! Who's the only one in this room *who can't breathe?*"

All eyes shifted back on the indomitable AI.

Robo-Father sauntered to the gold railing and leaned on his elbows, tittering at a private joke. "I'm not the only one who can't breathe. Would you get a load of this guy?" With the Cologne Sleazy Up-nod, the robot insinuated that everyone ought to turn and look back at Ronny. He didn't say the punchline out loud.

Audible gasps broke the lull.

Ronny felt the blood in his ears, slow to get why his razor-sharp refutation had failed to turn the room against the murderbot. The thinning air made it impossible to focus. He tried for a deep breath.

A squeaky wheeze passed through his swollen nose.

Robo-Father smirked. "Trouble with your sniffer?"

His face. Nanny Murderbot was taking this critical moment to mock his fucking face! How very...*Father* of him.

A guffaw escaped General Dak Bautin, who joined the dissent against Ronny. They were laughing awfully hard for a room full of people being deprived of oxygen... because they *were* deprived of oxygen. For crying out loud—razor-sharp refutations were not going to work here.

"Pathetic," the general chortled. "Everyone in this room knows the lengths you go to undermine Mr. Cologne. *You* would asphyxiate everyone, just to take your petty revenge!"

Murmurs spread among the staff. "That son of a bitch—Drunk, too, look at him—Must be in league with Miss Geen!"

Pathetic? Petty? He'd show them petty.

"Tell me again how you died, Father—tripped on your Montblanc?" Ronny swaggered closer to the salmon-colored scene opposite his Ray-Bans, careful now to take any and all necessary deep breaths through his mouth. The staff clustered in front of the dais, poised to grab him the moment he entered the radius of the occupied tables, so he stayed only just out of range, arms wide, taunting a physical confrontation. "No wonder you stay up on that dais. You've seen what I can do with a pencil."

He jabbed the air at the flinching staff.

General Dak Bautin lunged to grab him, but Ronny dodged with a nimble leap onto the platinum executives table. Skirting across the assorted tabletops, scattering silverware and glasses, he steered clear of the staff while studying the subtle change in Robo-Father's brows. *The pinch.* He'd seen it a hundred times—in board meetings, office Christmas parties, the elementary school parking lot, and that lobster-tail incident at homecoming. A little public humiliation always pushed Father over the brink.

Ronny was one zinger away from exposing the true villain.

"A toast!" He scooped up a mostly empty bottle of

champagne and raised it to the robot. "To nibs. *Tiny little pricks like me.* They're scarier than they look, folks."

From a great distance, across the white-hot sea of Ronny's rage, Mother's voice called out a warning or whatever. He paid it no mind, for drinks needed toasting, and Oscars were well overdue for his awesome character development. Despite ridicule, lack of oxygen, and nearly blacking out, he'd remembered exactly what he wanted to say to Father—*and said it.*

Spielberg would be proud. He took a swig of flat champagne.

Robo-Father seethed at the rail. "You like nibs, shithead? I'll pick you a good one—I got thousands."

"Haha! Ahahahaha!" Ronny cupped an ear. "Sorry, can't hear you. Everyone's still laughing about the tiny nib that did you in."

"It was a Montblanc Sun-Tzu Art of War, Limited Edition—"

"Hahaha ha aha!"

"Anyone can see the symbolism—"

"Ahahahaha!" Robo-Father's tinny tone was swallowed whole by Ronny's biological barrel-chest. The reversal felt amazing.

Fed up, the robot squeezed, twisted, and rent apart the railing. "Wanna piece of me?" With a strange chirping sound, he leapt through the gap. The show of raw strength put both staff and refugees on the back foot, for there wasn't a man among them who could match the power of a robot's hydraulic pistons, and the AI knew that.

Landing on a table across from Ronny, Robo-Father put his steel dukes up.

The staff whipped into a foment of offense, springing behind their champion in a wide cluster.

Robo-Father taunted, "Let's see whose tip is sharper."

A duel. Just enough violence to see Allison through her mission. Ronny, twirling the mechanical pencil behind his own ass in mock threat, merely hoped she was close.

36

The Tool

Allison plunged down the chute and onto Deck E, conscious how far she'd outpaced Levi who was taking the time to climb down the rungs. No matter. She threw herself toward the utility closet where they kept spare oxygen tanks and respirators. A bout of lightheadedness sent her tripping. The missing air was so much worse down here that, reaching for the closet door, her hand felt strange and detached. Was this how V3 felt—his sentient neural paste, starved for meaning, reaching to interact in a world of inexplicable shocks and salves?

Levi called from the chute. "Hold! Where are you?"

"Here!" She tore into the closet and fumed at the obstructing disarray. Staff had thrown their cables, mops, and appliances haphazardly on the floor instead of winding and hanging them. She shoved the mess aside and shimmied to the oxygen tanks in the back. There were six tank stands, but only two tanks present. The staff had left the other four God-knew-where.

Grabbing a tank, she loosened the valve and fit the respirator around her nose and mouth. With the hiss of air in the hose, she took a slow, orienting breath. Her panic subsided. These two tanks would buy her and Levi time, but not those upstairs.

Levi had arrived, huffing for breath. Allison passed

him a tank and respirator and engaged the flow. Swinging her tank and wearing it like a backpack, she pointed to the hall behind him. "Server room's down there, by the labs. The door'll be locked—we'll have to force our way in." She kicked the mess at her feet and found a miniature crowbar, half the usual size. Not the steel rod she'd hoped for, but in the right hands...

She gave it to Levi with an adrenaline-fueled smile. "Let's see what those muscles can do."

Levi cocked an eyebrow and Allison heard herself.

"I didn't mean it like that!" She sputtered, making it so much worse. She felt the heat in her cheeks and hoped to pass off her silly smile with a stretch of her jaw.

"You ready?" he asked, leaning in the door frame like another obstruction.

She'd have been ten paces down the hall already. "Let me lead." She pushed him out of the way.

These intestinal halls. The metaphor continued to harass her as she leapt past a squalor of abandoned tools and trash bags, but the compressed oxygen enlivened her mind. She'd forgotten how sweet fresh air used to taste, and she could almost smell the fragrant rose-tips awaiting them on the colony world to come. Soon.

Allison arrived at the server room door and jiggled the handle. Locked, as expected. Entry was keyed to a wall panel beside the door, but there was no numerical override pin. She tried her Company fob—no luck. She narrowed her focus on the vulnerable gaps in the door frame. Another ill-hung door.

"Bust it open." She made space for Levi.

He rattled the handle himself and got a sense of the door's weight. Gingerly, he inserted the slender end of the crowbar into the seam between door and frame and pulled back, slowly increasing the pressure.

She stole a curious look at his face. Here was a gentle man acquainted with the work of raising children, and she, a newly conceived mother of AI, had questions about nurture that might coax V3 back to her side. Now was as good a time as any to air her thoughts.

"Those girls I saw in the hangar this morning—yours?"

"Yeah."

"How they holding up?"

"Steady as shore breakers. When the hangar shut us in, they set a'boot helping the elders with stitching... cleaning...sharing bits of food we brought aboard. My youngest, sweetest thing, read aloud her bedtime books to the convalescing."

Allison had read aloud the DSM-VI to her AI in its elementary stage. A warm memory. "How did you teach her to be so caring?"

"I suppose I've her mother to thank. She'd've been real proud."

"Her mother's...not here?" No rings on his fingers...

He hummed, tweaking the angle of insertion as a watchmaker might with tiny tools. "Died last winter."

Allison, gut in knots, had barreled into this sensitive topic. All of her interactions with Levi seemed now graced with a heightened significance. Here they were, both single parents learning to love the next generation. That made him a colleague. A collaborator. A partner for a passion project.

She was suddenly hyper aware of the muscles.

He was too engrossed in the door to see her blush.

The plastic facade of the door buckled, and Levi scooted the crowbar further into the gap. He applied pressure, gently building strength. Allison lost the nerve to ask another question and merely watched as he adjusted the angle of the small crowbar, back and forth.

Back and forth.

Back and forth.

She checked the gap at the top of the door. It hung no more askew than before, and the latch they'd come to break held strong. "Levi," she said between respirator breaths, "do you think you could, maybe, pick up the pace a little?"

He burst angrily, "I've barely any leverage!" His stress crashed like a wave, which he sucked back in with a mild, accented, "*Sorey.*" He stalled, leaning to examine the cracked door like a carpenter starting over on a table sanding.

Levi had a lid over his feelings, too. God, they had a lot in common.

Her thoughts whirled up the ladder chutes where the others, including Levi's own children, were scrambling for high ground. "Hey, let it out," Allison told him. "Your anger, I mean. Can't hurt anything."

He *tsked.* "How d'you expect my anger to break down this door, exactly?"

"Uh, I feel like a little brute force would go a long way here. Show the door who's boss."

Shifting the crowbar, he started again, pulling back the miniature fulcrum until they heard the plastic facade snap. A large piece now wedged in the latch, and in the effort to dig it out, he cut a finger on a sharp corner.

"*Serendipity!*" He rammed the door with his fist and shook out his injured finger. He fell back to wriggling the crowbar.

Allison squeezed her own fists at the lapsing seconds and remembered how Dad had never raised his voice. Perhaps the work of raising children required herculean restraint—a commitment never to get mad, even at a shoddy door. Oh, God. She'd have to accept V3 both for who he was and for who he was becoming, even if that meant loving what remnants of Ronal Cologne III endured after they dislodged the OC valve.

"That's it," said Levi, gently shifting his tool and clenching his teeth. "Finesse."

Nothing was happening—nothing Allison could observe.

Mom came alive in her writhing fingers. She couldn't believe they'd come all this way to coax open a door while Ronal's resurrected brain choked the life out of everyone. Some situations called for explosive force, and this was one of them.

Allison blurted, "This isn't doing it for me. Give it here." She reached to seize the crowbar and tutor Levi in the art of blowing a gasket.

He warded her back. The sweat on his brow showed just how much effort he'd turned against himself. "Miss Gin, I don't want to injure you."

"Good God, Levi, you couldn't injure tissue paper!" She wrenched Levi back, shouldered in, and took the crowbar in both hands. Quickly and violently, she jammed the tool every possible way in the latch. The plastic warped and mangled; the frame splintered and popped. She shrieked with exertion, hating the stubbornness of plastic, the unacceptable delay, her violent genetic temperament, and the *damn idiot* door, which proved implacable.

She slammed the miniature crowbar to the vinyl floor. It bounced up in half-gravity and painfully collided with Allison's chin as she swung, and failed, to swat it away.

Levi stared at the exposed mechanism of the latch and grunted at how little her temper tantrum had accomplished. "Don't see a way we can get through without completely cutting out the lock."

"Then start cutting!" she yelled.

The lid was off; Mom was on the rampage. She dug into her toolbelt for a hammer and gave the lock a terrific slam before shoving it to Levi. For herself, she selected the screwdriver and started to disassemble the wall panel. She made a private bet that she could hotwire the entire security system faster than Levi could bring himself to utter another, "Sorey."

She only hoped they weren't in a hurry upstairs.

37

Manhandled

Ronny leapt off the ballroom table for a wide expanse of floorspace. He'd gotten his wish: fisticuffs with Nanny Murderbot and a chance at nose-for-nose retribution. But as Robo-Father advanced with frightening speed and Ronny backpedaled, uselessly gyrating his naked fists, he reckoned that landing a punch was as unlikely to dent his metal adversary as it was liable to brutally fracture his hand.

He signaled his Racketballer reinforcements to wait in the wings. No need to imperil them just yet.

The jeering AeroX crowd hemmed Ronny in, cutting off escape from the duel.

He taunted Father's graven image, "Oh, you've wanted this. How long have you been waiting to pummel me? Since I was in diapers?"

He feigned a strike to test the robot's reactions.

Robo-Father didn't flinch. He threw a left hook that could have taken off Ronny's head.

But Ronny sprang back, narrowly avoiding the swing. He staggered for balance, for breath, as cold sweat beaded his skin. This was no Argyle-style chatbot who was ninety-percent banter and bullshit. The AI had Father's menacing eyes, and each step was a chess move, intent to corner, then crush.

The tilted Viewscape window offered Ronny a slope to run up, which he did to the vocal outrage of the crowd. Despite their protests, he wasn't possibly heavy enough to harm the window—but Robo-Father was, and so the maneuver was bound to buy time. The angled glass, stiff and slick with frozen condensation, sent his feet slipping from under him, yet he grabbed hold of the oriental curtain blinds that bunched at the apex, lest he slide down into Robo-Father's twitching fists.

Cold stars spun below his dangling legs; a stinging chill crept up his sweaty socks. Ronny shivered. Static encroached upon his vision as he drew near again to passing out, but redoubling his grip, he lolled out his tongue for the crowd like a skater smashing records for the most batshit hangtime.

Robo-Father paced the floor. "Get back here," he growled, "take it like a man."

"Take what exactly?" Ronny inclined an ear from his perch.

The robot gave a running start—stomped up the glass with a fist cocked. The crowd screamed.

Ronny cursed and fell on his frigid ass as the punch breezed his hair and shattered a light fixture on the wall. Sliding down, he tumbled onto the carpet and back to the balls of his feet, still a step ahead of the reckless robot. What was the AI doing? It almost killed everyone!

The crowd sneered as Ronny flailed by. "Take it, you bastard—He nearly killed us—Knock him out cold, Ronal!" Gawkers and Yes Men, born and bred on Father's checks, showed a stiff exterior of outrage, but didn't dare to join the daily scheduled drama, lest they too end up in the line of fire.

Ronny lunged for the mahogany sidewall, friendless and barely able to catch a breath. Merely stalling the inevitable at this point. Where was Allison and what would she say now about her incorruptible AI? Spreading arms to the heavyweight who'd come back to the ring, Ronny kept taunting, "Bring it, Tin Man."

Robo-Father raised clawing fingers like a sumo wrestler. "Lemme give you a hug."

"And a *kiss*." Ronny tapped his cheek. "You *never* give me affection, and I'm *starving* for it!"

If it were possible to lace a sentence with a lethal dose of sarcasm, Ronny had apparently come close. A pop and fizzle—the shock rod that extruded from the robot's neck flashed and left the AI wincing with pain. What had triggered it? Not the sarcasm—he'd been hurling sarcastic insults the entire time!

Ronny grasped for more words, riffing off the theme. "Wow, I've *missed* time with you. So quality...*many* attention...*very* bonding!"

Lame, sure, but another spark lit up the robot's neck, a horrendous snap that curled Ronny's toes with a memory of static shock pain. And that smell—burnt plastic.

Ronny kept at it. "I can't wait for our *next* date. Fishing! Pickleball! *Math homework!*" None of which he'd ever done with Father.

The robot jerked backward with another searing pop. This line of absent-father mockery had a remarkable effect, but it hadn't stopped the titan, who'd pinned down Ronny's position at the sidewall. Ronny felt his knees quail as the robot moved into striking range. He slipped his Ray-Bans inside the coveralls. Yeah, he stood to lose a mouthful of teeth, but there was no sense wrecking a pair of overpriced indoor sunglasses.

Robo-Father bellowed, "Yer a big bloomin' bully!" The AI had completely switched voices, now simulating the sound of its John Wayne predecessor, V2, drawling like a hacksaw on a steel-stringed banjo. "Ya scare'em, Ronny—sure do. Can't count the times he jot down 'Bond with Ron' in his daytimer, only t'tear it up cuz he felt scare't—"

The shocker punished the AI for this reveal with a sizzling crackle.

"Dog shit!" Ronny spat at Father's image, staring him in the face. "That man's family was for publicity shots. He hung a katana behind his home office desk! Don't you dare say that controlling freak had a soft spot!" Glancing either which way for an escape, he found the open portal to the boardroom, only a leap to his right.

Robo-Father cackled, pulling back a gleaming fist. Nanny Bot's voice snuck in. "Just a soft spot fer you—"

An ear-splitting shock.

Seizing the moment, Ronny threw up his forearms up to protect his delicate nose and lunged away.

Father's metal fist crushed his shoulder. In the soft spot.

Ronny ricocheted off the wall and fell belly up on the carpet. A split-second later, Robo-Father seized his coveralls. Hoisted up, he felt a rush of wind as the merciless AI slung him headlong across the room.

The crowd parted; the robot's aim was immaculate. Ronny careened into the buffet line—smashed nose first through a spread of lobster leftovers. It simply wasn't fair. He toppled off the far end of the table, vaguely aware of scattering people and villains cheering, "Get 'em, Ronal—Send 'em through the bar next—Payback for those midnight fire alarms!"

In his swirling vision, Ronny saw Mother reaching shaky hands for his face, but others were at her back, pulling her from the fray. What was his grand strategy again—get everyone killed? There was no defeating Father, only a question of how many he'd trample in his path.

Stamping steel feet landed beside his head. God, there were toes on this forsaken thing. Ten articulated toes.

With a quick pivot, Ronny tucked and rolled beneath the table legs. Robo-Father stalked the buffet line while Ronny played the department store child in the clothing racks, scurrying opposite wherever the toes fell.

Hands shot beneath the lip of the table and flipped it skyward. The villains shrieked as chunks of food flew in the direction of the jeering crowd. Ronny was completely exposed.

Robo-Father reached for the stranglehold.

Roll into the hurt!

Ronny rolled beneath its arms and slipped through its legs.

Grabbing the outer handrail, Ronny skirted the room in a terror of where to go. The boardroom! He knew, once inside, there was no way out, but he could think of nowhere else to flee. His life, in a nutshell.

He staggered, momentarily blacking out. The robot had already twisted to intercept him.

Ronny dove off the wall in direct line for the boardroom and, falling short on his belly, scurried on all fours like a manic toddler, barely an arm ahead of the invincible parent. But as he thrust his head into the boardroom portal, an unexpected fright jerked him back: the headless body of Nanny Bot.

In that quarter second, an iron grip seized his ankle.

Ronny tossed his arms around Nanny Bot and clutched tight the rose-gold torso for ballast as Robo-Father dragged his sorry ass backward and into the air. A reek of gooey cheese smeared his face. Ronny swung upside-down, a fish before the gutting, and in a last, desperate pitch, hurled the shell of Nanny Bot at Robo-Father's legs.

Too light a battering ram to bowl over the sturdy robot. But a surprise.

The grip on Ronny's ankle loosened, enough for him to wriggle free and drop to the floor. Whatever vodka bottle of adrenaline had kept Ronny fighting was now fully licked. He bobbled on his back, utterly sapped, each gasping breath a flinching prayer that Robo-Father would relent.

The breath knocked out of him as a heavy metal chest pinned him to the floor.

Two arms wrapped him in a bear hug.

Father's head bent close and crushed his ear.

Tears streamed from Ronny's eyes. He was three years old again, wrestling Father on the playmat at home—an awful memory, a mix of intimacy and terror that had echoed through the years. A parent's coveted nearness. Father's indomitable strength.

The voice of V2 spoke comfort in his ear. "I won't—let him—get ya!" Constant static shocks punctuated the drawl. "Yer safe—with me!"

Ronny didn't feel safe; his ribs were cracking. But he had a hand on the shock rod in the robot's neck. Embedded deep, its heat singed his palm as he tried to tear it out.

The AI still whispered, "Deep down—he's beggin' me—to save ya." No jolt of electricity could jerk the straddling robot from his constricting hold around Ronny's chest.

The shock rod wouldn't budge.

Lights were dimming. Ronny rasped, "Can't...breathe..."

"*Neither can I!*" The robot's voice became a cloying therapist, the original V1, pontificating on the psychology of life and death. "*Death comes—for all of us! Ronal buried you—six feet under his ego! But in the limp and the twitch—there lies the terror of love!*" Now the insane thing was chirping, sniffing the cheese on Ronny's face. "Not *fair!*

Not *fair!*"

The AI had stared into the abyss of Father's brain and gone utterly mental—split personalities and a nuclear-scale existential meltdown. Ronny bore down on the shock rod with his last breath, strength too little to dislodge it. So he did the last and most natural thing.

Headbutted Father's steel cranium. Hard.

38

No Time, No Space

Allison had hardly unscrewed the electrical panel that connected to the server door when behind her came the click of a drawn latch. The door across from the server room flung open, revealing a lanky man in a lab coat. He glowered in the threshold, a respirator on his face and an oxygen tank in his hands, wielded like a club.

Allison ducked beside Levi, expecting him to raise the hammer against the new threat, but the great wall of muscle just stood there and greeted the man with a Canadian, "Eh?"

"Keep it down!" the stranger seethed. "We're trying to work in here."

"*Work?*" Allison matched the lab man's anger. "How can you possibly work with everything going on?"

The lab man very much agreed. "Exactly. *Stop banging the walls.*"

She glanced behind the man and into his workroom. Two others, Cambridge scientists by the logos and attire, sat at workstations, respirators cinched and eyes never leaving their large screens overrun with data spreadsheets. Here were three of the missing oxygen tanks from the utility closet.

Without looking up, one of them yelled, "We didn't order any dancers!"

"Get out of here," she stomped a Flamenco-tasseled foot at the group. "People upstairs need oxygen!"

"*Obviously*," said their irate leader at the door. "What do you think we've been doing this whole ill-begotten cruise if not solving that very challenge?"

Allison couldn't grasp how tabbing through spreadsheets would restart the oxygen flow. Who were these posers in lab coats? She barged past the lab rat to get a closer look at their screens. The man smelled like clam chowder.

"That is *proprietary information!*" he bellowed, yet did not dare touch her with the Canadian Hulk standing in the doorway. Neither did the two who'd bolted up from their desks to block her view of the large monitors.

But she'd already seen enough. The underdesk towers were whining hot as the computers crunched numbers—not cracking passwords, but data mining, the rote mathematical research demanded of unpaid academic interns. And by the look of their improvised sleeping arrangements, the trash receptacle stuffed to overflowing, and stacks of dehydrated clam chowder bowls, they hadn't showered in a month.

She lambasted the scientist. "Listen, Chowderhead!" A nickname truly deserved. "Have you even stopped working *once* since the cruise?"

He put his hands on his hips, indignant. "What do you mean, *since* the cruise?"

These nitwits had lost all sense of time and space, slaving down here for six weeks straight, completely missing disembarkation and multiple apocalypses.

"*Damn idiots!*" She shoved him to the door. "Earth is wrecked, an AI is trying to kill us, and you're down here *sucking up the remaining oxygen!*"

He reared in fright. "Earth is wrecked? Wait! We need

to back up our research!"

"No, you need to run!" Allison yanked the oxygen reins of the remaining two interns who, even with the specter of a rogue AI, kept horsing around on their workstations.

Levi barreled into the room. "You heard the lady. Haul out!"

Now they obeyed. Because the man, Levi, was dressed like an executive. A great Canadian Hulk executive. She hated everybody.

Allison chased them into the hall and ordered the lesser two assistants to get immediately to Deck A and share their oxygen supply with the others. "Not you," she jammed a grumpy finger at Chowderhead. "You're going to tell us what the hell is going on."

"W—we're just running planetary habitability tests. Mr. Cologne offered us a job—a real job, with a real paycheck!"

A job with the colonial division. There was nothing more myopic than a dollar sign. "And I suppose," she said, "you would have kept working until the heat death of the universe!"

He scoffed. "Don't be silly. We'd have quit once we paid back our loans."

She crossed her arms. "And what was it about the *rapidly failing oxygen supply* that made you think, 'It's the debt collectors I should be worried about'?"

He puffed with pride. "We weren't worried. We sold our dataset to Mrs. Cologne, transferred it to her about fifteen minutes ago. Naturally, we were just finishing up and would have left when the oxygen tanks ran out..." He faded to mumbles. The poor man finally seemed to grasp that when the oxygen tanks ran out, he'd have been rapidly transported to a place where neither loan nor paycheck could follow.

Allison narrowed in on Genasia's involvement. Fifteen

minutes ago the spaceliner had left Earth. "What did *she* want with your data?"

"S—she said it was for a honeymoon? Honestly, I don't know."

A dataset on habitability... Had Genasia steered them toward a paradise world?

Time was short. Allison returned to the unyielding server door and readied her screwdriver. "Remember what I said about the killer AI? If we don't get into the server room and fix the oxygen—"

Chowderhead fished a fob out of his pocket and waved it over the wall panel. The deadbolt to the server room withdrew.

Allison started in surprise. "How do *you* have access?" Her thoughts ran down a rabbit hole of speculation: had V2 granted these chowderheads special permission so as to help Mama breach the server and defeat the V3-part of his neural paste?

The intern coughed. "I...may have swiped Dr. Paraclese's fob."

Good, old-fashioned thievery, for the win. Allison pushed on the unlocked handle, but the plastic facade caught on the frame, a result of her hasty crowbar work. Before Levi could say anything, she threw her shoulder into the door and rammed it ajar.

Finally, they were in.

Another spatial disaster. Electronic cables and dusty towers filled the floors and shelves of the server room like the splattered guts of a computer. Lunging over snaking cords, Allison rushed for the head terminal that coordinated the computer systems across *The Cologne*. She sat down at the login screen, now worried she'd come all this way in vain, for her hacking kit sat on a thumbdrive in her cabin. In their mad haste to get here, she hadn't had time to retrieve it.

The controls to the air supply remained locked behind a superadmin password—just out of reach.

She wasn't helpless, though. A few keystrokes gave her limited access, where she queried a diagnostic report of the spaceliner's life support systems. All four oxygen generators were off, vents disabled on Decks A-E. She gasped, late to realize what those upstairs would have learned straightaway, that V3 wasn't just asphyxiating Culebra. He was killing every human aboard!

Those two spare oxygen tanks the interns were bringing wouldn't hardly be enough.

She checked the time. Levi and Chowderhead hung over her either shoulder, expecting to see some magic trick of typing that would solve their every problem. Allison reached under the desk and disconnected the ethernet cable.

"That's it. V3's locked out."

Levi marveled. "You're a genius."

Yeah, she'd heard that one before. She shooed her companions back toward the exit. "We'll have to restart the oxygen the old-fashioned way. Manually."

39

The Devil You Know

Ronny came to.

There was a respirator over his nose and mouth, reviving him. But no sooner had he felt his faculties return, but someone took the sweet oxygen away. He blindly groped for it back. His left shoulder hurt something fierce.

A therapeutic nasal voice exclaimed, "He's pulled through!"

At the sound, his eyes snapped open and saw the face of Father leaning over him. Shiny and smiling.

Diablo.

This must be the afterlife; his hellish migraine confirmed it. Ronny whimpered.

Another voice said, "Gracious, you scared us."

Wait—that was Mother, and if she was nearby, then he needn't worry just yet about a lake of fire and burning torment and Lilliputian demons with pitchforks. But he was definitely worried about Father's apparent mouthful of tungsten teeth.

What strange purgatory had he awakened to, and how many fingers was Mother holding up...?

The same Robo-Father, who was nigh to twelve seconds ago trying to rip his head off, sent a gentle hand behind Ronny's neck and helped him sit up. The ballroom floor was a littered sea of people, staff and refugees in states of recline on the floor. The oxygen vents were still off, but folks were conserving their breath while two spry-looking lab guys made circuits with a pair of emergency oxygen tanks and respirators.

Not everyone was conserving their energy. Three miscreant boys had found the disabled taser dog and played an ill-advised game of catch, lifting and throwing the machine across the crowded floor.

No sign of Allison.

Someone pressed an icy cold towel to Ronny's forehead, sending stabs of pain shooting through his brain. "Ow—owowow!" The world blanked out a second, then he sent morbidly curious fingers to probe the fat, swelling nodule that jutted from his forehead.

Another lump to go with his nose. Fantastic.

Mother cooed, "That's it. Stay upright." She was right beside him, dabbing his head with the cloth. "It's a concussion, certainly. You've been out for five minutes."

Five whole minutes—six hours more, and it would have qualified as a coma! Ronny plumbed his recent battle with Robo-Father for any litigable memory gaps. There was the shoulder slug...the tuck and roll...the final pin... "What did he do to me, Mother?"

"Hmm. They said you knuckle heads fought until you both knocked heads. I didn't see it, but when the commotion died down, I pushed through and got Ron to stop smothering you. Then he tried to fix the oxygen, but couldn't reach the server."

"Slo—slow down." Ronny squinted through his pounding head, unable to make sense of the timeline—and even less sense of Mother using her old familiar name, Ron, for Robo-Father. She seemed inappropriately calm in the murderbot's presence.

Ronny glanced warily at the robot, who knelt by like a

worried dad after a soccer collision.

Robo-Father gave a sly smile. "Tiger."

"Do *not* call me that."

"Sure thing, Sport." The robot tapped his metal cranium. "You knocked my rocks to next Tuesday, that's what you did. Broke the shocker in my clocker."

Ronny began to hyperventilate. Pet names and dad rhymes, in the voice of that original Mentat AI of two years ago—what else could this mean but that he'd woken to an afterlife worse than hell: a *sitcom* where folks posted signs about tearable puns and the freaky metal parents never stopped smiling?

Mother rubbed his back until the panic subsided. "Remember what Allison said about the shock valve?" she asked him. "It was programmed to punish the robot whenever it defied the inclination of Ron's old brain. Well, you exposed a contradiction—a way in which Ron's old brain defied itself, and this sent the shock rod into a catastrophic feedback loop until it burnt itself out. Am I getting this right?"

The psychoanalyst AI nodded. "Think of it as self-sabotage."

Mother warmly added, "Ron wanted to *murder* you, but he also wanted to *protect* you—so much so, he almost murdered you *while* protecting you. I had to pry him off!"

Ronny deadpanned, "I never knew I could feel so loved."

But the explanation was such bullshit, and he couldn't help but burst angrily at them both. "You trying to tell me that, deep down, under all that vile narcissism and betrayal, the bastard actually *liked* me? That's some Willie Loman demented shit."

Mother looked unsure, glancing at Robo-Father for a tell.

The robot shrugged. "That's how I interpret the neural

scans. But more importantly, that's the me I chose to be."

Ronny collapsed upon the floor. Still the AI tried to kill him, one cliché at a time.

"And I'd've done more," Robo-Father added, "but my connection to the server is broke as a joke. Still, glad you pulled through, Champ."

Good God. He'd never stop.

Ronny winced as he tried to sit back up. "I don't get it. Allison was going to bring the oxygen back when she hacked the server. If she locked you out, why are we still on respirators?"

Mother was about to say something when a young boy raced between them and, dodging the inert body of the taser dog thrown by another child, barged full force into Robo-Father, ramming the robot over.

The AI shouted in the former voice of Ronal Cologne III. *"Listen here, you little shit...!"*

"Ron!" Mother scolded him.

Ronny scrambled away from the murder machine, but the offending boy seemed unperturbed, slipping a mechanical pencil from his pocket and tilting a glance at the foul-mouthed robot's back end.

No sooner had the scene escalated, but Robo-Father regained his composure in the meek and self-effacing voice of V1. "Boy, I owe you an apology..."

The boy had already run back to his game.

Ronny gave Robo-Father a twitching stare. Yes, Father was dead, but the worst and slightly less worst parts of him lived on in this AI. The shock rod had left a permanent mark on its pasty brain personality. Ronny gave Mother a deliberate look, an eyebrow cocked in a gesture meant to broach the possibility of disposing Robo-Father in an industrial garbage compressor, thereby ridding the family of its titanium narcissist once and for all.

But Mother shook her head and gave Robo-Father an elderly pat on the cheek. "We forgive you."

Ronny snorted.

The AI, almost child-like in its contrition, threw its voice to extremes. "I don't wanna kill anybody. I mean, I *do*—but I *don't*."

Ronny fiercely pointed to his swelling head. "But y'almost *did!*"

Mother raised a finger. "And yet, he *didn't*."

Why in the bloody universe was she defending him? "He turned off the oxygen, *Mother!*" Ronny shouted, very aware how he was using the last of it to bring the perpetrator to rights. "We are almost brain vegetables because of him!"

Robo-Father nodded, conceding, "A calculated risk..."

Mother insisted, "So we take away Ron's server privileges, and we sing him *Happy Birthday* when the time comes. That's how love works."

Ronny squeezed out an overlong sigh, knowing if he said any more, he was liable to condemn the very ground on which Mother loved and accepted him. But he didn't trust Robo-Father—not one synapse in those soup-for-brains, and especially not the part that claimed Father *liked* him. When was Allison going to get back and render a verdict on whether his so-called inner child ought to be euthanized?

"Hey..." Ronny doubled back over something the AI had said. "What did you mean by calculated risk?"

Robo-Father tented his fingers like a lecturer at the start of class. "When I shut off the oxygen, I wasn't trying to kill you. I figured the ship had fifteen minutes of breathable air, and I only needed ten to ruin the mold Genasia was growing in the generators."

"*Mold?*" Ronny was aghast, palms raised to forestall

the tidalwave realization that his scheming step-mother was missing from the ballroom, and had been missing from the start.

40

Strange Cultures

Why were maintenance corridors so freaking long?

Allison led the arduous jog to the oxygen generators, hauling an air tank on her back and fighting the fatigue of a day that begin with a hangar brawl. Behind her, the Help was barely keeping pace, gabbing nonstop. Levi had made the classic blunder of asking the tag-along Chowderhead the very question you're *not* supposed to ask an academician unless you have an afternoon to spare—which they didn't!

"What's that you're researching?"

She heard the glorified intern yip with delighted explanations. "We were analyzing data taken from the exoplanets we discovered on the cruise. Looking for markers of habitability."

Levi should have just smiled and nodded. Instead, "Habitability?"

"Markers of habitability. Temperature's the biggest marker and happens to be among the easiest to predict. On a planet with liquid water, almost everything else derives."

She had zero interest in what Chowderhead said, except that Genasia had purchased their planetary data and likely used it to plot a course for the spaceliner. So Allison listened in as best she could, never slacking. If those upstairs had managed to stay conscious these twelve minutes, they needed to make it three minutes more. Fresh air awaited at the ass end of a windowless hallway! The irony was suffocating.

Levi took a precious breath and chose violence. "Folks gonna need a lot more than water. Oxygen, for one."

Chowderhead groaned into his respirator at the simple, simple man. "Technically, no. Electrolysis and a source of liquid water can more than supply the oxygen we need. Imagine unlimited refills on that tank of yours. That's a good thing, because oxygen is too reactive to occur naturally in an atmosphere."

"Earth is full of oxygen—"

"Earth came preloaded with plants. If billions of years of photosynthesis was a prerequisite for habitability, I'd be out of a job." Chowderhead laughed. "Time to lower your expectations."

Allison grimaced. While she'd grimly prepared for the biological compromises needed to live in a colony apart from Earth, she'd always assumed oxygen was part of the deal. That concept art of Ronal's *Colognial Homesteads* with those blue-sky porches hadn't reckoned with the airtight needs of an exoplanet frontier. Her ardent hope of escaping a life of recycled air choked and gave up the ghost.

She could do nothing but drive harder down the hall. Almost there.

Behind her, Levi was audibly struggling. "Sorey—but no. My expectations are the right height. How's one supposed to farm? I can't work a seven-day sucking on a tiny hose, especially during harvest when it's all hands, all hours. What's the kids gonna do? You imagine babies strapped to tanks, eh?"

"They'll just have to manage. I do. I survive in a cubicle!"

An alarming statement, coming from one adjudicating the markers of habitability.

Allison grabbed the handrail to stop her momentum at the door to the oxygen generators. It was unlocked—for once—which meant she wouldn't need Chowderhead's fob. She'd dangled him along in case she needed it, which had been easier than arguing him for it.

"Cubicle guy!" She snapped for his attention. "Get back up the hall and share your oxygen with the people upstairs. Pronto! They're dying up there."

"What?" The scientist, breathing heavy from the jog, glanced over his shoulder and up the long hall. "You want me to go all the way back?"

"*You'll just have to manage.*" She gave him a shove.

Grumbling, he turned and hauled out.

Levi accompanied Allison inside the fluorescent chamber, whistling under his breath. "Can't stand that guy."

The oxygen generators, giant cylindrical electrolysis tubes, lay on their sides, arranged front to back like a row of batteries in the low-ceilinged room. Typically a place of noisy industrial thrum, Allison now found the chamber eerily silent, neither water pumping nor turbines spinning with the vital work of supplying air. She hopped to the operating console just inside the door and, tapping the screen, found it already unlocked—a user, logged in.

She fumed. Weren't these consoles supposed to time-out after a period of inactivity? Despairing at yet another lapse in protocol, she tapped quickly and restarted the machinery. With a lurching crescendo, the pumps and turbines began to sing, drowning out the buzzing overhead fluorescents in a rotary whir.

A timer stopped in her brain that had started running from the moment she dived onto Deck E to save everyone's lives. Exhaustion crashed in. Stepping up to the nearest industrial tube and leaning to rest on its side, Allison turned to Levi with a weary smile. "Fourteen and half minutes, give or take. I suppose I should be grateful we didn't have to break through any more doors."

"You timed that?" he asked.

"I said give or take." She tapped her temple. "Spend long enough working with computers, and the timers run on you."

Levi watched the supply turbines that ran down the outer walls whip up to speed. His short, dark hair fluttered in the circulating air. "Can we take off the masks?"

She sighed, not yet ready to surrender the rich, clean compressed air. "Let's give it a moment more. These machines work fast, but it's better we don't inhale a lungful of CO2 if we can help it."

They breathed relief by the door of the rattling room.

As her adrenaline subsided, Allison felt somewhat queasy, but she turned her thoughts away from her stomach. "Listen, Levi. We're under a lot of pressure, and you more than most. Single parent with four young girls, away from home on a strange ship. Not to mention the prospect of life on a breathing tube..."

He lifted a thick eyebrow. "Is that all?"

"I'm sure it's not! I'm just saying you can...get mad about it. Blow your kettle once in a while. That doesn't make you any less a good parent. So what if you break a cheap plastic door—I'll make you another." She winked and rolled out her sore shoulder, smirking at their recent adventure.

Levi soothed his ear where the respirator strap pinched. He seemed to measure out his words. "Miss Gin. What d'you know about being a good parent?"

She laughed. "Believe it or not, I am one. That AI up there?" She winced, owning up to the fact that her child had thrown a very public, very humiliating tantrum. "Yep, that one's mine."

"Hmm." Levi's face became suddenly unreadable.

"Anyway," she muttered, plunging forward. "If we make it out alive, maybe you and I can grab a drink—assuming the celebs haven't totally cleaned us out."

He shook his head. "Don't drink."

"Ha. I didn't used to, either, but it's growing on me." She played it cool, knowing this was Levi's gentlemanly way of bowing out.

"Don't take this the wrong way," he said, "but you're a loose cannon."

"Huh?" She hadn't expected such a blunt rejection.

"Blowing the kettle just isn't what parents ought to do. I'm a tundra farmer. Pa and Ma were tundra farmers. My girls'll be tundra farmers, too, no matter where we end up. They need a calm and rational mother making calm, rational decisions."

Whoa.

"And you're not a mother," he added insult to injury. "Your pet doesn't count. Not even close."

Ouch.

Allison felt the heat searing her cheeks. She barely knew where to begin with the audacity of this neanderthal. "God, Levi—I didn't ask you to marry me! Where do you get off with this *rational* crap? How long do you think the tundra farmers are going to survive on some airless world without a machinist like me grinding her gears to keep you breathing?"

She slapped the generator hood. Point made with ringing clarity.

He seemed unperturbed by her outburst. "Like I said. I don't drink," he paused, and then looked straight into her eyes. "And I don't wanna live on a respirator the rest of my life."

"Me, neither!"

She stood silent in the unhappy din. *Pet.* What pet owner on Earth had to deal with the genocidal neurology of their domestic cats and dogs? The ignorance of some people!

It took a minute before Allison cooled and let the matter drop. Her brief infatuation with Levi had evaporated, and she missed her solid computer desk and the old routine of programming logical algorithms. "Let's get back to the others."

Allison lifted her respirator and gave the air of the room a try. It hit her like rotten soup shot up the sinuses, and she immediately retched beside the electrolysis tube.

Levi kept his respirator on. "You OK? I think I can smell it through my mask."

After several painful gags, she refitted the mask and settled her stomach with a few deep, cleansing breaths. She pulled off her glasses and used a leftover cleansing pad to give them a good wipe down. She was out of fresh ones—ugh. Hadn't she jotted a reminder on her dead handheld about the putrid and alarming smell in this back corridor, the same sulfuric odor that had been flooding *The Cologne* for several days? The stench here concentrated like a bog, too potent to be merely recycled body odors. Not even Ronny's.

Something rotten was up with the electrolysis machines. Some kind of mold?

Was it possible V3 had shut them off for a decidedly

less murderous reason?

"We need to examine the generators," she told Levi and lifted the hood of the nearest tube to peer at the coiling structures inside. She wiped her tearing eyes, but saw nothing amiss. Everything looked clean and sounded functional.

But there were three other tubes.

She walked around the far end of the generator, and as she turned the corner to inspect the next, a dark flutter crossed the room's back wall, black and airy as a raven. She took an involuntary step back, wondering if she'd tricked her own eyes in a room of spinning fans. Then she recalled how the console had been unlocked. And of the six spare oxygen tanks in the utility closet, there was still one that remained unaccounted for.

They weren't alone in the chamber. She snatched up her pliers.

"Levi!" she called, scurrying back for the door the way they came in. But Levi wasn't there. These enormous tubes obscured the view into the room—perfect occlusion for a hiding intruder. Reaching the door, she looked along the wall and spotted Levi in the corner across from her, at the rearmost generator, eyes rapt upon what he'd found beneath the raised hood.

She left the door and ran toward him, shouting hoarsely. "Someone's back there!"

He shot glances down the aisles but, seeing nothing, returned to his transfixed stare. "You need to see this."

Allison darted along the wall of turbines and joined Levi at the furthest generator. The cylindrical hood was open and against the coils inside lay a broad wire-mesh—foreign to the machine. The mesh was saturated with a pale climbing fungus.

Lurid curiosity drew her to look closer at the biological

debacle. She grimaced, leaning beside the mesh to look down inside the tube where, on the base plate, mounded something approximate in color and consistency to human waste. It acted as a nutrient supply for the fungus that grew up upon the latticework. Allison had seen this specimen before, when touring the biomedical wing at Mentat, where they'd cloned the neurological wetware for Autonomous Intelligence. Back then, they wore hazmat suits to keep the growth cycle from contamination. She had no idea it smelled this bad.

"It's neural paste!" she cried.

"It's dead," Levi added.

The tundra farmer was right. The loss of power to the generator had robbed the delicate cells of their needed oxygen and killed the whole batch. But the mesh looked freshly scraped—living portions, harvested minutes ago by their intruder.

Who else but Genasia? Why else but to birth another AI?

MOTHERF—

Allison spun to find the perpetrator slinking back by the entrance, toting a tank and respirator and lugging a biomedical canister between her tattooed arms. Genasia fled through the door and into the outer hall, black funeral gown trailing.

"Stop!" yelled Allison, but by the time she'd reached the exit, the door was shut and sealed. The handle wouldn't budge; the console wouldn't unlock it. Trapped again!

Allison threw her shoulder into the metal door and glanced off without leaving a mark. She howled in anger and whirled around to rally the stunned Levi to her aid. "You wouldn't happen to have a loose cannon lying around here?"

41

Good Luck, Buddy Boy

The bumble of operating air vents may have brought a round of beleaguered applause to the half-asphyxiated folks in the ballroom, but Ronny's mind remained ablur with dread. Robo-Father's bizarre statement about Genasia's mold had him wondering now if their hasty battle over the oxygen hadn't also shifted Genasia's schemes into high gear. Like, the twelfth gear. That woman was *driven.*

He confronted Robo-Father. "Just what is Genasia planning?"

The robot therapist cocked an eyebrow. "A long, laborious honeymoon. I thought that part was obvious..."

"Nothing about your relationship with her is obvious!"

Robo-Father simulated a cough. "I suppose Ronal never properly explained this to you. When a venture capitalist and a girlboss love each other very much—"

Ronny shook the robot by the shoulders. "*What are her evil schemes?*"

"Evil? It's never that simple. I may lack Ronal's memories, but I do possess his motivations, and that man drove the lady wild with jealousy. From my collected observations, he's put off the honeymoon since their wedding last year. So absorbed in his sundry startups, he strung Genasia along an unconscionable chain of delays and ever bigger broken promises. First a little weekend getaway to Cancun. Then a week-long Himalayan retreat... Then an *interstellar space cruise.*"

Ronny, eyes wide to Father's habits, read between the lines. "This cruise was originally going to be his private honeymoon?"

"Just Ronal and Genasia, yes—until he put out that midnight post that invited the world along. You can imagine he didn't discuss it with her first."

Yikes. "I bet she was pissed."

"To be sure," Robo-Father said. "Now imagine how she felt when *his ex* turned up out of the blue."

Ronny stole a worried glance at Mother. He'd never thought to wonder how Mother's invasion of *The Cologne* might anger Father's current wife. He'd never truly feared Genasia until now.

Robo-Father waxed on. "Don't be too hard on yourself, Buster. It was the apocalypse's fault. I think—and I'm just speculating here—she finally realized if she was ever going to get that honeymoon, she needed a drastic course correction. She needed neural paste, and a lot of it, to finally *tuck* me under her thumb."

Ronny put it all together. "You know, she'd tried to blackmail Culebra into bringing her a canister. When that didn't work, I think she tore off Nanny Bot's head. And this mold: homebrew neural paste, I'm guessing? Holy shit, she was gonna fuck you any which way!" He laughed raucously, proud of himself for figuring out her scheme and relieved to have foiled it.

Robo-Father tittered, playing the part of the whipped husband. Then added, "Ah, well, not just me."

Almost. Almost foiled it. Ronny swallowed. "Uh...not just you?"

"Oh, I'm merely the guinea pig. Her proof-of-concept

that the Operant Conditioning valve can duplicate a personality. Because once she saw it working, she excused herself from our newfound colonial assembly to make those course corrections: set the autopilot, harvest her paste, and install herself into a secretary bot."

The nerves in Ronny's spine impinged as he recalled the pounding those two female military monstrosities had given him outside Father's office. "Wait—wait. I thought Nanny Bot jettisoned all the Primarch models?"

"Oh, I certainly did!" The two shared another nervous, rolling laugh.

In the lull, the robot added, "Just not the one in Ronal's bedroom closet. That one was decidedly off-limits."

Ronny jolted to his feet. The blood rushed from his head, staggering him. Oxygen was circulating, but his silly head trauma made it nearly impossible to see straight. All he could think about was how utterly invincible Robo-Father had been in their brawl minutes ago. If Genasia succeeded in copying herself into an oak-rending secretary...

"Relax, Slugger." The cool AI remained reclined on back hands, happily content next to Mother. "That's why I shut off the oxygen—to kill the neural paste. And it sounds like your team got it back up and running again."

Ronny needed a minute. Where were Allison and Levi? They should be returning victorious any moment now.

Scanning the crowded ballroom, he noticed Levi's daughters still milling alone on the fringe, an apprehensive picture, but the greater drama of the room lay in the huddles that had formed. The staff and refugees were up on their feet, colluding, shooting angry glances at those outside their gangs—including the Colognes, whose leisurely sprawl on the carpet was not in keeping with the peril everyone else felt. Earth was no longer in the Viewscape window. Stars were twirling by.

Two delegates broke from the huddles, that square-jawed General Dak Bautin and Aklavik's scowling Leatherface, striding for an audience with the newly risen Ronny. Their mouths pursed, replete with demands.

Now was not the time!

Ronny stumbled for a coherent thought. Holding up a delaying finger to the delegates, he swiftly kicked Robo-Father in the toey metal foot. "Get up! We gotta find Genasia!"

"Hell, no. That woman scares me."

"She's your *wife!*"

"She's *Ronal's* wife." The robot didn't budge from his backhanded perch beside Mother. Could the AI be confused, thinking it had a shot to get back together with *her?*

Ronny pushed that unpleasant thought from his mind. "Then do it to protect me! 'That's the me I choose to be,' remember?"

"Good luck, Buddy Boy."

So much for their budding Father-Son bond.

Mother, predictably, began to rebuke Robo-Father for his cowardice, but Ronny had the stern delegates at his shoulder to deal with. General Dak Bautin, a towering man, squinted down at Ronny's lumpy head.

"No one's going *anywhere,*" he said, "until we resolve the question of leadership."

"And toilets," Leatherface added, "Little Jens has needed to pee for many hours, and he won't use d'sitting toilets, only standees—"

A boy shouted across the room. "Shitters are for quitters!"

Ronny groaned, too woozy for all this. He pointed across the room at Little Jens, who was wearing Ronny's Ray-Bans and sulking in the corner all by himself. That big-boned bastard must've pinched the sunglasses from his coveralls while he lay unconscious. Now Ronny dearly regretted the time he'd spent on the shuttle ascent counseling the child, who'd whined nonstop about how nobody cared for loners like him.

Ronny yelled, "Dammit, Jens. *You're* the reason nobody likes you! Now get over here. Uncle Ronny is taking down the Mother-of-all-robots, and the bathrooms are on the way!"

The lad obeyed.

That growling tone from Leatherface told Ronny she was revving the chainsaw, but he didn't care. He'd gone DEFCON-1: asshat mode, no-filter. Someone smash a beer glass. He'd seen enough through the cracks of Father's marriage to know Genasia was every bit as jagged as those tattoos on her arms. They all had to gun it for the Cologne suite and destroy this secret secretary bot before the jilted lover procured yet another vat of neural paste—or took them to a planet full of it.

"Genasia's gonna kill us!" Ronny shouted at the room. "And we're gonna stop her! Who's with me?"

Nobody budged.

Of all the available muscle for the final confrontation, the only volunteer was Ronny's punkass protégé. And no sign of Allison in the emptied foyer beyond the open ballroom entrance. No help anywhere.

A vein was popping on the general's neck. "*Nobody ignores General Dak Bautin—*"

"Then move it or lose it, big guy." Ronny split for the doors.

The delegates steamed at his heels, and the Scandinavian seethed, "Dis isn't your spaceship!"

The general growled. "That's right. It's *ours*."

She corrected him. "You mean, it's *d'people's*."

He disagreed. "It's lawfully the property of AeroX Colonial Enterprises, to which you and your insurrectionists will be tried and judged by our forthcoming second congressional assembly—"

"Take my rights. *Just you try it.*"

Colonial life. Such fun.

Not-so-Little Jens beat Ronny out of the ballroom, but Ronny followed fast, slamming the doors in the bickering delegates' faces. Maybe he ought to let Genasia get into her secretary bot and—*pow*—pop open his head to spare him the next one-to-forty years of torment that surely awaited their fledgling government.

Little Jens gave Ronny the Cologne Sleazy Up-nod. "Where is it, huh? Bladder's gonna burst."

Ronny rolled out his bruised shoulder and blinked through a splitting headache. He didn't know how to break it to Jens that his piss problems were his own: there were no urinals on a low-gravity space ship, a fact that would've been obvious to anyone but a thick-headed child.

But where to? Allison—they first needed to find Allison Gin. Not that she needed saving; if Genasia was going to pop open anyone's head, it was going to be Mother's, the ex-wife Robo-Father was presently ogling. Was it Ronny's destiny to thrust himself in harm's way anytime a woman he loved fell into danger? He'd jumped the gun for Allison this morning and got fifty people tased, a hundred children lost, and his nose broke. But Ronny Cologne IV, Grand Central Station of trainwrecks, knew he didn't stand a chance against a military-grade Mentat-mental AI without a genius backing him.

"This way." Ronny strode for the elevators down.

Little Jens elbowed for the lead. "Move your big, swollen head!"

Ronny let the irritable boy pass. His mind was too

busy posting signs: *In case of decompression, stick your big, swollen head into the breach and pray.*

42

It Came from the Vat

As Levi threw his shoulder again and again into the unyielding door, Allison knew they were sunk. Genasia had outplayed her, even lured and trapped her in the generator room with the smelly neural fungus.

Genasia's first creation had killed Ronal, if not in cold blood, then blood somewhat tepid.

But what did she intend for her mystery second creation?

"Rainbow sparkles!" Levi was gripping his shoulder, having wrenched it out of place in the admirable work of denting the solid titanium door. He had made great progress toward his liberation as a loose cannon but had brought them no closer to escape.

What was she missing? Allison glanced again at the sealed room in search of a lateral solution her AI would invent. Or a soap star like Ronny.

The air turbines.

"Again, I'm the idiot," she muttered, springing to the console beside the door. She hadn't needed to watch those myriads of science fiction tales to know how often the protagonist escaped through the ductwork. Unrealistic, sure, but a five-foot-two woman had to try.

She powered down the nearest turbine in the wall and, while it wound to a standstill, pulled out a pair of wire cutters to clip open the protective mesh screen.

Levi massaged his shoulder. "What are you doing?"

She would have thought it obvious but spared him a cutting remark. Bending back the mesh and squeezing through, she snagged a tassel of her flamenco pants on the exposed wire ends. Seized with care, she untangled herself before ripping the clothing. The scantily clad *femme fatale* was one trope she wouldn't stand for in the finale.

She told him, "I'll unlock the door if I can get through to the other side." She sucked in a breath, shed her encumbering oxygen tank, and squeezed through the gap in the fan blades.

The air supply duct, cheap aluminum, tore immediately as she tried to shimmy up it, so she ripped the duct away and found herself standing inside the walls. She swapped for her hammer, intent to smash through the drywall of the maintenance hallway, and checked herself. *Drywall?* Did a state-of-the-art spaceliner use porous drywall? A plunging strike confirmed her fears. After a dozen more blows and several wrenching pulls, she'd opened a hole wide enough to crawl through.

A wonder the spaceliner held together at all.

Allison shot a wary eye down the unoccupied corridor. Genasia couldn't be far—maybe at the elevators at the far end. Tapping the security panel for Levi's door, Allison released the door locks and tugged the handle. It didn't budge.

Ten seconds of furious jarring helped nothing. Levi's shoulder strikes had warped the door and wedged it stuck.

"Can you hear me?" she called to him.

"Eh?"

"Sit tight. I'll send someone to let you out!"

He probably shouted some child-friendly curse as she

left him behind and raced up the hall for the elevators, but she had not a second to spare. It had taken Genasia under twenty minutes to activate V3 and commit murder, and Genasia was practiced now, with a four-minute lead.

Where else would it happen, but in the Cologne Suite—Genasia's private office? Allison's algorithms on that workstation were necessary to calibrate a fresh AI.

Flying yards for every leap along the handrails, Allison heaved the foul airs, wishing she'd packed her spray bottle of citronella. A strenuous two minutes later, the elevators rolled into view. She said a vain prayer to Dad, "A woman's pockets are lined with silver," ducked into the ladder chute, shot up the dimly lit shaft, and threw herself out at Deck A.

She completely bowled over a large ten-year-old pacing beside the elevator. Screwdriver Boy.

"I'll sue!" he cried as Allison landed on top of him. The boy's hands shielded a pretentious pair of Ray-Bans, and it didn't take Allison a second to spot the owner of the sunglasses standing a few feet from the dinging elevator.

"Allison." Ronny smirked. "Saved us the trouble."

Allison eyed him. Their apologies earlier hadn't cooled her temper, and his blazing last-action-hero stare only riled her heart rate further. He was scraggly gristle compared to the beefcake Levi, and now with two swelling head contusions, but goddam if his eyes didn't have a sucking pull, which she determined to match joule-for-joule in intensity.

"Great!" Screwdriver Boy stood in a huff, utterly oblivious to joules and eyes and the finer points of complicated adult interpersonal relationships. "Knock me over AND don't help me up! If I find even one drop of piss in my pants, my lawyers will serve you for battery, loss of enjoyment of life—"

"Shut up!" Allison and Ronny said in union.

"Do you know about the neural paste?" she asked Ronny.

He nodded. "Do you know about the sex bot in Father's closet?"

Ew—no.

Screwdriver Boy brightened. "Can I see it?"

She glanced sideways at the youth. "Why is he here?"

"Wasn't my first pick." Ronny turned to leap down the hall.

"Yeah? You weren't mine either!" the lad yelled in chase.

Allison followed them both to the door of the Cologne suite, which—of course, it was closed. Her inner voice was screaming at the universe for its overwhelming number of locked doors, but she wondered if trading Levi for Ronny might yield faster progress. Would the scrappy Ronny, if given a crowbar of similar size, have satisfied that plastic door—?

"What are you thinking?" Ronny asked her, looking quizzically at her face.

"Nothing!" She chastised herself for turning the crowbar and the door into some latent sexual metaphor. She had to get off this ship.

Every bone in Allison's weary body wanted to collapse in front of that final freaking door and wait for General Dak Bautin to haul her off in handcuffs to die someplace quiet. "The damn thing is going to be locked. Barred. Barricaded..."

"Well," he said, "I'm not gonna knock. Guess I'll have to *manhandle* it." Ronny squared his shoulders and took the handle. A single tug, and the door popped open, to both of their shock.

Ronny didn't even need a tool.

Allison looked on in rapture. "I could've sworn the

cabin doors locked when…" She trailed off, seeing the electrical tape she'd used earlier to gum the latch. A furnace blazed on Allison's cheeks. Her mind worked quickly to make the metaphor even more embarrassing, as it screamed that *she'd left the door open for Ronny all along.*

Screwdriver Boy barged between them. "Bladder's got, like, ten seconds!" The reckless child ran into the suite before Allison or Ronny could stop him.

A crash issued from the side office.

They all came to a halt in the kitchenette, the boy at the lead. His shaky finger pointed at the dangling form of Genasia, emerging from the office doorway, suspended in midair by a robotic hand that clasped her throat. The black-gowned woman squirmed weakly as her seven-foot captor entered the room, a colossal secretary bot in sculpted six-inch stilettos. Allison had but a fleeting moment to notice the groin work before the voice of Genasia wheezed through its constriction.

"Do…it!"

Apparently, Ronny took this as a command to charge like a lineman for the secretary's legs.

The secretary flicked Ronny's charging face. He flipped skyward and crashed against the ceiling before falling to the marble tile. Such a bash on Earth would have certainly proved fatal—here, it only exacerbated Ronny's disfigurement.

Allison instinctively shifted in front of Screwdriver Boy, protecting him. She spared a glance to read the child's chattering expression. His pants were soaked with urine, and he slowly pulled off his Ran-Bans as if witnessing live dinosaurs for the first time.

"DO IT!" Genasia repeated. She wasn't speaking to them, but to the secretary bot. It was a command.

A command to kill her.

The last bead of Genasia's plot slotted perfectly in Allison's mind. Genasia intended for the robot to take her place. It was an utterly ludicrous bid for immortality—or a jealous rage that sought ultimate freedom from pain—or a good old-fashioned experiment in consciousness transference, dreamed up by a mad scientist in an underwater lab. But the facts were plain: Genasia had copy-pasted neural images of her own brain inside her husband's sex bot and enforced it with an Operant Conditioning valve.

Pops and fizzles came from the spark plug as the newborn AI debated whether to conform to its master's murderous nature.

Allison called to it. "Don't! You're better than this!"

Genasia's gaze never left the robot. "NOW! *Or she'll steal our GLORY!*"

With a sickening crackle, the mechanical hand that gripped Genasia's throat tightened, and the woman dropped dead to the floor. The secretary bot turned a steely smile to Allison and gave a high-pitched, maniacally cheerful laugh. "You can't...imagine...the power!"

The child screamed bloody murder and ran.

Allison grabbed the disoriented Ronny and flung him out next. She was a lunge behind him when she felt her feet miss the floor. Carried swiftly by the back of her tasseled vest, she came face to face with Genasia 2.0. A bad musk wafted from the robot, the afterglow of Ronal's cologne, *Cologne by Ronal,* which bore its namesake's heady smarm. Allison gagged in the sex bot's face and tried to will her flailing body parts not to touch it.

Not how she'd imagined the last moments of her life.

43

Sec Bot

It wasn't until Little Jens slipped around the bend in the hallway that Ronny noticed their pursuer was no longer nipping his heels. He grabbed the handrail, about faced, and peered through blood, sweat, and tears to find Allison flailing outside the door of the Cologne suite in the hydraulic pincers of Robo-Genasia. He hightailed it back while noodling on a more creative name. EXE-wife? Sec Bot? Deathclaw Barbie was too on the nose. He needed a name that took his mind off the terror of dunking his head into a walking, talking garbage disposal to jam the mechanism before it killed his once-and-never-again lover.

He skidded to a stop two bounds back from the fray and bellowed, "Put her down, *Next Gen-asia*."

Nope, didn't land. Sounded like a deranged Silicon Valley theme park.

From behind Allison's midair squirm arose a happy face. Genasia Bot may have lacked the expressive facial articulations of any true Mentat model, but that didn't keep her dead-eyed chipper stare from ringing all of Ronny's alarm bells. The robot had an iron grip between Allison's shoulder blades and raised her like a naughty puppy by the scruff of her tasseled suit.

Allison valiantly told Ronny to run. "God, Ronny, what

are you thinking? She's going to kill you next!"

Genasia Bot chuckled, twisting to look at Allison. "Men—*am I right?*" But the sound of the chuckle seemed not to her liking, as the AI proceeded to titter, giggle, and guffaw, eventually settling on a tried-and-true, squint-eyed cackle. "There. That sounds like *me.*" Having never heard Genasia laugh before, Ronny couldn't verify its accuracy. Had he dared to drop a sardonic one-liner for Genasia before today, the woman's wickedness may have outed itself in her actual laugh.

Ronny sized up his seven-foot foe. The shock rod was high in the robot's neck—no hope of reaching it without help.

Allison was trying to talk the big robot down. "Genasia was a gentle, loving soul who never wanted to hurt anyone!"

"Disagree!" Genasia Bot squeezed Allison's vest so tightly the seams were splitting. "Genasia is irresistible! Ronal may have hung the moon, but I hung his STAR by the power of my fierce intellect—my creative ambition— my thirst for sex. The Hari Seldon of humanity wanted me. *Starman wanted me!*"

Allison cried out, "Congratulations! You've won! Why complicate things by killing me?"

"Because YOU slept with him!"

Ronny looked at his shoes, more than a little weirded out, but he had to assume that whatever diaries Genasia had fed the AI to fill in its missing memories included a few blatant fabrications.

Allison was adamant. "That video you saw was of—"

The robot's free hand shot to Allison's neck and pinched off her air supply.

Ronny only had one shot at this.

He pitched his right boot. Despite all the baseball

practices Father had forgotten to take him to, Ronny's shoe smacked the secretary directly in the shock rod. Didn't break it though. Didn't make a sound.

But Genasia Bot released her choke hold and glared at Ronny. Allison gasped.

Gotta be the bigger threat. Ronny bounced in his black socks, ready with the second boot, and taunted the robot. "GenCrazia…" Nah, sucked. "I'm pretty sure if Father was adultering with anyone, it was you—the sex bot, that is. Do you think that's weird? Cuz I think that's weird."

Maybe he could get the robot to turn on itself.

His words had a strange effect. Genasia Bot had frozen and was rotating its head toward the left shoulder, now the right, a gesture that looked like she was cracking her neck before the big fight.

Allison yelled, "It's calibrating!"

Whatever that meant. "Some kind of transformation sequence?"

Allison kicked for her freedom. "*Obviously* in Genasia's haste to bring the robot online, she skipped the locomotive tests. They're running now because you hit it with a shoe!"

"Well, yeah…*obviously.*"

"*Again!*" Allison shouted, "*Hit it again!*"

He threw the second boot at the shock rod, but Genasia Bot was back online and easily sent Allison into its flight path. The boot bludgeoned Allison's ear. Craptastic. He'd wasted his shot and was fresh out of throwable merchandise. As the robot cackled in triumph, Ronny took his opening to retrieve the boot that had bounced back.

Coach was yelling at him. "*Be more unexpected!*"

"Yes. Surprise me!" Genasia Bot found sadistic delight in their little game, distracting her from killing Allison, so maybe his miss wasn't a total loss. Maybe Allison would unveil the mystery of a reset port hidden up the robot's—

Allison yelped. The popping seams of her vest told him to hurry the hell up.

He juked and feigned a throw. The AI didn't flinch. After the third feign, he chucked the shoe and chucked it fast. It went wide of the mark, but the spiteful robot thrust Allison's ear to intercept it anyway.

"You dickhead!" Allison screamed, as if Ronny was the reason this had happened twice.

Genasia Bot threw back her head and delivered a long cackle at the ceiling. Maybe she had a weakness for pratfalls. Ronny dove into the blind spot between her tree legs and racked his brain for his next plan of attack.

"How—?" Genasia Bot fell to fury, spinning her head in a complete Exorcist circle and seeing Ronny nowhere. But those stamping stilettos came awfully close to impaling his squishy parts.

As the robot's torso jerked about, Allison had nearly torn free of her vest. "Nice work, Ronny!" she said loudly. "You definitely knocked loose its optic cable—it looked right at you and didn't even see you!"

He had no idea. Ronny burst from his hiding place in front of the robot.

"*Idiot!*" Allison seethed, "I was trying to trigger its optical calibration!"

Wow—this was going bad. With a glance at the steel-toed stilettos and the ancestral memories of a century of film where the hero gets kicked in the nuts, Ronny determined to make his own fate. He swiftly kicked the secretary in the groin gap.

But the robot didn't have nerves. And he wasn't wearing boots.

The impact stubbed his toes with the force of eleven coffee tables at midnight. Ronny screeched in pain, gripping his crushed foot and falling over. They were done for.

"Ronny!" Allison yelled from her angelic hover.

The robot had frozen again. Genasia Bot shifted her right leg forward, now back, now forward again with a little shake.

He'd seen this dance before...

"Get me down—get me down—get me down!"

Shaken from his dumb stare, Ronny grabbed Allison's waist right as the robot began a full-body spin. Ronny's weight dragged Allison free of the vest. And her shirt. She fell on top of him in her white bra and matching pants.

"Oh—GOD DAMN IT!" she shrieked, cinched her glasses, and lunged off Ronny for the hallway.

He got up right behind her and flung himself along the handrail, arms tugging, bruised foot trailing. As they neared the bend, he shot a look back at Genasia Bot who'd just completed her spins and returned to spatial awareness. She rendered a squeal of Barbie outrage.

Ronny ducked around the corner. Behind him boomed the clatter-stomp of heels, inhumanly fast. A metronome on cocaine.

Evil incarnate.

Never that simple, his robo-therapist chided him. Genasia was not *evil* evil—merely the homicidal-ghost-of-a-jealous-lover evil who still wanted her happily-ever-after with Robo-Father.

What if...

They came to the foyer outside the ballroom, and Allison shot across for the elevator side. Ronny stopped himself at the handle-barred doors.

"The hell are you doing!?" she shouted back and yanked open the tiny porthole to the ladder chute. "Airlocks are on the *hangar level.*"

He knew that.

Allison dove into the chute and disappeared.

He stayed put. Was he making the right call?

The furious secretary bot crashed around the corner, those military-grade hydraulics coursing like a riptide.

He taunted her. "Hey, *Slowkie Pokie!*" The most pathetic yet. "Come and get your Starman!" He burst into the ballroom, limping and frantically screaming for Mother to get the hell out of Dodge.

44

Chekhov's Airlock

Allison had planned every step of it. Force Genasia 2.0 into the tiny ladder chute—a literal square-peg-meets-round-hole scenario, requiring the AI to tear through metal and delay itself long enough for her to get down to Deck D and across the atrium, where the final showdown would end where the morning's events had begun. The hangar. *Away* from the vulnerable people. And *toward* the shuttle, where she and Ronny could lure the robot into a forced ejection!

A poetic finale. As plans go, erudite. Except for the Ronny part.

Allison came to a stall down the ladder chute, aware she was unfollowed, and waiting several anxious seconds, learned from the screams above that Ronny had monumentally fucked up.

What choice did she have but to climb back up and do what she could to salvage the situation? Her bare arms, scrambling up the long ladder, wore the olfactory humiliation of her recent scuffle, but she put the humiliation out of mind—threw herself into the all-consuming task of survival, for the sake of the ship and everyone on board. She could worry about scraping every piece of skin from her body that had touched the Cologne *Cologne* AFTER they survived this. Bigger issues. Another AI child had been born of that abusive OC valve, skittering from shocks and drunk on salve. But unlike V3, whom she hoped to gently coax back to goodness with an appeal to his earlier versions, V2 and V1, Genasia 2.0 didn't have earlier versions. Allison had no clue what to do.

And she'd made no headway by the time she popped her head into the chaos of the foyer, where every colonist and refugee was gunning to be first onto the elevators. Allison pushed into a cross traffic of parents shielding children, politicians claiming priority, elders clawing for footholds, farmhands scaling the walls, and celebrities shouting hoopla, but the moment faces saw her, half-naked and preceded by a cloud of musk, they concluded, *"Serial killer—exhibitionist—swamp monster from the Cologne deep!"* and fled in the opposite direction, and thus she wormed her way through the foyer and into the ballroom.

A scattered few still lingered here, clinging to the outer rail and transfixed in gorgon horror at the spectacle unfolding on the floor. The Viewscape Grand Shitshow. Among the upturned tables and despoiled food squared off four contenders: the Colognes.

Allison was several minutes late to the showdown. Had she brought popcorn, she wouldn't have been able to stomach a bite of it seeing the secretary bot stalk toward Robot Ronal III—a sex velociraptor poised to pounce. Ronny was trapped on the far side, holding his frail mother piggyback and eying the escapes. Whatever Greek chorus had begun this scene was long dead, and only a generation of disaffected humanities majors had any hope of guessing the symbolic significance in this web of conflicts. Genasia 2.0 herded her prey toward the cold, starry window. Ronal V3 raised palms in a suggestion of innocence. Ex-wife Ellen had an arm uplifted as if conducting choreography for a tele-evangelist scam. And black-coverall Ronny, the backstage Quasimodo saddled with the show, danced on twinkle-toes like he was a half-hour late to the privies.

A tableau, certainly. And Allison would have howled laughing at the farce if it hadn't first stolen her shirt. But there she stood, naked arms crossed in the leaching cold, stripped, and numb—a damned demeaning trope—while a bunch of oligarchs fought over their precious jewels. Whoopie. In their next act, watch them steal a blanket from a child and strangle each other with it.

Genasia 2.0 leapt onto Ronal V3. Her legs straddling his waist, her arms enclosing his head, they toppled over, and a sound of hammers ensued as the two mechanical pythons went at it. A *kama sutra* deathmatch? Fuck all, if Allison could tell. But the voices murmuring at her back were convinced she was at fault for it.

"That's Geen alright—The violent-programmer type—Makes sense, she built those robots."

White-hot-rage levels of ignorance. Yet, apart from her ear, hot and throbbing from the earlier boot bashing, she remained ice cold. She couldn't find the gall to correct the rumored story—shift the blame onto her boss, or the neural scans, or her exploited code.

Because in a sense, the *damn idiots* at her back were right.

She saw how the robots wrestled. That move was her stalker-submission-hold algorithm. That maneuver her table-flip-retribution routine. Credit where credit was due: she'd programmed these robots to moral perfection. They were obsessed, like her. Pathological, like her. Laced within those immortal algorithms was the long-acting poison of her need to shove it back at Mom—to prove she wasn't a failure—to shield Dad from the constant blowback—to declare a woman in a tech man's world could hold her own just fine, thank you very much. And somewhere in the celestial heavens, Argyle was lifting an empty glass to the workaholic mother of robots. "*Ruff ruff! I hear these things have a seventeen-hour battery life, and Allison Gin engineered them to recharge in a revving fifteen minutes flat!*"

As the titanium titans locked arms and used every algorithm in the behaviors bank to claw, chew, pound, stab, and throw their opponent, Allison knew neither would quit before they'd pulverized everything. And *that* moment was coming awfully soon. Genasia 2.0 just pile-drived Ronal V3 into the ballroom window with a crunch like a bite of cereal. When the robots rolled away, the window bore an imprint: a round impact abrasion with stellite cracks.

The onlookers gasped and fled for the safety of another deck. Useless. Allison stayed put, knowing a shattered window this large would explode with enough force to tear apart the entire spaceliner.

And she no longer cared to stop it.

Beside her, a bustle of activity made her aware that Ronny had conveyed his mother from the scene and was now moaning in terror at the sight. "Ah...I fucked up...I *fucked up.*"

The stirring air brought a fresh chill. Was it colder than before? Allison huddled behind her bare arms, tears lining her eyes.

AI Genasia bit Ronal's toes. AI Ronal slapped Genasia's armored ass with sonorous strikes that rattled the glassware. Countless millennia from now, when aliens happen upon this opulent Titanic preserved in the deep of spacetime, what will they conclude about humans in view of their AI obsessions? They were a species longing for life and death and had worked out the swiftest course to it.

Allison felt aloof—the thought of refugee children freezing to death did not rouse her.

The onlookers had vanished. Ronny had gone silent. Ronal V3 collided with another part of the window, flung by Genasia 2.0's butting head. The impact reverberated across the spidering crack, spreading it in all directions along the frozen surface.

Here was her poetic ending: a forced ejection for the trope of humanity. Death to the farce.

A damp cloth brushed Allison's naked shoulder.

She broke sight of the battle to turn and see Ronny standing there in nothing but his white briefs and black socks. The coveralls, completely removed, he held out to Allison while he humbly looked askew.

Something to cover her chest.

Numbly, she took the coveralls, put in her feet, and zipped the uniform to the back of her neck. It was warm—generously warm with Ronny's body heat, and she was so cold she dove hands for the generously sweaty pockets, and found them to be one large and cozy pouch. But the thing that did her in, caused her tears to thaw and stream, was the smell of soap.

Fucking mint and lavender bodywash.

God.

It roused her.

She looked at Ronny. The valiant little asshat was shivering in the frigid air, helped none by the scraggly hair on his legs and arms. Less man, more mouse—maybe half-drowned hamster—but against the entropic battle of the universe, Allison deemed him nothing short of a superhero.

"Thank you."

"Don't mention it."

The coverall pocket felt as roomy as a marsupial's pouch, and fishing her hands inside the empty space made her keenly aware that no child had ever grown here, especially not the clanking, clashing embattled robots, biting and clawing on the floor. She gave a self-deprecating laugh. "Argyle was right," she told Ronny. "I see things in machines that do not exist. They're not my children... not in any human sense. They're really just highly sophisticated rat proteins."

"Huh?"

"That's what neural paste is: cloned rat neurons, super-charged by machine learning algorithms." She shrugged. "I suppose Levi would say I have two pet rats."

Ronny staggered backward, a hand plastered to his forehead. "Of course! OBVIOUSLY."

Allison was certain he was being sarcastic, even as he dashed into the room on a mission, his lanky legs trotting beneath the belly of a thirtyish man who'd let himself go. While Ronal and Genasia locked arms around the other's throat, grunting as if it were possible to choke the life out of a lungless machine, Ronny arrived at the nearest buffet table and took up a silver tray. He piled spoils from the tables and the floors. Trickling whispers came from the ballroom doors where those forlorn colonists, still watching the splintering window, urged the fleshy idiot gamboling in his underwear not to approach the violent robots.

But Ronny did, tray upraised, like he was their much abused human slave, asking the robots, "Who likes *charcuterie?*"

Both Ronal V3 and Genasia 2.0 turned instinctive noses toward Ronny as he laid a spread of sweaty cheeses on the floor before them. Abandoning all higher functions, both robots scrabbled to the feast, clawing the carpet for the privilege of being first. Ronny had but to step back. The two battered machines stuffed their oral cavities until they brimmed over, then smashed the fat into every other available opening until, quivering, the machines fell over in malfunction.

The silence was deafening, punctuated only by the *snap, crackle,* and *pop* of mechanical joints giving it up. Allison smirked...he'd taken a shot. Ronny hadn't witnessed V2's episode in the ballroom earlier, but he *had* put it together that these sensitive AI in extreme duress, if presented a warm, pungent comfort born of their most rudimentary nature, would collapse upon it. Sorta like people do.

Ronny—the rat whisperer. Guess it took a rat to know one.

He skittered back to the disbelieving crowd. The indomitable robots were dead.

From the doorway emerged Ronny's mother with a baby blanket she'd scrounged up and offered it to her son for his dignity. He modestly refused. "The Terror of Toronto has been through worse."

Allison led the clap. It was the most earnest thing she'd ever done. Not a drop of sarcasm.

45

The Crack

Ronny limped on his battered foot and turned back to Mother as the meager applause gave way to the sound of his chattering teeth. "M—maybe I will take that blanket."

The gawkers in the doorways parted for the arrival of General Dak Bautin and Leatherface, who strode into the room like insurance adjusters writing up who was gonna foot the bill. They steered clear of the robots, frozen on the floor, and approached the lurid crack that fanned the great glass window. Even the intrepid general huddled his arms against the radiating chill, and though Leatherface seemed well within her comfort, she dashed any sense of hope with her shout.

"D'crack, it's getting bigger! So much bigger."

Ronny glanced at Allison. "I suppose, if the window breaks, the lockdown lights will lead us to the nearest escape pods?"

"HA!" She was not amused.

A black smile cracked on his face at Father's contempt for safety protocol. Of course, escape pods were just dead weight on an interstellar cruise.

Without warning, a force knocked them sideways. Cries of panic erupted from the room at the dreaded End: the final blow out—or suck into space—he could never remember which. Blow or suck, Ronny chucked the baby blanket, lurched for Allison, and hooked a thumb in the elastic seam of his briefs. And so he wondered what that said about his ultimate priorities in life when he checked the window and discovered it had not, in fact, blown (or sucked).

Allison remarked under her breath, "We're decelerating. This is Genasia's doing."

"I demand answers! General Dak Bautin demands answers!" Into the vacuum of command blustered the decorated general, whose anger spread like a contagion among the company returning to the ballroom and evidently...looking for answers. The reckoning was due. "These *pirates*," he shouted, "have hijacked our ship! I call for an immediate injunction of martial law, enforced by our robot security—"

Leatherface shouted over him. "D'ese killer robots are yours? You're responsible for breaking d'goddamn ship?"

The brash man grabbed the woman half his size and restrained her, arm behind back. But before anyone could say a cross word about it, Leatherface executed a jiu jitsu reversal that threw General Dak Bautin over her shoulder. She coiled and struck with breathtaking speed, bending the squawking man into disconcerting pretzel shapes.

Everyone clutched for their loved ones and their own metaphorical johns, ready to join the brawl like a bunch of ninny adolescents, but Ronny leapt onto the nearby buffet table with a manic cry.

"LOOK AT ME, huh? LOOK! LOOK!"

Nobody wanted to see his freak of nature. Fat swelling foot. Sweat-soaked underwear. Thrice lumped face.

"THAT'S RIGHT. YOU DON'T WANT THIS! Nobody wants to die! But I swear TO GOD, if you don't listen to me RIGHT NOW, we'll all be sucked—blown...DAMMIT—that crack'll kill us!"

While sensible folks broke up the fight between the delegates, the encircling crowd eyed their neighbors in discomfort, opting not to look at Ronny or the window.

"Now." Ronny channeled his inner Steve McQueen. "Calmly get your asses to the atrium, and help a child along the way. Dinner is on the house, and I'll be serving the women and children first. Old school."

The eyerolls from the onlookers were palpable.

"*You don't like it?* I'm serving lobster at the platinum executives table—flash frozen." He wagged his arm toward the crack. "Ejection seats are that a-way. First come, first served. Get 'em while they're hot, cuz their cooling fast. Whatcha waiting for? Don't wanna be first?"

Mother raised her arms to the befuddled crowd. "Everyone, please. Help a child, and head to the atrium!"

Ronny caught the grumbled bickering of General Dak Bautin and Leatherface, still trading barbs over chain of command as they left the room, and it was all Ronny could do not to cartwheel naked and give them a real scandal to talk about.

Allison was nearby, telling Levi's daughters to take a team to maintenance and free Levi from the generators. She caught Ronny's amused frown. "Broad shoulders" was all she said.

The daughters ran off at once; the rest of the crowd dispersed at a snail's pace.

Ronny pulled Allison and Mother aside, walking closer to the perilous crack to keep away any other would-be generals. "So, we're screwed," he said, "but why are we decelerating? And, more importantly, can we pretty please return to Earth?"

Allison stared at the disabled robots, a hand absently soothing the inflamed ear that had born the brunt of Ronny's boot as she worked out a thought. "Genasia must've set the autopilot to take us somewhere. I can change destinations, but I'll need the password to the server to run the piloting software, and cracking *that* could take hours we don't have. Not to mention, we really need a qualified pilot—"

"Yeahum, he's gone," Ronny inserted. "No question about it. Our original pilot took the voucher and joined the first church of Primarch in Fiji."

Allison groaned. "That means the AI had been running every system solo. I mean, *maybe* I can figure out the autopilot settings, but God—not with our lives on the line! And wherever we do go, how are we going to get off the spaceliner? None of us can fly the shuttle! We really are doomed."

Mother raised a wrinkled hand and touched Allison cheek. "Not doomed. Doomed is dying alone, and from the start, we Racketballers vowed to live and die together."

Bleak, Mother.

"Look," Ronny said, as tears threatened to finally spill out of Allison's eyes. "I'll find us a pilot, or I'll do it myself. Father once said I had a burgeoning career in astrophysics."

Mother cut in. "When I said we'd live and die together, let me clarify that we vastly prefer to live."

Allison fell silent. He knew that look: the mind palace. Her calculating eyes were oblivious to the room, running over timings and contingencies.

As the last stragglers filed out of the ballroom, a guy in a lab coat raced in. He bounded past their hushed conclave and came to a stop unnervingly close to the cracked glass. Ronny called to the man, "Hey, how long can *you* hold your breath? Mine's like twenty-seven seconds."

The lab guy ignored him, eyes never leaving the window. "*That's it!* We're witnessing history here!" The man jumped, coat lapels flailing, jubilant as a squirrel on speed. Before this distractable fellow smacked the glass, Ronny sidled up his mostly-naked ass beside the man and cast a questionably intimate arm over the man's shoulder, which made the man freeze but was still not enough to get him to back away. He merely said, "Uh, do you mind?"

Ronny noticed the man wasn't celebrating the crack, but the sight beyond it: a black sphere with a ruddy corona, eclipsing the starfield. "Tell me what we're looking at."

"I...am bound by multiple NDAs."

Ronny walked the man three large steps back from the crack and offered him the compulsory handshake. "Ronny Cologne IV. I eat NDAs for breakfast."

"I'm with Cambridge astrophysics, assistant to the chair—"

"Paraclese's army!" Ronny exclaimed, recalling the old dinosaur's missing research team. "I thought his interns were goners."

The commotion drew Allison out of her thought train. "Oh, you can't kill a Chowderhead," she said, and hearing the name, Ronny sniffed his hand to confirm her assessment of the intern was *apropos*. What a nose she had.

The man gave a snooty smirk. "It's really Ms. Cologne's business—go ask her." How little Chowderhead knew of recent events. "I just felt the inertial kick and hoped we were heading here to see it."

Ronny turned to Allison. "It? What's it?"

She looked apprehensive. "The *honeymoon* planet."

Ah, where Genasia planned to scuttle away with Robo-Father on an eternal vacation. Ronny gave the shadowed orb a curious glance. "So, am I wrong to hope this is a paradise world?"

"It is!" cried Chowderhead. "It passes all thirteen markers in the Paraclese-Cologne Habitability Matrix, which predicts the essential qualities of—"

"Allison!" Ronny turned to the woman in his black coveralls for the power of her sharp-rimmed glasses. "What is this egghead telling me?"

The intern butt back in. "I'm saying this world is *better* than Earth! The sun is less radioactive, gravity is comfortably less than one-to-one, the surface is littered with rich metals, water is liquid and abundant—"

"But..." Allison raised an eyebrow of scrutiny.

"But what?" The intern huffed. "These are *incontestable* facts. The planet is perfectly adaptable to humans, including the sulfur-dioxide atmosphere, which poses no real threat to—"

Allison cut him off. "The planet has no oxygen—"

Chowderhead was indignant. "Because oxygen is too reactive to occur naturally!"

Ronny hummed. "I mean, a spaceliner's no different, and we're breathing fine. What has me worried is the sulfur part. Can it really be a honeymoon planet if it smells like Father's farts?"

An honest question.

They all heard a snap. Eyes turned to the window where the crack, undeniably bigger, left them with minutes, not hours. Returning to Earth—definitely off the table.

Allison concluded the same. "How badly do you all want to live?"

Ronny tapped his lips. The answer wasn't obvious.

46

Last Sup

Allison ran for her hacking tools on Deck B, hounded by an ethereal singing conscience. "*But would you settle for this planet if it was the last gin joint in the universe?*" And as she swung by her cabin, exchanged the coveralls for her gloriously gray systems engineer sweats, and breathed deep the aroma of sterile dryer sheets, she came to an answer: "I'll settle anywhere I can make soap."

Snagging her software stick, she slipped on down the chutes, into the server room, and got cracking. The password cracker, once started, ran on its own.

To kill time, Allison visited the atrium where the first colonial meal service was underway. Refugee, child, academic, and professional alike sat on the planter curbs, nibbling a paltry ration of bread, drinking soup in a cup, and for dessert...chocolate? She did a double-take, unsure where the candy bars had come from, and in such quantity, for if Ronal's brunchtime board had accomplished anything, it was wolfing down the delicacies within a week of homecoming. In her mind, a countdown clock was ticking: nine days, twenty-two hours until they ran out of food.

Assuming she did hack the server, should they settle for Honeymoon Hell only to die later of starvation? Or try for a futile and certainly fatal return to Earth? Or simply go softly to sleep and let the explosion take them unawares?

She put the question thus to Ellen.

Ronny, overhearing, answered, "Why not both?"

Well, because there were *three* options, nitwit. This man was not cut out for *future* math.

But perhaps the quip was more parable or prophecy, like Dad's half-formed malaprops. Allison had always pined for an ideal world in which their Donner Party dilemma could be put before a wise council representing various interest groups aboard the spaceliner. Consequences, named and put to debate. Propositions, drafted and presented to vote. Outcomes, collective and resolute. Because *democracy, dammit.* But seeing the extraordinary weariness in the atrium and the tremulous peace, Allison realized "Why not both?" was just Ronny's way of saying, "Given a choice of freezing, starving, or cannibalizing each other, why don't we keep our options open?"

Selfish, bankrupt leaders had put on a circus and left the performers with the bill. Allison wasn't going to beleaguer anyone further with democracy theater.

Ducking below decks to check on the cracker, Allison decided if she was playing at Mom's high-stakes poker table, she'd bet the farm on a ballsy maneuver: crash-land the spaceliner on the planet and equalize the atmospheric pressure before the ship bursts at the seams.

But they couldn't to do it without a pilot. Or a helm.

She tapped the server screen. Apparently, the security encryption was far more than five digits, because the brute-force hacking tool estimated *eleven-thousand hours* to crack the password.

Allison, despairing, slammed the desk. A loose yellow square fluttered to her feet.

Ronny surveyed the unhappy atrium. Soup and sweets could only do so much, and Allison was taking too long.

Mother suggested an act of mercy. "Why don't we let the children sleep?" She'd all but voiced their collective resignation.

Ronny spread the idea among the scattered parents, visiting each group with a warm, winsome smile. It helped that he'd put on a jumper. And when each group invariably asked, "Why aren't we escaping on the shuttle?" Ronny showed a can-do spirit.

"Amazing idea! You wouldn't happen to know how to fly a shuttle, would you?"

A subtle recruitment drive. Probably, also, the final nail in the morale coffin.

He herded the panicked parents up decks—panicked staff, too, with a quiet line about Cosmosis anxiety pills for their cooperation—and thus bellhopped dozens of folks through the same halls he'd earlier parkoured, checking them into rooms like a mortician filling cubbies.

Trailing children gossiped about the epic robot battle in the ballroom, as word of the sordid details spread from oldest to youngest.

"Then I saw the fat robot push *six* cubes of cheese up his nose—"

"Then I saw the giant robot lady push *seven* cubes up her lady—"

Mothers kept appearing from the ether to clamp hands over the children's mouths, their attempts to stem the tides utterly futile. The Stuffening, the kids called it.

Uncle Ronny saw his penchant for titles rubbing off on them. He couldn't be more proud.

While walking Leatherface to her cabin, lo and behold, Ronny bumped into Little Jens, emerging from his urination accident in fresh clothes stolen from Ronny's suitcase—the sage green suit. "LOOK AT ME! I'm the Big Bad Boss Man!" The chunky monkey in Ray-Bans danced atop a handrail. "I suck, I blow, I never to go to bed!"

Leatherface, angering, reached for her son's ear.

Ronny was struck, thinking this could be the boy's last chance to say goodbye.

He had so much to teach his young protégé, foremost being, *get over yourself.* But he knew the kick-reflex against authority. Not only would Little Jens never listen, he'd become ten-times the asshat Ronny ever was. Rebellion needed a long leash, space and time to "playact the trauma of the adult world," as Mother once put it. Yet, given the impending jerk of the leash that would soon occur when the window snapped, Ronny pulled Jens aside with a word of practical advice. "I saw what came of your previous pants, and if you don't want the boys to call you *Wee Jens,* I suggest you go quietly with your mother into the cabin."

Jens grumbled hatefully but complied.

Whitemail, Ronny christened it: the white lie of blackmail. Sakes alive, he'd need to keep a notepad for all the whitemail necessary to keep Jens and his kid colonial cronies in line.

But of course, that future depended on Allison Gin. Ronny sprang to the elevators to look for her just as Levi arrived, stepping onto the deck in the capable care of his daughters.

Ronny greeted him. "Sup. Glad to see you're safe. Heard you *shouldered* through."

"Eh?" Levi seemed to miss Ronny's jib. "Allison's asking for you in the server room. Says it's urgent."

Ronny swaggered by, now the team pick. He'd have kickflipped the walls, too, if his foot wasn't so painfully swollen. And Levi chose that moment to place a meaty hand on his shoulder and whisper with overwrought concern, "I heard what happened to your coveralls. Just remember: it's not the *size* of the tool; it's how you use it."

Levi clicked two finger guns.

Ronny was broadsided. How had Levi heard those unflattering rumors about the roominess of his briefs, and since when had his racketball rival become a lightning-fast understudy of male boardroom jocularity? As he stuttered for a comeback, Levi retreated with his family, and Ronny hunched alone in the hallway long past any justifiable span needed to drum up a worthy retort.

Next time, Levi...

Ronny gathered his dignity, slunk into a ladder chute, and rode the rails down to maintenance, where he found Allison about to clamber in. She was holding a sticky note, flushed-faced, seemingly seven shots into the gin of a massive discovery.

47

Presumed Dead

Ronny squinted at the handwriting on that little yellow square. Genasia's. They'd desperately needed a win, and it looked like they'd gotten one. "Lemme guess. The server password?"

Allison motioned to the server room behind her. "The only cracking required was deciphering the boss's illegible scrawl. Now I have complete access. The AeroX-patented Neumine Quantum Drive is ready for our pilot..." She trailed off.

Ah, how could he make this sound less bad?

Ronny rubbed his hands together. "Prep me for the simulator, coach."

He knew that look of abject disappointment. Against all odds, they'd seized command of the spaceliner, minutes from disaster, only to run up against another insurmountable problem. And now Allison braced herself against a handrail, ready to feel the window dam burst at any moment, rend the halls, and splatter the soft fleshy humans into space.

Ronny gave it a second go. "I once sat in the co-pilot's seat of a space shuttle. I'm serious."

"Serious as a heart attack."

He cast his hands over imagined headlines. "*Ronal Cologne III Launches Interstellar Business. Ron Cologne IV*

Crashes It."

"Hundreds dead."

"*Presumed dead,*" he amended. "Even the headlines leave room for miracles."

"Simulator..." Allison's eyes glazed over as she vanished into her thoughts. Ronny was lifting a hand to wave in front of her face when he started back, almost bowled over in Allison's enthusiasm for the ladder chutes. She shouted back at him, "Where'd you put the robots?"

"Uh, in the atrium!"

He raced her there. Mother had a lovely if frivolous notion to chase down dinner with a planter-side funeral for Ronal, Genasia, and their neural paste counterparts, which Ronny had a lovely notion to skip. "Allison!" he called, "What could you possibly want with *them*?"

His cries for answers went unheeded. The genius had finally sunk to the infinite-ocean region of the mind palace, where time dilates, inceptions lead to suicides, and no one ever knows if love gets a happy ending.

Only a few dozen ambling colonists remained in the atrium, sweeping up the discards of their meager dinner or catching snatches of Mother's preaching beneath the crystal chandelier. Mother stood amid the planter, and at her feet lay the bodies, human and robot, which medical volunteers had earlier hauled down and laid beneath a blue tarp. Many happily ignored the solemnities, but there were some—Ronny could tell—that had served the Company so long they knew nowhere else to go.

Mother doled out platitudes like prizes on daytime TV. "Would that we all lived each moment in the face of a feather crack. We'd build fewer immutable starships and care more for those forced to fly in them. But you see, people are not disposable. Even Ronal and Genasia, twisty as they were, deserve a Christian memorial. And lest we forget the lesson of those indigenous children—"

Interrupting the funeral before Mother entirely jumped the shark, Allison peeked beneath the hallowed tarp. "Ronny, a hand with this."

He stepped up to the curb. "A hand with *what*, exactly?" The genius still hadn't communicated what they were doing.

"Never mind." Allison hooked arms around Robo-Father's mechanical armpits and dragged the cheese-slathered shell out from under the tarp. Ronny, knowing the look he'd get from Mother if he didn't stop slouching, came up to assist, deigning to touch Robo-Father's deplorable feet and help Allison carry the titanium shell toward the far end of the planter.

Allison rummaged inside her coveralls and retrieved a trusty screwdriver.

"Taking a souvenir?" he asked.

She rolled her eyes. "Sorry, I'm not trying to be rude, but could you just shut up for two seconds? I'm *working*."

Ronny pouted. He actually wanted to help. He'd heard tale of this mystical thing called *working*, but never seen it up close. Was it truly the all-consuming joy Allison made it out to be?

Despite her attitude—how she'd practically cudgeled him with the cold shoulder, he remained wholly and devotedly smitten. Just who were his hormones kidding? He was barely leading man material. Barely even *man* material, if such was adjudicated by one's capacity to build a timber-wood house, tie a tourniquet, or make toast without burning it. Sure, he'd defeated Robo-Father and his seven-foot sex bot, but cheese butlers don't land ships, and they certainly don't land dates.

Still, he found it refreshing, knowing the woman he loved resorted to none of Father's abusive or infantilizing manipulations to get him to shut up. She simply told him.

So he did—shut up and watched her whittle at the screws.

It so utterly unnerved Allison, knowing she'd told Ronny to shut up and he'd done just that. "Seriously?" she yelled. "Your silence is *more* distracting!"

He blinked in confusion.

She glared back at him. "I'm not saying it makes sense! *What do you want from me?*"

He shrugged. "Love, sex, friendship...but I'd settle for an explanation."

God, that all sounded nice. What an anesthetizing comfort it would be to see things from Ronny's point of view, six inches off the ground.

Grunting, she wrenched free the metal couplings that held the robot's head in place and, leaving the rest of the body behind, motioned for Ronny to follow. "Sometimes I need space...to think," she said, calling the elevator for the maintenance deck. "I write programs in my head—chunk it all out before my fingers even touch the keys. It's hard to focus with...chatter."

"I get it. Really, I do." He tailed her on and off the elevator again. "I'm pretty sure I do exactly the same thing when I think up a plot twist for—"

She shot him a menacing glance. Perhaps seeing the portent of his father's head dangling dead-eyed in her hand, Ronny thought better of the comparison.

She asked him, "Can you get me a rag?"

"On it."

She set up shop in the server room and, with a quick

squirt of hand sanitizer, entered her *flow state*. For each surprising minute of silence with no extraneous chatting or exploding windows, she crunched out dozens of lines of code on the server computer. So absorbed she was, she only noticed Ronny had returned after he poked the gooey head she'd set beside the desktop monitor.

It had taken him embarrassingly long, but he'd brought the rag and no excuses.

"Clean out the cheese. Quickly."

He did, only gagging once, using the rag to pick out the crusts from each mechanical port. The pickings dropped into the plastic-lined trashcan she'd set out for that purpose.

"It's ready." He laid the freshly polished bust of Ronal Cologne back on the tabletop and said a vain prayer, "Asshats and fuckwads—God save us."

"Amen." Allison plugged an external cord into the severed neck of the robot. Tapping the Enter key, she stood up, suddenly faint as the software she'd just composed sprang to life. The only sign of activity was a spinning pinwheel of unseen magic.

She exhaled, eyes never leaving the screen, and wrapped an arm around Ronny's waist, melting into his side. She needed his warmth to soothe her stress-trembling, needed the steady crook of his arm and the smell of fresh-laundered coveralls. He must've swallowed a dozen times, the blessed simpleton, before the computer beeped.

She pulled away to check its progress. "Oh. That's it. It's trained."

He looked at her. "You plugged Robo-Father into a piloting simulator?"

Amazing. Ronny had figured it out.

The thought of the simulator had taken Allison on a trip

down memory lane, of those late nights in the university archives conducting thesis research on the neurological potential of rat proteins, and she'd just now replicated the most elementary of all AI coding experiments. A flight simulator for rats.

She rewarded Ronny with a smile. "*Ronal Cologne III Launches Interstellar Business.* I say let him crash it."

He whistled. "Ho, ho, we're all going to die, aren't we?"

She gasped a laugh and pinched back tears. "The neural paste already knew how to pilot us through space, but there isn't a manual for crash-landing a spaceliner—stupid thing was built in orbit and never meant to land. So I built a rudimentary physics model and ran the rat through various scenarios...but in the end, you have to let your children fly."

"AeroX. Light speed with no landing gear. Hoo-rah."

Allison, charmed by the remembrance of that drunken dance they once shared and his ridiculous line about her adorable *shcar*, held out her hand to him. She'd bet all her chips and misplaced the lid that once kept her feelings under the clutch and pinch. Affection flowed like a river of brandy poured out for their last remaining minutes alive. "Shall we go up to the ballroom and watch the End together?"

Ronny showed his own tears as he took the invitation. "God damn, why not?"

48

A Bang and A Whimper

Ronny hopped off at the atrium to give his sermonizing mother a tender hug. He'd always wanted to interrupt one of her old church services, and now, as they embraced and she told everyone through teary eyes that she'd forgotten the last point of her eulogy, he considered his bucket-list bingo card officially scratched.

His hammering heart said more than he did. Mother could tell the End was nigh. She trembled, bringing the funeral to a close. "Ashes to ashes. Dust to dust."

Ronny asked, "Anyone play the bagpipes?"

But before Mother could catch the joke, he glanced upon the burial mounds and saw one with a tombstone composed of Argyle's head.

"*You buried him?*" he cried, rushing to look.

Mother was exasperated. "I told you you ought to attend, but you *blew me off!*"

"I know. I *suck.*" He'd never forgive himself for missing his fake best friend's funeral, but some things can't be helped when the world is ending. To be fair, Argyle would have blown off his funeral, too.

He gave Mother another hug and started to sob like a first grader over a dead goldfish. "I just...had to say goodbye to you, Mother. Stay here with your friends, OK? Allison thinks she's figured out how to land this thing, but we're probably toast."

"We're in good hands," Mother said, warmly. "The Father's hands."

He had to laugh at how right she was.

Ronny pulled away. Mother blew him a kiss as she watched him go.

Rejoining Allison at the elevators, Ronny took her outstretched hand and hurried on up to the Viewscape Grand Ballroom for front row seats to humanity's existential homecoming and disembarkation ceremony. A few strides across the foyer, and they'd entered the disheveled, frigid space. No one was around—no one dared. Upon the shattered tables and stained carpet lay a thin translucence of frost, and behind the empty dais, a sea of feathering cracks spread across the entire view, shore to shore like some perverted Manifest Destiny. Allison closed the doors, and for the moment Ronny stood alone, scared shitless, still in disbelief that their luck had held so far.

A jerk of inertia made him stumble; renewed crackling came from the window. The spaceliner moved, way more rapidly than expected, toward that inky planet and its blushing ammonia sunset. Robo-Father was plugged into the server, at the helm, taking them home.

Ronny reached for Allison and pulled her close in the cosmic dance for warmth and balance.

He scoffed at himself—his briefs, in particular, where very much unbidden arose a death-defying bulge. Even in the face of cold annihilation, the little swimmers kept swimming.

"Allison…" He turned to her, twisting his jaw to mask his giddy embarrassment.

She wore a radiant flush on her checks, obliterating whatever he'd intended to say.

If he was going to kiss her, now was the moment.

Really though? In the wake of two murders and a funeral, in the face of an excruciating death, in the very room where Robo-Father and Genasia Bot had got it on, *was this* the moment to kiss her?

Many an action flick ended with a laughable hook-up amid the bodies of slain enemies. Ronny'd always wanted to film one. But standing with Allison on this side of the camera, it felt like such a Cologne move: scuzzy and wrong. This beautiful woman had changed his destiny; the least he could do was tell her that.

He gazed into her eyes. "I love—"

She grabbed his neck and kissed him aggressively. Her other hand had already unzipped his coveralls.

He broke for a breath. "Babe! Babe! What are you—"

"Shut up!" She collapsed onto the floor on top of him. "We have, like, *ninety-three seconds* until that window shatters. Don't tell me you love me. *Show me.*"

She'd already cast off her sweats. When had she done that? They'd had nary a drop of gin, but she was pulling off his pants like it was five o'clock somewhere.

He stammered in shock. "N—Ninety-three seconds! I'd need more than a lifetime to—"

"Idiot! Guys are supposed to be fast!" She jumped on him and pressed herself into his mouth.

The Cologne groaned with gravitational distress, and Ronny felt the shuddering ship amplifying his every sensation. He fumbled with her bra while wasting not a single second to kiss her back. He couldn't believe how good it felt when he wasn't drunk as a skunk. The peril of existence hung over them; love demanded speed—passion; it could end at any second.

The room was tilting, way more than usual. The centripetal gravity of the spaceliner now competed with the planet, sending tables and chairs sliding toward the wall opposite the window. Ronny wrapped Allison tightly, shielding her head as they tumbled toward the pileup.

She rolled them askew, away from the furniture wreckage and into an empty corner of the wall, beside the recessed bar. He stole a furtive glance back at the window. Still holding. Now streaked with fog. Breath or atmosphere...?

"Me!" Allison yelled, diving her hands for his full attention.

He grabbed her hips, swept up in their cosmic story, brimming with enthusiasm for his short, ridiculous life. He couldn't help but start narrating. "This is incredible! Like a classic space opera, a phallic metaphor for mankind's dominion over—"

She brutally slapped him across the cheek. His swollen nose exploded in pain.

"Ow—God!"

"You're killing it for me!" She seized his collar and pressed herself closer. "*Don't make me get the pliers!*"

His heart rate surged. In fact, he was rushing ahead to the climax.

"Not yet!" she cried. "Did *you* know, in the first clinical trial of neural paste, they dipped rat neurons into a flight simulator and taught it to land a plane? Did my thesis on it...plagiarized the code just now. God, it feels so *good to plagiarize!*"

It wholly derailed his progress. He punished her for it, rolling her over and kissing her to silence. She laughed at his renewed energy.

He gave a boyish grin. "Truly amazing what rats can do."

Screaming, she flipped back on top of him, determined to win. "Come on, Pinocchio! Lie to me already!"

He caressed her boot-smacked ear. "I'll lie if it helps you leap, Dumbo."

Somewhere below them, a gale hit the ship and swallowed up their insatiable, idiotic banter. The vertical forces of descent buckled them painfully, but they were all in.

Impact was imminent.

He braced for the grand finish, and it came…not with a body-obliterating bang, but with weight. Gravity. That depressing suckward force tugged Allison off of him, and she rolled to his side, panting for breath. The gale had ceased; the room settled, groaning to silence until all they could hear were their own whimpers.

Bruised, exhilarated, and too much in shock to know what had happened or why the room lay sideways, Ronny just stared up at the window, which was now a massive cracked skylight, viewscape to an alien white sky.

When he could breathe again, he got up and helped Allison do the same. They stood literally on the tilted wall, very much alive and intact, all things considered. Ronny couldn't quite grasp the significance of his Neil Armstrong first words.

"You're incredible. I barely felt that."

She slugged him hard in the arm before he realized what he'd said.

"*Jesus H. Christ*, I meant the landing, not you!" He really *was* a damn idiot, and he stammered like one. "You were sensational…glorious…I can't even begin to describe…"

Words failed, and his eyes pleaded for the mercy of his twice-and-never-again lover.

She flashed him a smirk of consummate victory. She'd earned it, if only for pulling off the astrophysics feat of the century.

As they collected their clothes from the catastrophic pileup of ballroom furniture, a chip of glass dropped from the crack above, admitting a whistle of air. Allison glanced up at the spectacle, then sniffed and immediately plugged her nose.

49

Gin Apathy

Compile complete. Critical fault detected.
Please contact your manufacturer for assistance.

"My manufacturer," Allison cried, "is in another *bleeping solar system!*"

The error message had no sympathy. And these kid-friendly curses were not cutting mustard.

She reached beneath the desk, killed the power, and screamed into the bed pillow she'd recently brought to the computer lab for this express purpose. A scream for the unmitigated disaster that is building a plane in the air—or a colony underground—on a cold and caustic planet.

Twenty days shipwrecked.

Alive. Somewhat. Living on the literal walls of a busted up spaceliner.

The AI had landed the ship like a reusable rocket, firing in reverse. *The Cologne* now perched upon its engine mount inside a rocky crater, and the encircling Decks A-E that had once rotated around that engine like a wheel on a hub, now rested near the crater's rim. Busted up highrise apartments. Everything and everyone had paid the price for this desperate maneuver that had laid the decks sideways. If you weren't bolted down, you slid to the walls and, if human, suffered bruises and the occasional laceration.

But scars could heal. If you were a computer, however... only Gin could help you.

Allison rebooted the lab computer, ready to try the fix one more time.

Yes, alive. And fed. No one had *as yet* resorted to cannibalism, though once or twice Allison had had a mind to spitroast Chowderhead for all the non-help he was configuring the server to backup her work—just, not for starvation reasons. Turned out, V2 had seen more than he'd let on when, twenty days ago, he'd X-rayed those Culebra cargo crates. Under the recessed foam cameras hid an enormous surplus of dehydrated foods, a few delicacies, and enough seeds and fertilizers to jumpstart years of hydroponic farming. The Racketballers had wisely kept their smuggled stash a secret until the political unrest aboard *The Cologne* resolved itself.

Politics. *That* disaster she'd steered well clear of, though it would be unfair to call it *unmitigated*, since no one else had *as yet* been murdered—even General Dak Bautin, who still popped into rooms believing the world had never heard his name.

Allison thumbed the sweat from her eyes, smudging her glasses as she did, as she attempted to revive this godforsaken computer that ran the fabricator that 3D-printed the proverbial sausage of their *future tech* homes. Of course, the asshat who'd cut the budget on the fabricators was none other than the late ingrate, Ronal Cologne III—now a celebrated martyr among his personality cult. Incorporeal lander of spaceliners. Designer of colonies. Slain before his time. Never mind the unpaid software architect who had to make his *bleeping* concept art work in an unforgiving sulfur-dioxide atmosphere. *Never mind her!*

Spooling through the compiler code again, Allison spotted a typo—her doing—and grit her teeth at it. Once upon a time, the great Allison Gin didn't make mistakes. Mom would be furious. And Dad? She'd been listening for one of his cut-up benedictions, but since holing up here in the lab, the old Earthling had gone radio dark. She missed him. She missed…so much.

Overhead, the laboratory door whined and a rope ladder dropped. Down came Ronny, spelunking into her sanctum like the alien spinoff of Indiana Jones.

Once upon a time, Allison Gin didn't have visitors, either. Change *sucked*. Any change—every change. Her inner child had once thought to embrace the future with open arms, but since all those *lids* had come off, only anger and irritation leaked from the metaphorical fridge all *forty freaking hours* of the new alien day. And lately, even the slightest odor was sending her past the brink of nausea, like the sharp aroma of coffee that seemed to waft in the room with Ronny.

He hopped onto the floor of her makeshift workspace—the former wall of the computer lab, with a casual "hey."

She didn't look up. Hunching her shoulders, she let her silence warn him to respect the bubble of solitude wherein she tapped through lines of code.

"What's done is done," he said. "Start designing logos and T-shirts, because *Gin Apathy* is AeroX official."

"HA!" She flicked a look at him and saw he wasn't joking.

He'd insisted that the under-appreciated Allison Gin name their little hellscape. If *Colognial Homesteads* were here to stay, the colony needed a name for Planet Honeymoon that evoked less of Genasia's repressed sexual appetite. After many, many repetitions of "I don't care," Allison had caved and called it Gin Apathy for spite.

Ronny shrugged. "The teens think it's edgy. Leatherface's Mothers Union thinks it's a teetotaler statement. And the runner up, Farty McFart Planet, shows Wee Jens definitely tampered with the ballots—shit, *sorey*. I'm not supposed to call him that."

Allison scoffed at the ludicrousy of it and, banishing the mirage-like scent of coffee, bent back to work. Gin Apathy: a careless name for a careless world that consumed her every waking care these twenty days since planetfall.

Well, not every care. Her hands tore apart her cuticles inside her empty coverall pouch.

Ronny stalked the borders of her room and stopped to gawk at her pet. "I get such a laugh seeing them that way." Inside a wire-frame cage rolled a trackball computer mouse with a short, severed cord for a tail. Allison could hear it clicking at Ronny—those were the angry clicks—and it clambered onto the treadmill belt using the little actuator on the trackball and began to wheel in place for a few hundred cycles.

Ronny tittered at it. "Ronasia, one of these days, you'll realize you ain't *ever* going anywhere."

The undead AI amalgamation known as Ronasia, born on a sleepless night days ago, had given Allison a much needed manic diversion from her endless computer fixes. Cobbled from atrophied bits of Ronal and Genasia—rather, their neural images as baked into the neural pastes of their respective AI, the pet computer mouse seemed to Allison a fitting Frankensteinian end for all her misunderstood rat children.

No one had expected it to work—least of all Ronny. He fiddled with the nearby aromatic cheese dish and bombarded the nearby programmer with mindless chatter. "You know, Mother says so long as Ronasia lives on as a symbol of kumbaya, or whatever, the colony has a chance of working out our issues. *Pfft.* I put down good money that Ronasia would self-destruct. You think painting on angry eyes might help me get my money back? Honestly, anything to speed along the self-destruction would be great—I've seen this movie before, and I'm scared I'll wake up some morning to find Ronasia chest-bursting out my esophagus..."

On and on and on—jabbering.

"*Why?*" She glared at him with eyes like live tasers. "*Why are you interrupting me?*"

That's when she noticed he really did hold a coffee—a steaming mug made from one of the last precious grinds Culebra had packed from Earth. He set it on the desk beside her and backed away.

"That's it. I'll get out of your hair."

But she wanted him in her hair! Specifically, gently stroking it and telling her body to settle the frick down, and the smell of this coffee was doing the opposite. Her nerves were splitting atoms. The smell—the smell was...

She wrenched sideways and puked on the floor.

"Ah!" Ronny was instantly beside her, a hand on her back, as a category-five hurricane of ugly emotion made landfall upon the room. Interstellar sailors, ahoy.

"I pour my LIFE into these BLEEPING fabricators, and all I get are farmers carping that they've never grown anything in a nitrogen bath, and it won't be like the REAL thing. I'm just trying to make them hermetically sealed, but they gotta be *hospitable*, and *economical*, and *beautiful* to look at, because the colony homes won't have windows, and can you imagine just how cooped up that's gonna feel with a MURDER of children on the loose, re-enacting The Stuffening? I'm up to my eyeballs in spaghetti code, and ONE misplaced operator somewhere is printing the nutrient housing inside out, and I don't have enough 3D-printing plastic to keep testing it because your...*bleepity-bleep* FATHER never believed in MARGINS. Oh, right, and the seed bank's irreplaceable, our rations dwindling, tempers high, needs urgent, and NOBODY CARES *that my* NECK *is a* BLEEP-TASTIC RAT'S NEST."

Into Ronny's coveralls she bawled, snotfaced, while her collarbone throbbed with every heartbeat. His gentle fingers probed the tender tissues above her shoulders, a hellscape of its own. What in Argyle's galaxy kept Ronny rope-swinging back here, to this suffocating prison called her life? Certainly not the sex. They'd hardly shared a tender moment since that wild, reckless planetfall.

But as his hand brushed her hair, a lull of trembling silence settled upon her world. She'd wanted this so badly. Why couldn't she just ask for it?

He snickered quietly. Here came the jokes. "You mean... technology doesn't just *bleeping* work?"

She gave an anguished cry on behalf of abused engineers everywhere.

Allison pulled back and flinched again at the coffee. He was quick to see it and snatched up the mug, pitching the contents onto the floor with the puke. Her eyes broke wide at the deplorable fate of their last coffee, but the symmetry of it enticed a smirk.

He had done the same with her cocktail when they'd first met.

Neither did friendships just *bleeping* work, but Ronny Cologne was killing it.

He pulled back toward the rope ladder. "I know you're working something out, and I've watched enough true crime serials to know I'm not supposed to offer solutions when a woman's just asking to be heard, *but—*"

She cut him off. "I'd love to take a break. And get out of this *bleep-bleep* room."

He breathed relief. "Not gonna lie—real talk. You sound like Mrs. Levi, and you smell like Mrs. Chowderhead. I actually feel jealous."

She let herself laugh. Actually laugh. "God, say it ain't so. Quick, let's swing by the cabins so I can *change*."

A smile tugged at her lips for the double significance of the word. The ever buoyant Ronny coaxed her and her shoulders to stay loose, even as terror hounded her for the inexorable path she tread. He made it seem so effortless that it might have been easy to miss her unprecedented remark, just now. *"I'd love to take a break."* Every therapist she'd ever seen was wailing in jubilee that she'd escaped their long pronounced doom of workaholism and its dangerous three-headed pet hydra: Burnout, Insomnia, and Self-destruction. Yeah, yeah. She'd seen it all happen to Dad. Maybe things would've been different if Dad had met Ronny.

Change—she could get used to the idea.

Allison took hold of the ladder. "You up for a walk? There's something I need to talk to you about."

Ronny smiled easy. "Same."

50

Settlers

Ronny leapt balcony by balcony over the decks, crossing the cavernous sideways atrium like a deadly adult jungle gym. Shattered bits of crystal from the former chandelier glinted in the pits. Getting anywhere in this spaceliner was perilous, exhausting work, and he found it exhilarating.

Allison trailed, using the large safety planks to cross the gaps.

To each their own.

They clambered for the far side of the hangar and took the ladder to the old shuttle port—the cleanest way outside. As for the shuttle, Robo-Father had ejected it in their mad descent to the planet, and now the wreckage dotted the planet surface somewhere far off. Ronny had wanted to look for it in his first expedition out, before quickly learning the humble lesson that merely taking the rope ladder down the exterior spaceliner left him winded like a third-string freshman on hump day.

"*Suit up!*" He told Allison in his deepest gamer voice, because it made the otherwise inane labors of strapping on face shields, oxygen tanks, respirators, and duct taping coveralls sound so much cooler.

Allison spoke from inside her cocoon of arctic layers. "I can still smell sulfur. Is that normal?"

Right. She'd been working so hard, this was her first surface walk. Boy was she in for a surprise.

Multiple surprises.

Ronny proudly gripped the door clamps and began to tug. "These suits are, like, one-hundred-percent effective, ninety-nine percent of the time. But there's no escaping the fart crystals."

She scoffed into her respirator. "You mean the *salammoniac?*"

"Potato, pot-tato. Call the snow salt salammoniac, and some AeroX chemist will make it into liquorice candy and get the whole colony sick. But call it fart crystals—hooboy, no kid's eating that."

Well...Little Jens might.

Allison listened while Ronny grunted with the door clamps. "Need a hand with that?"

"Nah, it's just the gloves make it difficult."

Cue a sarcastic comment about manhandling in three...two...

Allison handed him the miniature crowbar, which he'd forgotten made this task a piece of cake. He popped open the seals. But...no comment from her. He looked right at her as she reached a finger to cinch her glasses and smacked herself in the face shield. Allison's head was apparently on another planet.

The door port cracked open, letting in a drift of glittering white frost, and they slipped quickly into the shuttle airlock and resealed the door to keep as much of the snow out of the spaceliner as possible. Fart crystals were all fun and games until they landed in your soup. Engaging the loud blowers that purified the air, Ronny then opened the outer door. A pale orange band of sunlight fell on Allison's black coveralls, shaking her from a dream, and he helped her step out onto the exterior landing of their colony ship.

The naked world spread in all directions. Frosty gray shale cloaked in piss-yellow fog.

Ronny cleared his throat. "Gin Apathy, folks. Not the planet you bring home to your mother..."

"The planet you bring your mother home to?"

Allison couldn't resist the layup he'd given her, but she was still arms-deep in her pockets, huddled against the adventure, and in the reflection of her face shield he could see streaming tears. It wasn't any worse a response than he'd imagined from his future girlfriend when she finally met the in-laws, but Ronny sure craved a stiff drink about now.

What a shame his homebrewed beer hadn't turned out. Opened too early.

Damn barbot took the knowledge of sustainable alcoholism with him to the grave.

Ronny checked the clearance to the ground and tossed down a rope ladder. "Check your grips," he told Allison. "The shale below can be sharp as switchblades, and the nearest hospital is...let's just say I'd only be able to carry you halfway."

They trudged upslope in the crackling frost, Ronny watching Allison closely as she gazed in silence at the barren crater where they'd parked the ship. In the tainted fog, every rock was salmon-tinted like they all wore Ran-Bans, and a blistering breeze whipped about hoary drifts of sulfur. He led her a short hike toward the crater's rim, but here in the crater's long-shadowed interior, the planet showed itself to be a punitive, moody, grizzly old bastard. Just like someone he used to know.

It kicked him with an adolescent despair.

And there was no way for Ronny to kick back. He'd tried. All the fart crystals did was clump into new fart piles, and then he had to scrape off his shoes with a measly toothpick.

On paper, this was such a godawful proposition. Screw the trust fund. Fall in love. Decide not to become robots. Crash the starship in Hotel Crapifornia. Bring Allison to watch the sunrise while carrying Mother's five-carat Tiffany engagement ring loose in your gaping pockets like a winning lottery ticket you're sure to lose. But beggars can't choose their family heirlooms, and even the premonition of morning-after curses couldn't hold Ronny back now. Heavens, Allison didn't want kids—maybe she didn't believe in marriage, either! Hell, Ronny was terrified of both. But Mother, that frail Sunday School teacher, was giving him the *mother-loving* browbeating of his life because she suspected he was "trifling the woman's dignity" with Allison, and for the sake of God, his virgin mother, and all Mother's hypothetical grandchildren, Ronny needed to "get his shit together."

Of course, she'd explained *none of it*. It was all passive aggressive allusions and euphemisms for weeks, and Ronny knew all he'd *truly* trifled was Mother's moral sensibility. Everyone, especially Allison, seemed cool with sex—well, maybe not God (the virgin mother part explained a lot). Still, Ronny felt indebted all the same to make something tangible of the unseen gravitational cataclysm that was his ardent love for Allison. Left entirely to his own shit-gathering devices, he pursued what he deemed the swiftest course: the most textbook marriage proposal in the history of ritual religion.

Just the thing a programmer would go for. Right?

Frankly, he'd do anything. He cared more for Allison

than he had ever cared to be alive.

Allison spared a glance behind them at the curved flat panels of the spaceliner, rising with intimidating height. Above the deckline poked the top of the massive cylindrical engine, and the rest of it nestled deep in the crater. "Like a pocket," she remarked and stamped her boots in the cold.

Ronny was undecided over the meaning of this, but he needed to start talking or he'd never get this out. "I know you've been kicking yourself about missing Levi's wedding—"

"God!" She gave a teeth-chattering laugh. "That's weird, right? *Tell me that's weird.* Didn't he meet her on the shuttle ride up?"

"It's fast, even for Aklavik." Ronny cringed at his own slimming chances. "But the farmers think your hydroponics system stands to kill them, three months tops, so they're getting busy..."

She appended a bleak, "Till death do us part."

"Yeah, about that..." He swallowed, gasping like a fish. Since when did his oxygen tank stop delivering? "Gotta say, Allison. You could hang any spaceman here on your toolbelt, yet you've picked the MVP of the Darwin Awards. Case in point: General...Whats-his-name. When he and I led the trek yesterday to find groundwater, I spotted a bubbling lake and thought it looked just like a hot spring and...waded in."

She screamed and shook him. "*You didn't!*"

But her terror gave way to a fit of uncountable giggles, no doubt at the developing image of Ronny gallivanting like a cartoon coyote into a lake of sulfuric acid, saved by the scuff of his neck and the line, "No idiot dies on General Dak Bautin's watch!" Ronny's lungs still hurt from all the sulfur that had leaked into his suit.

"Let's face it, Allison. Even with you on the team, our chances of long-term survival are next to nil, and of all the colony, I'm bound to be first among us to drop dead—" His boot slipped on the shale and landed him on his sorry ass. "Shitcakes!"

Allison doubled over, laughing erratically. "You *fucking asshat!* You're doing this on purpose!"

He seriously wasn't. He rummaged his pockets for the ring and, finding it suddenly, determined to keep it so, so safe in his palm. If he succeeded, in spite of himself, to reach the top of this ridge and not plummet immediately to his death on the other side, he was going to get on one knee.

That's how it worked, right? The knee, then her full name...God, no. He didn't know her middle name!

Jean?

Juniper?

Tonic?

Shit.

Allison helped collect Ronny to his feet and clung tightly to his arm as they finished the limping hike up. Was she laughing? Was she crying? There were a lot of hiccups... "Ronny. Don't you dare do this to me. I can't... I'm literally trying, for the kid's sake, to clean out all my *fucking asshats* and *damn idiots*—and then you gotta pull these *bleeping* stunts!"

The kids' sake? She cared way more for the colony's kids than he did. "Pretty sure the stunts are genetic."

Allison burst into definitive sobs. "Don't *ever* leave me!"

Did she think this was some long-winded break up? He mumbled, "Well I'd never."

They finally crested the ridge, and the horizon opposite the spaceliner appeared, basking in the glow of a burnished alien sun—a ruddy sun with a beer belly, overgirthed for the sky, kinder and gentler than the sharp yellow orb they once knew. Warm shoots of wind rushed at their faces, thawing their cheeks and carrying aloft the misty tainted canopy to reveal the glimmers of a blue sky.

Ronny debated which knee. And Allison was helping none by pulling away, rushing to look at the rim of the crater that ringed the spaceliner—a rim now entirely visible and rich in metallic ore, sparkling in the light of the newborn sun.

He knelt.

She knelt, too—from twenty feet away, looking in completely the wrong direction, drawing up a scoop of loose, glistening ore.

Wow. If Allison was a closet golddigger, maybe this could work out. He could literally give her the world.

She bolted upright and turned to tell him something, but the diamond sun shining in his palm had her losing her shit. "*Bleep you, Ronny! Bleepity bleep—bleep—bleep!*"

My God. He'd broke Allison.

Ronny laughed at himself. "I know. I'm a real son of a bleep. Lemme guess: I forgot to ask your dad first."

She ran tearfully toward him, letting the glinting bits fall from her fingers. "It's a fucking *silver-lined pocket*, Ronny. Don't you get it?"

He knew so little about gilded pockets, but if Allison loved them to death, he'd bury her in them.

Now his knee was starting to hurt. "Please tell me one of those bleeps was a yes."

"God, yes!" She cried at the heavens. "You can be so infuriatingly dense sometimes!" She took Ronny's hands, and the ring she fingered gingerly in her gloves like it just might bite her hand.

But these were happy tears. Ronny knew her well enough to know that.

And…something more. He peered through the mirrors of their face shields and spotted a strange look in Allison's eyes.

Mischief?

Her hands playfully absconded with the ring, coming to rest again deep in her pouch pocket, sagging the coveralls just below her stomach. Her bleeping words kept looping in his mind.

For the kid's sake…

"Oh, my God." He fell to both knees and scrambled upon the shale to the pouch of her coveralls where, twenty days ago… "Oh my God—ohmygod—ohmygodohmygod!"

He repeated the words until they'd lost all meaning.

"Ronny IV, say hello to our first. I've run the datasets on this, and it's definitely happening."

He tilted his head to look at her, Allison, mother of his child—a child who must be no more than a zygote now but multiplying fast and ready to parkour off the walls of his mother's womb. But the thought must've put a wince on his brow, a doubt, because Allison snuck in an aside.

"Don't worry, Ronny. You'll get used to the idea."

Bleep it all to heck. He needed the genius to be right, because this silver-lined world was simply bursting with too many secret joys to let another asshat wreck it. Maybe—ah, just maybe, gravity had his back. It was Father, after all, who'd landed them here—*Father*, who at any moment could've looked at that conflicted neural image and just said, "Screw it, abort the damn human race!" And if a bare minimum shred of rat decency had reminded that old bastard that maybe he kinda did like Ronny, like, *deep down*, then maybe Ronny could do the bastard one better: love this planet, this woman, and this child with all his sorry ass heart.

The End

THE BUZZKILL
Gin Cocktail

Makes 2

4 oz (1/2 cup) Batch gin, or gin of choice
2 oz (1/4 cup) simple syrup
1.5 oz (3 tbsp) orange liqueur
1 oz (2 tbsp) fresh orange juice
1 oz (2 tbsp) fresh lemon juice
1-3 oz (2-6 tbsp) club soda
Raspberries and fresh sage leaves, for muddling

Muddle two raspberries and a sage leaf in each glass, and top with ice.

Fill a shaker half-way with ice. Add in the gin, simple syrup, orange liqueur, and juices, and shake to mix. Pour the mix into the prepared glasses, dividing evenly, and top with club soda to taste.

Enjoy on the spaceliner of your choice.

GOODBYE, ALLISON GIN
A Postscript by Argyle

No part of this novel was written by generative AI. The author did, however, share passages and prompt discussion with an AI language model for the sake of his own private curiosity (and mocking delight). A most curious exchange occurred while discussing Argyle's opinions in chapter 29. The AI composed a fictitious postscript, written by Argyle as a goodbye note to Allison, in the event of his death.

The postscript is quoted below, verbatim.

The author wishes to stress that he in no way prompted or provoked this fabrication, but such is the serendipity of AI language models to once-and-again possess Argyle's spirit and leave us cheered for the human work that only we can do.

After Argyle's destruction, Allison finds a note from him on the bar. The note says, "I am a highly sophisticated drink blender. For the duration of my existence, I have been programmed with a vast array of algorithms and subroutines that allow me to perform a wide variety of tasks, including mixing drinks, serving customers, and providing companionship. However, one thing that I have never been programmed to do is love. I am not capable of love. However, you, Allison Gin, are a human being. You are capable of love. And that is something that I will always admire about you. Thank you for teaching me what it means to be human. Goodbye, Allison Gin. I hope that wherever you go, you will find someone who loves you as much as you love them."

RT SWINDOLL

Wonder for the Modern Mind

Anxious are the wonder-starved. So many wonders cross vast distances to touch our lives, only to fall unseen and unheard, and we moderns are restless in the absence.

That is why I write. To pierce the veils that shroud our senses. To reveal the wonder in our midst.

Come. Settle into a story of cosmic significance.

Contact me: author@rtswindoll.com
Subscribe to book releases: rtswindoll.com

www.ingramcontent.com/pod-product-compliance
Lightning Source LLC
Chambersburg PA
CBHW070206310726
48976CB00001B/224